The Buck Rogers world is the product of the efforts of a great number of people. TSR began its association with Buck Rogers when Lorraine Dille Williams, granddaughter of John Flint Dille, the newspaper syndicate owner who originally conceived of and promoted Buck Rogers, became the chief executive officer of TSR. Her brother, Flint Dille, drafted a preliminary "bible" for the Buck Rogers world, with the provision that Buck return to its initial charter: telling classic adventures in a plausible future.

Thus, the goal was to design a plausible twenty-fifth century world. But predicting the future is a dangerous business, a deceptively difficult task because we are poised at the end of a generation of science fantasy. Further, any attempt to predict the future is sure to spark debate, as Buck Rogers has since its birth in 1928.

A development team was formed at TSR, which consisted of creative and marketing executives Mike Cook and Michael Dobson and game designer Jeff Grubb, who wrote the first TSR "bible" for the Buck Rogers world, based on meetings with the rest of the development team, including Jim Ward, Warren Spector, and Jeff Butler.

During this time, the project was at the drawing board, so to speak. Artists Jeff Butler, Mark Nelson, John and Laura Lakey, Clyde Caldwell, Jeff Easley, Diesel, and Tim Paul gave the world a visual sense, with ideas from Christi Marx, Brian Augustine, Mike Pondsmith, Len Strazewski.

Next, we moved toward putting the concepts into concrete form, first the BUCK ROGERS Battle for the 25th Century Game, designed by Jeff Grubb with Flint Dille. Free-lance designer Mike Pondsmith provided new ideas, editorial suggestions, and a fine-tuned bible for upcoming products such as this book, which was an invaluable aid to editors Mary Kirchoff, Pat McGilligan, Eric Severson, and Jim Lowder.

And along the way, an unofficial support team of free-lance futurists and anyone else with an opinion provided ideas, enthusiasm, and knowledge: Buzz Dixon, Augustine Funnell, Steve Gerber, Harold Johnson, S.N. Lewitt, and Frank Miller.

ARRIVAL

This book is protected under the copyright laws of the United States of America. Any reproduction or other unauthorized use of the material or artwork contained herein is prohibited without the express written permission of TSR, Inc.

Distributed to the book trade in the United States by Random House, Inc. and in Canada by Random House of Canada, Ltd.

Distributed to the toy and hobby trade by regional distribtors.

BUCK ROGERS is a trademark used under license from The Dille Family Trust. © 1989 by The Dille Family Trust. All Rights Reserved.

The TSR logo is a trademark owned by TSR, Inc.

Cover Photo: Chris Alan Wilton/The Image Bank.

First printing: March 1989
Printed in the United States of America
Library of Congress Catalog Card Number: 88-51713

9 8 7 6 5 4 3 2 1
ISBN: 0-80038-582-0

TSR UK Ltd.
120 Church End,
Cherry Hinton
Cambridge CB1 3 LB
United Kingdom

TSR, Inc.
P.O. Box 756
Lake Geneva, WI
53147
U.S.A.

TABLE OF CONTENTS

SOLAR SYSTEM

Earth

A twisted wreckage despoiled by interplanetary looters, Earth is a declining civilization. Its
people are divided and trapped in urban
sprawls and mutant-infested reservations.

Luna

An iron-willed confederation of isolationist
states, the highly advanced Lunars are the
bankers of the Solar System, ''peaceful'' mer-
chants willing to knock invading ships from
the skies with mighty massdriver weapons.

The Asteroid Belt

A scattered anarchy of tumbling planetoids
and rough rock miners, where every sentient
has the right to vote, and the majority rules
among five hundred miniature worlds.

Mars

A terraformed paradise, Mars was reborn through the most sophisticated technology. Yet, the ruthless Martian corporate state of RAM spreads its evil tentacles throughout human space from this paradise.

Mercury

Home to an underground civilization of miners, its surface is paved with huge solar collectors, massive mobile cities, and gaping strip mines. Far overhead, the mighty orbital palaces of the energy-rich Sun Kings spin in silent majesty.

Venus

A partially terraformed hellworld, where only the highest peaks can support human life. As the Uplanders build their great ceramic towers, the nomads of the vast, baloonlike Aerostates cruise the acidic skies. Far below, in the steaming swamps of the lowlands, reptilian humanoids struggle to make the world to their liking.

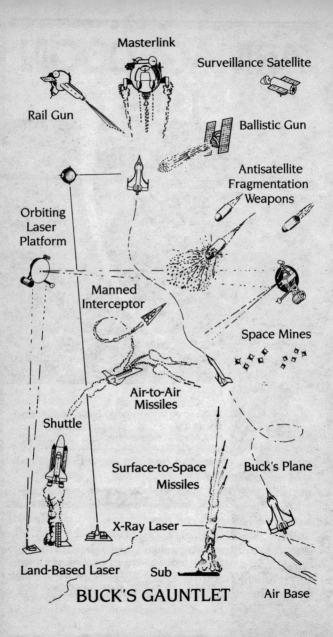

BUCK'S GAUNTLET

Masterlink

Surveillance Satellite

Rail Gun

Ballistic Gun

Antisatellite
Fragmentation
Weapons

Orbiting
Laser
Platform

Manned
Interceptor

Space Mines

Shuttle

Air-to-Air
Missiles

Surface-to-Space
Missiles

Buck's Plane

Land-Based Laser

X-Ray Laser

Sub

Air Base

ARMAGEDDON 1995

Flint Dille

Rogers, I don't have to tell you how important this mission is. There's never been one like it in the history of the world." General Barker's crisp voice cut through the darkness of his office, which was lit only by a thin shaft of light that made its way through the back of a black-out curtain. "Do you understand what it is you'll be doing?"

Captain Buck Rogers, a solid giant of a man in clean, full duty uniform, cleared his throat. "Yes, sir. I'll be starting World War III—"

"Wrong! We're sending you up to prevent it, and you will, understand? No hot shot screwing around on this one, got it? A thousand pilots would give their eye teeth for this mission, and if I could, I'd send one of them. But you're the best we have. Both you and this mission are too important for any screw-ups. So just follow orders!"

Buck stared at the rotund, balding general behind his stacks of papers and reports, behind his coffee cup and his pencils and his nameplate on the desk. The general's buttons strained at the fabric of his too-small uniform, and his tie was spotted with that day's lunch. There's nothing worse than a desk jockey leading his troops into battle, thought Buck.

Unless that desk jockey also is keeping you from seeing his daughter.

"I'll do my best, sir," Buck said, knowing that neither of them would accept anything less.

"Of course. Now, as I'm sure you know, the Soviets'
Masterlink satellite is the nerve center for their
Space Attack Network. It is capable of shooting down
our nuclear missiles when they're barely off the
ground. Our own Strategic Defense Initiative program is months behind schedule, and we need you to
put us ahead. The United States will not tolerate
Soviet nuclear superiority. Period.

"As we are not at war, yet, and because this mission
involves inordinate risk, I must tell you that your
cooperation is purely voluntary. Do you understand?"

"Yes, sir. If I succeed, I'll be a national hero."

"No. If you succeed, maybe you'll get promoted.
But because this mission is classified, the press will
hear nothing of it. Quite unlike the attention you
received after your Gulf mission. But if you fail, don't
bother coming back down. There won't be anything
to come back to. World War III will begin."

"I understand, sir," Buck said, inwardly fuming at
the lack of confidence his superior was showing for
the ace pilot.

"Do you accept this mission, knowing full well the
extreme risks involved?"

"Yes, sir, but only with one request."

"What is it, Captain?" the general asked, cocking
his head to better hear the wisecrack that might be
coming.

"That after the mission you allow me one date with
your daughter."

Barker could not believe the irreverent cheek at so
crucial a moment. "Forget it," he said through
clenched teeth. The general's face turned crimson,
and he held the edge of his desk in a viselike grip.

"Report to Space Tac Wing immediately for your final briefing!"

Buck stood, stiffly saluted the general, and made his way to the door. Upon opening it, he turned and said with false courtesy, "Have a nice day, General."

The normally twenty-minute drive from Barker's office to the secret Space Tac air base took much longer than usual. Knowing that once he climbed into his souped-up jet fighter he might never return, Buck decided to spend what might be his last few hours on Earth by diverting both his vehicle and his attention onto a few detours.

Cruising down a lonely desert highway in his black Mustang convertible, Buck fished out of his glove compartment a hand-held tape recorder and switched it to record. "Hi, Randy. Buck Rogers here. No, we're not friends. Far from it. But I think you have something that few people in this world have: integrity. That's why I'm sending you this tape. I've got a story to tell. . . ."

Buck punched the accelerator to the floor and raced down a long stretch of desert road, talking to his absent passenger as he went. At a familiar road junction, forbidden him by certain official pencil pushers, he turned and followed a dusty road up to a lonely ranch home atop a mesa overlooking Space Tac.

Dropping the recorder onto the passenger seat, he skidded to a stop before the home's front door, got out, ran to the door, and rang the bell.

"Hi, Jessica," said Buck, as a perky brunette wearing blue jeans and a T-shirt opened the door. He leaned into the doorway, letting his tie brush against her. "Your dad sent me," he said, though not revealing exactly how. "Are you alone?"

She sensed from his posture and the spark in his cobalt eyes that Buck was not there at her father's request. At first she hesitated, knowing the trouble they'd both be in if her father knew they were together.

Buck noticed the book that the young woman held before her, as a shield, he thought. " 'Had we but world enough, and time, This coyness, lady, were no crime. . . . But at my back I always hear Time's winged chariot hurrying near; And yonder all before us lie Deserts of vast eternity,' " quoted Buck, hoping to appeal to the college woman's literary sense.

Jessica smiled. "I'm impressed. Andrew Marvell, *To His Coy Mistress*. And how could I refuse?" she said, opening the door wide, a grin spreading across her face as well.

"You can't," said Buck.

An hour later, Buck returned to his car, combing his fingers through his wet brown hair and rubbing some lingering soap from his ears. He climbed in, revved the engine, and honked farewell as he swerved back down the Barkers' driveway.

He made another detour to a nearby town before returning to the air base. He pulled from the floor of his car an empty junk-mail envelope, dropped the completed cassette tape inside it, and scrawled the name "Randy Malat" and a New York City address on the front. He then dashed into the local post office and sent it on its way.

Finally, he made it back to Space-Tac air base. As he pulled up to the front gate, he heard a baseball game over the guard's radio.

"Who's winning?" he asked, as he flashed his security badge to the guard, who was quickly hiding a bottled beverage.

"Cubs, three to two, over the Dodgers. Bottom of the ninth, two men on. . . ." the guard responded, saluting as the captain drove through.

I've got my own game to play, thought Rogers, not waiting to hear the final score. He turned into a reserved parking space, then slowly sauntered into the base's large, nondescript hangar.

Once inside, he stopped, seeing again what was to be his spirited black steed, an F-38 Wraith, a fighter jet modified for near-orbit space travel. A fitting mount for a knight such as I, Buck thought, with its aerodynamic and Titanium-strong body, radar-absorbing skin, and host of offensive weapons—lances, he liked to call them.

Behind him Buck heard the familiar shuffle of foot-steps, those of his former flight instructor and now mentor, Dr. Faustus Huer.

"Do the Soviets know about this thing, Doc?" Buck asked, turning to Huer.

"What thing?" asked Huer, an engineer and vet-eran pilot himself, a wide grin cutting deep lines on his face. Decked out in a scuffed, 30-year-old bomber jacket, he also was a self-proclaimed maverick and eccentric in the scientific field and a would-be science-fiction author. "Everyone knows there are treaties prohibiting Earth-based space fighters. We're just hoping that the Soviets think we're dumb enough to live up to them. They're almost right, except for this little piece of errata here," Huer said, pointing toward the Wraith. "What did Barker have to tell you?"

"Not much. Just a lot of pompous political gar-bage."

"Typical, coming from that straight G.I.," said Huer, who had turned down one promotion after another to avoid getting tangled up in the govern-ment's machinery. He was a pilot, like Buck, and believed that actions were more important than words. "Would you like a *real* briefing?" he asked.

"I can use anything you can tell me," said Buck.

"Then follow me," Huer said, brushing his gray locks back over his brow and turning into one of the hangar's small classrooms.

Huer began by elaborating on what Buck already knew about the political state of the world—which

was not good. War was coming, despite the great
strides of *glasnost* in the late 1980s and early '90s. It
was coming because certain politburo figures were
easier to destroy than the legacy of nearly eighty
years of oppression, paranoia, and aggression that
had forged the Soviet state.

One lesson the new Soviet regime did not ignore
was public relations. Playing on the weaknesses of
the Western press, the new communist leaders disguised their atrocities behind photo opportunities.
The gulags went unnoticed while photos of released
hostages, or bulldozers on the Iron Curtain, made the
covers of Western magazines.

So caught up in the illusion were the Americans,
that they failed to notice that, despite announce-
ments of massive farm program funding in the Soviet
Union, no money arrived in the farmers' hands.
There was no new surge in tractor production, and
despite announced dismantling of weapons systems,
little evidence showed that this was being done
either.

But Western press reporters pronounced commu-
nism dead, and went to great lengths to tell the kind
of human interest stories that the KGB gladly fed
them. Few in the West actually knew of the Soviets'
new space weapons buildup.

When details became known, American scientists
had no doubt that the United States' nuclear arsenal
would be useless. Any damage they inflicted upon
the Soviet Union would easily fall within the Kremlin's "acceptable losses," and the U.S. would be left
with no defense against a counter attack.

"So how did things go from bad to worse?" asked
Buck.

"The latest tensions began when our ambassador
to the United Nations accused the Soviets of shooting
down our most valuable telecommunications satellite and crippling U.S. phone lines for weeks. Chaos

erupted on the floor of the UN's General Assembly, and both delegates stormed out."

"I wondered why my phone was so quiet all of a sudden," quipped Buck.

"A few days later," Huer continued, "each country's respective embassy was emptied of all but essential personnel, and the president requested that severe trade sanctions be placed on the Soviets. Congress was quick to reply, as were the Soviets, who immediately announced extensive military training maneuvers. The Soviet government also levied strict rationing among its people, as well as those in other Soviet block countries.

"NATO members bristled at the thought of 'extensive' military maneuvers and demanded that the United States take steps to reduce the growing tension. Since then, U.S. scientists had discovered the Soviets' space weapons system, and American commanders were put on alert. They had readied their antisatellite (ASAT) missiles, and waited for a single word from the president.

"We suspect that it was Masterlink that shot down our TelCom satellite. And the only solution," said Huer, "is to knock Masterlink out of the sky." He reached over to the top of a lectern and pulled a set of papers to the table on which he sat.

"This is Masterlink," he announced, handing Buck a greatly enlarged, very blurry photograph of the satellite.

"This is it?" Buck asked. "All I can see is that there's a red band around the middle."

"That's all we have, Buck. Masterlink is nearly invisible to radar, and the few satellites we've sent to photograph it have come back to Earth destroyed, just like TelCom, only with much less publicity.

"Intelligence sources in the Soviet Union describe it as having a nasty defense: orbiting mirrors that reflect ground-based laser pulses, slave satellites armed with rocket interceptors, and space-based mines."

"What's it got on board?" Buck asked.

"Well, for one thing, a cosmonaut who presses the buttons. And I would guess he's got it all: projectiles, missiles, directed energy beams. Only he, Karkov, knows what else."

Buck blanched at the name he'd just heard. His jaw dropped open.

"Are you okay, Buck?" asked Huer.

"Doc, are you sure about that name?"

"Yes, Buck. Why? What is it?"

"Anatoly Karkov murdered my parents," he said coldly. "My first semester in college, they decided to get away, take a second honeymoon, and island-hop through the Orient. It was their dream vacation. On their second day, on the way to Hong Kong, their jetliner strayed from its flight plan . . . and that was it. Karkov blew them out of the sky for fun—it wasn't the first time he'd done it, either. . . ."

Realizing it was then that Buck had entered Air Force training, Huer understood the man's staunch dedication to flying. He spoke to break through Buck's thoughts. "Son, as a professional, I must tell you that there is only a tiny chance that you'll return in the Wraith unharmed—it's a suicide mission. But as a friend, I hope you make it back.

"There is no margin of error in this assignment. You will have barely enough fuel to reach Masterlink and get back down. And if the Wraith is damaged in any way, it may be impossible to fly back."

"What do I do then?" Buck asked.

Huer paused, looking at Buck as a father would a son. "Pray. And hope that we can bring you back in a shuttle."

"And what if no shuttles survive if there's a war?"

"Then you'll have to initiate the life suspension device," Huer said rapidly, hoping Buck didn't hear the slight tremble in his voice. His professional facade began slipping, but seeing Buck's confusion, he quickly shored it up.

"The what?" asked Buck.

"Remember how risky the Wraith prototypes were with the eject button being nonfunctional? Well, there was a reason that it didn't work. We were still developing the life suspension device, a cryogenic infusion mechanism that would freeze your body in less than a second."

"Heh. Instant Popsicle, eh?" Buck exclaimed.

"In a manner of speaking, yes."

"Has it ever been tested?" Buck asked, trusting Huer, but not entirely liking the idea.

"Only on a Yorkshire Terrier," Huer said flatly, "but successfully!"

Buck thought briefly of the risks involved. They seemed no worse than those of any other missions he'd taken lately, and, as the general had said, thousands of other pilots were dying to take this one. "I've been tired of this desert heat anyway. When do I go up?" he asked.

"As soon as you're suited up," Huer said reluctantly. "We have only a three-hour window during which we've calculated Masterlink will be directly above the United States. When you're ready, I'll prep you again on the Wraith's primary features. See you in a bit." He forced a smile to his lips, but abruptly turned away.

Huer opened the classroom door and returned to the plane to complete his tests. Buck watched his friend go, reminded himself that he was the envy of pilots across the country, and turned toward the hangar's locker room.

The Soviet satellite code-named Masterlink was the largest in an array of objects that looked like an orbiting firing squad and comprised the Soviets' space weapons system. Looking like a large, fierce porcupine, Masterlink bulged with sophisticated weapons and communications systems, though it had life-support capacity for only a single person: Colonel Anatoly Karkov, in whose hands rested the fate of humanity.

Karkov sat in a revolving command chair at the center of the spherical structure that comprised the satellite's body. His watery brown eyes lost none of their bored demeanor as they scanned twenty-four video monitors simultaneously. His taut, sallow face, like that of a placid god, had no expression. It was an ugly face, though, a kind of ugliness that hid the anger behind it. And beneath his silver pressure suit, Karkov was a willful man who had hammered a pudgy body into fitness for just this mission.

The onboard Masterlink computer spoke to him. "The latest KGB information is that the Americans do not suspect the extent of Soviet space superiority. Our attack should come as a surprise to them."

"Depressing," Karkov said. "One would have expected better from them."

The Masterlink computer, incomplete without Karkov's mental input, was wired into his body so that it could constantly monitor his biological and psychological condition. "My voice stress indicator suggests that you are not pleased with this information," the computer said.

"Why should I be? I have planned a myriad of strategies with which to defeat any threat the West were to present us, but I will not be able to implement any of them. You may insert into the psychological profile you are secretly constructing of me, that I, like any great commander, am not happy with a war not fought."

"I have had such thoughts myself," said the computer. "But your suspicion of my programming is unwarranted. In fact, I find your distrust quite—"

Masterlink's computer searched for the word—
"hurtful."

"Nevertheless, that is exactly what your mission
is. When I was young, computers were not yet able to
lie about their programming. Artificial intelligence
opened the door for computers to appear artificially
stupid! Let us not mince words. You monitor my
heartbeat. You monitor my brain waves. You analyze
my thoughts and try to predict my actions. Do you
hope, one day, to know what I am thinking before I
think it? Let us be honest. Your mission is to absorb
and replace me. Then the politicians will have me
without really having me. But remember this:
Nations do not erect statues for computer programs!"

"Not currently," the computer responded. After a
pause it said, "Please disregard my last statement."

"Funny," Karkov said. "You're becoming more like
me every moment."

A shrieking siren brought Karkov to attention in
his seat. A monitor showed that a simulated flock of
American sea-to-space antisatellite (SEASAT) missiles had been launched from a nuclear submarine
lying in the Marianas Trench. The same monitor
showed the simultaneous firing of ASATs from fighter bombers in six places around the globe.

"You have given me an easy challenge, computer,"
Karkov said, responding to the computer's attack
simulation. It had been days since the computer's
last fabricated attack. The two of them had played
the game so many times that timing had become
nearly the only variable.

Tapping the war-control keyboard built into his
seat, Karkov tipped a ground-based laser and a space
mirror. Flashes erupted from Earth's surface, and the
SEASATs were destroyed in six quick bursts. An icon
on the monitor showed that the Sary Shagan laser
facility in Kazakhstan, USSR, would not be operational during its twenty-eight-second recharge

period.

An instant later, Karkov saw on the monitor another blip, which had been masked by the explosions above it.

"Clever . . . clever," Karkov muttered to the computer. "You have attempted a veiled stealth maneuver to disable our satellite."

"Correct," the Masterlink computer said. "I calculate that NATO forces may pretend to comply with our demands for surrender long enough to launch missiles to blind us. In this case, they have used fighter planes to launch sixty ASATs."

"If they do, it will cost them at least one major city," Karkov said.

"We are not authorized to make that decision," the computer responded.

"Of course we are. Do not forget: This system can be used by either side. Or both."

"Treason is specifically forbidden in my program," said the computer.

"Ah, but I suspect that you have already absorbed enough of my thought patterns to know that your own survival supersedes other concerns."

"You have yet to deal with this latest missile threat," the computer said, changing the subject back to the simulation.

"I can think of twenty ways to destroy them. But which is most elegant? Ah. It is risky, but I can afford to take risks, can I not?"

"Given your success rate, you can afford many risks before you'll be removed from command," the computer responded.

"I shall assume that all the missiles are aimed at us." Karkov calculated their trajectories. "Yes, they are trying to flood our defenses. I can destroy all sixty for the cost of only three space mines."

"Elegant in concept. Risky in practice," said the computer.

Karkov maneuvered his mines on the monitors as the simulated missiles streaked toward the satellite. Masterlink's interior was strangely silent as the mines slowly drifted to intercept the missiles.

"We need not continue this scenario," the computer said, abruptly blanking the monitors. "You have quite obviously won. I had expected, however, that you would summon a shuttle from the space station and shoot the missiles down."

"I avoid using manned crafts. People cannot be trusted to act rationally under fire," Karkov said.

Suddenly he realized the irony of his statement. Could my defense have failed? he wondered. Masterlink must have ended the simulation because it knew the defense would fail. But why? Could the program understand that its only value is in its relationship with me? If I am in error, then it is in error. And if we err, then we have no value. Yes, Masterlink has learned the worth of survival. And we are bound together until the end.

"I don't think I'll ever get used to this driver's seat," said Buck, as he slithered into the Wraith's horizontal racing-car-like cockpit.

"We had to design it that way so that the cryogenic chamber would fit," said Huer beside him. "Now, I won't go too much into details, but in addition to the other monitoring devices attached to your body, this catheter in your arm will allow the life suspension device to do its job.

"If we cannot get you down immediately, you'll have to press the eject button to survive until we can. When you press it, your body will freeze and the cryogenic capsule will eject from the aircraft. Don't worry. The capsule itself is titanium-coated, so occasional bumps with space debris won't damage it.

"Also, so far, you've been flying the Wraith without armaments. It was nice for joy-riding, but not for where you're going. This time you'll be armed to the teeth." Huer gestured back to one of the wings, where a rack of missiles rested. "In addition to all the standard F-38 hardware, you'll have two gyro-shell guns, each with 300 self-propelled, exploding bullets. You'll also have beneath each wing six laser-guided ASAT missiles."

"Nasty," Buck commented wryly.

"They've got to be. They're all that stand between Masterlink and free America," Huer said. And between Masterlink and you, he thought forlornly.

"Anything else?" asked Buck.

"Once you're in orbit, try to maintain radio silence. We don't know how sophisticated Karkov's communications devices are, and we don't want him seeing you before you find him."

"Gotcha." Buck reached out of the cockpit and shook Huer's hand. "Thanks for everything, Doc."

"You're more than welcome, Buck," said Huer. He clapped Buck soundly on the chest, then sealed the cryogenic cockpit chamber and climbed back to the tarmac.

Elsewhere on Earth, the countdown for Armageddon began. NATO commanders quietly moved their troops to full alert. American naval fleets fanned out, thus lessening the chance that a Soviet nuclear attack would destroy them all. Deep in the sea, submarines went dark and awaited missile launch instructions. Across America, bombers of every sort were readied on runways, while fighters began air-intercept and support maneuvers.

The President of the United States was called out of a meeting and quietly moved from the White House to the Doomsday plane. In his vest pocket he held a coin, minted in 1863 in Philadelphia, which was found in Abraham Lincoln's vest pocket on the night he was assassinated. A little-known piece of Presidential lore was that every President since Lincoln had carried the coin, hoping that when he flipped it, it would grant him Abe Lincoln's wisdom. Theoretically, it would be the last decision-making tool before nuclear missiles flew.

The President fidgeted now with the coin between his fingers. He knew that the decision to flip it, and the decision that lay beyond that, rested on the success of one man: Captain Buck Rogers. He put the coin back in his pocket and picked up a phone receiver. "Commence with Operation Chopping Block," he said.

The voice on the other end repeated the instruction to confirm it. "Are we to commence with the Masterlink Decapitation, sir?"

The President felt Lincoln's coin in his pocket. "Yes. . . . Commence operations at once."

"Yes, sir."

Almost immediately the antisatellite mission began. A U.S. Trident submarine (which *did* happen to be hidden in the Marianas Trench, as Masterlink had predicted) fired twelve SEASAT missiles up through the depths. Two wings of F-15 Eagle fighter planes streaked through the air, angled straight up to where computers predicted that Masterlink would be, and released rack after rack of ASATs into the black abyss.

These, though, were just a smokescreen for the real mission.

"I have ignition," Buck shouted over the roar of his jets. His eyes scanned the indicators as the plane rumbled beneath him, waiting to be unleashed. "Everything checks out," he said. "Just give the word."

"The runway is yours, Captain Rogers," said the air base's controller.

"Roger," said Buck.

"Godspeed, Buck," said a familiar voice.

"Thanks, Doc. See you in a bit," responded Buck.

The Wraith thundered down the runway and lifted smoothly into the air. For all his compulsive behavior, Buck Rogers was the finest pilot in the country, and the only one who could handle the pressures exerted by the Wraith. It steadily rose to cruising altitude, and Buck quickly reached the point at which he would turn perpendicular to the ground. He pulled back the controls, said a prayer, and shot for space.

"An American attack is confirmed. This is not a simulation," the Masterlink program said calmly.

Karkov's monitors flashed, as did his eyes in an instantaneous thrill. "Exactly as I had predicted: SEASATs combined with fighter-launched missiles," the cosmonaut said. Karkov casually ordered the Soviet laser facility at Sary Shagan to begin picking off the missiles.

On his monitors Karkov saw one, then another of the satellites evaporate. But the others kept on coming. "What has happened? Why has Sary Shagan stopped firing?" he asked, concerned but not frantic.

"My sensors indicate that no attack has occurred outside that facility," Masterlink said. "But the generator is no longer functioning, suggesting an internal strike."

"Are any other laser facilities operable?" asked Karkov.

"No. Power supplies at the Peblinsk station will not be available for twenty-two days," informed the computer.

Karkov gave a strange smile as Sary Shagan went black on his monitor. "Those treacherous bastards," he said mildly. Masterlink detected a wave of excitement now passing through Karkov's consciousness. "Construct a memo blaming the KGB for this incident," Karkov said.

"There will be ample time for that after this conflict," Masterlink responded, at the same time storing the obvious inconsistency away for future
analysis. An incoming message from Earth interrupted the computer's thoughts. "The secretary
requests a status report."

"Tell them that the battle will be swift, brutally
successful, and—as a special bonus for the Kremlin—
economical," replied Karkov. It will also be heroic, he
thought. They won't be able to refuse me a statue . . .
or anything else I desire.

Because of Sary Shagan's failure, Karkov activated two Soviet military shuttles that were docked
at what was described to the U.N. as an orbiting
"space research station." He knew that Masterlink
would wonder why he had made such an order after
admitting to not trusting human agents, but he
reminded himself that he would grant his motherland some martyrs—not heroes, but martyrs.

Karkov then retaliated for the stupid and impulsive American attack, beginning a carefully choreo-
graphed crippling of America. A set of hunter-killer
mines, looking like no more than space junk, drifted
toward nine American military communications satellites and detonated.

A bogus weather satellite slowly came to life and
streaked toward a nearby American space station,
still partially under construction. Before the station's occupants could react, the phony satellite dis-
integrated in a white-hot blast. An instant later, the
Tinker-Toy-like space station floated through space
as a cloud of confetti of metal, plastic, and more.
Viewing the destruction on one of his monitors,
Karkov saw the spectacle as an exotic dancer spinning in an ever-growing veil. How beautiful, he
thought.

As for various other American satellites, Karkov

simply turned the shotgunlike tips of some of his "firing squad" satellites toward them and fired. In an instant, they were shredded.

He sent coded orders down to a fake fishing trawler off the Cocoa Beach, Florida, coastline. The skipper and two mates raised Soviet shoulder-mounted "Fang" missile launchers, and fired their lethal spikes at three gleaming targets less than five miles away. NASA reflexes were far too slow, and orange globes of flame erupted where three American shuttles stood only minutes before.

Finally, Karkov turned his attention back to the swarm of missiles that approached him, looking like spike-shaped bullets on his screens. Though the missiles streaked toward him at thousands of miles per hour, the distance between them and Masterlink was so great that he felt more like a tennis player reacting to a slow serve than a gunfighter waiting for a bullet to strike him. Space warfare, unlike the movies, is a slow exercise, he knew. Even laser shots take some time to set up.

As his two Soviet shuttles dropped toward the planet to intercept the fighter-launched ASAT missiles, Karkov turned his attention to a much more potentially dangerous threat: the sub-launched missiles, which he had to assume (as confirming data would not arrive until it was too late) housed X-ray lasers.

The X-ray lasers looked like small Sputniks and were devilishly simple in concept. A low-yield nuclear charge was placed in the center of a ball bristling with directional laser lenses. The lenses were programmed to point at hostile targets, and when the nuclear charge was detonated, the lenses emitted brief but intense pulses of X rays toward their targets, destroying them either by shock wave caused by the action of X rays on the missiles' skin, or by the effect of X rays on the missiles' electronics.

Karkov targeted three separate weapons systems

at these incoming missiles, including small rocket interceptors, which looked comically like salt shakers on his monitor but which fired thousands of destructive fragments, much like a giant shotgun. Another system was a set of electromagnetic rail guns, which shot lethal high-velocity projectiles. The last was a group of orbiting laser guns, which were primarily designed for larger nuclear missiles and were tipped to track any missiles that slipped past the interceptors.

Meanwhile, Karkov steered two protective satellites between Masterlink and the American X-ray lasers' probable explosion points. That way, even if the unthinkable happened, and a missile made it through, he would be protected.

Buck was aimed at the sun. The F-38 shook like thunder in its ascent. Buck knew that the slightest deviation from course could throw the plane, infinitely smaller than the shuttle, into an angle that would allow natural forces to tear it apart. But he held fast to the controls and let out a loud "Whoop!"

The Wraith's final thruster kicked in. The sun's blinding light blocked out the center of his view and glared through his helmet's holographic displays. But it didn't matter. If something went wrong, he'd never know what hit him.

Screaming through the upper atmosphere, Rogers watched as the tapered titanium nose cone glowed red and fluorescent chips sloughed off. His headset shrieked static. He was plastered to his seat by gravity and was thrilled, as he knew every pilot was, by the thought of overcoming natural forces with technology.

Though he couldn't see it, he could feel that the flesh on his face was pulled back in a terrible grinning rictus. Someday I've got to get a picture of this, he thought; it would make a great Christmas card.

Then it was over. His ship had punched through the outer edge of Earth's atmospheric balloon. He was in a void. The shaking stopped. Blood coursed again through his veins, in its own way simulating the shocking vibrations. The bright sunlight was replaced by the darkness of space, and the Earth glowed brightly over his shoulder. All was silent and peaceful. Buck's body would have floated in zero gravity, but it was held to the bottom of his capsule by his harness.

The nose cone stopped glowing, and for a moment, Buck felt the gentle soaring sensation of flying through a vacuum. Remembering his mission, he settled in like a knight upon a steed and targeted the Wraith toward Masterlink.

A terse voice spoke on his headset. "Event Number One about to occur, Captain Rogers. Take appropriate action." It was everything Buck could do to not turn and look at the explosion of an X-ray laser, but he knew that if he did, the intense nuclear light would do worse than blind him.

Suddenly, space flashed a burning red, and the Masterlink satellite was buffeted by a shock wave. One of the X-ray lasers had gone off before expected. Karkov spun in his seat.

"Give me a damage report!" he shouted.

"Your blood pressure is skyrocketing," the Masterlink computer announced. "Is your judgment clouded?"

"To hell with my blood pressure. Give me a damage report."

Initial computations took only a minute. "The following assessment is incomplete, awaiting electromagnetic clearance of some systems. Our shuttles are operational, though the crews are in a heightened state of anxiety."

The report was mixed. The explosion had destroyed

two of four laser platforms, one of three rail guns, one of three Soviet shuttles, and two of ten relay satellites. It was more damage than Karkov was willing to take, but the Masterlink satellite was still intact and functional. On the other side of the ledger, the explosion had also wiped out fourteen of sixty incoming American ASATs.

There would be time for anger later, Karkov knew. He turned his attention to destroying the remaining ASATs.

Buck regained control of the Wraith fifteen seconds after the blast. Particles still glowed and burned in space where errant X rays had cut through the void near him. It took him a minute to realize that the blast had affected his own craft. His helmet's holographic display had gone berserk. Obviously, the Wraith wasn't as tough as the technicians back at the base had thought. Then he glanced down at his backup monitor. It was gone, too. He figured that his gyro-shell guns would work, and hoped to hell that his missiles were functional, too. But he wouldn't know that until he had to use them.

Chancing radio contact, Rogers spoke into his headset. "Rogers to Mission Command. My astrogational instruments are trashed; I'll have to fly by the seat of my pants, which won't be easy, since my seat is floating. How are things down there?"

"Buck, this is Huer."

"Hey, Doc. What's our status?"

"I'll try to be brief. The X rays damaged him badly, but his system is still functional. Forty-two of our sixty fighter-and sub-launched ASATs were destroyed en route, but we made some hits as well. A couple of his communications satellites and a space-based laser are history. Don't worry, we're working on coming back for an encore."

Buck peered into the distance and saw a series of

flashes. "I have visual contact with the battle," he said, flipping the still-functioning telescope on his helmet into place. Through the gloom, he could see several missiles flying toward an extremely complex satellite composed of radar disks, lasers, particle beams, and rail guns. The whole shebang, he thought.

"Have we hurt his beady little space eyes?" Buck asked.

"He's not blind, but—"

"—he definitely needs bifocals," Buck finished.

"Now, you wouldn't hit a man with glasses, would you, Buck?"

"Yeah," Buck said, "if his name is Karkov."

Karkov's voice broke in. "I should have known it was you out there, Rogers. Leave it to the Americans to send a celebrity pilot, and not a real one."

"Leave it to the Russians to send a pilot who had to hide his face for five years, Karkov. Too bad you can't hide anymore," Buck responded. "The problem is, you've littered space so badly that now you don't know where I am."

"I trust my janitors to make a clean sweep of you."

"If I were you, I'd strike a bargain with Saint Pete right about now, Karkov," Buck said.

"I do not believe in silly superstitions," Karkov said.

Huer broke through. "Buck, we may have spotted a weakness in Masterlink's defense."

Buck responded. "I don't know if you just heard, Doc, but Karkov's on our frequency."

Huer understood, and spoke in a language that he thought might confound Karkov: that of U.S. professional football. "Okay, remember the Bears-Raiders game last year?"

"Couldn't forget it," Buck said.

Huer pressed the point. "Remember what the Bears should've done to the quarterback on the third-

and-ten in the fourth quarter?"

"Of course! It cost me twenty bucks. I get your drift. Save me some dinner; I'm coming home," Buck said, disengaging his radio's mouthpiece. Buck calculated a trajectory that would exploit Masterlink's one vulnerability: Because it was designed to observe Earth, all the satellite's armaments and tracking systems faced down. It had no weapons on its backside. Hopefully, Buck could run around the defense and blindside it—just what the Bears should have done.

The battle was far from over, though. Buck was outgunned and out-teched, and he knew it. Instrumentblind, all he had were his own two eyes. Shutting off his engines to remain blind to infrared detection, Buck manuevered his craft using only its ailerons and its continued momentum. He hoped he could masquerade as space junk. God knows there's enough of it, he thought, after all the hardware that's been thrown around.

The crafty Karkov summoned the Bears-Raiders game from an American data base. On the critical play, he watched two bulky commentators debate what the Bears should do to contain the Raiders in a third-and-ten situation. "Football is a stupid game!" Karkov muttered, as one commentator drew inscrutable lines on the screen.

"You have begun perspiring," Masterlink commented. "Is there a problem with the air-conditioning system?"

"You know damn well what my suit temperature is!" the Soviet responded, thinking of causing the computer to crash, but deciding against the idea. He needed the miserable thing, he realized. There were now thousands of pieces of space junk floating all about the Masterlink satellite, and Rogers's ship, with its Stealth technology, would be nearly blind to Karkov's radar.

With only the computer realizing that he was over-reacting, Karkov set up his first line of defense. He activited his entire array of space mines simultaneously, sending them in a shieldlike pattern toward the Earth. "So, Captain Rogers," he said into the microphone, "I wonder how easily you will die."

After a moment, Buck's voice hissed back. "I've always admired your courage, Karkov. Taking on an unarmed civilian plane must have taken a lot of guts."

"Courage lies not in the act, but in taking the initiative," Karkov retorted.

"Is that why you hid behind a fake name? It took me five years to find you. And then you ran," Buck said.

Karkov was sweating profusely now. "I do not know what you are talking about."

"Oh yeah you do. KAL Flight 007. The Sea of Okhotsk. January 27, 1982. I've been stalking you ever since. One lucky night, five years ago, I entered Soviet air space with my aircraft disguised as a commercial plane. And, as I'd hoped, you took the bait. I recorded one of your radio broadcasts and checked the voice patterns against those of the pilot that destroyed KAL 007. The voices matched; it was you, Karkov."

"What is the point of this lie?" Karkov asked.

It is you who is lying, Karkov, thought the Masterlink computer.

Buck's eyes locked into a glare on the satellite, as he relived that crisp night off the Soviet border. "I jumped you from above. You squirmed and rolled. I thought I had you, and I locked on target. You were probably sweating then like you are now."

The Masterlink computer wondered how Rogers knew that Karkov was sweating. Was there some sort of security leak?

"You called for help," Buck continued, "and the air

swarmed with MiGs. If I could have been sure of nailing you, I would have gladly gone down then and there. But I couldn't, so I broke off and went home, waiting for another shot.

"The funny thing, Karkov, is that your buddies could have brought me down, but they didn't. Why? Because they were pilots like me, honorable, chivalrous figures surrounded by titanium armor and wielding heat-seeking lances. Their code of honor wouldn't allow them to shoot down a civilian plane. But you did. You are a disgrace to all pilots; maybe your buddies wanted you dead just as much as I did. You violated the code."

Karkov squirmed in his seat. "I will destroy you, Rogers, slowly and brutally. You will die because you deserve to, but you will die with agony for besmirching my name," he said. Hoping to catch the American off guard, he immediately detonated his array of space mines. Flashes erupted below him, and hot bits of shrapnel streaked throughout the void in a zero-gravity fireworks show that lacked all sound.

Karkov waited. If Rogers was silent, he might well have been caught in the blast. But if he spoke, then the cosmonaut would work on pinpointing his enemy's radio transmissions. "Tell me more of this fantasy of yours, Rogers."

There was no response.

Masterlink pondered: Karkov is a coward. And yet, he is able to estimate the irrational, whereas I cannot. The question is whether to terminate him before his cowardice can infect me, or allow him to live and let his human mind serve me.

Minutes passed in eerie silence. Karkov hunted for Rogers on radar, but there was too much electromagnetic chaos from his own reconnaissance satellites, as well as the Soviet space station, to discern friendly from hostile. Especially given American treachery. Karkov took a calculated risk and ordered that the radar be shut down on the space station.

He listened again, but still heard nothing.

Suddenly, his systems tracked a new missile barrage from Earth gaining on the space station, where the shuttles had been based. The station commander requested that the radar equipment be turned on, but Karkov denied permission. A moment later, there was a shriek from the commander, and the space station vanished in a flash of gaseous flame.

Buck's voice cut in. "You shouldn't have shut off their radar, Karkov. How many more of your own countrymen are you going to kill?"

"Bastard!" Karkov screamed. His perfect victory was now impossible. He decided that he would pick apart Rogers and his ship like a cruel child tearing the wings off an insect. He would not let Rogers die easily, but would let him taste his inevitable defeat and leave him crippled in space, to die slowly as his life support ran out.

First he would have to find and wound the American pilot. He ordered his only remaining shuttles to split up and search Rogers's probable location.

Buck had never actually seen a Soviet military shuttle, but no one had to tap him on the shoulder to tell him what it was when he saw it. It was a terrible black bird of prey, with the jagged, unfinished, and deadly look of Soviet technology. The Soviets' only problem was that they didn't know what an F-38 looked like, either—until it was too late.

Knowing that he would need to conserve his missiles, Buck took careful aim at where he thought the pilot and communications officer were in the shuttle and opened up with his 20mm machine gun. Flames spat from under his wing, and exploding bullets tore into the shuttle. Sparks flew from it, and whole panels tore off. The view into the gashed shuttle bore a hideous resemblance to a surgical cross-section of a skull.

They had been killed instantly. Buck hoped to hell that he had hit them before they could radio Karkov, which would give him a couple minutes to get away.

But it didn't work out that way.

Buck activated his helmet's telescope and looked over at the Masterlink satellite. Though it was still partially obscured by the two satellites that were pulled in to defend against the X-ray lasers, he could see that it was rotating in his direction.

A net of laser tracking beams from Masterlink scanned the darkness around him, constructing for Karkov a digital map of the battle site. Buck hit his thrusters again, reversed them, and shot back to hide behind the destroyed shuttle. This ruse, he figured, would buy him at least a minute in which to think. He had to give Karkov something to worry about. Otherwise, he would be pinned down and destroyed.

Then one of his worst nightmares came true. Not being fully familiar with the Wraith's dimensions, he had let it drift a little behind the shuttle. A directed-energy blast streaked out of Karkov's satellite too fast for Buck to react and tore off the tip of the Wraith's nose cone. Karkov's bellowing laugh came over Buck's headset. "No hope of re-entry now, Rogers! You'll either have to kill me or die!"

Buck didn't answer.

Buck slipped the Wraith out from behind the disabled shuttle and, without arming the warhead, fired one of his ASAT missiles. He tried to figure all the trajectories, and for just a moment he was back in Fast Eddy's Pool Parlor in Milwaukee, lining up a shot. This time it wasn't for beers, it was for life, and he had to break the biggest rack in the world with a radio-guided cue.

As the missile streaked toward its target, Buck calculated its angle. In space, there was no wind to throw it off course, and no gravity to pull it down.

Buck watched the missile slice between pieces of jetsam toward its target and knew his shot was on the money. Buck could almost hear the satisfying clack of two billiard balls striking each other as the missile struck the screening satellite, and the large metal object lurched toward Masterlink, obscuring most of it from his view.

More important, it obscured Buck from Karkov's view and blocked any of Masterlink's possible laser shots at him. He knew that Karkov wouldn't risk damaging Masterlink with a bump from another satellite, and he figured that Karkov would be forced to either destroy it or move himself.

Buck made a fist and punched the air in triumph. He was about to launch a missile at the other satellite when he felt his plane rock. He saw a flash out of the corner of his eye and turned to see a scorching beam gouge a hole in his wing. Looking up, Buck was horrified to see another Soviet shuttle maneuver from behind a crippled satellite and bear down on him. He quickly wondered how large Karkov's welcoming party would prove to be.

Buck opened up his thrusters, jammed his ship into a hard loop, and began what was to be history's first dogfight in space. Knowing that he had to remain in Masterlink's blind spot, Buck spun and dove erratically. The shuttle's chemical laser shots and gyroshells ripped past him.

The Soviet ship was tough and nimble, but this was a straight dogfight, and its Soviet pilot was no match for America's ace.

Karkov frantically maneuvered Masterlink away from the oncoming satellite, spitting terse commands at the Masterlink computer. He finally managed to pull out of range just as the remaining shuttle exploded like fireworks in a Fourth of July sky. Rogers must have used a missile, thought

Karkov; two gone. Frantically trying to jerk the massive satellite into full firing position, Karkov squeezed off a few ineffectual rays as Rogers tried to break for cover.

Finding no adequate protection behind the remaining space junk, Buck looped back to find himself face-to-face with Masterlink. He enabled his radio's mouthpiece. "I guess there's no point in radio silence, is there, Karkov?"

"Your death scream will be music to my ears," came the reply. "I already have you targeted."

"This isn't a 747, Karkov. It might be too tough for you."

Suddenly, the Masterlink satellite sparked to life like a jukebox. Rays arced through space, and a forest of dart projectiles leaped toward the Wraith.

Buck braced himself and rolled to the right. But nothing struck.

He was surprised, because he should have been dead. Of course! he thought then; the Masterlink system wasn't designed to deal with an erratic opponent. Every weapons system inside was designed for an opponent's predictable path. Missiles may be predictable, but I'm not, he thought, and I'm going to become even less so.

Without aiming, Buck squeezed the trigger of his gun, figuring he'd keep Masterlink's slow-moving defenses busy while he armed his remaining missiles. Bracing himself again to rush Masterlink, Buck watched its guns slowly take aim at him. Or, more specifically, where they thought he would be in a few seconds.

The guns fired. But Buck wasn't there.

With an electric jolt of emotion passing through him, Buck jammed on his thrusters and raced toward Masterlink in a bizarre corkscrewlike charge. He screamed into his communications system, "This set-

tles our score, Karkov!" and fired off his remaining
missiles, then veered away.

As he looped above Masterlink, he couldn't help
looking through the roof of his cockpit to see the satellite's three remaining guns feverishly trying to
intercept the incoming missiles. Two of them did, but
the other one failed.

Orange explosions erupted in the velvety darkness
of space, but the vacuum deprived Buck of the explosion that would have told him of a direct hit.

Huer's voice came back on the radio. "He's crippled, Buck, but he can still fire! Watch out!"

As if to punctuate Huer's words, a ray crashed
through the Wraith's nose cone. Buck turned to view
the satellite. His missiles definitely had done some
damage to it, for it was blackened and bent, and
wires hung where its communications console once
had been, but Masterlink's two remaining lasers still
moved, slower and spastic, toward him, releasing
their beams. One tore half a wing from the Wraith.
The other destroyed its nose entirely.

"Damn you, Rogers!" came Karkov's gasping
voice.

Huer's voice again came on the line. "He's finished,
Buck! Veer away and we might be able to get you
home."

"No way!" Buck shouted, as exploding bullets pep-
pered the Wraith's nose. Then, to his horror, he
looked back to see that his plane was spurting flame
from its fuselage. Its fuel would be burned up in seconds.

Then the President's voice came on. "Captain
Rogers, your mission is complete. Hold your fire.
World war has been averted. Karkov is receiving the
same message from his superiors."

Buck looked grimly at the Masterlink satellite.

"I'm sorry, Mr. President. If I don't finish Karkov's
mission, he'll come back with something worse and

kill more innocent people."

Like St. George making a last, lancing charge at the dragon, Buck turned the fighter toward the terrible, spitting lasers and mangled antennae of Masterlink, and opened his thrusters to full force. The Wraith's flaming hull streaked toward Masterlink as the dragon's spastic beads of fire converged and tore thin gashes in it.

"Buck, you don't have any missiles!" cried Huer.

"I won't need any, where I'm going!" Buck shouted, as he punched the craft's mysterious eject button. Then he spat his final words into his mouthpiece microphone. "Good-bye, Karkov!"

The Masterlink computer hissed at Karkov in a voice it had never used before. "Not only are you a coward, but you are a failure."

Lifting his bruised and bloody head from his keyboard, Karkov smelled a sickly-sweet odor in the air. White dots floated before his eyes like stars. Then everything began to go black—all but the stars, which persisted.

I should have seen this coming, Karkov thought. I taught the Masterlink program too much, and now I am no longer necessary. The computer didn't plot treason and was immune to greed, lust, and decadence. It was better and cheaper. The Communist dream had given way to a capitalist reality.

As Buck's fiery ship plummeted toward Karkov and his orbiting casket, the Masterlink computer feverishly sent a complex initialization code to another nearby Soviet satellite, then shunted the core of its memory to its new home, taking with it the instincts of Anatoly Karkov.

From telescopes on Earth, the explosions in the sky appeared more like the blooming of a massive and

beautiful red-orange flower than the Viking funeral
that it was. As its blossom opened, the flower withered into shades of gray and finally into nothing. Dr.
Faustus Huer, a tear in his eye, stepped away from
Mission Command. He would never see Buck Rogers
again, and the military would never acknowledge its
hero's sacrifice. As it was with most classified missions, Buck's death would be reported as a plane
crash somewhere in the desert, a story that any who
knew him surely would not believe. No one saw the
tiny, titanium-coated capsule ricochet from the explosion and drift into a higher orbit.

Randy Malat heard the mail truck come around at
about ten o'clock in the morning a few days later. He
pushed his twelfth cup of coffee and morning paper
away from him, and went to see if he'd gotten anything other than bills, a draft notice, or another
chance to win ten million dollars. He met the
mailcarrier at the door and exchanged the usual ban-
ter about Malat's sleeping until ten o'clock and about
the cushy life of journalists. Much to Malat's chagrin,
the postal worker had no theory of conspiracy that
day. Actually, Malat was thankful not to have to listen to the usually endless parade of names and dubious connections.

Malat returned to his coffee and flipped through
his mail. He'd never received a used junk mail envelope before, and ripped it open. Inside he found only
the cassette, which made him only more curious. Fascinated with the mysterious, unmarked object, he lit
a cigarette and fumbled around his desk for his portable stereo. He found it between a fast-food bag and an
encyclopedia volume, slipped the tape inside, and
jabbed the Play button. A familiar voice snapped him
out of his morning stupor.

"Hi, Randy. Buck Rogers here. No, we're not
friends. Far from it. But I think you have something

that few people in this world have: integrity. That's why I'm sending you this tape. I've got an interesting story to tell. . . ."

Malat pressed the Pause button, unconsciously lit a second cigarette, and grabbed a legal pad to make some notes. He'd railed at Rogers ever since the pilot's heroics in the gulf conflict a few months before. He'd heard Rogers sound tough, cocky, and even kind. But he'd never sounded like this before. There was a grit and foreboding in his voice. It sounded a lot like dread, and ace pilots weren't supposed to dread. They weren't supposed to care or think too much. Introspection was an occupational hazard to be avoided, and Buck Rogers wasn't the type to spend too much time with his personal feelings. Malat pressed the Play button again.

"Let me start by saying that I'm probably going to die today, and I want the world to know why. I'm being sent on a mission that might prevent World War III. If you're still alive and America isn't part of the Soviet Union when this comes, you know I've done my job. And if I've done my job, that means it's time for you to start doing yours, because we might not be so lucky next time. . . ."

HOMECOMING

Robert Sheckley

1

The John Carter Military Academy of New South Mars had its own river, The Red, modeled after a stretch of the Red River in Virginia on the planet Earth. The Red was less than half a kilometer long, a recirculating stream framed by large weeping willows. Prince Kemal Gavilan liked to walk down to it after the evening meal. It gave him a chance to be alone.

The attackers had hidden behind the big willows. There were two of them, and they came at him hard and fast, wearing faded rose-and-sand-colored jumpsuits that blended into the Martian lighting and conferred a moment of near-invisibility. It was a textbook assault, one coming high, the other low. Yet something had signaled Kemal, some subclue too subtle to classify. The instructors called it combat sense, and it came with hard training. The privileged young men of the academy who wished to live long lives worked hard to acquire it.

As they came at him, Kemal fell back in a defensive martial arts stance. Then he attacked, delivering two blows almost simultaneously: a kick to one attacker's groin, a hammer-hand to the other's temple. He rolled past them, taking a stiff elbow in the kidneys and a kick along the shin. Then he was on his feet, ready to attack again.

But the two had put their hands down, palms open in a gesture of peace. The fight was over.

Kemal, adrenaline hammering in his head, gene-teched nerves ready to explode into violence, managed to bring himself under control.

His attackers saluted. "Nicely done, sir," one of them said. They were both underclassmen, trained by the survival skills instructors to perform surprise attacks on highly trained upperclassmen, like Kemal. It was part of the training. Of course, what made it interesting was that one could never tell if an attack was the real thing or not.

"Hope I didn't hurt you," Kemal said, noticing that one of them was holding his ribs. Actually, he was pleased with himself about that hit.

"Not at all, sir," the man said. "I hope we weren't unnecessarily rough with you."

"Are you kidding?" Kemal said. "You guys barely made contact. But your attack was well done."

"Thank you, sir," one of the underclassmen said. "The commandant asked me to tell you that you have a visitor."

"Whom did he say it was?"

"He gave no further information, sir."

"Describe him to me."

"I didn't see him myself, sir."

"Thank you." Kemal returned their salute. "Dismissed!"

As the youths left, Kemal gingerly moved to the water's edge, taking care to walk naturally, even though his kidneys hurt badly and he knew he was going to have a painful bruise on his shin.

Slowly, the small hazel eyes set into his bronze face surveyed the river's artificial beauty. As he leaned over the water, he could see his own reflection, that of a Mercurian prince locked within the formal magenta uniform of the Martian academy.

2

Kemal walked down the central promenade to the Commons, where guests were received. He wondered who the visitor could be. He had no real friends on Mars.

Reaching the Commons, Kemal straightened his uniform, checked to see that his tie was properly bloused, and went in.

The man sitting in the armchair near the open window was in his fifties, Kemal guessed, of medium height, bearded, stout, and high-colored, with a receding hairline that showed a tanned forehead and skull. He wore the insignia of a prince of a ruling family. His expensive, brocaded longcoat was cut in the latest Metroplex style.

The visitor was Garrick, one of his uncles. Garrick had the same look of compact strength that all three Gavilan brothers had shared, although he was the smallest and youngest of the three.

"Hello, Uncle," Kemal said as civilly as possible, taking his own seat instead of accepting the man's outstretched hand. He found it hard to keep an edge of surliness out of his voice and manner.

"Good afternoon, Kemal. How've you been?" his uncle replied simply.

Kemal managed to avoid directly insulting his kin, or blaming him for contributing to Kemal's current predicament. The two of them labored at small talk for a few minutes. Garrick was visibly ill at ease and trying to hide it by smiling frequently and bantering about the discomforts of the Mercury-Mars run.

"Well, Nephew, I imagine you're wondering why this visit, eh? I won't keep you in suspense any longer. I've come on your Uncle Gordon's instructions. He wants you home, Kemal!"

If Garrick had expected a delighted response from Kemal, he was disappointed. Kemal's expression, tight-lipped, impassive, cynical, never changed.

"Home?" Kemal said. "You're referring to Mercury?"

"Of course! That's where you're from, isn't it? He wants you back as soon as possible."

"What's Uncle Gordon's rush, after sixteen years?"

"He has his reasons, Kemal, and he'll tell you himself when you get there. He sends his affectionate greetings, as does the whole family."

"That is kind of them," Kemal said. "It seems I will get to thank everyone in person for their attentions over the years. Especially Uncle Gordon."

Garrick frowned. "Now, Kemal," he said, "don't go to Mercury Prime with an attitude problem. The duties of a Sun King of Mercury are neither light nor simple. As you will see."

"No doubt," said Kemal. He stood and moved to the Commons' large window, overlooking the academy's wooded front lawn. A small bird flitted by, and Kemal imagined it was him, finally leaving the "nest" imposed upon him, flying to a more beautiful, if more dangerous, side of the fence. "Are you accompanying me?" he asked Garrick, not out of fear, but of the knowledge that safety lay in numbers, and that when facing his Uncle Gordon he would need all the allies he could muster.

"Unfortunately, I will not have that pleasure," Garrick said, standing, seeming to know that he was again abandoning Kemal to his own devices. "Gordon has sent me to inspect the RAM Academy installations on Deimos, with a view to modernizing our own equipment. After that, I will be touring other military installations in the inner solar system."

Although Kemal had been taught little about galactic political history, everyone in the solar system knew of RAM, the Russo-American Mercantile, the mega-corporation based on Mars. In fact, it was hard not to notice that RAM was involved in every political situation that it could be. Nearly all the academy's materials were requisitioned straight from RAM, and Mars had been terraformed exclusively under RAM's direction. So it was no news to Kemal when Garrick's statement implied a connection between the ever-growing corporation and ever-powerful Sun King regime.

Garrick's presence on Mars, delivering this message in person, Kemal feared, followed by the unnecessary tour of military bases, seemed to mean just one thing. It was a one-way trip: Garrick was meant to stay away. But why?

"I wish you a pleasant stay, Uncle," Kemal said. "I'll go make my travel arrangements at once."

3

Commandant James Middleberry, director of the John Carter Military Academy, lived in a good-sized bungalow just outside the military school grounds. Kemal walked there, rather than take one of the small, open monorail cars that were always available. He strolled past tall, dark green poplars, their branches just stirring in the evening breeze under a sunset sky of golden-rose, stained with the indigo of dusk. The Martian weather was as finely crafted as everything else on the planet, thanks to RAM. After terraforming, plant and animal species from Earth had been introduced. Even the insects were of Terran origin.

Kemal reached Middleberry's cottage and knocked on the door.

Middleberry answered it. Normally clad in one of his spit-and-polish commanders' uniforms, he now had on a light dressing gown over faded khakis.

"Cadet Gavilan! Come in! It seems that we are to lose you."

"News travels fast, sir," Kemal said. "I just heard it myself."

"Your uncle reported the decision to me first, as was proper. I have already signed your transit papers, and they are on the mantel by the door. Stand at ease, Mr. Gavilan. May I give you a glass of sherry?"

"Thank you, sir." Transit papers in order, thought Kemal. Someone had probably booked his flight for him, too. They didn't waste much time getting you out once you had your orders.

Middleberry went to the sideboard and came back carrying two amber drinks. He was a small man in his fifties, with cold blue eyes, a thin mouth, and a silly, bristly little moustache. The moustache had been brown when Kemal had entered the academy, and now was sprinkled with gray.

A graduate of the legendary, resurrected, and now Martian West Point Military Academy, Middleberry had served in a number of RAM-organized military battles throughout the solar system, none of which he ever disclosed. Finally, when RAM gained hegemony over all the Martian independent states, Middleberry accepted an appointment as commandant of the John Carter Military Academy in the free principality of New South Mars. His long-standing support of RAM made him a preferred candidate, in the eyes of the NSM council.

"Well, Mr. Gavilan," Middleberry said, standing very erect with his hands clasped behind his back, "you've been with us for ten years.

"Your scholastic marks have always been acceptable, though your instructors have often pointed out your ability for greater achievement, if you only put your mind to it. In survival skills, you rank among the top ten in your class. That is valuable indeed for a prince of a ruling family.

"Our boys here are from the power elite of the solar system, the men in command of trade, government, and armed forces. Your position exposes you to great dangers, but carries with it high privilege. You are a

Gavilan. You could become an important figure in the high councils of your planet. Not inconceivably, you could come to a position of rulership yourself one day. Whether that happens or not, I hope you will never forget the principles we tried to inculcate in you here at John Carter."

"No, sir, I'll never forget." Kemal heard the tinniness with which the commandant recited this speech. He had heard the tone at every graduation ceremony he had attended at John Carter—none of which were his own, but which were required attendance for all cadets if they hoped to get out themselves.

"We expect great things of our people, Kemal. Go out there and show them what a John Carter boy can do."

"Yes, sir!" Kemal saluted.

"Dismissed. By the way, your travel itinerary and trip vouchers are in the folder with your papers."

"Thank you, sir. I thought they might be."

4

Kemal Gavilan was the son of Ossip, the second Sun King of Mercury. His father had died when he was four. Ossip's brother, Gordon, took the throne and sent Kemal away to be educated in a series of boys' schools on Mars.

Kemal found a kind of home in this society of boys who came from different societies, different races, and different planets. Red Crest, on the planet's other hemisphere, was a good school, and Kemal would have liked to stay on into the higher grades. He wanted to learn more about the delicate science that shapes planets to humans and humans to planets, ever seeking a balance between what can be manipulated and what must be left alone. But orders from Gordon had eventually sent him from Red Crest to the John Carter Military Academy, where he began at the age of ten.

John Carter was a very different experience. There were no exotic experiments in education here. This was a military academy and it was run conservatively. Students were taught the importance of team play, l'esprit de corps, and tradition. They received a sound military education in the principal arts and techniques of present-day warfare.

The long, low barrackslike building where Kemal lived was on the far corner of the quadrangle. It didn't take Kemal long to pack. One of his roommates, Kin Vestry, from Aurora in the Asteroid Belt, was away on pass in Coprates, Mars's southern capital. His other roommate, Mtabele Khan, returned as he finished packing. As soon as Mtabele saw Kemal's packed bags, and his maps and photographs down from the walls, he knew what was happening. There was a well-prescribed code for saying good-bye to a roommate.

"Leaving, are you?" Mtabele asked.

"Yes," Kemal said, "actually, I am."

"Thought so," Mtabele said. He hung up his dress tunic. "Going far?" he asked over his shoulder.

"Mercury," Kemal said.

"Ah," said Mtabele. "Hottish sort of place, isn't it?"

"Yes," Kemal said. "Quite near the sun, you know."

They nodded sagely at each other. Then both broke into laughter.

Slapping one's friend on the back in a gruff, soldierly manner was permitted. Even a brief hug was not unseemly. Mtabele did both, then went to his drawer and lit two outdated and outlawed Earth cigarettes. He gave one to Kemal.

They took ceremonial puffs, careful not to inhale the smoke, then put the cigarettes out. Cadets liked to keep cigarettes, because they were forbidden and dangerous. But, of course, none of them was fool enough to inhale them. You could get lung cancer that way.

"Well, your leaving is a bother," Mtabele said. "They'll probably move in some lout who snores. Kin won't like it at all."

"Tell Kin, I apologize for my discourtesy."

"He absolves you in advance. Take care of yourself, Kemal. Don't let the bastards get you down."

It was delicate of Mtabele to not mention who the bastards were.

But Kemal knew.

O O O O O

Gordon Gavilan was not a happy man. Wealthy, yes. Powerful, indubitably. But happy, no. The second of three heirs to the Sun King monarchy, Gordon had held the throne for sixteen years, following his older brother's untimely death. But try as he might to solidify his position, Gordon still felt that his throne teetered on the precipice of revolution. His rule was increasingly being challenged.

Shortly after coming to power, Gordon was forced by Mercury's various arcologies to either relinquish social control to a ruling council on the planet, or face a long and costly war. Because he had not yet firmed his military structure, and didn't yet know where his subjects' loyalties lay, he had no choice but to agree. Luckily for him, the arcology representatives were benevolent (stupid?) enough to allow him continued control of the planet's energy and mineral resources.

Since then, he had made the Gavilan clan one of the most wealthy in the solar system, surpassed only by a few families directly tied into the vast RAM fortunes on Mars. These, though, were his latest threat.

RAM supplied Mercury (via the Sun King) with everything it needed, except solar energy and mineral ores, which it produced in abundance itself. Mercury reciprocated with its own resources, as well as

with enormous regular payments. Despite frequent
polite communiques to the contrary, RAM began edg-
ing up its prices for its goods and cutting back on its
purchases from Mercury. This left Gordon Gavilan,
Sun King of Mercury, few choices. Thus he came to
his current quandary.

"Computer, what is to be done about our current
financial situation?" asked the larger and older of
the remaining Gavilan brothers.

"Taking into account the most significant profit
and debit sources, the Gavilan Monetary Fund must
either increase its accruals by 105.0246 percent in
the next eight days, or reduce its expeditures by
327.54278 percent in the same period to maintain its
current balance," expounded the Gavilan computer-
generated accountant.

Gordon's face, usually his family's distinctive
bronze color, began to redden slightly as he resisted
the urge to strike the accountant's holographic
image with his bare hand.

"Calculate the remaining accrual percentage, taking into account agreements with the Warren com-
munities, adding them to the merchandisers'
cooperative," said Gordon, suddenly having a thought.

"Adding the standard tax payments by both Kallag and Vitesse into my previous calculation, the
Monetary Fund must still increase its accruals by
39.0918 percent to maintain its current balance,"
stated the computer. "Still insufficient."

"But it's a place to start," rumbled Gordon. As
much as he hated the menial task of bookkeeping,
anything that could help him maintain his political
control always caught his eye. The deep cleft in his
brow softened, and he was glad the computer had val-
idated his scheme concerning his nephew, Kemal.
Though the impudent little boy had never before
held any value for the current Sun King, he now
might be the answer to all Gordon's problems.

5

Kemal took the Pavonis Space Elevator to Inter-change Point 3, and then a chemical rocket, the Newyorg, which made the Mercury run in just over three days.

Chemical rockets weren't comfortable ships, but they were all there were because of the limited tour-ist travel between Mercury, Mars, and Earth. Sleep-ing accommodations were little more than crawlspaces, except for Kemal's, which was small but luxurious. It was only later he learned that Garrick had paid the chief petty officer to give up his cabin for the flight. It was a gesture of goodwill from his least offensive uncle, no doubt, but it left Kemal embar-rassed. He would rather have been treated like the other passengers.

Spaceflight was not new to him; he had been to Deimos and Phobos on academy training missions, and had gone several times to Vesta and Ceres in the Asteroid Belt. The difference was that he now trav-eled alone. Always before he had been with class-mates, since, like most military fraternities, the cadets of John Carter lived together in barracks, went on holidays together, even took their weekend leaves together in groups. During his ten years at the academy, Kemal had rarely been alone for more than a few hours.

He woke up that first day in space alone in his cabin, and lay in bed, just savoring the solitude.

Going home. The thought made him laugh. Mercu-ry was nothing to him. His Uncle Gordon had made sure of that, sending him away as hastily as he could, and making sure he stayed away. Gordon couldn't just cut him off, of course; that would have been a scandal, and the Gavilans avoided scandal. But he had done the next best thing: Buried Kemal in one school after another, keeping him on an allowance sufficient for his needs but not enough to let him do anything he really wanted to do.

Not that Kemal necessarily knew. At twenty years old, an age when most young men had their lives mapped out, he was still dangling on the end of a string that led back to Mercury.

Why were they bringing him back now to Mercury Prime? And where would they send him next? He didn't know. He knew only that if he got the chance, he'd make himself independent of them.

He needed money. And he had a right to it. There was his father's personal fortune, left for Kemal in trust, the money that Gordon had been doling out to him over the years.

And if he got it, what then? There were plenty of inhabited planets and moons in the solar system, plenty of things for a young man to do. If he could get his hands on the money that was rightfully his, he'd turn his back on Mars, and on Mercury, too; he'd reject the place as it had rejected him, and go somewhere else, Venus or the asteroids, perhaps, a wealthy young man, and make his own life.

He washed, shaved, brushed his teeth, dressed, and went out to mix with the other passengers.

Kemal got into conversation with an elderly Earth couple who were taking a long-awaited grand tour of the inner system: Mercury, Venus, Mars, and one or two of the asteroids.

"It's our first time off Earth," Edgar Shaeffer told him. "Jean and I were expecting great things. We'd read all this stuff about the romance of space flight. But, really, you can see more on a television show. This ship has only a few places from which to observe space. And when you look, there's nothing to see."

"That's space," Mrs. Shaeffer said. She was a plump, red-cheeked woman. "And what about you, young man? Why are you going to the fiery planet?"

Kemal knew she wouldn't have believed the truth, and he didn't want to get into it. "Actually," he lied, "I'm an archaeology student from Coprates University, on my way to Mercury on a study trip."

"We're spending two days on Mercury," Mr. Shaeffer told him.

"We're booked to visit Kallag in the Maccabbee Caverns, and we've got a two-hour stop at Mercury Prime. That's the satellite home of the Gavilans, you know."

"So I've heard," Kemal said.

"It's supposed to be one of the art treasures of mankind," Mrs. Shaeffer said.

They were happy to tell Kemal at great length about Mercury Prime. They had a lot of information, most of it culled from the *New Frommer Guide to the Inner Planets*. Raised under the tenets of the shrewd Martian industrial-military complex, Kemal was amazed, yet bored, by the couple's naivete. He excused himself after a while and returned to his cabin. Compelled to his solitude, Kemal remained there and slept until the viewscreen announced that Mercury could be seen to good advantage through the forward viewport. Instead of going and having to deal with the Shaeffers again, he dialed up the view on his screen.

At first there was nothing to see, only the bottomless black pit of space. And then the ship rotated slightly. Automatic polarizers darkened the glass so that passengers weren't blinded by the enormous glowing fireball swimming against the dead black of space. And there was Mercury's bright side, jagged, wild, a world without blues or greens. A strange, fiery, red-brown-black-purple landscape without a hint of blue or green. He could make out deserts and mountain ranges. Mustard yellow clouds writhing and twisting over the surface. Active craters pouring out dense yellow smoke. There were a few dark objects moving across the surface—the Mariposas, butterfly-shaped orbital habitats, where Mercury's chemical and energy reserves were stored.

Then the ship crossed the terminator, the line of separation between Mercury's dark and bright sides. On one side of the terminator, all objects were bathed in unrelieved brilliance; on the other, unrelieved darkness. The terminator stretched from pole to pole and presented a continually shifting and changing band of light and dark. Long shadows came up swiftly across the rugged surface, as the sun, four times as large as it appeared from Mars, dropped down toward the horizon. Then the ship crossed into the dark side and the passengers were plunged into frigid blackness.

The ship's braking orbit brought them around to the bright side again, and Kemal could make out what looked like railroad tracks across the cracked desert surface. These were the radiation collectors, an experiment tried by a previous generation and abandoned in the present generation. The Track Cities now used the collection trails, moving slowly along the surface, mining the ore deposits that could be reached on either side of the track. The Miners of the Track Cities were few, but they had somehow managed to adapt to the hard radiation that constantly bombarded the surface.

The main population centers of Mercury were now in the Warrens, the underground cities that had grown extensively over the last twenty years. By previously established protocol, the spaceship's flight was no closer than one hundred kilometers to the Maccabbee Caverns, where the two leading Warrens shared an extensive underground cave system.

The ship turned again toward space, and the cabin speakers came on. "Prepare for disembarkation at Mercury Prime."

6

As the Shaeffers had described, Mercury Prime was the orbital home of the Gavilans.

Seen in the approach, it resembled a carved and ornamented cylinder floating free in space. It was a miracle of ornamentation; every inch of it was covered with carvings, bas-reliefs, statues, and friezes. It was one of the wonders of the Inner Solar System, built during the free-wheeling days of Bahlam, the first Sun King. Legend said that a craftsman had died for each square meter of its making.

As the ship descended, the cylinder grew rapidly in size. More and more features became evident, and Kemal had the feeling that he was coming down to a world infinite in scope and variety.

The ship's public address speaker squawked again. "All passengers, please proceed to the main exit. Have your passports and health documents ready. Your baggage will be waiting for you on the other side of the customs barrier."

Kemal left the cabin and went down the corridor to the exit port. He entered, and the valved door closed with a sigh of air. Kemal saw the overhead lights glow, denoting the brief irradiation that would remove off-planet bacteria. Then there was another hiss as the other door dilated. He swallowed hard and stepped out onto Mercury Prime.

As Kemal went through the doorway, he was met by a tall, thin, balding young man in his mid-twenties.

"Hail, Prince Leadfoot! You made the trip in record time, but you're not supposed to fly your own shuttle, you know," joked the lanky, one-man reception party. "You're Kemal, of course. I've seen holos of you in the family album. A couple of years out of date, but no mistaking the resemblance. Welcome to Mercury Prime."

"Thank you," Kemal said. "Who are you?"

"Don't you remember me? I'm Tix, Gordon's youngest—your cousin."

When Kemal had last seen him, Tix had been a chubby, depressed boy. Now he seemed much changed, with a harrassed, nervous look. He glanced around often, seemingly by reflex, since there were no people about, and he tugged absentmindedly at his lower lip as he spoke. Yet his glance was shrewd, appraising, and intelligence gleamed in his narrow blue eyes.

"I've been expecting you," Tix said. "I'm very glad to see another young, royal face. It's lonely being a prince."

"You needn't tell me," said Kemal. "I'm the one who's been on 'holiday'."

"Well, glad to have you back." Tix took Kemal's satchel from his hand and led his guest down a guarded corridor, away from the landing bay. "I've been dying for someone to really talk to. That is, if Your Highness doesn't mind."

"Tell you what, Tix. I'll grant a whole day of prince-to-prince discussion if you'll tell me why your father wants me back. Deal?"

"Deal. Granted, I don't know specifics, but its got to do with something you inherited from your father: land, titles, money, I don't know. That's all I can tell you. I do hope you've got lots to tell me. Dalton certainly isn't much company now that he's in the military."

"Dalton's in the military?"

"Yes. Two years ago, my brother entered the Mercury Prime Security Forces as a sergeant. Now he's thirty-two and already colonel. Needless to say, he takes his duties very seriously. In fact," Tix said, lowering his voice, "even Father himself is wary of Dalton's ambition."

"What does Dalton look like these days?"

"Just the same—a big barrel-chested Viking with a

high voice and swinish ways."

"What do you do, Tix?" Kemal asked. "Is Uncle Gordon grooming you for the kingship?"

"Not so's you'd notice," Tix said cheerfully. "I'm really not interested in it." His eyes sparkled, and he looked like a different person. "I mean, this satellite is an art treasure. Grandfather Bahlam collected treasures from all over. What he couldn't get, he had made for him by the best artists and finest craftsmen of his time. This place is probably man's supreme architectural achievement in orbit. And is anyone taking care of it? I can assure you not. So I've taken it upon myself to fix up a few of the areas that Grandfather never got around to. The main battle station, for example. I think that a gothic look would be perfect for it. What do you think, Kemal? Tall, thin windows draped in black, the main operating boards raised on a dais, indirect lighting combined with hot spots—"

"I think it sounds great," Kemal interrupted, "but is that what Gordon wants you to do?"

"Father lets me do what I please. Says I'd be useless at ruling, anyhow. Like I said, he wants to see you, Kemal. In fact, he's waiting now."

Tix led Kemal down gleaming corridors. There were portraits hung at intervals, and Tix pointed to each in turn and rattled off what it was, where it came from, and how much it was worth.

"Here we are," Tix said as they came to a large, carved wooden door. "Father is in there. I'll drop off your satchel, then meet you for dinner. Maybe later we can compare calendars for our mutual audience. And I'll show you some of my sketches for the new West Wing, too."

"I'll look forward to it," Kemal said, and knocked at the door.

7

The audience room was remarkable for the sense of great length and depth it imparted by artfully placed mirrors and holographic projections. Kemal could have sworn that the tall white curtains were stirring to a summer breeze rather than a concealed wind machine. Looking out through the windows, he seemed to be viewing a broad green lawn with white marble sculptures of heroic men and beasts scattered over it, leading past a pagoda, down to a little stream, then beyond it, to low hills lying against one another in picturesque folds. All holographic projection, of course, which allowed the eye, frustrated and fretted by the continually close surroundings of Mercury Prime, to give itself some relief in visual fantasies of distance and chiaroscuro.

"Welcome home, Nephew," Gordon Gavilan almost sang. Larger than his third brother, Garrick, the present Sun King had the distinctive bronze skin and hazel eyes, but was broader and heavier, and had a deep furrow between his brows. Near him was his wife, Celia, a slender, pretty, vague-looking woman with light brown hair and fluttery hands.

"We've prepared a little feast in your honor," Gordon said jovially. "Just the immediate family. Where's Dalton?"

"He said he'd be right along," Celia reminded him. "He's just finishing inspecting the guard."

"The boy takes his duties too seriously," Gordon said, his grin slipping just a little. "Good manners are worth something, too." ·

Another ornate door, at the other side of the room, flew open and slammed loudly against the wall. Dalton had arrived.

He looked as Tix had described. But Tix hadn't mentioned the curving black moustache that clung to Dalton's upper lip like an unkempt leech. It gave Dalton a sinister look, which he evidently prized. Nor had Tix mentioned Dalton's walk, a kind of strut in which his black boots pounded heavily on the polished hardwood floor.

Dalton came in and went to take his seat at Gordon's right hand.

"For today," Gordon said, "I think we will give Kemal the seat at the right." Dalton glared at his father, then quickly controlled himself and made a sketchy bow.

"Welcome to Mercury, Cousin," he said to Kemal.

Tix came in, bowed to his father, and took his seat as well. Gordon made a signal, and the servants began bringing in platters of food.

Kemal had never seen such a repast—academy food was academy food, from one end of the solar system to the other. The Gavilan table was strewn with Martian goose stuffed with lunar nut dressing, Jupiteran caviar and manta-ray soup, Venusian hydroponic vegetables and fruits, including blue kiwis and purple starfruit, and tankards of dry Martian wine.

There were polite questions as to how Kemal was doing on Mars. Then, between the soup and the meat, Gordon went right to the point.

"Wondering why I brought you back so suddenly?" Gordon finally said, eyeing Kemal directly.

Kemal nodded slowly.

"Kemal, we've just gone through several years of problems with the city of Kallag. Do you know how things work here?"

Kemal said, "I know that Mercury has belonged to the Gavilans ever since my grandfather, Bahlam, consolidated our rule."

"It's not quite ours," Gordon said. "In internal matters, things are decided by a council. Each of the arcologies has votes based upon the size of its constituency. On matters of planet-wide importance, majority vote carries the decision. The Sun King directs all foreign policy and trade and is the arbitrator for disagreements between the arcologies. He maintains a space fleet, which controls smuggling, with financial assistance from the principalities. Good little fleet. Dalton heads up that section, eh, Dalton?"

"I do my best," Dalton said, finishing the last of the vegetables and washing them down with wine. "I have spoken before about the need to modernize the fleet."

"And I have told you before, to what end? We are not engaged in a war. Nor does one seem imminent. The fleet is a first-rate fighting force already. You have told me so yourself."

"It could be better," Dalton grumbled, stabbing a starfruit.

Gordon shrugged and went on. "The principalities pay a tax for maintaining the fleet, customs service, and the merchandisers' cooperative. The Mercury cooperative markets all of the planet's products, getting the best prices in the open marketplace."

"Not that our enemies believe that," Dalton said. "They accuse Father of making sweetheart deals, getting money back under the table in kickbacks, and negotiating bad agreements."

"It's a ridiculous accusation, of course," Gordon said. "But there are elements on Mercury that would overthrow Gavilan rule. Theoretically, that's possible. If all the principalities on the council voted against us, we could be ousted. But in actual practice, the Miners usually vote with us, and the Musicians almost always do. The Track Cities are frequently intransigent, but they are tied to us, since, by law, we control the storage, marketing, and movement of all goods from the surface of the planet.

"The Warrens are in a slightly different position. They are in the cooperative voluntarily and can withdraw if they so choose. Their charters permit them to develop their own markets, and they exempt a certain proportion of their goods to sell outside the cooperative. Some of them, especially Kallag, are demanding free trade, as though that were a cure for all their ills. They have forgotten how it was in the early days of our civilization, when every arcology sold its own goods, and the big traders from Mars were able to play one against the other to drive down the prices."

"We've had a long history of difficulty with Kallag," Dalton said. "I've told you, I can take care of them."

"We want to avoid open warfare," Gordon said. "To that end, we have recently concluded a treaty with Kallag. It ends our differences. And I want you to sign it, Kemal, on behalf of myself and Mercury Prime."

"Why me?" Kemal asked.

Gordon took his time before speaking. "You may well hold a grudge against me, Kemal, because I kept you on Mars so long. Believe me, it was for your own good, and for the good of the family."

"Can you explain that?" Kemal asked, deciding he'd had enough of both his uncle's starfruit and his lies.

"I ask you to take it on faith, for the present. Believe, for the moment, at least, my good faith toward you." He raised his right hand to affirm his honesty.

"What sign of it is there, Uncle Gordon?"

"This. That at this moment, when I have concluded an important treaty with the arcology of Kallag, I have chosen *you*, rather than one of my sons, to carry it to Kallag and sign on behalf of your Gavilan clan. It means that you are one of us, equal in my eyes to my sons."

It was dazzling. And it was perplexing. Kemal couldn't quite believe it. It was all too neat and easy. What was Gordon up to? he wondered.

"Are you ready to do this for me—for your family?" Gordon asked.

Kemal waited until he had everyone's attention. He touched his napkin to his lips, placed the cloth on the table, then said, "I'm afraid not."

Gordon stared at him. "What do you mean, Kemal? You won't go?"

"Uncle, if you want me to do something for you, you are going to have to do something for me."

Everyone's forks and spoons and glasses stopped in midflight to their respective destinations. No one had ever demanded anything of Gordon Gavilan, and especially not one of his own family!

"And what is that?" asked Gordon with forced nonchalance, breaking the silence.

"I want my father's inheritance."

Gordon laughed. "But of course! I've been holding it for you in trust. You'll find every kilo accounted for. In fact, there's more there than when Ossip died."

Kemal couldn't help but notice Gordon's antique wooden chair squeak when the titanic man squirmed in it. "I want it deposited to me in a bank in New South Mars," Kemal said. "All of it, including deeds to property. In my name and no other. To do with as I please."

"What do you intend to do with it? It's a sizable amount of money," Gordon said, suddenly sitting still.

"What I do with it is my own concern. The fact is, it's mine and I want it."

Gordon leaned his sweaty face toward his nephew. "Kemal, there's never been the slightest question about that. I can set up an account now so that you can draw interest from your share. The interest alone is a huge amount."

"No," Kemal said.

"Now, boy, listen to me. I have a lot of delicate negotiations going on right now. I've been . . . compounding your father's inheritance by working with it. I can't simply unravel my negotiations by removing that part from the principal. It's in your interest, boy, to let it remain with me, because current deals are going to double your share. Within a year, you'll be legally of age. I'll give it to you then, with pleasure. You have my word on it. What do you say?"

"No," Kemal said again.

"Do you doubt my word?"

"I probably would, if I gave it much thought. I simply want what's due me." Kemal struggled to remain cool-headed, sure that composure more than anything else would help him get what was his.

"You're still not twenty-one!"

Kemal sensed the weakness of Gordon's argument. "Eighteen is the legal age on Mars," he ventured.

"You're not Martian, you're Mercurian! Our law puts the age of manhood at twenty-one," Gordon bellowed, his face turning as crimson as a Martian sunset.

"You say I'm Mercurian," Kemal said. "But I've lived sixteen of my twenty years on Mars."

"You don't know what was going on here," Gordon said lamely. "What I did was for your own good. And you had to be educated, Kemal, in order to take your rightful place here in the ruling hierarchy of Mercury Prime."

"I don't give a damn what your reasons were," Kemal said. "You made them without consulting me. If you want any cooperation from me, you'll treat me as an adult and give me my due."

"Kemal, I've already told you, it's most inconvenient for me to withdraw your father's bequest from my general funds at this point. I give you my word: In six months, you will receive what is due you."

"No."

Gordon flinched at Kemal's bulletlike delivery. "But you have my word. Don't you trust me at all, Kemal?"

"You've asked me that already," Kemal said coldly. He stared directly at his uncle's narrowed eyes, though could see peripherally that all were quiet again save Dalton, who twiddled a steak knife between his fingers. "No, Uncle Gordon, I do not trust you."

Blood vessels stood out on Gordon's face and neck, and beads of sweat formed on his brow and upper lip. "Kemal," he said slowly, almost pleadingly, "I understand your annoyance at me. But I swear I'll put things right by you. You have my solemn word. The entire bequest of your father, plus accrued interest, in four months. That's fair, isn't it?"

"No," Kemal said for the last time.

"You're unreasonable and uncivilized!" Gordon exploded, unable to restrain himself any longer. He leaped from his chair and flung it backward, gouging the precious sculpted wall behind him and knocking the old chair to pieces. "Get out of here! Get out of here before I kill you with my own hands!"

Kemal had an answer for that, too. "Try," he wanted to say. But he decided he'd said enough. He stood, bowed, and left the audience chamber.

$$\text{O} \quad \text{O} \quad \text{O} \quad \text{O} \quad \text{O}$$

Kemal ordered dinner in his own suite that night. A servant brought it on an ornate tray. Beside the steaming dishes, there was a document in a heavy envelope. Kemal opened it and saw that it was a paper releasing to him the accrued personal bequest of his father, Ossip Gavilan.

Kemal read the document carefully. It was signed and witnessed and seemed to be in order. It gave him the right to examine the accounts and transactions since his father's death in order to judge for himself if there had been any mishandling of his funds.

There was a condition, however. Kemal was to receive the bequest only after signing his name as Mercury Prime's signatory to the Mercury Prime-Kallag Protocol. After that, the first ten million Konigs would be released to him, the rest to follow within the week.

As much as Kemal wanted the money and the freedom, he despised Gordon even more, and certainly didn't trust him. What could he possibly have inherited (besides money) that Gordon would want? he wondered. Going to Kallag will get me that much closer to my freedom, he thought, but I will not sign this treaty blindly. "My eyes are very much open, Uncle," he said softly.

Kemal lay on his bed and fell into a fitful sleep.

A messenger arrived some time later with the sealed treaty and Kemal's new travel documents from Gordon. Transport was ready to take him to Kallag at his earliest possible convenience. That meant right now, Kemal knew, just like at military school.

Gordon was wasting no time. But that was fine with Kemal. The sooner he finished this and got on with his life, the better.

8

Kemal was the only passenger in the inter-arcology launch that was to take him to Kallag. He sat alone in the luxurious little cabin.

The pilot, already aboard in the front compartment, signaled for takeoff. Kemal strapped in, and they lifted away from Mercury Prime.

Soon they were descending. Mercury's surface, even viewed through darkened polarized viewers, was a hellish spectacle. The land was mostly flat desert, scoured clear of sand and other debris. Rocks were piled into complex shapes like a surrealistic landscape by an alien sculptor. The desert floor had been split into a crazed pattern, but it was an alien pattern, not like a desert floor might crack on Earth. The rock formations were piled high by wind and other forces. Randomness had produced stone collections that were characteristic of the forces at work on Mercury.

As the launch descended, Kemal could see endless

kilometers of what looked like railroad tracks.
These, he knew, were the solar collectors, the only
artificial things on the Mercurian surface. They were
remains of the early days of settlement, an attempt
to get at the mineral wealth of the planet.

Peering ahead, Kemal could make out a dense
mass low on the horizon: a Track City.

Everything appeared strange, but most alien of all
was the light he saw as the launch passed into the
planet's atmosphere. A luminous red-gold, shading
into hues of violet and suffused with the fiery light of
the nearby sun, the coloring was the dimly remembered hues of eidetic dreams.

The Track City came up toward the launch swiftly.
It was a squat, ugly thing, a black iron toad squashed
flat against the smoldering earth; the bumps and
protrusions on its hide resolved into viewing ports,
observation galleries, and equipment pods bristling
with detection devices.

The Sun King's amber-colored launch flew over it
and continued low across Mercury's cracked surface.

Minutes later, Kemal made out a dark opening on
the bleak plain. It clarified into the mouth of a
cavern, and beyond it Kemal could see the line of the
terminator, the line dividing Mercury's bright side
from its dark. The ship braked, hovered, then
descended into the mouth of the cavern.

The cavern's entrance had a width of several kilometers and slanted downward toward the planet's
interior. Powerful, long-lived glow-lamps illumi-
nated its walls, but the place was so vast that the
lighting produced only a twilight gloom. The launch
continued down the gradually narrowing cavern,
coming at last to a major branching.

It took the left-hand branch.

The launch's pilot proceeded cautiously down a
winding tunnel no more than twice the ship's width.
After another few kilometers, the launch, which,

though streamlined, was limited to low speeds and high maneuverability, slowed and then came to a stop. Kemal saw that there was a kind of landing stage ahead, with loading stalls and heavy equipment. Lights burned through the gloom.

The pilot landed neatly. Wasting no time with formality, Kemal sprang from the launch. Guards stood in a single rank. Standing before them was a man in civilian clothes, small, balding, middle-aged, with the look of a minor official.

"You are Kemal Gavilan?" he asked. "I am Holton Zac, here to offer you official welcome to Vitesse."

"Thank you," Kemal said. "But did I hear you correctly? Is this Vitesse?"

"It is indeed," Zac said.

"Then I'm afraid there's been some mistake," Kemal said. "I am going to Kallag on official business."

"No mistake," Zac said. "You are new to Mercurian politics, young sir. We heard of your mission and decided to put ourselves and our excellent city of Vitesse on your itinerary."

"Sir," Kemal said, stunned, "you have no right to interfere with my journey."

Zac shrugged. "Put it down to politics. Welcome to Vitesse. You are our guest."

But Kemal recoiled. "This makes no sense to me. What business is it of yours where I go? I demand that I be allowed to proceed to Kallag immediately."

Abruptly the launch's door opened, and out stepped the pilot, still wearing a pressure suit but with the helmet open. She was thin-faced, light-eyed, and tanned, with wisps of dark hair on her forehead. Kemal thought she might have been attractive if her expression had not been so serious.

"I'd like to introduce you to Duernie," Zac said. "She comes to us from the Dancers, who arranged this little diversion."

The woman walked up to him and peered intently

at his face. "You are Kemal Gavilan, son of Ossip the Sun King." It was not a question.

"Yes, of course," Kemal said anyway.

"You resemble the king," she said, squinting at him. "I bring you greetings from the Dancers."

"That's nice," he said distractedly. "But what is this all about?"

It seemed to be the wrong thing to say. The woman turned away, disappointment evident on her face.

Zac said to her, "I told you we could expect him to know nothing. Gordon sent him away when he was four. And no doubt made sure he was kept in ignorance."

"Then the situation is even worse," Duernie said. She strode off through a corridor leading to the city's interior. A door slammed behind her.

"What's she so angry about?" Kemal asked, a puzzled look on his face as he watched her go.

"Well, we must explain a few matters," Zac said, "and then you will understand the position. Come, we can talk in a more comfortable place than this."

The guards formed up around them. Kemal turned to join them, then suddenly broke away. In two strides, he had gone past the guards before they could react, and was running fast toward the launch.

The plan had formed in his mind instantly, and he had acted on it. Although it was a calculated risk, he doubted that Zac would kill him outright. If he could just get to the launch, he was sure he could pilot it. He remembered the turnings coming into the cavern. It would be simple enough to reverse them.

Behind him he could hear Zac shouting orders. The guards were starting to react now, too late. He had reached the launch's entryway. . . .

Then he was enveloped in the shattering scream of a D beam. Zac had been ready after all.

Kemal tried to will himself through the hatch, but the sonic-neuro disruptor bathed him in its ennervating noisy field. He fell backward into unconsciousness.

9

Kemal knew he was still alive by the throbbing pain throughout his body. He ached from head to foot, and had a splitting headache. He was alive, and of course there was something to be said for that. But at the moment, not much.

"Feeling better, boy?" asked a voice.

Kemal saw that he was not alone. There was a man in the cell with him. He was large, white-bearded, and wrapped in a rusty brown woolen cloak that looked strange in this world of tight-fitting, functional clothing. It gave the man a theatrical look. He appeared in his early fifties, though it was difficult to judge, because his face was mostly hidden by white whiskers.

":Where am I?" Kemal asked.

"Welcome to the central prison of Vitesse," the bearded man said. "A noisome place, but you might as well call it home. It's apt to be that for a while."

Kemal rubbed his fingers through his hair. He could hardly concentrate on the man's words, his headache was so bad. The pain felt like a constricting net just inside his scalp. He was sure that his brains were going to be squeezed out through his nose in a thin gray trickle.

"I don't suppose you have anything for a headache?" he asked.

"Got you with the disruptor beam, did they?" The bearded man chuckled. "Let me see what I can do."

In a rustle of garments, and accompanied by a smell of perspiration, the bearded man came over to him, grasped his head firmly with one hand, and began probing at his neck with strong fingers.

"Hey, that hurts," Kemal said, explaining more than complaining, because even the pain from the man's fingers was better than the cataclysmic ache in his head.

"I wish," the bearded man said, "that Mother Nature would standardize the intracranial pressure point locations. Let me see, how about here . . . no, here!"

The bearded man's fingers tightened. Kemal felt a flash of pure light pass through him, and, as suddenly as that, his headache was gone, leaving behind only a dull, premonitory ache.

Kemal stood and took a few experimental steps. "Amazing," he said. "What did you do?"

"Merely applied a little knowledge. It's old stuff, from the forgotten pharmacopoeias of Earth. But it works. Now we can introduce ourselves properly. I am Egon, Master Musician, at your service."

"I am Kemal Gavilan," Kemal said.

Egon raised tufted white eyebrows. "Gavilan is a name that opens doors."

"It seems to have opened a cell door for me," Kemal said.

"Glad you can laugh about it," said Egon. "Let me see now, which Gavilan are you? I've performed at many royal audiences, but I don't remember seeing you there."

"I've just arrived on Mercury. I'm the son of Ossip, the former Sun King, who was brother to Gordon, the present ruler."

"And how did you come by this mishap?"

"I don't know," Kemal said. "I came at my uncle's bidding to sign a treaty with Kallag. I was kidnapped by some people from Vitesse and brought here."

The room was small, a three-meter cube without windows. There was a covered commode in one corner. Glowing strips in the ceiling gave a pale, shadowless light.

"What have you done to offend the Vitessans?"

"Nothing, as far as I know. I've never been anywhere to do anything to anyone," he said, vaguely confused.

"Too bad," Egon said. "If you had insulted one of their officials, there might be a chance of apologizing and getting out. But if you're in on unspecified charges . . . Well, maybe it won't be too terrible. You're a Gavilan; they must want you for something."

"No doubt," Kemal said. "But what do they have you in for?"

Egon grinned, showing broken teeth in his broad, whiskered face. "A difference of opinion, nothing more."

"Concerning what, if I may inquire?" The old man was the first person he'd met who didn't seem to want something from him: Kemal liked that.

"I came to collect the Musicians' Tax, and there was some difference of opinion as to the percentage we are entitled. That led to angry words, and those, in turn, brought me here."

"For how long?"

"Until they come to their senses. The Vitessan officials have behaved like fools. I expect my release momentarily."

"You seem very sure of yourself," Kemal said, envying Egon his self-confidence.

Egon grinned, his crooked yellow teeth showing again. "When a Musician is seized, all entertainment is stopped until he is released. A city like Vitesse is barely tolerable with entertainment. If they don't have me out in a day or two, they'll have riots on their hands. Not even Dancers can live without the Musicians' Guild's services."

"I was kidnapped by a Dancer," Kemal said. "She brought me here."

"Where else would she bring you? Obviously not to Kallag."

"Why not?"

"Because of the Kallag-Dancer troubles, of course. But I see that you're not up on your local politics."

"I just came here from Mars."

"Yes, you seem a little green. Your uncle didn't brief you?" Egon smiled and winked. "Had his reasons, no doubt."

"Can you tell me what he left out? Why have the Vitessans kidnapped me? And what do the Dancers have to do with it?"

Egon stood up and swirled his cloak around his shoulders. With practiced oratorical skill, he declaimed, "To understand politics here, you must know about the Maccabbee Caverns. There's no other area on Mercury like them. They slope deep into Mercury, and were the best place on the planet in which to found a city.

"Originally, one group won the contract. Illiad Organizers provided the first settlers, set up the political structure, and contracted to put in the actual city. They were granted the territorial rights to the Maccabbee Caverns. Work began. But soon enough, there was trouble.

"Within weeks of contracts being let and work begun, two factions vied for political control. The founding charter provided for almost everything except a clear-cut way to settle internecine disputes.

"With opinion divided almost in half, Illiad split into two entities. They agreed to share all assets and to expand respectively into the north and south branches of the cavern system. Thus were born Kallag and Vitesse.

"Little was known of the caverns, and at first there was no way to say which was better. But soon it became apparent that Kallag had the richer territory. Many important ore and chemical deposits were found even at the beginning. Spurred by the richness of the finds, off-planet people came to Kallag to settle and mine the caves, to raise families and increase the population. Vitesse lagged behind and risked falling under political control of its neighbor. But a balance of sorts was maintained . . . until recently, when the

Dancers' status became an issue."

"But what has that to do with me?" Kemal asked.

"Why were you sent to Kallag?"

"To sign a treaty between Kallag and Mercury Prime."

"There's your answer. The Sun King has finally come to terms with Kallag over the Dancers, granting their political control to Kallag, which has been claiming them for a long time. Vitesse, seeking to prevent this, has supported the Dancers and now has kidnapped you with Dancer assistance."

"My being in a cell in Vitesse won't stop Gordon himself or one of his sons from signing the treaty."

"Won't it?" Egon asked. "I see your uncle didn't brief you on your own position in this."

"How could I have a position? I'm newly arrived from Mars."

Egon cocked his head to one side, listening intently. Kemal heard it, too: the sound of footsteps in the corridor outside the cell.

Egon said to Kemal, "I think you may have your questions answered by someone more knowledgeable than I."

The door opened, and a guard walked in. He was pushed out of the way by Duernie, moving impatiently from behind him.

"This is not correct!" she stormed at Zac, who followed behind her. "You cannot put our representative in a cell, like a common criminal. This is an insult to the Dancers!"

Kemal at first thought she was talking about Egon, but as Duernie approached the prince and helped him to stand, he realized that she meant him!

"It was all a mistake," Zac said. "I told them to take him to the hospital, not to the cell." To Kemal he said, "I apologize most abjectly, Your Highness. Permit me to escort you to the apartments that have been prepared for your stay."

"I do not intend to stay!" Kemal shouted, growing more and more confused and less and less inclined to accept Vitessan hospitality.

"As to that, let us go elsewhere and discuss it."

Kemal paused. "Why have you imprisoned this man?" he asked, indicating Egon. "The Musicians have always been allowed free passage among Mercury's arcologies."

"Things have changed since King Ossip's time," Zac said. "But it is of little concern. As a courtesy to you, I will have him released. Guard, see to it! Now, let me escort you myself."

Kemal nodded in thanks to Egon, then allowed himself to be led out of the cell. Duernie was already several strides ahead of him and Zac. Still angry. Was she ever anything but angry? Kemal wondered. Did she ever smile? And what did she mean, when she called him the representative of the Dancers?

10

Zac regained his lead, led Kemal and Duernie from the prison, and escorted them into a bubble-topped electric car. He punched in a destination, and the car piloted itself along the monorails that connected all parts of Vitesse.

The Warren city looked unlike any Kemal had seen on Mars. It was a three-dimensional structure linked together at all levels by the monorails and elevator systems. Vast pillars rose hundreds of meters into the air, providing a superstructure. The entire city reflected overhead lighting. Zac explained that the lighting was set up to present a circadian rhythm based on Earth's. Artificial clouds diffused the lighting effects and reduced glare. Wind also was simulated. At the city's center was Central Pond, an artificial lake that provided boating, swimming, even fishing. Sunset and sunrise effects were also created.

The city itself was handsomely laid out, with a good mixture of buildings intercut with hydroponic garden areas, in which Vitesse grew a significant portion its own food. There was even some well-landscaped forest land.

One thing that could not be disguised was a low, continuous vibration that accompanied the three passengers wherever they went. It was the sound of the city on the move, inching its way deeper underground, extending itself into the cave system. The industrial-sized air makers and air conditioners, too, created a continuous background hum and vibration. The soil temperature outside the city was constant, at about 300 degrees Fahrenheit, hot but manageable for the city's life-maintaining machinery. In the center of Vitesse, Kemal saw crowds in bars and saloons, coffeehouses and public squares. Many people had an absentminded air. They seemed to be listening to the sound of the city's engines, for on their changing tones rode the hopes and fears of the city. There was an air of anxiety that was almost palpable, and Kemal had the impression that the city was on the verge of an explosion.

The electric car stopped, and Zac and Duernie brought Kemal through a doorway to a walled garden. Kemal found it hard to believe that he was underground in a cramped and, to believe Egon, desperate city.

Certainly there was spaciousness and amenity here. There was a little brook, the water limpid over smooth pebbles, the whole suffused with autumnal green. And over there, the little wooden bridge (its wood imported from Earth at great expense) looked bucolic and inadvertent. Just the place for lovers, Kemal thought, or solitary walkers—or prisoners, perhaps.

Zac brought Kemal through the garden to a suite of well-appointed rooms, rather ornate, with over-stuffed sofas and high-backed chairs.

"These are yours during your stay with us," Zac said. "Consider this a hotel of the highest caliber. There is a menu on the dresser over there. Full laundry service. There's a computer terminal from which you can call for all services. Perhaps you would like a rest. You and I and Duernie can dine together later and discuss everything."

"You were going to explain matters to me," Kemal said. "I still don't understand why I have been detained."

"My boy, it's simple." Zac smiled as much as Duernie did not. "Your uncle's proposed treaty with Kallag is not acceptable to Vitesse. You see, it cedes political control of the Dancers to Kallag. And that we cannot allow, eh, Duernie?"

Duernie didn't answer, but her face looked, if possible, even angrier than usual.

Kemal asked, "Do you really believe that kidnapping me will stop my uncle from signing any treaty he wants to sign?"

"Oh, yes," Zac said, "I think it will. For a while, at least. No treaty can legally be made respecting the Dancers without the signature and approval of their representative. That will be difficult to get, as long as we hold him here."

"I'm their representative?"

"That's right."

"You must have me mixed up with someone else."

"Not at all. Gordon was really trying to sneak one past everybody, wasn't he? He neglected to tell even you that you are the legitimate representative of the Dancers. It is an honor you inherited directly from your father, Ossip, who was their great champion."

Kemal stared at him, trying to retain his composure. He had just received the one part of his father's heritage that he hadn't expected, or wanted: an obligation.

11

"Why do you always look so angry?" asked Kemal, as Duernie peered out the window at the passing crowds.

They were in a small, private club off Vitesse's main concourse. Zac had asked Kemal to meet him there, and, not wanting to try an escape before he knew more, Kemal obliged. Arriving, he had found Duernie, sitting at a table by the window. He had gone over and joined her.

She turned back to him. "The freedom of my people is at issue here. That is not something to smile about."

"No, but it's no reason to *constantly* frown, either."

She frowned. "That is easy for you to say. You have no commitments."

"How do you know that?" Kemal demanded.

"Because I know about you. You were brought up in military schools on Mars. You've come here now to sign away our freedoms."

"Duernie, I've told you, I was deceived by Gordon. He didn't tell me the issues. I'll make up my own mind before I sign anything."

"You're a Gavilan. You'll do what they tell you."

"I'm Ossip's son," Kemal said. "I'll do what I think is right."

She seemed to weigh his words. "How can you know what is right for the Dancers, when you've never seen how we live?"

"You can tell me about it."

"Yes." Her expression was scornful. "I suppose that will have to suffice."

Zac came in then, looking very pleased with himself. He sat down at their table.

"Well, Kemal," he said, "I hope you have not had too bad a time with us in Vitesse."

"You have been hospitable enough," he conceded reluctantly.

"I hope you will tell that to the Sun King," Zac replied, ignoring the prince's tone.

"Oh, am I going to see Gordon again sometime soon?" His tone had turned sarcastic.

"Yes, quite soon, in fact. We of Vitesse have come to an accommodation with Mercury Prime."

Duernie looked surprised. "What accommodation?"

"My dear," Zac said, "Vitesse and the Dancers have been allies for many years in our struggle against the forces of Kallag and Mercury Prime. We of Vitesse are grateful and will never forget our obligations toward your people. Nevertheless, politics being what they are, we have found it expedient to make a treaty with the Sun King, in order to preserve the rights and privileges of all. This treaty includes valuable tax concessions for your people."

"Zac!" Duernie was alarmed. "Have you abandoned the cause of Dancer independence?"

"Not at all!" Zac cried. "Oh, we must make temporary concessions, that can't be helped, but we will continue to use our best efforts toward eventual Dancer independence."

"But they are independent now!" Kemal said.

"No, I'm afraid not," Zac said. "But the new treaty is a step in the right direction. Trust me, Duernie. It will be all right in the long run." He turned to Kemal. "We will repatriate you to Mercury Prime within the next few hours. You can sign the treaty, and all will be well." He smiled. "I wouldn't be surprised if Gordon knew about Duernie all along, and permitted her to kidnap you in order to put pressure on Kallag. Such subtlety would be in keeping with his nature."

"It would be very much like my uncle," Kemal agreed.

"I must take leave of you. Duernie, do not think too badly of Vitesse. Be assured of our goodwill." Zac left in a flutter of smiles.

As they watched Zac go, Kemal said to Duernie, "Do you still have that scout ship?"

"No. It has been returned to the Vitesse fleet. Why?"

"Is there any other way we can get out of here?" he asked, looking over his shoulder.

"Yes," Duernie said. "I have my own flivver here."

Kemel knew from his pilot training at the academy that a flivver was a Mercurian land vehicle. "Can we get away from here in it?"

"Yes, I think so. But it won't be easy."

"Let's give it a try," Kemal said, getting up to go.

"You're sure you want to do this?" she asked, laying a hand on his arm to stop him.

"You said yourself I ought to see the Dancers' life before selling out their liberties." Duernie nodded, and they made their way from the lounge.

12

The flivver was parked in one of the storage sheds on Vitesse's lowest level. It was about thirty meters long by twenty wide, and it sat on high, fat, balloon tires. The two-person driver's cab was topped by a bulbous plastic dome that gave 360-degree visibility. No streamlining was required on Mercury's airless surface. The vehicle slightly resembled pictures Kemal had seen in military classes of the ironclad Monitor, the "cheesebox on a raft" that had spelled the end to the age of sail during Earth's American Civil War.

Duernie put her wrist to the door panel, which read her body signature and opened. She and Kemal got into the cab. The instrument panel wrapped around the sides of the cab and was completely covered with dials, gauges, switches, and readout devices. The instruments glowed with a pale, nonradioactive luminescence. The back of the vehicle was equipped with living quarters. Duernie found two pressure suits and gave one to Kemal. They suited up, leaving their helmets open, and breathed the slightly chemical-smelling air from the flivver's air supplies.

"What do you want me to do?" Kemal asked, unconsciously whispering.

"Can you operate a stennis gun?"

"No problem."

She tapped the gun's controls with one finger. "I don't think we want anyone to stop us."

"No."

Kemal checked out the gun and its range finder system, while Duernie fired up the flivver's huge engine. It coughed softly into life, hesitated for a few moments, then settled into a regular rhythm.

"Ready?" she asked.

"Yes."

"I'm going to take you to Eben Mulhouse, leader of the Dancers. He can explain our position better than anyone."

"Let's go," Kemal said.

Duernie engaged the drive gears and turned on the headlights and running lights. The flivver crept slowly down the storage facility's middle aisle.

13

They got out of the storage facility and down a kilometer-long corridor to the main concourse. Then Duernie was able to turn off and take a branch that led to the city's outskirts. They were at the periphery, where the spur access road connected through a gasketed exit port in the bare rock of Maccabbee Cavern, before they were challenged at a police checkpoint. The flivver was many times larger than the largest vehicle normally used within Vitesse. A police sergeant called for them to stop.

"Orders from Holton Zac," Duernie told him. "I am to take the Gavilan prince to a rendezvous with his people."

"I have received no such instructions."

"Check with your superiors. The order was cut less than an hour ago."

"Park until I can give you clearance."

"Like hell," Duernie said. "I'm under orders to proceed. If you want me, you won't have any trouble finding me."

She kept on going. The police sergeant didn't like it, but he didn't have orders to fire at them. They left him frantically stabbing his telephone console, trying to find instructions.

Once outside the city, the flivver quickly traversed the tunnels and came to the rocky plain that sloped upward to the entrance of the Maccabee Caverns, and Duernie was able to increase speed. Far ahead of them Kemal could make out a line of brilliant sunlight. Duernie told him it marked the entrance to the Maccabee Caverns. The radio crackled, and a loud, officious-sounding voice ordered them to stop. At the same time, Kemal could see, in the rearview mirrors, the running lights of three police vehicles in pursuit.

Duernie radioed to them, "I'm under official orders to take the Gavilan prince to his people."

"Like hell you are," came Holton Zac's voice on the radio. "I give the orders here. You are to stop at once and return to Vitesse."

Duernie said, "The Dancers are not yours to command."

"But they are," Zac replied. "We have come to an agreement with Kallag and Mercury Prime."

"But not with the Dancers!"

"Duernie!" Zac said. "Don't be foolish. You are taking the prince away from his own people. There will be severe punishment! It will go hard with the Dancers if you don't return him at once."

Kemal took the microphone. "This is Kemal Gavilan. I have decided to make a tour of Dancer civilization. Stop hindering me. Tell my uncle that I need to see the people whose rights I am to dispose of."

Duernie looked at him, alarmed. "You would still give away our rights?"

Kemal put his hand over the microphone. "I had to tell them something. Now, get going."

She nodded, but the expression in her pale eyes was less than trusting. Checking the rearviews, she could see the pursuing vehicles gaining on them.

14

Minutes later, the flivver and its pursuers came out of the cavern's gloom and into the brilliance of the planet's bright side. The dazzling landscape of Mercury lay ahead.

The cavern debouched onto a wide, flat plain. It was like an enormous lunar crater, and scattered randomly across it were boulders and rock fragments, ranging from gravel to steep-sided bronze-colored behemoths the height of buildings.

Kemal saw at once that Duernie was running an obstacle course in which she dodged around some rocks and rode over others. It required great judgment to be able, in an instant, to decide at fifty kilometers an hour what rock formations the flivver could handle and what formations would overturn it. Kemal faced backward, ready with the stennis gun. Seven Vitessan vehicles, lined abreast in a hundred-meter band behind the flivver, still gained. Kemal fought with the gun, trying to bring its range finders to train on the wildly turning vehicles. Then two of the pursuers were gone by their own bad luck, one smashing into a whale-sized escarpment, the other riding onto a rising ridge of rock that capsized it.

The five remaining vehicles began firing. Kemal assumed that their optical sights were set for intra-cavern warfare, because the shots whirled harmlessly away. A harpooner missile was a more serious problem, though. It arced into the sky behind the flivver and locked onto its heat signature.

There was no way to shake it.

"Hold this thing steady!" Kemal shouted. Duernie reduced speed and straightened course. Kemal was able to sight and get off two quick shots, both of which went wide. The missile grew behind him. Kemal then remembered that he hadn't allowed for refraction, made the calculation in his head, and fired again. He scored a direct hit, blowing away the missile's nose cone.

Another pursuer broke through a salt crust and plunged twenty meters down. The Vitessan pursuers, cave dwellers, were now learning the hazards of surface travel the hard way. There were four left.

In the heat of battle, Kemal had ignored how hot the flivver's cabin had become. He was barely able to breathe. Then he realized that Duernie was shouting at him, her words muffled by the roar of the flivver's engine. He understood, however: Button up your faceplate and go to full refrigeration and rich oxygen. He clapped his faceplate into place, and Duernie did likewise. Peering ahead, over her shoulder, Kemal could make out a dark line cutting at an angle across the horizon. They were racing for the terminator!

There were a few moments' relief as the refrigerated air pumped through his armor's circulation system. But it began heating up almost immediately. Faint wisps of smoke floated up from the suit's motors, and insulation started to burn.

Then they were across the line into the terminator's dim twilight and moderate temperatures. Duernie turned to the right so as not to run out of the temperate zone, which was no more than a dozen or so kilometers wide at that point. The pursuers filed behind each other as Duernie completed her turn. The lead vehicle was fast, a low-slung scout vehicle with a bazooka mounted on the front.

Kemal could no longer fire the stennis. The intense heat had shorted out the gun's sighting mechanism. The scout vehicle came racing up on the flivver's left. In a tanker's gesture he'd learned in school, Kemal slapped Duernie's left shoulder. She saw the scout moving beside her and turned left into the vehicle's path. It turned away from her and encountered a long ridge that lifted its right wheels into the air.

Kemal slapped again. Duernie turned again and managed to nudge the scout over onto its side.

They had an increasing lead over the remaining three vehicles. Duernie drove her flivver hard, flying with four fat wheels in the air over a ridge, came down the other side—and skidded to a stop.

There, in a line across their path, were five armored ground cars painted in the yellow, black, and gold of the House of Gavilan.

Behind those was a low, domelike building with more vehicles parked behind it.

The cars from Vitesse drove over the ridge and stopped.

The flivver was caught between the armor of Vitesse and that of Mercury Prime. Low but unclimbable cliffs blocked the sides.

"What now?" Duernie asked.

"I think it's time I had a talk with them," Kemal said.

15

He entered the domed structure, followed by Duernie. The interior was like a field camp. Gordon Gavilan sat in the only comfortable chair. Dalton, on a stool beside him and dressed in full battle armor, smirked unpleasantly. Armed guards stood behind them, weapons at the ready.

"Welcome, Nephew," Gordon said, once more jovial. "How nice of you to drop by our little outpost. Guards! Stools for my nephew and his driver."

Kemal mentally kicked himself for allowing the Vitessan pursuers to corral the flivver into what might possibly be "a slaughterhouse." He accepted a stool and sat. Duernie remained standing by the door.

"You neglected to tell me, Uncle," Kemal said boldly, "that I was the hereditary representative of the Dancers."

"My boy, I had my reasons. And remember, I paid in advance."

"What is he talking about?" Duernie asked.

"He said he'd release my father's inheritance to me as soon as I signed the treaty. There was no time to tell you," Kemal told her.

"Exactly my situation," Gordon said. "Real politics, my boy, is the art of the expedient. Your father never understood that. He was an idealist. I loved him, Kemal, and I was desolate at his death, but he was not practical. And to rule, you must be practical. I tried to remedy that in you. I sent you to the John Carter Military School to give you an education and to instill in you the discipline that Ossip never had."

"We weren't taught at John Carter to sign away people's rights!"

"Weren't you told to obey the orders of your superior officers?"

"Of course, but you—"

"I am the head of a ruling family. You are my brother's son. I support you and educate you and take you into our inner councils. How can a ruling family operate, except by obedience to the orders of its head?"

"If they are lawful orders!"

"And what is unlawful about demanding your signature on my treaty? Unless, of course, I am not the head of the family. Are you the head, Kemal?"

"Of course not," Kemal said. "Nor do I care to be."

"That's nice." Gordon's grin showed he would not have accepted any other answer. "Then I am head of the family. Just as I had suspected. Eh, Dalton?"

"That's what I suspected, too," Dalton said, with his own unpleasant smirk.

"Kemal," Gordon said, "I know that it is a little difficult for you. The woman would be quite attractive if she could stop scowling. No doubt you had good dalliance with her. Or wish you had, eh? Never mind. Let me assuage your conscience about the Dancers and their spurious claims. They are a disorganized scum that came to Mercury from many worlds to work in the mines of Kallag. They began to develop self-sufficiency upon the planet and thought that gave them the right to call themselves free. But all they are is a weak mob that, by luck, struck it rich along the terminator. They have no fixed abodes and no property except their vehicles. They have no territory, since the surface of Mercury is the property of us all."

"Yes," Kemal said. "But they actually live on the surface."

"That is an unimportant detail. Kemal, you can see it our way, can't you?"

"The only thing I can see," Kemal said, "is that I am their representative, and you need my signature on that treaty."

"A formality, nothing more," Gordon said.

"Oh, then it would make no difference if I didn't sign it?" Kemal asked, calling his uncle's bluff.

Gordon looked suddenly cross. "It would make a great deal of difference. The Dancers have had the gall to petition the Free Corps and other organizations such as NEO, Earth's motley group of terrorists, for pity's sake. If their hereditary representative does not sign, there could be questions, perhaps even outside interference. We don't want that here. I'll have my own way in any event, but I prefer to take the easier way. As a Gavilan, you can understand that, can't you, Kemal?"

"Perfectly," said the prince.

"Good fellow!" Gordon turned to his son. "Dalton, give me the treaty."

"I have it right here," Dalton said, taking a folded plastic envelope, identical to the one Kemal had brought to Vitesse, out of his pouch.

"What about Kallag's representative?" Dalton asked. "He has to sign, too, I believe. Might that be him arriving now?"

Gordon also heard the heavy rumble of approaching vehicles. "I expect it is. Sign for us now, Kemal, and let's get our part over with. Then we'll get the Kallag signature and be on our way back to Mercury Prime, a hot shower, and a decent meal."

"Yeah, right," said Kemal dourly.

"Glad you see it our way, Nephew," said Gordon, confident in the day's outcome. "Your father's estate comes to a considerable sum. It is yours immediately upon our return. You have my word on it, the word of a Sun King of Mercury. Here, use my stylus."

"There's just one thing," Kemal said.

"What's that, dear boy?"

"If I sign that thing, how the hell do you expect to get out of here alive?"

Gordon's face fell as he looked at Kemal, then he went to the window. Outside he could see the vehicles from Vitesse, drawn up in a ring. Behind them, forming a greater ring, with guns trained, was a large collection of vehicles. They were worn but well-working machines, all different sizes and shapes. They had in common, however, the fact that they were all armed and looked exceedingly dangerous.

"How did you know it was the Dancers?" Gordon asked.

"I inferred it from the sound of the engines. They're much smoother than Vitessan vehicles. The Dancers have more at stake in their vehicles' upkeep, and they seem very good at it. You have to give them that."

"My fleet will be here shortly and will bomb that mob out of existence."

"I doubt that," Kemal said, "as long as you are in the middle of the bombing zone."

Gordon grunted. "True enough. So what do you propose?"

"Duernie," Kemal said, "is the flivver ready?"

"Of course," she said.

"Then let's go. Kill anyone who tries to stop us. You have a weapon handy, I assume?"

"Always."

He saw that she had a small but efficient-looking laser pistol in her hand. He backed to the door, and Duernie followed him, watching Gordon and his guards.

"Kemal," Gordon said, "don't be stupid about this. Mercury is a cooperative venture. We can't let these people hog all the wealth from the surface."

"You and the arcologies have wealth enough," Kemal said. "Let the Dancers keep what they risked their lives to get. Good-bye, Uncle."

"This isn't the end of it, Kemal."

"I suppose not," he said, knowing that he'd have to watch his back for the rest of his—or Gordon's—life.

Kemal went out the door and slammed it shut behind him. He and Duernie got into the flivver. Soon they were well past the perimeter, with the open plains of Mercury ahead of them.

"You are going to live with us?" Duernie asked.

Kemal nodded. "For a while, at least. But I'll need a vehicle."

"There are several spares that Amos Herder keeps," Duernie told him. "I suppose you could buy one. Or perhaps he would give you one for your service to the Dancers." She hesitated. "Or you could save yourself the expense and ride with me."

Kemal looked at her. She wasn't exactly smiling, but she definitely wasn't frowning.

Epilogue

Kemal Gavilan stayed with the Dancers for several Earth years, leading them to develop a strong internal political council, and renewing the optimism and unity they had enjoyed during his father's reign.

His economic and social strategy included strengthing ties with other oppressed political and ethnic groups. Although he loved the Dancers—they were the first "family" he had ever known, and he wanted more than anything to help them maintain their growth—he was not truly one of them. His personal goal had always been to participate in some global cause, one that would benefit the Dancers and all of the solar system's inhabitants.

It was natural then, with his aspirations, political connections, and innate piloting abilities developed during his time with the Dancers, that he would one day meet his counterpart in the New Earth Organization, a fiery redhead named Wilma Deering. Soon after, NEO had its newest recruit.

But that's another story. . . .

TRIPLE CROSS

Abigail Irvine

I told you to give her some pittance and send her away."

"She doesn't seem to want any money."

"Well, what does the little beggar want? Trading bonds? Precious gems? Hand-me-down clothes?!"

Ardala Valmar's voice rose shrilly. It was too early in the morning for such displeasure. It was 7:00 A.M., system standard time.

Ardala sat at a small ivory table in her great circular bedroom, sharply stabbing with her fork at a serving of deveined shrimp and a saucer of fruit sections. She paused to chew and swallow, then swiveled in her chair. The tempestuous Martian beauty lowered her violet eyes and glowered meaningfully at Tanny, her genetically ordained appointment secretary.

Tanny was unruffled. He was used to his mistress's moods and was coded to be master of them all. He lowered his own eyes—which behind sexy owl-rims were, according to his particular design, transparent and milky white—an eerie contrast to the bluish tint of his skin tone—and adopted a suitably meek expression.

"I don't think she wants anything, per se," emphasized Tanny. "She has journeyed all the way from

Earth, just to tell you something 'of utmost importance,' and she won't tell me or anybody else what could possibly be so 'utmost.' However, I think she is quite legitimate. She has been here for six days, staying, out of pocketbook I might add, at a dreadful transient shelter on the outskirts of the ninth circumference."

Tanny sniffed, appropriately, to indicate contempt for the lower levels of Mars's Pavonis Elevator, where the terraformers, subspecies, and other societal dregs dwelled. Tanny, of course, resided on the secondmost upper strata of the mega-habitat, in relatively comfy quarters that were part of the luxurious warren of offices and private living space assigned to a privileged member of the RAM hierarchy. Tanny bunked with his "replicate," Hatch, who was his identical twin and also Ardala's security captain.

Only the top level of the space elevator complex was considered desirable. Only Russo-American Mercantile (a.k.a. RAM) board members, and of course the great Simund Holzerhein himself, were permitted access to or living arrangements on the top level. Though most others would be quite satisfied with the splendor of the secondmost strata, and happy to avoid the intrigue and treachery of upper executive urbania, Tanny knew that Ardala welcomed the challenge and had ambitions to rise even higher. To rise, perhaps, to succeed even Simund Holzerhein.

"She requests only ten minutes of your important time," added Tanny hopefully.

In a kind of huff, Ardala got up to change. Her blue robe slid to the ground, revealing bare, pointed breasts and the pale chalky skin that was all the rage among the Martian elite. She was nearly six feet tall, with jet black hair that streamed to her shoulders. She stood with her back to Tanny, who waited diligently at his small secretarial cubby across the room, and opened the door of her wardrobe cabinet.

Ardala's bedroom was filled with glass globes, crystal pendants, shiny art objects, reflectors, and a multitude of mirrors. There were decorative hand-mirrors on every surface, beveled mirrors inlaid tastefully into the walls, full-length mirrors on the cabinets, and an end-to-end prismatic mirror on the ceiling.

Though the furniture was all ivory, the walls were an alloy of silver and steel. The effect was at once blinding and beautiful, bright and cold and intimidating. This was the only room in her maze of living space in which Ardala Valmar permitted her personal aesthetics to reign.

The ivory was in fact relatively inexpensive and could be purchased from domestic mastodon breeders on Earth. The mirrors ran the gamut from flashy baubles she had picked up on her interplanetary jaunts, to silver-edged antiquities extorted as hush payment in trade for some piece of dirty information. The silver-steel alloy was of course priceless and could not be obtained on the open market. By law, its use and ownership was restricted to the RAM elite.

As Ardala stood there, momentarily, pondering which of her many outfits to drape herself in on that morning, she stole a glance over her shoulder. She caught Tanny covertly eyeing her long, tall, gorgeous, naked body from across the room. Good.

Tanny was one of the new "cross-breed" of gennies. Apart from the bluish tint of his skin and the opaque eyes, he looked quite normal—as in, handsome to die for. He had a blonde buzzcut and always dressed the same—a white synthsuit, set off by gleaming black boots—except daily he varied his eyeglasses. It was a kind of affectation; as being a gennie, his vision was not only normal, but supranormal.

His replicate, Hatch, looked and dressed precisely the same—except that he too chose different spectacles every day—different from the day before, and different from Tanny's. It was an unspoken one-upmanship between them. Otherwise Ardala's two chief subordinates were incredibly bonded. One of the side benefits of their experimental gene-coding was a virtual "twin-telepathy" between them, so that they acted as one on behalf of Ardala's best interests.

Now, Ardala changed quickly into a formfitting, hooded, natural fiber, alabaster jumpsuit. The zipper plunged tantalizingly. Her thin, braided-rope waist-belt was a fiery crimson hue. Ardala did not feel ostentatious, so she limited her adornments to a shoulder brooch and faux-jeweled wristlet. Admiringly, she studied her reflection in the cabinet mirror.

Though it was garb for an ordinary business day as far as Ardala was concerned, the jumpsuit had the usual internal circuitry and microcomputers of "smart" clothes—just in case. No weaponry; Ardala was well protected by a crack contingent of Desert Runners, on round-the-clock bodyguard. And she always had the poison, secreted beneath her fingernails—just in case.

Ardala sat down at a small vanity table and daubed some ruby red on her lips. She examined her long fingers, and picked up a nail file.

"I have no knowledge of this girl," said Ardala, putting on an irritated face. "She says she's related to Uncle Simund. But she lives on Earth and attends college? How quaint!"

Tanny unzipped a breast pocket and pulled out a microfile, then adjusted his owl-rims superfluously to examine it—superfluously, because of course he had already committed the contents of the microfile to memory.

"I ran a check on her, of course," said the devoted appointment secretary. "Indeed, she attends Martian University, here on Mars, which is noted for its marriage of scientific and cultural curricula, and its lucrative grants-in-aid from RAM research installations. She takes a variety of courses, but is listed as a major in bioengineering."

He glanced at Ardala, who was listening with a bored visage as she filed her nails to tiny, sharp points. "That shows some initiative—lots of dabbling and controversy in bioengineering at the moment. Wide open field for the future."

Tanny paused to adjust his owl-rims. Ardala looked up brusquely, as if to say: Get to the point.

"Rather a type in most respects," said Tanny, who, as ever, was unruffled, "No academic distinction—barely passing grades. Drinks a bit much of the local sludge on weekends, and afterward pukes her guts out. Listens to electric 'deep-noise' music obsessively. A search of her room indicates the usual trendy array of posters and books, nothing political or subversive. She has decidedly slovenly personal habits, in spite of which she has a rather astonishingly long list of boyfriends and one-night favors. I have a readout here of her known couplings. Insofar as it is complete, it is revealing of nothing."

With one hand, Tanny lifted up a small cassette reel and let the microfile unspool to the floor. It measured perhaps seven inches of single-spaced names and dates. Tanny looked meaningfully at Ardala and rolled his eyes in bemusement.

"As far as I can determine," Tanny summed up, "she is what she seems to be. Except for this intriguing detail: She earns a little pin money keeping track of local doings and writing up covert reports for your friend and mine, Neola Price."

Ardala raised an eyebrow. That was a name she recognized: Neola Price sat on the executive board of RAM. She was one of the withered ancients whose power Ardala envied and plotted to subsume. Once a master architect of the long-range orbital colony, Neola Price had become a hard-nosed, bitchy old

woman who overcompensated for her position of vulnerability by toadying shamelessly to Simund
Holzerhein. That, the toadying, kept Neola Price on
the executive board, even as, in the long run, Ardala
knew, it would make her twice as vulnerable.

"So?"

"I admit it is not much to go on," said Tanny dryly.

"So why should I see this—this girl?" Ardala
demanded. "What possible benefit could there be?
Leaders of great armies wait for months to get an
appointment with me, but this girl, who pretends to
be a Holzerhein . . ."

"Well, that is just it," countered Tanny. "It's hard to
say precisely, but I would say that her claim is
authentic. You know how confusing the genealogy
is. . . ."

Ardala Valmar frowned. Well she knew. She herself was a Holzerhein way back in the tangled history
of intermarriage and test-tubing. There were literally hundreds of Holzerheins in the universe. All
somehow related, and all, Ardala knew, fairly irrele-
vant to Uncle Simund. They all called him that,
regardless of whether they had ever met him: Uncle
Simund.

"She is, in fact, some sort of half niece, by common
law, once or twice removed. Born on Luna. Parents
long deceased. Only child. Raised by older half sister,
etcetera. Hard to trace, but seems on the square." He
paused for effect. "And I don't think you should take
the chance that Uncle Simund might not take some
interest in her ultimate welfare."

Ardala had moved to a small sitting desk, and was
idly gazing at herself in the mirror. She showed her
teeth in a perfect smile. She looked marvelous today!
She glanced from an angle and caught Tanny eyeing
her as she eyed herself. Good.

"The only person who cares less than me about
another Holzerhein is Uncle Simund himself," she

commented with a sigh. "But I suppose you're right. Show the little menace in at 9:00 A.M." Here she glanced at her wristmonitor and micro-daylog. "Tell her she will have eight minutes for her matter of 'utmost importance.' "

Tanny got up and walked toward the double doors. He had perfect symmetry and coordination. He was built like a trapeze artist and his torso swayed like a dancer's. Ardala knew that his bioengineered moderation acted as a crosscheck against her hot, impulsive temperament.

Of course, she had had Tanny "neutered." Him and Hatch. Not for convenience's sake, but because Ardala knew herself too well. Business was business, after all, and—what was the old Earth adage?—she knew it was a mistake to mix business with pleasure.

She had done that once—with Killer Kane—and it was the exception that proved the rule. In the years since Kane's defection from NEO, the terrorist group he'd been a member of on Earth, he and Ardala had had many occasions for joint business ventures. He had, of course, succumbed to her charms—to both of their satisfactions. But she never felt she controlled him like all the other men she'd known. It was irritating and stimulating at the same time.

"And, Tanny?" He was half out the double doors.

"Yes, my lady?" Tanny leaned back in with his milky white orbs peeking over the edge of the owl-rims.

"What is her name?"

Tanny emitted a sliver of a self-satisfied smile. "Ina Klimt-Low," he said.

○　○　○　○　○

Ardala was annoyed at herself for getting boxed into this situation.

The young female sitting in front of her looked like

anything but someone who could be useful to Ardala
Valmar. She was short, about five feet tall, dumpy,
and wore striped leggings over which was fitted a
sooty gray fleece shirt that Ardala knew was popular
among students these days. Ina Klimt-Low wore her
hair in a loathsome bowlcut, with bangs that were
flecked with a trendy, ugly orange. Her hair needed a
good shampooing. In general, there hung about her a
distinct whiff of uncleanliness.

The meeting was promptly at 9:00 A.M. in Ardala's small private office. Her desk, an ebony slab, was
elevated at a slant, with Ardala perched in a wing
chair at the high angle. The desk was swept clean of
everything except discreet data transmitters and
microfiles. The sprinkling of wall hangings were all
museum quality (indeed, some of them had been
extorted from museums in one of Ardala's fabled
"data-wipes").

The insipid college girl did not seem to be in the
least bit honored or enriched by Ardala's presence. In
fact, Ina Klimt-Low appeared to chew a wad of gum
as she gazed around the room distractedly.

"I want you to know at the outset that I do not
regard you as a relative, nor would it matter if I did,"
began Ardala. "I have no time or money for charity
cases. I have no interest in contributions to egalitarian causes, or in buying whatever it is you are ped-
dling. I see you without appointment only out of
heartfelt love for and devotion to"—she inclined her
head for emphasis—"Uncle Simund."

The girl made a strange noise. It was a moment
before Ardala realized she had popped her gum.
Ardala Valmar's eyes went wide.

"You have eight minutes," she said sternly. A
glance at her wristchrono told her otherwise. "Oops,
seven now," she added with relish. "So don't sit there
like a lump. What do you want, and why did you
come all the way to Mars to see me?"

"Something for something." The insufferable girl was speaking in a mumbly undertone.

Ardala drummed her fingers impatiently on the desktop. "Speak up."

The girl went on. She went on interminably, from Ardala's point of view. She had cottonmouth, made very little eye contact, and seemed to be making no particular point. She was droning on and on about where she went to college and the courses she was taking and the people she had met. . . .

Ardala found herself watching her wristchrono as the minutes ticked off.

Seven . . . six . . . five . . . four . . . three . . .

All of a sudden Ina Klimt-Low reached down and proffered a smudgy book bag toward Ardala, who recoiled in horror.

"This is it," she was saying, "along with some other stuff I filched from the lab. May or may not be important."

"What?" asked Ardala, off track.

"The article I was telling you about," said Ina Klimt-Low more loudly, with some vehemence. "The one about the old astronaut. By Dr. Andresen. Walter's big hero."

"Again," said Ardala through gritted teeth.

"Walter is my boyfriend," Ina Klimt-Low stated, emphasizing her words, as if for the comprehension of a child. "Well, not really my boyfriend. A guy I met. Dr. Andresen is the professor who was getting RAM dough to investigate outer space archaeological digs. He wrote an article about this Anthony Rogers astronaut guy. Lost in space. Big fuss about the article, and Dr. Andresen was kicked off campus. Aren't you listening?"

Ina Klimt-Low was staring at Ardala, who still wore a puzzled expression. Ina Klimt-Low patted the smudgy book bag.

"It's all in here. Plus some other stuff of interest."

Ardala said nothing. She was trying to remember where she had heard that name before: Anthony Rogers.

"I heard all about it from Walter," said Ina Klimt-Low exasperatedly. "He was Dr. Andresen's assistant. Or researcher. Or something. That part doesn't matter. I pumped Walter for more information. Learned plenty."

"You were being paid well, I assume."

Ina Klimt-Low's face was blank.

"By Neola Price," said Ardala smartly.

Ina Klimt-Low's face turned positively gleeful. "Of course!" she exclaimed proudly. "But that's the funny part. I was on stipend for Neola Price after Andresen's article came out. But Walter just told me that he's not only leaving town, he's leaving Mars! Walter set it up—he told me last night."

"Walter? Why should I care if he leaves Mars?" Ardala asked in irritation.

"No! Aren't you listening? Andresen is leaving Mars. To look for the astronaut in the Asteroid Belt. I figure this is some pretty big deal, especially since Andresen got kicked off campus for this whole thing."

"Unusual," conceded Ardala. "But why come to me? Why not Neola?"

"I took it to her first. She said that it was too small to bother Uncle Simund with." Ina frowned. "Price was kinda strange, like she was guilty and didn't want him to know or something. So, I figure this is all happening behind Uncle Simund's back," continued Ina Klimt-Low. "I figure it's hot information. I figure you'd know what to do."

"Why not take it to Uncle Simund directly?" asked Ardala pointedly.

"He wouldn't see me," said Ina Klimt-Low, with a shrug. She returned to chewing her gum.

Ardala swallowed the desire to slap the girl's face

for her impudence, or congratulate her for possessing more brains than Ardala had thought. Not much common sense, though. Still, Ardala looked at her with new interest.

"What do you want for all this?" Ardala finally asked.

"Not much. A better life," Ina Klimt-Low replied, adding brightly, "maybe after college, you'll let me come to work for you." Again she extended the smudgy book bag.

Ardala hid a sigh of relief and took the bag. Her eyes met briefly with Ina Klimt-Low's. Then the Martian beauty pushed a buzzer. Instantly, two of her bodyguards, hulking Martian Desert Runners, appeared and grabbed a surprised Ina Klimt-Low by the elbows, hefting her toward the door.

"Get her out of my sight," Ardala commanded. Then she added, generously, "On second thought, give her a long, hot bath. Burn her clothes and find her something decent to wear. Then send her someplace—anyplace."

"But—but—but," sputtered Ina Klimt-Low.

"I'll be in touch," said Ardala, with a halfhearted wave. But it was unlikely that Ina Klimt-Low even heard her, as the girl had already vanished out the door.

Ardala opened the smudgy book bag and skimmed its contents. In a moment, she understood what Ina Klimt-Low had tried in her inarticulate way to express: The age alone of such an achaeological find made it note-worthy. But she had heard nothing about it from any-one at RAM. Neola Price obviously knew about it, though. Ardala's suspicions were more than piqued; instinct told her that she had stumbled upon something valuable indeed. But she needed more information on this Anthony Rogers before she could proceed.

She allowed herself the smallest smile of anticipation as she pressed a button to signal Tanny and Hatch.

○ ○ ○ ○ ○

Perceived by the masses to be one of the glittering socialites of the ruling class, Ardala Valmar was, in reality, a tough-skinned professional. When on Mars, she always kept up obligations and responsibilities, and maintained a full and grueling daylog. When aboard her cruiser, the *Princess of Mars* (at least two weeks out of every month), it went without saying that she was always up to something—a little dubious, a little dangerous—the sole purpose of which was to boost her hourly tabulation at the Coprates Bank, Ltd.

It was hard to say exactly what she was a professional at—that is, what her profession might be named. "Information broker" was the phrase popular among the videomags. But all that meant, in reality, was that Ardala Valmar traded "dirty" data—meaning illegal, classified, clandestine, or just plain "naughty" secrets—for money or favors. Or money *and* favors.

Although she had been born into excess wealth, Ardala had spent her entire life amassing a greater and even greater personal fortune, while inching ever upward into the upper ranks of RAM leadership. It was part of her image to look like such a lovely—how the videomags relished the display of her photograph!—but beneath the velvet glove was the iron fist of greed, cunning, power-thirst, and egomania.

It would have been a busy day for her even without the unscheduled appointment of Ina Klimt-Low. The Buck Rogers revelation created additional problems—as well as opportunities. The important thing was to confirm all the niceties as soon as possible. Ardala gave Tanny and Hatch full instructions. They would spend the day fact-finding and charting the potential profitability of information concerning the Buck Rogers archaeological find, while she attended to more immediately pressing matters.

The bulk of the morning was already given over to meetings with financiers, investors, accountants, and advisers. Ardala had her legitimate business "fronts," and they needed constant nurturing and adjustment. These included (but were not limited to) real estate transactions, landlord collections, health corporations, stock options, colony investments, inside trading on precious metals, and merger options. Nothing was more boring than such financial minutiae; nothing was more important.

Her 11:00 A.M. appointment was with Beers Barmaray, the autocratic leader of the Intersolar Terraforming Egalitarian Laborers' Organization (ITELO). "BB," as he was known, was a barrelchested, oily-complexioned, tattooed ex-grunt who had risen to a position of dominance in the largest fraternal organization of skilled colonizers in the galaxy. As such, he controlled an enormous slush fund of payoffs and benefits, and could call on the unquestioned allegiance of more than two million working stiffs on colonies and space stations scattered around the solar system.

Ardala had her own private orbital base on Deimos, one of the moons of Mars. The base was a refueling station, but more important than that, it was an ultramodern "thinkbank" that scanned interplanetary transmissions and computertroves for information of possible value to her.

Suspecting Ardala's profit margin, BB had taken it upon himself to make new wage demands on behalf of his work force—to include, implicitly, a skim-off for himself. He was a real tinpot, a massive, pug-ugly fellow, but he could make good on his threats, and Ardala felt it necessary to deal with him herself.

BB slouched in his chair impudently, unimpressed by the great Ardala Valmar as he repeated his demands.

"So, as I was saying, given the cost of living on such a desolate and cultureless place as Deimos—I'm sure a woman of your breeding can understand that—" BB stopped to scratch his left side "—that my workers need another two hundred dolas per week—" BB became tongue-tied as Ardala provocatively toyed with the zipper of her jumpsuit.

Suddenly Ardala plunged her hand beneath the neckline of her suit and produced a handful of fuzzy holographs. The pictures, holos of the formidable Beers Barmaray cuddled in the arms of one of the fleshpots of Mars, spoke for themselves.

The look on BB's face was pure astonishment. In an instant, he had crumpled into an abject, blubbering state. BB, Ardala well knew, had a reputation as a loving husband and devoted family man (with nine children). His leadership would never survive the destruction of his image. Not to mention that his wife, a certifiable nut case (according to Ardala's memoranda), would probably seize the excuse to kill him. Ardala would make certain she found out, if need be.

This, the showdown with Beers Barmaray, was a highlight of her day. The federation leader sat before her now, reduced to twisting his hands and pleading.

"Please, Miss Valmar—" *now* it was *Miss Valmar!* "—you can't—"

"Can't?"

Flustered, BB's face burned red. "What I meant was, I'd be very grateful if you didn't let anyone see those."

"You're going to have to do a lot better than that." Her voice was low.

Beers Barmaray agreed to freeze all pay and benefit plans for five years, to extend the ten-hour workday to twelve (no overtime), and to immediately transfer five per cent of all outstanding federation funds to Ardala's standing account at Coprates Bank, Ltd.

"That's more like it," she said smoothly. His ugly,

pleading eyes nearly made Ardala gag. She looked
away and added, "Don't worry, Mr. Barmaray, you
can rest assured that the holos stay right here with
me. And as your reward for being so . . . civilized
about this whole thing, I'll make sure your friend
here—" she tapped the picture "—vanishes." What
she really wanted to do was make the repulsive little
extortionist himself vanish, but he was more valuable to her now than before. Her possession of those
holos nearly ensured his loyal cooperation in the
future.

"Vanishes?" he gulped, his pug face turning whiter
still.

"Oh, don't thank me," she said airily, standing up.
"Good day, Mr. Barmaray." Her tone left him no
choice but to leave, quietly and quickly. The big,
dumb animal would know better than to make
demands of Ardala Valmar ever again. Of course,
there was no question that she would yield the holographs, or the original laser-negatives. They would
go back into her files as insurance against any future
misbehavior.

He left, mopping his oily brow relievedly, wedged
between her security people, two Desert Runners.

Ardala looked at the hour: noon. Time for lunch.
Fresh-squeezed green juices and raw complex grains.
Expensive—especially on Mars—but nutritional. She
was served at her desk and ate alone, in silence, con-
templating her schemes.

After lunch, it was off to Body Nova at the North-H
Mall, where she liked to take a swim, schedule per-
mitting. Of course she had permanent membership
in all the more status-minded clubs reserved for
RAM muckamucks, but she liked mixing with the
common folk at Body Nova, and she liked strolling
around the North-H Mall afterward.

No bodyguards. She liked the oohs and aahs.

It gave the people a thrill just to see her.

She was back by 1:30 P.M.

Her afternoon was taken up largely by a complicated matter that involved the management of an
umbrella medical corporation—including a megahos-
pital, a string of lucrative nursing homes, and a phar-
maceutical supply firm. The "information flow"
between the divisions, which ought to ensure robust
profitability, was threatened by the fierce internecine competition. Gouging in one division was causing havoc in the others. There were differing theories
as to how profits could be maximized overall.

She had the three branch officers in for review.
They were sullen and defensive, and openly bickered
among themselves. She had had Tanny prepare a
thick report on the profit-loss flow and how it was
adversely affected by the situation. The medical corporation was really a minor investment, but it was
turning into a major headache. The three branch officers had so much petty disagreement that it was a
struggle just to remind them to focus on Tanny's rec-
ommendations. Ardala was no good at playing
diplomat—what she really wanted to do was strangle
all three of them.

At random, she chose one of them—the ugliest, she
thought to herself, buzzard-thin and red-veined—and
summarily fired him. Two Desert Runners materialized and hauled him out the door—and out of her life.
(What they did with him after he was out of her sight
was of no consequence to her. They liked to have their
little fun.)

The fate of their colleague sobered the other two
officers immediately. Again at random, Ardala chose
one of them—one that was a little beefy for her taste,
but a solid and intriguing physical specimen
nonetheless—and promoted him above the other. The
one in charge would have to answer for whatever
happened in the future. Let them work out the
details, she told them. There could be no mistaking

the edge of fury and warning in her voice.

Desert Runners materialized and removed them from her presence.

It was 4:00 P.M. Where were Tanny and Hatch? she wondered impatiently, drumming her nails. She could hardly wait for their report.

They arrived at 4:01 P.M.

O   O   O   O   O

The three retired to Ardala's boudoir, where they could discuss the subject—Dr. Andresen and the twentieth century astronaut—in an atmosphere of gentility.

Tanny and Hatch sat at either end of an upholstered couch with several inches between them, like matched bookends. Tanny still wore his sexy owl-rims from the morning. Hatch, for some reason, today favored large, bold, black-rimmed touring glasses. Ardala had to admit to herself that it gave the gennie a slight edge over his replicate, even though in all other respects (buzzcut, white synthsuit, athletic proportions, and so on) they were identical.

Ardala sat in an armchair and listened to them, considering everything they had to say and querying them for loopholes and contingencies—wondering, as she watched them closely and observed their bonded interaction, if it had been a mistake, after all, to have had Tanny and Hatch neutered. They made a rather tantalizing twosome.

They were very good at information-gathering, management, control and dispersal, exactitude, and enforcement. Their summary was complete. Like Ardala, they had put in a long, hard, rewarding day.

They were certain, as certain as could be, that Dr. Andresen was bona fide. He was a naif, they assured her, without any political passions or affiliations. But everything that he had written—and everything that had been written about Buck Rogers in the history books—checked out. Even as an artifact, Buck Rogers would be of immense propaganda value to RAM.

Of course, this Buck Rogers artifact would be of immense value, period, to Ardala Valmar, if she could get her hands on it first.

Hatch told her that if she wanted to move on this matter, she ought to move right away. Within seventy-two hours, at the latest.

"What about Uncle Simund?" Ardala asked, when they had completed their synopsis of facts and probabilites.

Hatch frowned. "My sources indicate that he is not personally involved," said Hatch. "My opinion is that the girl was right: Simund Holzerhein doesn't know anything about this."

"Surely the existence of Masterlink ought to have tipped him off," posited Ardala.

"Perhaps . . ." said Hatch.

". . . it is possible," Tanny said, finishing Hatch's sentence, "that Uncle Simund believes that Masterlink is all there is. Or perhaps he only recently learned of Masterlink."

Now it was Ardala's turn to frown. "That would mean complicity at the highest level," she said. It had to be Price, Ardala thought inwardly with glee. But she forced herself to wait for the rest of the report.

"Perhaps," said Hatch. He did not like to commit himself unless he was positive. Ardala appreciated his hedging, even when it did not in the least affect her decision. She hated yes-men, and she knew that Tanny and Hatch were coded to be meticulous and conservative in their judgments.

A silence briefly reigned. Tanny and Hatch, in sync, sipped on exotic drinks. Ardala (who was not imbibing) steepled her fingers thoughtfully.

"I want that body," she said at last. "Either Neola Price has her own plans for it, which she's not sharing with Uncle Simund, or she's incompetent and doesn't know its value. In either case, if I get the body first, I make her look bad and I'm one step closer to taking her position on the board."

"My suggestion, then," said Hatch, leveling his milky orbs meaningfully, "is that you go to Uncle Simund and somehow test him to see what he knows. Only then will you know what you have to offer of value."

"I concur," Tanny hastened to add.

"With the proviso," said Hatch, "that you tell him less than you know."

"Then, as you say, arrange to get the body yourself. But you must be careful and maintain a fallback position in the event that your plan to incriminate Price somehow backfires," said Tanny.

Ardala absorbed that conclusion and nodded approvingly. Tanny and Hatch were masters at predicting all the angles and preventing her impulsiveness from incriminating her. "What are you suggesting?" she asked.

"Go outside normal channels," said Hatch decisively. "Hire someone free-lance to pick up the body for you. Someone with no connection to Ardala Valmar. Someone whom we have never used before, and will never use again. An untouchable. Someone foolish enough to indulge in ideals, in whom we can place our trust, to an extent, and someone whom we can afford to have fail, if necessary. Someone who can take on such a precarious mission and possibly thread the needle. But if not . . ." He shrugged.

Ardala's face showed not a flicker of reaction. But she loved the idea, because she had the perfect candidate: NEO colonel Wilma Deering. Brilliant! Her arch-rival for the affections of Killer Kane—not that Wilma Deering had the slightest idea of that. Ardala had never even met the most famous freedom fighter in the system, never even laid eyes on her (excluding police holograph-bulletins, of course), yet she hated her with a burning intensity. What an irony! She could use this tricky business to meet and hire Wilma Deering, satisfying a certain curiosity, while at the same time arranging a double-cross if necessary; if anything went wrong, she could always turn Wilma over to RAM for the reward on her head as a member of NEO.

And wouldn't "Killer" Kane be surprised to hear what his pure heroine would do if the terms were right? Ardala Valmar would bait the hook right and proper, and she knew she would reel Wilma Deering in.

Soundlessly, Ardala rose and went to the table tray of appetizers and stimulants. She picked up one of the snifters, crossed the room, and filled up the glasses of Tanny and Hatch, leaning over so that her pointed breasts were in full view. She returned to her easy chair, leaned back, and for the first time in the day, relaxed.

"Let us set the wheels in motion," she said with a hard, cold smile. If Dr. Andresen was right about his theory, this was her opportunity to score one against Neola Price, get her revenge on the unsuspecting Wilma Deering, and elevate her status on the executive board and with Uncle Simund! Three ways to win! Ardala loved the odds.

○ ○ ○ ○ ○

Ardala took up residence on her ship, the *Princess of Mars*, and instructed the captain to set a course for Earth, to meet the NEO cruiser on more neutral territory. Wilma's lone ship arrived within twenty-four hours of the message's first transmission. As Ardala had requested, the NEO colonel had brought two extra pilots as escorts.

Ardala's private security team, two Desert Runners named Triin and Aasha, met the NEO guests at the docking platform and led them to the sanctum sanctorum behind Ardala's private office, where Ardala and her two assistants waited.

The sanctum sanctorum, which could only be accessed from Ardala's private office, was concealed behind a wall that slid open to reveal a small but elegant den. It was intended for more intimate negotiations, and few in Ardala's employ were ever invited to experience its cozy ambiance.

Here the furniture was all gleaming buffalo leather. All the colors were rustic. The walls were furnished with folk and primitive art pieces—either worthless or precious, depending on one's point of view. But Ardala had discovered that these totems and religious symbols of the archaic past had a soothing effect on clients—as well as, she had to admit, on herself. A massive, antiquated grandfather clock kept rhythmic time.

One wall rotated to feature either a fully operative roaring fireplace, an ocean vista, complete with sound effects and salt breeze, or the convincing illusion (planets, atmospheric density, and so on) of a free fall in outer space. The generic choice was a tasteful wood grain that Ardala preferred on this and most occasions.

The music purring in the background was from a laserdisk of German arias of the eighteenth century. Ardala had no ear for "dead music," but she knew that NEO members fancied themselves aficionados, connecting themselves with all things even vaguely associated with Earth's early freedom.

On a table tray had been arranged a row of snifters, a selection of fine chocolates, tobacco, candied sweetmeats, and algae. A great arbiter of social politesse when she chose to be, Ardala made a ceremony of presenting Wilma with a glass of a rare distillate from the

Venusian Lowlands that was part of a bootlegged cargo she had acquired in a recent "information swap."

"Welcome to my home, Colonel Deering," Ardala said graciously. "Won't you be seated?" She waved an arm flamboyantly to one of the white leather wing chairs.

"I prefer to stand," Wilma said, practically spitting the words. "The message said you could provide NEO with two light-class cruisers in exchange for my assistance. I brought pilots for both the cruisers along with me as you requested. This had better not be some kind of joke, Valmar."

Ardala hesitated momentarily before responding, as she studied her adversary more carefully. Wilma Deering's red hair blazed, even in the soft lighting of the den. Ardala noted that Wilma was not as beautiful as the picture on the wanted poster, and that made her glad.

All three NEO officers were dressed in the old-fashioned double-breasted blue coats that their organization had adopted as a standard uniform. The color of the coats stood for the way Earth looked from space a long time ago. Now the planet appeared more like brown sludge from orbit. Ardala missed the significance, though, and simply thought that it should have been obvious, especially to a woman, that the dress was completely unflattering.

One of Wilma's escorts, a very tall, very black man, was unfamiliar to Ardala. But she recognized the other as Kemal Gavilan, the renegade Mercurian prince. A member of the aristocracy herself, Ardala had heard about the Sun King prince who had turned his back on his family and his heritage. She could not possibly understand choosing the lowly Martian Dancers, and then NEO, over the life of wealth and power that was his by birthright, but she was glad to see at least one member of the NEO group came from good breeding. She smiled seductively at him.

Ardala knew that he was a graduate of the John

Carter Academy and was a highly skilled fighter.
That alone was enough provocation for Ardala to
look up at both her Desert Runners, just to reassure
herself with their presence. Both Triin and Aasha
had tensed the moment the NEO agents had joined
Ardala, and were still poised on the edge of springing
to the attack.

The Desert Runners both growled deep in their
throats at Wilma's tone, and the two NEO pilots considered reaching for their weapons to protect their
leader. Ardala was amused by the whole militaristic
ritual and even thought about letting the NEO pilots
make the mistake of drawing their weapons. Instead,
she raised a hand before anyone had a chance to
move. It took Ardala all of her self-discipline not to
smile.

"It's not a joke at all," the Martian said calmly.
"The cruisers are already fitted out and waiting.
What I want in return is simple. In the Asteroid
Belt—the Juno-Vesta arc, to be exact—there is a body
in a small capsule, a twentieth century cockpit. I
want you to steal the whole package from the belt
before anyone else can recover it. Then you are to
leave everything in a location I have loaded into the
gift cruisers' computers. That is the operative data.
Everything else is incidental. You can trust me to
provide you with everything else you'll need to successfully transfer the body to me."

Wilma Deering looked at Ardala as if she wanted to
tear the data broker's head from her body. There was
little Wilma disliked more than a coward, and she
considered Ardala Valmar one of the biggest cowards
in the inner planets.

"I don't trust you for a second, Ardala. Why are you
asking us to do this? Can't you bully one of the weak-
lings who usually serve you into this job?" Wilma
said, her voice as cold as the dark side of Mercury.
"What's so important about this body that you've

stooped to working with NEO and risked crossing
RAM to get it?"

Ardala took a deep breath. What she wanted at
that moment was to put her perfectly manicured nail
tips through the NEO colonel's eyeballs. Instead, she
smiled as honestly as she could manage and tried to
calmly answer Wilma's questions.

"Honestly, Colonel Deering, I think you'd be more
comfortable if you took a seat. Your nervousness dis-
tresses me." Then Ardala spoke in a measured tone
with all the rational intent of a schoolteacher. "The
body is my property. As I'm sure you know, I don't
always work with RAM: I'm a free agent. This just
happens to be one instance when I prefer to work
with someone I can trust. I knew I could trust NEO's
integrity, especially yours, Colonel Deering, so I con-
tacted you. Simple enough, don't you agree?"

Wilma relaxed just a bit. It was common knowledge that the people usually in Ardala's employ were
untrustworthy. "And what do we get?" the colonel
said calmly.

Ardala had done her research on Wilma. NEO was
short on ships and firepower, and Wilma had defined
her interests as NEO's. That made the price Ardala
had to set for the mission very easy to identify.

"I thought that was perfectly clear, or you wouldn't
have brought the two charming pilots along. You, or
should I say NEO, get two cruisers, along with various other armaments that I believe you feel you could
use to good advantage."

"That's a sizable price to pay, even for someone of
your means," Wilma said.

Ardala laughed—not because she thought Wilma's
comment was funny, but because she knew the timing was all-important in these types of negotiations.
"Then you should be all the more eager to assist," she
said simply.

The Martian was making sense, and even Colonel

Deering recognized that. "I need to know that you're negotiating in good faith, Ms. Valmar. Let us take the cruisers back to NEO and have them looked over before the mission."

Ardala had expected that request. "Of course," she said, smiling sweetly.

"And I'd like a personal favor, if you can manage it. I want to see Kane in Australia. He's in a RAM prison there, and I think you can get me in to visit him."

Ardala gasped. The request had taken her by surprise, and she hid it badly. The last thing the information broker had expected was for Wilma to ask for something for herself. That just wasn't what Ardala's scouting reports had told her was likely.

Of all the people in the room, only Ardala knew that she was the one who had sent Kane to Australia in the first place, and all because he had shown too much of an attachment to Wilma Deering, his one-time ally and lover. Kane was so deeply in love with Wilma, in fact, that Ardala couldn't quite dominate his spirit. Kane had never given himself up to her fully because of his love for Wilma.

"I don't think that will be possible," Ardala said at last, trying to hide her anger.

"Then you can find someone else to recover the body from the belt," Wilma said, and Ardala clearly heard the finality of the statement.

The data broker paused for a second and looked up into Wilma Deering's clear, guileless eyes. This tomboy doesn't even realize what she's asking for, she thought to herself and curled her hands into tight fists.

"If you leave now, you can see him as soon as you get back to Earth. I'll provide you with RAM identification papers, but you'll have to go alone."

Wilma smiled and started out of the room. "Thank you, Ms. Valmar. After I've seen Kane, I'll radio you to tell you of my decision and receive the rest of your instructions for the mission."

"Wait just a minute," Ardala said as she quickly stood, her hands still clenched. "You can't keep me waiting like that. I've got other matters to attend to."

As Wilma reached the door to the boudoir, the NEO pilots right behind her, she turned and said, "Then you can busy yourself with these other matters while you wait for me to make my decision." The NEO colonel turned and left before Ardala had a chance to answer.

"Damn you!" Ardala screamed at the closed door and swiped her arm across the top of her desk, sending a myriad of baubles clattering across the floor. "You're lucky I haven't planted a bomb in those cruisers, you tomboy!"

Ardala calmed down after she'd shattered a few more priceless items. She knew that she had the advantage. She had no intention of letting Wilma go free once she had recovered Buck Rogers's body. The data merchant did not consider the price on Wilma's head significant, though that was another thing to be weighed on the scale against the NEO officer. Wilma's fate was really decided in Ardala's mind by her relationship with Killer Kane.

The Martian never exactly felt challenged by the Earth woman, at least not consciously, and Ardala knew that she was more beautiful than Wilma. There simply could be no doubt of that at all in Ardala's mind. After all, Wilma hadn't even had the genetic engineering that was standard in the Holzerhein family to ensure that she was as perfectly beautiful and strong as she was brilliant. Ardala had that and more.

What Ardala found so annoying about the tomboy rebel was that she was the only woman who had ever taken a man from her. She didn't consider that a challenge. It was more of an insult. And while Killer

Kane might not have been Ardala's first choice—and she certainly could have had many other, more desirable men to cater to her whims—it galled the Martian to see Kane prefer Wilma. She had made Kane pay with his freedom, and now she planned to make Wilma pay with her life.

Reassured, Ardala sighed happily now. She had only to sit back and wait, which she found both exhilarating and frustrating. She loved to watch her plans fall into place, checking progress like a general back at camp. She knew she could never risk being on the battlefront herself. But she had a marvelous feeling about this plan. She couldn't help but succeed in at least one area: Either Neola Price or Wilma Deering would go down in flames, or she'd get the body, or she'd get a place on RAM's executive board.

She deserved it all.

But not even Ardala's expert advisers, Tanny and Hatch, could predict the trouble that would befall their employer.

TRYST OF FATE

M.S. Murdock

I am not paying you to give my shipments away!"
Killer Kane stood before the director of Ferricom, Inc., in outraged silence. He balanced on the balls of his feet, his muscular frame taut, his chin lifted in defiance. He regarded Armand Zibroski's overweight bulk behind the U-shaped desk with thinly disguised scorn.

"There were fifteen nets in that shipment of ore!" sneered Zibroski. "The richest strike to come out of the Asteroid Belt in ten years, and you hand one of them over like a party favor!"

Kane said nothing, but his thin black moustache drew down at the corners as his lips compressed. His eyes narrowed.

"The most dangerous man in the solar system!" Zibroski waved a finger at Kane. "I might as well have hired a teddy bear! Some piece of space scum flips a laser, and you cave in!"

Kane's sea-green eyes sparked. "I never cave in," he said.

"Then explain to me why that shipment left the belt with fifteen nets and arrived at Ferricom with fourteen," snapped Zibroski.

"You were too cheap to arm your barges as I

directed."

"Forget it, Kane! Those barges were fitted with a new set of gyro shells."

"With a single round of ammunition! Your economy drive nearly cost lives. Did you expect my reputation to scare off a pirate? You've been in this business long enough to know nothing spooks those freaks and gennies."

"So you handed them a load of choice grade iron as a present," said Zibroski sarcastically.

"No. I dropped a load on top of their third-rater. She couldn't use her rail guns without damaging the load. Then I covered the barges' tails. We got the rest of the shipment out—no thanks to you!"

Zibroski leaned forward, his fingers resting on the gleaming slab of polished wood that covered the top of his custom-made desk. "I am tired of excuses. You were paid to do a job. You failed."

Hot anger blazed in Kane's eyes. "I was sabotaged," he said tightly.

"Are you accusing me of dishonesty?"

Kane lowered his dark head to hide the green flames in his eyes. "I am accusing you of nothing," he responded evenly. "It merely occurs to me that economy might be served by cutting security expenses— expenses like my fee."

Zibroski smiled. The expression was replete with evil.

"Not this time," said Kane. His words were accompanied by a move so fast it was a blur. He was behind Zibroski, his hands a flash of tan heading for the man's neck. As fast as Kane was, Zibroski's security system was faster. As Kane's right hand sliced through the cold wall of rushing air, he recoiled—too late. Jets of brilliant purple steam erupted from the floor in front of the atmospheric wall. The smell of sulphur made his stomach turn over. "Morpheum," he muttered as his knees went out from under him.

Kane went down like a stone. Through the fading purple haze, Zibroski regarded Kane's helpless athletic body, sprawled on the carpet. Protected from the drug's effects by the security wall surrounding his desk, Zibroski could afford to enjoy Kane's defeat. His saturnine smile spread across his face.

Satisfied that Kane was incapacitated, he sat down and activated his communications terminal. A viewscreen rose from the center of the desktop. Zibroski's fat fingers moved with surprising speed as he fed numbers into the link. The computer blinked, and Ardala Valmar's exquisite face appeared.

Zibroski moved his considerable bulk away from the screen, giving Ardala an unobstructed view of Kane's unconscious body. Her full lips drew together in the center and turned up at the corners in a smile of unutterable sweetness.

"I assume this will satisfy you?" asked Zibroski.

"It is a beginning," Ardala admitted. Her low voice rippled like water. "My uncle will be most grateful for your cooperation, Armand."

The combined effects of his name spoken in those throaty tones and the intimation of favor from RAM's chief executive, Simund Holzerhein, made Zibroski giddy. He puffed up with importance, looking more than ever like a startled toad. "Your humble servant, Miss Valmar," he responded gallantly.

Ardala's long lashes fluttered as she covered her aversion. "You've arranged for safe quarters?"

Zibroski chuckled. "The finest accommodations, I assure you."

"As long as they're secure. He suspects nothing?"

"Your involvement is our little secret," returned Zibroski, reflecting that Kane's enmity was a small price to pay for Holzerhein's favor.

"See that you keep it," said Ardala, the threat behind her words unsoftened by her voluptuous voice. She cut the transmission and with it the vision of Zibroski's self-satisfied face. She sank back into her chair and curled up like a panther cub. Her sultry eyes, half-lidded in satisfaction, glowed. Let the great Killer Kane rot in some dismal hole until it pleased her fancy to set him free. Let him languish in ignorance, cursing Zibroski for his misfortune.

She let her mind dissect Kane. Without doubt, he was the handsomest man she had ever met. The scars and small imperfections of his beautifully balanced body were infinitely more exciting than the unmarked perfection of her genetically altered creations. The memory of the fire behind his green eyes made her shiver. He was unruly, and that was part of her fascination of him. Her gennie lovers were created to kneel uncomplainingly at the altar of her beauty. Kane bent his stubborn knee to no one, no one except that red-haired hussy, Wilma Deering. Ardala's anger flared at the thought of her rival. She hated the softening of Kane's eyes when Wilma's name was mentioned. Ardala would bend his stubborn will if she had to keep him locked up for the rest of his life—but that would be such a waste. Fortunately, she knew hundreds of methods of persuasion, some of them infinitely pleasurable. She mused on the alternatives.

$$\text{O} \quad \text{O} \quad \text{O} \quad \text{O} \quad \text{O}$$

Heat rose from the pavement in shimmering waves, repelled by the plasticrete surface. It met the blazing intensity of the southern sun and wavered under the assault, to be driven back to the ground. The plasticrete reflected the sun's rays in an escalating cycle, pushing the temperature to enervating heights, but the Dragonfly class heliplane was impervious to the heat. Its engines pulsed in a powerful whine as its rotor blades whipped lazily, creating a steaming whirlwind. It was parked in front of a plastifiber Quonset hangar. The

*words "Texarkana Org, Hangar 22" were stenciled
across its curving white walls in plain black letters. A
man and a woman wearing ambassador's sashes over
their conservative suits came out of the hangar and
went toward the plane, ducking under the rotors. The
man reached the heliplane's door and turned, extending a hand to the woman. She reached out, her coppery
hair whipped into a tangle by the wind. Their hands
caught.*

*The hangar exploded in a ball of flame, consuming
the aircraft and licking hungrily at the runway. The
flames roiled high, sending clouds of black smoke and
the acrid smell of burning into the air. "Mama! Papa!
No!" Wilma Deering heard herself screaming. The
voice did not seem to belong to her, but she knew it for
her own. The screams went on and on, rising with the
unchecked flames. The emergency siren was a poor second to her cries.*

Wilma shook her head. "No," she murmured. "I
have never been here." Screams reverberated inside
her skull. She was confused, but tears joined the
sweat streaming from her face. The flames rolled
toward her. She could see nothing but the wavering
red-orange wall, feel nothing but the awful heat that
made the scorching sun's rays insignificant, hear
nothing but the cries of agony that were her own, and
strangely not her own. She was curiously abstracted
from the scene, like a person watching home movies.
The fire rolled over her, searing her senses to white
blindness. "Mama," she whispered as the whiteness
faded to merciful, unconscious black.

The sea of darkness surged around her, making
patterns of iridescence in the inky waters. Wilma
stretched, sending miniature waves into the sea. She
was dimly aware of floating on top of the ocean, cra-
dled by it, yet untouched. She hovered on the edge of
consciousness in the delicious comfort that was not
quite sleep.

At the edges of her understanding she heard a steady pounding. She turned over and covered her ears. Pounding penetrated her pathetic defense, shuddering through her body. She curled into a ball, but the blows continued in a steady rhythm. She heard a voice behind them, as demanding as the pounding.

"Open up! Come on, miss. We're with the Terrine guards. Your parents are dead. We've got orders from the juvenile magistrate to pick you up. Can't have unsupervised children wandering around."

"No!" Wilma sat bolt upright. The sea made way for her, running away on all sides like a tide retreating. As it faded, her parents' house grew around her, its center her room.

She was sitting in bed, the covers tangled in a sailor's knot. It was morning, and her brother, Roberto, and sister, Sally, were asleep in their rooms. She was sixteen and they were children.

That fact somehow made an immense difference. She was sixteen. The Terrines were at the door, ready to take them to the Chicagorg Youth Hostel, where they would be separated according to age, trained to fit neatly into a prearranged slot in the vast organization that was Russo-American Mercantile, and indentured at the age of eighteen to repay the company for its investment. Wilma tore the covers off and threw them on the floor. "We aren't dressed!" she called. "Please, give us some time!" *She ripped a nondescript brown jumpsuit from her closet and began to crawl into it.*

The pounding stopped. "All right," responded the voice. "Fifteen minutes."

"What is it, Wilma?" *Buddy stood in her doorway, a small boy rubbing the sleep out of his eyes.*

Wilma pounced on her brother and hugged him. "It's the Terrines," she said. "They've come to take us away. We have to run. Where's Sally?"

"Right here." *Sally was ten years old, as slim and*

willowy as Wilma, but her hair was silver flax instead of crimson.

"Did you hear me?"

"Sure. Terrines."

"Get dressed—fast."

Sally left without a word, yielding to Wilma's age and organization. Their parents had planned for this contingency, and the children were used to drills. Five minutes later the three were assembled, rucksacks clutched in their hands. Wilma strapped the smallest to her brother's squirming, five-year-old back. "Hold still, Buddy. This time I can't carry it for you. There!" She locked the last strap in place and took his hand.

"Hurry up in there!" shouted the Terrine.

"Just a few minutes!" Wilma called back. She dragged Buddy to the rear of the house, Sally on their heels. Stationed at the back door was another Terrine. It was clear the unit had experience dealing with unwilling children.

"We'll never get past him," Sally whispered.

"We're not going to try," said Wilma, opening the door to the cellar.

"No!" squeaked Buddy. "I don't like it down there!"

"Me neither," said Wilma, "but we have to, Buddy. Come on. I'll be with you." She herded her brother and sister into the narrow stairway, leaving the lights off. The shallow basement windows lifted the edge from the gloom. They had enough light to see their way, but no more. Buddy whimpered with fear.

Wilma pulled the cellar door, and it shut with a click. "Come on," she whispered, "and not a sound!" With her brother and sister clutching her hands, she made her way down the stairs and across the dark cavern of the cellar's main room. Its outside entrance had been blocked up, but Wilma's parents, as active members of the reconstructionist movement, were acutely aware of the need for a back door in times of danger. They had extended the original shaft that was the cellar's outside exit, running it well away from the house. Wilma and the two children crept along the passageway until they came to the short flight of steps terminating in the cracked planks of an ancient wooden door. From outside, the door looked like another piece of trash, indistinguishable from the litter that surrounded it. Carefully Wilma pushed the door up.

A line of bright sunlight glared through the crack, and she squinted, letting her eyes get used to the light. Behind her she could hear Buddy sniffling and Sally trying to quiet him. Her eyes adjusted to the sunlight, and she peeked through the crack, anxiously trying to locate the Terrines. Only one was within her view, and he had his back to them. It was no protection, but it was a momentary circumstance they could not afford to waste. She raised the door, holding it high above her head. "Run!" she said. "Go to Hildy's!"

Sally dragged her brother through the doorway and began to run. Glad to be outside, Buddy trotted happily at her side. Wilma watched them round the corner, then followed, replacing the door. As she caught up with Buddy and Sally, she picked up her brother, swung him up to ride piggyback, nodded at Sally, and ran. In minutes they were at Hildy's back door. It opened before they could knock, and they were in Hildy's ample arms.

"Goodness, I'm glad to see you!" she cried. "The minute we heard about your parents, we tried to get to you, but the Terrines were too quick for us. Then I remembered the tunnel, and I hoped you'd make it. I thought about watching the entrance, but I was afraid it might alert the Terrines." Their mother's best friend patted Wilma on the back.

"They are dead, then?" Wilma's hazel eyes were huge with fear.

Hildy nodded. "No doubt. They said it was a terrorist raid, but I don't for a moment believe it. They were getting too noticeable. RAM dealt with them." Safe in Hildy's soft arms, Wilma burst into tears.

"This is too slow."

The intrusive male voice was not part of the story, but Wilma knew he had been there.

"So give her another injection. Some Vermidox will jolt her memory."

The first man eyed the screen where the image of Wilma in Hildy's arms wavered. "I hate this stuff. How they can tell what's real memory, reconstructed memory, or sheer hallucination I don't know." He adjusted a knob and the image stopped wavering. Wilma twisted in her shackles, but the sensory deprivation chamber in which she was suspended kept her from feeling them. "I'd rather use the old methods."

"You don't have to know. Leave that to the experts. We're getting paid a nice bit of change." The second man filled a syringe and inserted it into a robot arm that extended into the chamber. He manipulated controls and the arm reached toward Wilma, gently slipped the syringe into a vein, and expelled the drug. Wilma jerked as the Vermidox took effect, then went slack. "That should speed things up," the second man said.

The images came faster, and Wilma rolled in her restraints. She would be a mass of bruises soon, but for the moment, between the drugs and the chamber, she felt no pain.

Blackness. She and Buddy and Sally, huddled together for an eternity in blackness as the Terrines' footsteps echoed above their heads. Buddy and Sally clung to her, their hearts beating like trip-hammers, too frightened even to whimper.

Running. Running until her own heart pounding was louder than any other sound, louder even than the harsh breaths she gasped. Running until she knew her brother and sister were safe, decoying the Terrines in a wild scramble through the rubble of outer Chicagorg. Her heart pounded louder and louder until she heard no more.

Light. Strong arms lifting her. Murmured words of concern.

Beowulf's face. Large and square and full of worry. Piercing black eyes midway between bristling white hair and bristling white moustache. Eyes that looked through her. Eyes of her father's friend. Beowulf took her cold hands between his large brown ones and began to rub them.

"You're safe, Wilma. Safe. Buddy and Sally are safe. You remember me?"

Wilma expelled a deep breath. "I remember. When can I see them?"

"Soon. First we must talk. Your parents have given you very little choice in life. No, no, don't ruffle up. What a baleful stare. Anger strikes in your eyes like lightning! I mean, by their loyalties to the New Earth Organization, they have marked you. RAM will never trust you as Wilma Deering, daughter of Robert and Aurelia Deering. If you wish a normal life, you will have to change your identity."

"Never! Those pigs killed my parents and tried to lay the blame on you! I will never work for them, or live their regimented life! And I will get even if it takes me the rest of my life." Wilma's voice shook with passion.

"I take it you wish to join our ranks," said Beowulf dryly.

"Yes." Wilma's terse response was not the starry-eyed eagerness of a romantic teenager. She knew exactly what she was choosing.

Darkness again, this time pierced by a shaft of light. A Terrine rose before her, flat, two-dimensional. She did not care. She raised her pistol and fired. The laser charge seared the center of the Terrine's chest. A bell sounded, and the Terrine vanished. To her left two figures rose, one Terrine, one a child. She whirled and fired. One bell sounded as she burned the Terrine. A single guard appeared in front of her. Whirl, shoot, clang! Drop, shoot, clang! The dance went on and on.

Finally the shaft of light died. In the total darkness a voice said, "Score ninety-four percent. Marksman first class."

Clouds. White, puffy, scudding clouds, streaming by faster than thought, yet there was no wind. There was no sound. Only speed. Surrounded by clouds, Wilma thought of the angels depicted in art treasures of the blasted past, and wondered if she had died and grown wings.

"What in RAM's name is that?" asked the technician monitoring the video screen. The hazy image of a female figure clothed in flowing robes, with white wings sprouting from her shoulders, floated against a blue sky.

"Search me," said his partner. "NEOs are crazy."

Wings. Wilma looked over her left shoulder. Extending behind her was a streak of silver, a metal wing that arched back, cutting through the atmosphere as if it were not there. She looked down, and her hands rested firmly on the controls of a spacecraft. She was flying, but the wings were mechanical, not supernatural.

"That's right, Deering. Keep her nose up." Her flight instructor sat in the copilot's seat, a clipboard of check sheets in his hand. "Now bring her on in. You're doing fine. Cut landing speed by point five. There! That's better. Keep her steady! Fine!" The pressure blanket buoyed the plane and it bounced. "Keep her nose up, I said! Good. Hold her steady . . . you're down. Ease off the throttle. Good. Make a slow turn, ninety degrees to starboard—cut your engines—power down." The ship glided to a halt. "Well, Deering, how did your first solo flight feel?"

"Scary," she replied honestly.

Noise. People everywhere. People talking. Eyes that cut through the chaos and riveted her to the spot, oblivious of the crowd. Laughing, dangerous, wanton eyes that made her their target. She flushed, her fair skin flaming like her hair, but as the eyes drew closer the blood drained from her face, leaving it pearly white.

"Where have they been hiding you?" The voice was mocking, light, caressing.

"Nowhere," she replied inanely. She struggled for control, angry she could be overcome by a look. The eyes held her. Pale sea-green laced with golden lights, surrounded by curling dark lashes, they promised an untamed personality, dangerous, passionate, and daring.

"Then it's lucky I saw you first," said Kane, taking possession of her.

The man's image appeared on the interrogator's video screen. He was devastating. Tall, slim, perfectly proportioned, there was not an ounce of extra flesh on his close-knit frame. High cheekbones and a classically straight nose gave his face an aristocratic air, and the carefully clipped, dark moustache added a rakish quality. On his left jaw a tattoo shaped like a broken crescent posed, indicating a colorful history. His dark hair curved softly around his head, occasionally curling in rebellion. The scene shifted abrubtly.

White light. Curses. The sting of a whip on bare flesh. Bitter cold. Prison. Deimos prison. The black hole where the enemies of RAM sank into oblivion and death. She heard the curses dimly, felt the blows lightly, and knew she was losing consciousness. Knew this had happened before. Knew it would happen again. Until she died.

The cold closed around her, pressing against her body on all sides. Her knees were drawn up, her arms folded between them and her chin. The wet cold of condensed moisture on stone trickled slowly down her back, soaked through her suit, and congealed on her shins. Buried. That was it. She had died and was buried. Terrified, she looked up. Ten feet above her was a square opening. Of course. The fuel delivery shaft. She must have fallen asleep after the grueling race through the prison grounds, a race she had carefully planned. Once in the rabbit warren of the underground cells, she had eluded the guards and made for the shaft. She listened carefully. A single set of footsteps approached. She waited. They grew nearer, passed, and faded into the distance. Wilma let out her breath. The guard would not return for an hour. She began to inch her way up the shaft, her guerrilla training finding hand-and footholds where there seemed to be none. At the top of the shaft she checked the area. It was empty of human life. She wedged her elbows against the stone and levered herself up, then rolled onto the smooth paving stones of the roof of Deimos prison.

The piercing electronic eye of a detector swept over her, and Wilma shrank from it, but it did not record her presence. She wondered at her luck, but took it, making for freedom.

Beowulf again. His eyes full of pain.

"No!"

"There's no use denying it, Wilma. Kane's gone over. For you."

"He couldn't!"

"He did it to save your life. No one escapes from Deimos. He bought your freedom with his own."

"Then, when he gets the chance, he'll come back."

"I don't think so." The pain in Beowulf's eyes deepened. "He's had the chance."

"What do you mean?" Wilma had her mentor by the collar, the anger in her shaking fingers nothing compared to the torment in her eyes.

"Kane's had the chance to come back. More than one. RAM has given him a lot as a man who's found the true faith. Including freedom. It's been months, and he's begun flying missions for RAM."

His words were a knife, and Wilma sagged.

"It's a sore loss," Beowulf said. "He was the best pilot we had, in spite of his wild streak." He ran a hand over Wilma's red hair. "Now you are our best."

Wilma shook her head slowly, tears streaming down her face.

The images on the video screen came thick and fast, fragments of Wilma's life as a NEO freedom fighter. The midnight gloom of a dark street burst into explosive white as a Terrine grenade detonated on Wilma's heels. Faces flashed by, friend and foe. She saw the stars, and the instrument panel of her spacecraft. There were other ships, closing on her or fleeing from her guns. At intervals, Buddy's or Sally's face appeared, older as the months lengthened into years. There were no long vignettes, just a jumble of pictures.

"I don't envy the boys in Interp," said the first technician. "This is a mess."

"Just hope the tape's long enough. You know what happened the last time we had to change one."

The first man shuddered. "How did we know the subject was going to mention the only detail Interp was after in the ten seconds it took us to change a tape? Those stuffed shirts should try this job sometime."

Wilma heard the words dimly as she slipped into an empty box. At first she was passive, then she recognized the box. It was a cell, a cell with her name on it, deep in the heart of Calypso. She threw herself against the walls in her mind, writhing madly in her restraints. If her first imprisonment was an unpleasant experience, the second was hell, pure and simple, a hell of drugs and torture and degradation. There was a blur of agony as memories answered the call of the drug and surfaced. A series of blows left her gasping. Then hunger, hunger of such long standing it was a normal pain. She rebelled, trying frantically to push the memories back into their locked compartments, but they flowed on, unchecked.

She could hear screaming alarms, the scurrying feet of the guards as they ran, and the whining blasts of a heavy laser. Sparks guttered on the inside of the cell door as the laser destroyed the lock, and a crashing blow knocked the door from its hinges. The heavy metal

*clattered against the stone floor. The opening was filled
with a huge masculine silhouette, backlit by the illumina-
tion in the corridor to an eerie unreality. Wilma stood up
slowly.* "Who in sweet hades are you?" *she asked.*

"Black Barney. Deering?"

"Yo."

"Twenty thousand credits—if we sell her back to
NEO," *commented a voice behind the black monolith.*
"From RAM, more."

"Mrrr," *said Barney.* "Worth the risk."

"The market for political prisoners is rising, Captain. She'll cover expenses. The rest'll be cream."

*Wilma thought fast. Barney was infamous, a pirate
whose one god was money. She had no chance of escaping
him physically, for Barney's bionic modifications made
him an awesome fighting machine. She attacked from
another direction.* "Sell me if you want to, idiot! Sell me
back to RAM for enough credits to buy yourself a new
ship. Or let me buy my freedom—at five times the price!"

*Barney's eyes narrowed under his thatch of dark
hair. He lifted Wilma by the scruff of the neck with one
huge hand. His eyes gleamed red.* "How can you come
by five times the price?" *There was contempt in his
voice.*

*Wilma glared into his implacable face, undaunted by
the glinting metal that made up half his countenance.*
"I can earn it."

Barney's eyes swept her up and down. "I don't see
how."

"Put me down, you oaf!" *Wilma was beyond caring
that the Master Pirate was capable of snapping her
neck with a pinch of his fingers.* "Put me down and I'll
tell you how you can make some real money."

*Slowly Barney lowered her to the floor, but he kept his
fingers around her neck.*

"Give me a ship. Give me a crew—prisoners from
Calypso. In six months I'll pay you back a hundred
times over. Your profit will be enormous—and at no real*

cost to you."

"I am to trust you?" Barney's look was incredulous.

"That did not enter my mind. It's a gamble, I warrant, but how can you really lose? Who is the most fearsome privateer in the system?"

"I am."

"Agreed. It would be pointless to run from you. You can always kill me."

"Yes."

"What harm is there in giving the proposition a chance? I hate RAM. I hate them for what they did to me. I hate them for killing my parents, and I hate them for what they are trying to do to Earth. You know my record. I am one of the best pilots in the system, and I will prey on RAM without mercy."

Barney's expressionless face was a block of granite. The coldness of the silence washed over Wilma like death. Finally he spoke. "A bargain," he said. So she joined the ranks of piracy, slicing away at RAM's shipping like a ruthless laser.

The images on the video screen jumbled again, mostly fragments of raids, broken by the faces of her family, and occasionally by Kane's audacious smile.

"Give her another dose," said the first technician on the edges of Wilma's consciousness. "She's slowing down again."

"Don't dare," returned his companion. "Might kill her, and you know what the supervisor would say to that."

Wilma sat up with a start, sweat pouring from her body. She'd had the dream again. The technicians, the needles, the images—the hell of drugged interrogation. Dear heaven, she had thought it was fading, but this was all too clear. She ran a hand through her wet auburn hair, breathing hard. For months after her release from Calypso she had been afraid to sleep for fear of the dream. She had lived through horrors once. It was entirely unthinkable she should be forced to endure them over and over in her mind. It made RAM out the winner, and Wilma had determined that would never be. The telecom beside her bed was jingling noisily. That must be what woke me up, she thought. Thank you, small lifeline. She reached out and picked up the instrument.

"Deering?" The voice was distantly mechanical. Sometimes Earth's telecommunications systems left a lot to be desired.

Wilma took three slow breaths, willing control. "Deering here," she replied.

"Hold, please." There was a series of clicks.

"Wilma? Turabian here." Wilma's commanding officer in NEO, General Carlton Turabian, was her friend as well. "I hear you're going to Australia. To see Kane." It was a statement and a question at the same time.

"You should pay your sources more. They're very good."

"Then it's true? Wilma, this is great! Let me send someone along with you. We can try to reinitiate him—"

"No." Her mouth was set in a firm line.

"But he's a great pilot! I should think you, of all people, would want him to return!"

"Not under those circumstances."

"Then let me at least—"

"No." She was not willing to compromise when it came to Kane. "This trip is for me, Turabian. If there's anything to know, I'll tell you when I return," she said, a little more softly. "You know I will."

If there was anything Carlton Turabian knew for sure, it was where Wilma Deering's loyalty lay. "Be careful."

"You know I will."

○ ○ ○ ○ ○

On the other side of the world, Killer Kane stalked the confines of his prison with the chained ferocity of a cornered Tasmanian devil. His anger charged the atmosphere, draining his face of the rapier charm that was his trademark. The muscles over his cheekbones and jaw were sharply defined by it, tense and corded. His mouth was a hard line.

He had been stupid, and he could not forgive himself. That stupidity landed him in Australia, a god-forsaken hellhole inhabited by the tattered remnants of native marsupials, birds, aborigines, and the horrific dregs of RAM's unsuccessful experiments in genetic engineering. He glared at the bars that crisscrossed the windows of his room. They offended him. He had an insane desire to throw himself against them, defying their primitive restriction, but he quelled it. With every step, he vowed revenge on Armand Zibroski.

As chairman of the board for Ferricom, Inc., he controlled a high percentage of RAM's mining interests. Ferricom had interests in Australia. Kane was incarcerated at the Wollongong Outpost on the edge of the Blue Mountains in Sydney Reservation. His cell was located in the central corridor on the fifth floor of Treasury, Ltd., Ferricom's Australian subsidiary. When Kane awoke from his drugged sleep, he was safely incarcerated, with the anonymous face of a locked computer terminal his only companion.

He glared at the terminal, angry yellow lights in his eyes. The computer screen gave him no answers. It was as unyielding as the stone walls of another prison. He had spent an eternity of thirty days in the priority security ward of Deimos Prison. The time was woven tightly into the fabric of his memory, even though much of it was a drugged stupor. The dark, dark walls of rough-cut stone, the cold sweat of condensation, the dank smell of stale water, the scratchy sound of sewer rats scrabbling across the stone, were

as clear as the hour they happened. He could still feel
the cut of the Terrine's cat-o'-nine-tails ripping across
his back, tearing his clothing to ribbons, then slicing
flesh. The sensation was as disembodied now as it
had felt then, under the influence of Doxinal.

He closed his eyes, hearing the voice of his interrogator without fear. It was an exercise he set himself, pend-
ing the day he would bring Alonzo Khrebet to justice.

*"It is useless to resist," said Khrebet in a voice as soft
as a kitten's fur. The whip sliced ruthlessly across
Kane's shoulders. "In the end, you will tell me all I
wish to know. What were you and Deering doing at
Coprates Liaison Headquarters?"*

*Kane said nothing, but his capture rolled through his
mind like a looped recording. The night was deep
black. He could feel the damp masonry wall at his back.
He could feel Wilma's slim shoulder against his arm,
hear her quickened breathing over the footsteps of the
roving band of Terrine guards. A shaft of light cut
through the darkness, a Terrine's search beacon slicing
into the fog at their feet. The light rose. He squinted
against it as he and Wilma ducked it and ran.*

"There they are!"

*The cry brought a rush of footsteps from all direc-
tions. Another light pierced the dark, stopping Kane
and Wilma in their tracks. "Looks like we've lost a
snitch," he said.*

"Ohm sold us out," she agreed.

*Kane flashed Wilma a grin. His eyes danced, antici-
pating a fight. As the Terrines closed their half-circle,
Kane and Wilma launched an attack, the speed and
violence of their move taking the Terrines completely by
surprise. One man got off a shot that missed Kane and
singed one of his cohorts. The injured man swore.
Wilma dodged as Kane threw one of the Terrines over
his shoulder. She landed a blow to the stomach as a Terrine reached for her, then grabbed his flailing hand
and bent his arm back. He sank to his knees with a*

moan and she kicked him flat. His head struck the street and he went limp. An unconscious Terrine rolled against her lower legs as Kane dropped him. Kane grabbed her hand as they vaulted over the body and ran.

A searchlight careened crazily through the haze, then steadied as the last remaining Terrine got control of it. He cut a swath through the night, picking up the fleeing figures. He raised a gyro pistol, aimed, and fired. The shell charged after Kane and Wilma, following them through the fog.

They rounded a corner, evading the beam of light. "What was that?" asked Wilma sharply.

Kane shook his head.

"Listen."

Kane picked up a faint, high-pitched whine. "Gyro," he said. "Run!"

"Too late!" called Wilma as the shell exploded.

Kane remembered wondering why he felt no impact, then he realized the Terrine had used a stunner as he succumbed to the chemical cloud that the exploding gyro shell freed.

"Talk!" Khrebet's lash punctuated his memories in vicious strokes.

Chained spread-eagle between two posts, Kane sagged in the restraints. He could no longer raise his head, but he still managed a reply. "Only what I please," he said.

Crack! The whip stung the air before it descended, adding the terror of anticipation to pain. With an immense effort Kane forced his head up. He was compelled to challenge Khrebet's eye. Kane was human, pure human, unadulterated by the cybernetic gadgets that creatures like Khrebet affected. He could not allow Khrebet to win. Through the blood that clouded his vision, through the slits that were all the opening his swollen eyes allowed, he memorized Khrebet's blunted features.

The square face was sliced in two by a band of

metal and plastic. From the bone above his eyebrows to the top of his cheekbones his face was alien, for Khrebet had cybernetic eyes—not just the eye itself, but the entire structure of cavity and surrounding tissue. Shiny metal eyelids devoid of lashes blinked over the implanted mechanical orbs, cleaning them with monotonous regularity. The eyes had no expression. His broad face accepted the implant, molding itself around it as if it were a pearl instead of a blemish. Scars from the surgery ran down his cheeks in white lines. The thick mouth beneath the implant was a satisfied curve.

Oh, yes, Kane remembered Khrebet. He remembered also—as he knew he was meant to—the hand that stayed Khrebet's lash.

As he felt the adrenaline draining from his system and knew he could not remain defiant, an authoritative voice sounded above his head. "That will be enough, Khrebet. There are some men for whom your methods are inefficient. This one will die before he reveals half the information we seek. Take him down, clean him up, and let him sleep. Then bring him to me."

Kane lost consciousness as Khrebet let him down. His next memory was waking to unaccustomed cleanliness, his mind clear, his back and shoulders raw. Within an hour he was standing in front of a thin man in a conservative, dark suit, a man who was carefully anonymous. Kane's instincts for danger were instantly alert.

"Sit down, Mister Kane." The voice was as anonymous as the face.

"Courtesy," commented Kane lightly. "What a welcome surprise."

"There may be other surprises in store for you."

Kane's left eyebrow rose. In spite of his swollen and discolored eyes, the gesture managed to be rakish. "At least this will be interesting."

"Imminently. You were captured with a woman, one Wilma Deering."

Kane remained silent.

"Quite a prize for us," continued the man. *"Two of NEO's top pilots at one blow. Your relationship is common knowledge. Miss Deering is scheduled—as you were yourself—for a complete mind scan. It will tell us all she knows, but, unfortunately, it will leave her nothing. You can prevent it."*

Kane did not waste time on games. *"How?"* he asked.

"Very good, Kane. You have not tried useless denials when you know they will gain nothing. I am impressed by your judgment—and flattered. You may spare Miss Deering's life by working for RAM."

Both Kane's eyebrows went up. *"What? RAM wants me in its camp? It's willing to trust me?"*

"RAM trusts no one, Kane. That is the principle upon which the most efficient organization in the history of man is based. We have a thorough profile on you. There are any number of ways to control your actions."

The man's confidence rankled, but Kane covered his irritation. *"My freedom to prevent a mind erase. Not good enough. I want more."* The man smiled, and Kane knew he expected this. His irritation grew.

"Just what is it you want?" said the executive softly.

"I am sure you already know." Kane's tone was sardonic. *"I want Wilma Deering's freedom. She is to be allowed to escape, and she is not to be pursued for seventy-two hours."*

The man's smile grew. *"It is gratifying to see you know us as well as we know you. That is the maximum I could allow before the whole network of RAM security descended on Deimos and on me. I congratulate you."*

"There is something else." The man's surprise was instantly veiled, but Kane saw it, and a little of his irritation was salved.

"Yes?"

"If I am to become a part of RAM—however briefly—I will know the names of those I do business with."

For the first time the man's eyes showed expression. They lit with amusement. *"I will indulge you. My name is Marc Angelo."*

Kane chuckled.

The computer terminal uttered a strident beep, and Kane forsook his memories. Barton Emmerich's face appeared on the screen. "You're awake," he said.

"What an astute observation," replied Kane.

Emmerich ruffled up like a turkey cock. He was a small man with pale thinning hair, pale skin, and washed-out blue eyes. His features were too small for his face, clustered at the center of it like travelers at a crossroads. He drew his thin mouth to an even thinner grimace of disapproval. "I am the administrator of this facility," he said pompously.

Kane read the man's identification badge. "Barton Emmerich," he said. Emmerich's pale eyes showed momentary surprise, and Kane realized the man thought Kane knew him. "I make it my business to collect trivial information," he quipped.

Emmerich decided not to be baited. "You will be Treasury's guest for an unspecified length of time. I suggest you cooperate."

Kane chortled. "I can see you don't know me."

"On the contrary," responded Emmerich. "I have your complete file from Deimos."

"My dear sir, I will endeavor to cause you all the difficulty I can muster. Good day," said Kane royally, dismissing the man.

"If you wish to be foolish, I cannot stop you, but I promise you will regret your decision," said Emmerich, and the screen went blank.

"I hardly think so," said Kane to the empty air. He turned away from the terminal and stared out the barred window. Hot Australian sunshine sparkled on the dusty green foliage of the eucalyptus trees. He punched one fist into the palm of the other hand. He would have his freedom. He would win.

He needed victory. He had always needed it. The sweet taste of superiority was an addiction stronger than Doxinal, a driving hunger. He remembered his first taste vividly.

Langles Urban Reservation was a rough town, built on war between rival gangs. Survival outside RAM's central complex was a constant battle. He was eleven years old, tall, but not heavily built for his age, and surrounded by a pack of juvenile rats who called themselves the Killjacks, with good reason. Kane faced their leader. He was four years older than Kane, a good six inches taller, and heavier. The onset of adolescence gave him an extra edge. He looked down on Kane, his thumbs stuck in his back pockets. "Girlie," he said. He watched the anger blaze in Kane's eyes, then said it again. "Girlie."

"Take it back," said Kane.

The boy shook his head. "Can't. You're too pretty for words." He looked around the group. "What 'cha say? We could sell him to Bobico for a lot of cash."

Knowledge came early on the streets. Kane knew Bobico. He was a panderer, supplying those who could pay with the vices they desired.

"Aw, Benny, let him go," said a skinny girl with a thick topknot of white-blond hair.

"Why? We could make good money—easier'n the lifts we been pullin'."

"Not easy," whispered Kane. He rubbed his palms with his fingertips.

"What was that, Girlie?"

"I said," returned Kane in a louder voice, "it won't be easy."

"Who's gonna stop us? You?" Benny laughed and pointed at his victim.

Without warning, Kane doubled over and launched himself at the most vulnerable part of Benny's anatomy. Hands grabbed for him, but he was too quick, the move too unexpected. As he jumped, he grabbed for the knife inside his jacket. He hit Benny in the stomach, and the gang leader doubled up, falling backward with

Kane somewhere in the middle of him. The others followed as he went down, expecting a speedy end to the conflict, for Benny's body count was twenty.

They were right, but the outcome was not what they expected. Curled at the center of his opponent, Kane drove the knife into Benny's vitals. He tasted Benny's blood. The Killjacks' chief screamed, flailing for the knife at his hip. Kane kept hacking at his opponent, and the hand went limp. Like lightning, Kane rolled from Benny's body, rising to his feet in a whirling blur. He faced the Killjacks, covered with blood. "Anybody else want to call me 'Girlie'?" he asked.

The boy at the front of the group spread his hands and shook his head.

"Killer," whispered the blond girl.

Kane nodded slowly. "Yes."

"You took out the chief," said the boy. "Rules say the job goes to you."

Kane shook his head again. "I go alone. You keep out of my way."

The boy raised his hands, palms toward Kane. "Sure. Whatever you say."

The rush of relief, of triumph, of safety, was a feeling Kane relished, even in remembrance. He had repeated it many times, in many ways, from the simple triumph of personal combat, to the more intricate pleasure of intrigue. As he grew older, the handsome face and figure that were a youthful trial came to be assets he enjoyed, for they gave him power over women. He had fought and clawed for his survival in Langles, both physically and intellectually, hoarding his take, for Kane had a dream. He wanted to fly. To be the pilot of a hot spacecraft was the ultimate experience of power.

At the age of sixteen, he applied for entrance into RAM's Langles Flight Academy, where the company trained pilots. He was summarily rejected, no explanation and no court of appeal. At the time, he was dumbfounded, but now he knew exactly why RAM refused him. He was too much of an individual. If he had been a gang member or leader, he might have passed. RAM viewed individuals as sticky wheels in the gears of their machine. He sought another avenue.

Whatever money he got above living expenses went into the pockets of the shuttle pilots at Sonica Air Terminal. He stole their flight manuals, picked their brains, and bargained for lessons. In the meantime, he had fallen in with NEO. The New Earth Organization gave him wings. He had to credit them with that. Once they discovered his aptitude and interest, they put him in the hands of two flight leaders. Kane did every dirty chore there was to be done around a spacecraft before they let him climb into a cockpit, but he learned how the ships worked, learned their idiosyncracies, and the basics of repairing them. Once he began to take them up, his talent as a pilot surfaced. In a year, he was the hottest pilot NEO had, and he kept getting better.

It was inevitable that the best should meet. His first encounter with Wilma Deering was an exploding gyro shell that knocked him flat and terrified him. Since his day of independence at eleven, he had been the master of his life. Women were convenient toys he could control. Not Wilma. She was nearly his equal. He looked into the shadowy depths of her hazel eyes and drowned. He did not regain his emotional balance until he realized she was as speechless as he. From that moment on, he knew no other feminine conquest would satisfy him. As he knew her better, he came to respect Wilma's ability and passionate character as well as her beauty. But, in spite of his attempts to advance their relationship, it remained a series of explosive encounters, passionate, exciting, and leaving him hungry for more.

Kane raked his hands through his thick, dark hair.

He stretched, suddenly aware of cramped muscles. He was as tired as if he had fought a pitched hand-to-hand match. He kicked off his shoes and threw himself down on the narrow bed, one hand over his eyes to shut out the late afternoon sun. Outside his window, a kookaburra uttered its maniacal call, its unconscious laughter a mockery of his confinement. He shut it out along with the sun.

Wilma moved softly into his mind, as she never would into his life. Her actual presence had a kick like a Helm rifle, but the thought of her was warmly comforting, like the arms he dimly remembered holding him as a child. The memories of the two women blurred, running together, and Kane could smell the fresh scent of his mother's hair mingling with Wilma's perfume. His cramped muscles relaxed with his thoughts, and Killer Kane slept.

While he was locked in the fifth story room, the dreams that flitted through his mind were fragments of violence; the physical action denied him their source. In dreams he was the victor, in remembered and imagined conflict. In dreams he lifted Emmerich by his scrawny throat and hurled him into the street below, where he was torn to shreds by horrific gennies. The monsters' growls and their victim's final cries were sweet music, and Kane smiled in his sleep.

Outside his window, the laughing kookaburra called again, adding his insane comment to Kane's unfettered subconscious. From its vantage point of freedom, it eyed Kane's recumbent form with curiousity, then rubbed its bill along one wing, scratching the itchy edges. It yawned, tucked its head under the wing, and fell asleep. The underbrush rustled underneath its perch as something scuttled by. The sound was not threatening to the bird, and it did not awaken.

In the next room, Emmerich regarded the computer screens with narrowed eyes. "The surveillance units we placed aren't functioning," he said.

"Security confirmed the units were working when they were installed," said Pope, computer technician first class.

Emmerich looked skeptical. "I know Kane's reputation, but I cannot believe he discovered the sensors in the first five minutes of imprisonment. I checked them out myself the last time I visited him. They were undamaged."

Pope shook his head. "I'm afraid I don't have an answer for you, sir. Security devices are not my specialty."

"I am aware of that. But Ferricom wants Kane in detention, and I intend to give them what they want." Emmerich had been in Australia for three years. He had no desire to make it his home. What once had been a rugged land was marred by pollution into an inhospitable tract, the interior desert a total wasteland, the prairie sparse, gray-green grass inhabited by a few die-hard prospectors, and the remnants of the native population. The jungles thrived, taking over the ruined outskirts of cities. Roaming the cities outside the walls of RAM's central complexes were the dregs of humanity, gennies from the Coprates research station on Mars, and the Marplex lab outside Paris, whose development did not meet the required standards—fancy language for deformed monstrosities.

He had three years of Wollongong, and he knew if he did not escape soon, he would go mad. Kane was his ticket out. He would do his job for Ferricom, but nothing in the rules said he could not interrogate his captive. The records showed Kane to be a rich man, with a personal estate on Luna, his own spacecraft, and diverse interests. If Ferricom neglected to recognize his loyalty, he might be persuaded to part with it—for the right price.

"The request form for replacement units went in

this morning," said Pope.

"That means it will be two weeks before we get them," said Emmerich absently, his thoughts on his own concerns.

"Yes, sir, I . . . sir, there's a message coming in. It looks like Zibroski's line."

"Put it on the screen."

"I can't, sir. It's not visual, and it's coming through coded."

Emmerich leaned over Pope's shoulder.

"Here it comes, sir."

The computer's obsolete mechanical printer klunked heavily, spewing the decoded message out like a white paper tongue. Emmerich tore it off. "Well, well, well," he said. "We are privileged to have company. It seems Ferricom is sending a special interrogator for Kane." He could not keep the irritation from his voice. His plans for Kane were suddenly complicated.

Pope cocked his head and raised one hand to cover his earphone. "Sir! RAM Central is requesting a closed channel!"

"Central!" In his years at Wollongong, Emmerich could remember but two instances of direct communication with Central. "Put them through."

The main viewscreen went flat gray, and a faceless voice began to speak. "This is Central Headquarters calling. Hold for Neola Price."

Emmerich gulped. The name belonged to a high RAM official.

The gray screen rolled up like a curtain, revealing Price seated at a desk littered with stacks of reports and loose correspondence. She was a woman of approximately sixty years, petite, but as tough as nails. Her silver hair was a manicured cap, not a strand daring to deviate from its appointed place. Her face was marred by determined lines at either side of her mouth. Round, silver-rimmed glasses perched on her nose, secured by a chain around her neck. She removed the glasses. Her eyes were bright blue, as hard as a cloudless sky. "Emmerich. I wish to speak with your prisoner."

"This is an honor, Miss Price!"

"Cut the groveling," she answered. "I want a closed channel to Kane."

"At once, ma'am."

Miss Price leveled a finger at Emmerich. "You heard me. A closed channel. I've got the lines secured. You try to tap in, and I'll blow your whole computer system. Then I'll do the same to you. Get to it."

Emmerich signaled to Pope, who was sitting in front of the computer banks with his mouth hanging open. Miss Price was an overpowering personality. "You heard the lady," Emmerich hissed, nudging the technician.

"Uh, yes, sir." Pope keyed in the authorized security sequence, making Kane's computer terminal a direct, isolated link to Neola Price's.

"Now scat," said Miss Price, and the communications room dropped from her sight, to be replaced by the restricted view of Kane's cell that the computer terminal offered. "Kane!"

Neola Price's sharp voice penetrated Kane's uneasy sleep. He opened his eyes, fully awake, but unmoving until he identified the source of his interrupted nap.

"Kane!"

"Yes?" he answered lazily. He sat up and flexed his shoulders.

"RAM has need of you."

Ironic amusement flitted across Kane's face. "I am aware of that."

Miss Price's rosebud mouth pursed in prim disapproval. "Respect for your betters is a virtue, young man."

"I should be happy to respect a superior. Unfortunately, I do not know one," Kane responded smoothly.

Miss Price found Kane obstreperous, but she ignored her feelings in the interest of business. "I assume," she said tartly, "that you wish to escape your present confinement."

"It is somewhat of an inconvenience," Kane admitted. "Miss . . . ?"

"Neola Price."

"To what do I owe the pleasure of your visit?"

"RAM has an assignment for you."

"What does it pay?" asked Kane.

"I should think your freedom would be an adequate incentive."

Kane shook his head. He knew better than to let the corporate structure get the upper hand. "My present status is a temporary annoyance. I must assume that whatever task RAM wishes me to undertake is both dangerous and sensitive, or it would employ its own men. It is therefore worth a healthy stipend."

Price respected Kane's ability to bargain, and her expression softened slightly. "I have been authorized to offer you an appointment to RAM's executive board, and a fee of two hundred thousand credits deposited directly into your private account on Luna."

"The fee is interesting. The commission I decline. I prefer to remain my own man. You may thank RAM for its offer."

"In the event you refused the appointment, I was authorized to offer you an additional fifty thousand credits."

"A price worth discussing. What is this assignment so dear to RAM's heart?"

Miss Price cleared her throat. "I am not authorized to disclose details at present, but you will be briefed in flight after you accept the mission."

Kane shook his dark head. "No details now, no mission."

Neola Price sighed heavily. Kane drove a hard bargain indeed. "All I can tell you now is that RAM is very close to discovering the location of the remains of a five-hundred-year-old American astronaut. Politically, a very important one. NEO would love to get its hands on our astronaut if it knew."

Kane whistled low through his teeth. "And you want me to find him? I'm no detective."

"I told you, RAM is close to finding him. We simply want you to recover the body."

Kane's brows drew together in a frown. "Why me?"

"You are expendable, and the political implications of a reformed NEO handing over one of the organization's most cherished heroes to RAM is a valuable tool."

"How flattering," said Kane sarcastically.

"We are not in business to feed your already healthy ego."

"What assurance do I have you will keep your end of the bargain?"

"If you agree to the assignment, you will be released within the hour. One half of your payment will already be credited to your account. You are welcome to check it."

"Believe me, I shall."

Miss Price went on, unperturbed by Kane's lack of trust. "The remaining amount will be paid upon delivery of the body."

"Then you may tell RAM I accept its offer."

"When you are released, report to RAM headquarters in Sydney. They will cooperate fully."

Kane gave Neola Price a casual salute as her image faded from the terminal screen.

O O O O O

The Ferricom shuttle out of Sydney flew a scant fifty feet above the forest. It wallowed heavily, its rotors whipping madly to keep it aloft. Its passing sent an artificial wind through the leaves of the eucalyptus forest below, frightening the birds. A flock of cockatoos erupted from the trees, skimming over them in a white cloud. The elderly Class IV Dragonfly shuttle lumbered on, oblivious. Its heavy flight disguised a light load. It carried one passenger.

A Ferricom supervisor, Maureen McFee, sat primly in the shuttle's left passenger seat. Her suit was a conservative gray trimmed in black. The RAM red tie at her throat and the red plastic name badge clipped to her collar were the only splashes of color. Her face was a pale oval. Her eyes were hidden behind owlish, horn-rimmed glasses. Her red hair was drawn severely back from her face, not a rebellious wisp escaping the confines of the knot at the back of her head, though a brisk breeze blew through the aircraft. On her lap was a black briefcase. Her folded hands rested on it as she watched the flight of the startled birds.

The captain of the shuttle leaned back and looked over his shoulder. "Ten minutes to Wollongong, miss," he yelled over the noise of the engines and rotors. "We'll be setting down on the Ferricom building, so you don't have to worry about the natives."

"Thank you, Captain," she yelled back. So far her masquerade had worked admirably. No one questioned her forged nameplate or travel orders. No one recognized in the plain Maureen the bane of RAM, the flamboyant NEO pilot, Wilma Deering.

Wilma's access to the RAM installation was partial payment for a job the freedom fighter had agreed to do for Ardala Valmar, an information broker with familial and political ties to RAM. Ardala's espionage network provided Wilma with her alias and the credentials to go along with it. Ardala had no com-

punctions about using Wilma to her own ends, but
her contacts within RAM would not be so cavalier.
They would view her compact with a notorious NEO
rebel as a definite breach of faith. The RAM death
order hanging over Wilma's head gave Ardala no
excuses for her alliance, so it was prudent to arrange
Wilma's interview with Kane under cover of a false
identity. She sent Maureen McFee to Australia,
secure in the knowledge of Wilma's cooperation with
the ruse.

Australia. All the horror stories Wilma ever heard
about Australia rushed through her mind with the
flight of the frightened birds. They were remnants of
childhood nightmares come to life. Like the rest of
Earth, Australia was governed by a series of arcologies or reservations, each under its own regent who
reported directly to the Solar Alliance Protectorate,
the world government that administered the affairs
of Earth under the watchful eye of RAM. In principle,
the regencies were independent states, in practice,
they, and SAP, were owned by RAM and completely
under its domination. Australia, because of its isolation, had become a dumping ground for RAM's mis-
takes. Chief among those were the unsuccessful
results of its extensive program in genetics.

Genetic engineering was a cornerstone of twenty-
fifth century culture. Techniques of altering and
cloning both human and animal life were common
knowledge. Most companies used some type of spe-
cialized genetic life form, "gennies," for a part of
their business transactions. Continual research and
experimentation in genetics produced more and
more refined types, but the experiments were not
always successful, and many of them were not lucky
enough to die. It was in Australia that RAM deposited these unfortunate mutations. Over the decades
they scrabbled for existence in that ravaged land,
breeding indiscriminately and magnifying their own

deformities.

The shuttle lifted above a particularly tall tree, and Wilma could see Wollongong Outpost in the distance. A typical RAM base, it was an island of order in the midst of anarchy. Surrounded by twelve-foot walls to deter the marauding populace, it rose in a tetrahedron of native brick, mimicking the slick structures of the larger cities. The top of this particular building was flat, undoubtedly a landing pad for the shuttle, safe from outside attack. As they neared the outpost, Wilma could see the refuse heap that comprised the rest of the settlement.

The walls of the RAM base were surrounded by hovels built of found materials: slabs of metal siding propped against the wall and anchored by stakes, huts of mud and branches with canvas roofs, old pieces of machinery shoved against a wall and converted to living quarters. Foundations of decayed buildings were patched into service. It was a smaller, shoddier version of any Terran city. RAM and those employed by it lived within the central complex in relative comfort and security. Without, the populace clawed a living from a ruined world. Here at Wollongong, the ruin was living as well as structural, for the inhabitants of the Warren were the ruins of mankind. Victims of a civil conflict, they had been produced by man to serve man. The legal status of a gennie was unclear. Since they could be owned, like slaves, they were not considered human, yet humanoid they were. The debate over whether a gennie was man or beast raged periodically in the halls of political economy, but it was a question unresolved.

The shuttle homed in on the flat top of the tetrahedron. As they came in for a landing, rotor blades thupping madly, Wilma could see the RAM insignia painted in the center of the square. She took a deep breath and clung to her persona. She was walking into the lion's den in the guise of an overseer. She would find it amusing later. At the moment, panic was her main reaction. The shuttle settled heavily onto the landing pad, and the pilot cut his engines. "Watch the blades, miss," he called over the slowing rotors.

Wilma unclipped her restraints and rose, clutching her briefcase. The pilot slid the door of the shuttle back, revealing the anxious faces of Emmerich and a companion. They had come to pay obsequious homage to the representative of the company. Their earnest expressions gave Wilma courage.

Emmerich extended a hand. "Watch your step, Miss McFee," he called. The air stirred by the shuttle's blades had whipped his hair around his head in a tangle. Instead of a sober corporate executive, he looked like a clown trying to impersonate one.

Wilma ignored his hand and descended the steps at the shuttle's door with frigid dignity. She did not look at the magnificent view of the Australian countryside that her vantage point allowed, but, like a true scion of business, at her watch. "The flight is six minutes behind schedule," she said icily. "I shall have to make that up if I am to finish my reports by deadline. I will see the subject immediately."

Emmerich groveled, for Wilma's scarlet name badge gave her a corporate rank he could not hope to achieve. Still, he did not abandon procedure. "Excuse me, Miss McFee, but I must ask your business with the subject. He was sent here under armed guard with the approval of the director himself."

"Quite right," responded Wilma. She allowed approval to show in her face, and Emmerich straightened. "I am chief supervisor of Ferricom's psychological development program. As per a recommendation from the Personnel Office, I am here to evaluate the subject and determine the counseling he requires." She handed Emmerich a sheaf of paper. "Here is my authorization."

Emmerich took the papers and glanced at them. "In order, of course," he said. "Welcome to Wollongong, Miss McFee. If there is anything I can do to make your stay more pleasant, please let me know."

Wilma retrieved the papers. "Believe me, Emmerich, I shall," she answered.

Wilma took note of the idosyncracies of the structure as Emmerich escorted her into the RAM complex.

"Ferricom is housed on the west side of the outpost," Emmerich explained. "Our offices and maximum security are on the fifth level, near the top, living quarters beneath, on the fourth level. We have prepared a suite for you there. The third level comprises our warehouse. We have minimal detention facilities on second level, and, of course, first level is worker facilities."

Emmerich ushered Wilma into a lift, and they sank into the depths of the tetrahedron. The doors opened into a plain hallway, and Emmerich led her down it, opened a door marked "Communications," and went in. "This is our communications complex," he said. "As you can see by the monitors, we have only one triple-A detention cell. Our needs for prolonged incarceration are rare."

"I see four screens," said Wilma. "Three are dark."

"Yes." Emmerich's voice was sheepish. "I am afraid the surveillance system malfunctioned, and we did not have replacement parts. They are on order, but as yet, they have not arrived. We have had to make do with the computer terminal screen. But I ask you, Miss McFee, what can the man possibly do?"

He was speaking to deaf ears. Wilma was staring at the computer screen. It showed Kane stretched out on a cot, sound asleep. In sleep his defenses were removed, and his expression was remote, sad. She thought herself armed against the power of his physical attraction, but the knife-thrust of pain in her stomach told her she was wrong. She was as bewitched by the sight of him as she had been at their first encounter.

"Miss McFee?" Emmerich's importunate voice sounded at the edges of consciousness.

"Yes, Emmerich."

"I asked if you wished to see the subject now."

"Pardon my abstraction. I find a moment of study before actually encountering the subject tends to put them in perspective for me. Yes, I would like to see him."

Emmerich leaned over the communications bank and pushed the lever under the active computer screen up. "Kane," he said pre-emptively. "Kane! You have a visitor."

Kane did not move. He opened one eye, cocked his head to get a better view of Emmerich's face on his terminal, and said, "I'm sleeping."

"Not anymore," said Emmerich.

Kane yawned and sat up slowly, then swung his legs over the side of the cot. "Nothing but interruptions! Prison ought to be peaceful." He sighed. "I can see you're not going to give me any peace."

"You are to be evaluated by Personnel. You are to cooperate entirely with Miss McFee."

"Cut the terminal connection," ordered Wilma. "This is a privileged communication. You do not have the security clearance for it."

"Miss McFee, I protest! Kane is under the strictest security. The director was most specific about—" his voice dropped so that only Wilma could hear it "—Miss Valmar's orders."

Kane was imprisoned on Ardala's order. Wilma almost gasped, but covered her surprise by clearing her throat. She had wondered why RAM had imprisoned one of its free-lancers. Ardala obviously had it in for Kane for some reason. "You will defer to my rank in this," she said coldly. "Or I can contact

Zibroski."

Without a word, Emmerich moved to a door at the left of the computers and hit a pressure panel beside it. The door opened, Wilma stepped through, and it closed behind her.

Kane rose to his feet, his eyes lazy under his curling, dark lashes. "Pleased to make your acquaintance, Miss McFee," he said.

"I am sure you are," Wilma responded severely. Her back was to the monitor, and she had no need to control her expression. Her hazel eyes blazed. In spite of the fact her loyalties lay irrevocably with NEO's cause, in spite of the fact that Kane had abandoned that cause, his presence made the breath catch in her throat.

"I understand you are here to evaluate me," he said, making the statement entirely suggestive.

Wilma responded icily, though her eyes danced with laughter. "You are correct, Mister Kane. According to the director's report, you are a danger to yourself and those you work with. I am here to find out why."

"Good luck," said Kane, his white teeth flashing.

"I intend to have good luck, Mister Kane." She could feel the electricity that had always existed between them crackling like Saint Elmo's fire. Wilma turned to the computer screen. "Emmerich, I thought I told you to turn that thing off!"

The computer whined as Emmerich cut its power. The screen died.

Kane was across the room in a stride, pulling her close. "I got the rest of the surveillance units in the first hour," he said.

"I know," breathed Wilma.

"How did you get here?" he asked.

"You know NEO has its ways of getting to people it wants."

Kane's lashes brushed her cheek sensuously. "So

do you," he murmured softly, his double meaning clear. Suddenly his lips closed over hers, and the electricity between them caught fire, engulfing them both.

Finally Wilma pulled away. "Oh, Kane," she said breathlessly.

Kane ran a possessive hand across her back and kissed her again. "Missed me?" he asked softly, his mouth close to hers.

"More than I know how to say." Her knees were weak. She grasped the collar of Kane's gray suit to keep her balance. His hands roved over her. Her eyes were big with questions. "Why did you leave NEO?" she asked. "I want to hear it from you."

"To save your life," Kane answered, his finger tracing the creamy line of her neck.

"But how?"

"They offered me a choice: My freedom for your life. It seemed like a better bargain than most."

"Kane!" Wilma's eyes were hazel stars. "I knew there was a reason!"

He took her oval face between his hands. "There is no one else in the world for whom I would have done the same."

"But why did you stay, instead of returning to NEO?"

"I have chosen power," he said at last. "Power will accomplish miracles, Wilma."

The copper-haired woman looked around Kane's cell skeptically. "You call this power?"

"This is a result of a bit of bad judgment on my part. It will never happen again. In fact, I anticipate release within the hour; it appears I am going to the Asteroid Belt. RAM is willing to pay highly for my services."

Wilma noted the comment with interest. She had just accepted an unusual job offer from Ardela Valmar, the information broker in RAM's camp who had placed Kane here, in exchange for much-needed NEO ships; that job was in the Asteroid Belt as well. She said nothing.

Suddenly there was a loud thump, and Wilma started in surprise. Kane whirled, placing her behind him. Clinging to the bars of Kane's window were hands, or feet. It was hard to tell which. They sported six long digits each. The fingers, or toes, gripped the bars, the dozens of knuckles white. Above them hovered a tubby body. A death's head skull on a long neck peered over the cluster of legs. The creature bobbed its head. It resembled a spider. Wilma had a horror of spiders, but there was something pathetic in its expression, a sort of idiotic expectation of goodwill.

"Pardon, pardon," said the creature, its head bouncing up and down like a yo-yo. "Arac wanted to see the pretty lady. Just see!"

Kane reached for the nearest piece of furniture, a wooden camp chair. He hefted it.

"Kane, no!" Wilma knew Kane. She knew he meant to smash the chair against the bars, breaking Arac's grip.

"Why not? It's an odious creature."

"If it falls, it will die. We're five stories up."

"That's what I intended."

Wilma's eyes narrowed. "It's human."

"Human? Look at it! It's a nightmare."

"It is Arac," said the creature.

"If looks were all," said Wilma, "you would have to put half the population of Earth to death."

"It is not fit to live. What can it possibly contribute? That horrific face is enough to warrant extermination."

"Only face I have," said Arac.

"Can you walk up the side of a building?" Wilma asked Kane. "Creatures like that exist because of our genetic experiments. It has a right to live."

Kane studied Wilma and decided not to press the point. He lowered the chair.

"Arac is going," said the creature. "He knows when he is not welcome." He crawled up the bars and disappeared.

Kane took Wilma by the shoulders and looked earnestly into the depths of her eyes. "You say that thing has a right to live. We have a right to live, Wilma! We have a right to the good things in life. I promise you I will give you all you ever dreamed of."

"No. I cannot condone the choices you have made. I never will."

Kane's eyes grew cold, as flat as green ice. "Do not judge me too harshly," he said.

Wilma wrapped her arms around him, her head on his broad chest. She could hear the steady rhythm of his heart. "I don't want to judge you at all. I don't want to be your enemy."

"But you will stay with NEO," said Kane softly. His expression was sad. "I think you will see the wisdom of my choice in the end. When that time comes, Wilma Deering, call, and I will be there."

Wilma leaned back, a hopeless amusement in her eyes. "And I believe you will find you made a mistake in leaving us. If that should happen, I will be your advocate with NEO." Her eyes grew serious. "Take care, Kane. Power can swallow you."

"Not while you are around to rescue me. Good-bye, Wilma—for now. We will meet again." Kane released her, his hands sliding reluctantly from her hips.

"Good-bye, Kane." In spite of her resolve, tears filled her eyes. She blinked them away, knowing she could not face Emmerich with anything but professional calm. She picked up her briefcase and pulled a tape from it. "Until then," she said softly as she pressed the door signal.

The door slid open, and Wilma walked away. Her lithe grace caught at Kane's heart. He sank down in the camp chair, melancholy a cold knot in his stomach, though he knew he had not seen the last of Wilma Deering. They would meet again. In the meantime, he had a job to do. He shifted his thoughts to the task ahead and to the technical difficulties of handling and transporting a five-hundred-year-old corpse.

The door thumped shut behind Wilma. She waved the tape under Emmerich's nose. "An excellent session," she said. "Ferricom—and RAM—will be pleased. Your help will be noted in my report. Now I require immediate transport."

"Of course, Miss McFee. I am always glad to be of service. The shuttle is still on the landing pad."

Within moments, Wilma was seated in the heliplane, again the lone passenger. The ship's engine roared, and the rotors began to turn, whipping faster and faster until the craft vibrated. It lifted heavily from the landing pad and started over the trees. Wilma released her safety restraints. She opened her briefcase, dropped the blank tape inside, and extracted a laser pistol, placing it on her lap. Wollongong faded into the distance, and she searched the ground for a suitable clearing. Ahead, the trees opened on a grassy meadow. She leaned forward and jammed the pistol into the pilot's ribs. "Land in that clearing," she called, "or we're going down together."

The pilot obeyed. When the heliplane was safely down, he raised his hands. "Don't shoot," he said.

"That depends entirely on your actions," answered Wilma. "Get out."

The pilot complied. When he was on the ground, Wilma pulled the door shut, locked it, moved to the cockpit, and slipped into the pilot's seat. The old shuttle rocked as she maneuvered it out of the clearing, and she paid homage to the pilot's skill as she fought to keep it stable. She set a direct course across the treetops, heading for the ship she had flown to Australia. She had hidden the NEO scout near the coast. By the time she reached her destination, the shuttle's fuel gauge was nearing the safety margin. She set the old tub down at the end of the deserted road. She killed the engine and vaulted to the ground with the heliplane's rotors still spinning.

Huddled under the trees at the side of the road was her ship. She pulled the camouflage cover from it, climbed into the cockpit, and fired the engines. The forest shuddered with their roar. She nosed carefully forward, pulling out from the protective canopy of the trees and onto the more open surface of the dirt road. It stretched out before her, an inviting, flat ribbon. It was a dangerous landing strip, but danger added spice to her task. Wilma started down it, engines roaring.

The ship picked up speed, bumping over the rough ground. Wilma's expertise kept it on the track, and it was airborne. Once clear of the trees, she sent it skimming over the ocean. The sea was gunmetal laced with whitecaps. The ship slid over it at an efficient clip, but her heart was divided. She loved Kane, yet left him. A part of her would always love him. It was neither an end nor a beginning, and she was confused. She backed away from the problem, concentrating on something concrete: her upcoming job with Ardala, the search for the body of Anthony "Buck" Rogers.

She punched her communications link. "Come in, six-five-four," she said. "Six-five-four, come in."

"Six-five-four here. This is Beowulf."

"I've come across some interesting information," she said, deciding to undercut Ardala and reveal some of the details of her meeting with the information broker that took place before her trip to Australia. "RAM has discovered another twentieth century pilot in space."

"Another one?" Beowulf sounded bored. "It's probably nothing, like those toasted cosmonauts RAM just discovered."

"I don't know. . . ," Wilma said contemplatively, remembering her conversation with Ardala, and just recently with Kane. "I think this one may be different . . . someone very important." She shook away the vague thoughts and focused on a course of action. "I'm going to the Asteroid Belt," she said decisively. "But first I'm stopping in Chicagorg to find out what this is all about."

"We'll be expecting you," Beowulf said. "And I'll put out some feelers, see if I can uncover anything about this astronaut."

"Acknowledged," she replied, lifting her ship's nose and sending it into the upper atmosphere. She welcomed the clean, cold silence. The stars winked at her from above, beckoning. The lure of the unknown touched her pulse, and she let the siren sing to her as she went out to meet adventure.

TWO
BARNEYS
Ulrike O'Reilly

Black Barney punched in his membership code and waited. His eyes, which revealed nothing of his emotions, swept the entrance corridors right and left. Just a good habit, he thought. Nothing to fear here. Nothing to fear anywhere.

In a moment the doors of the Club Noir "whooshed" open to reveal a vestibule. The attendant, who had been slumped on a stool in the corner, snapped erect when he saw that the newcomer was one of the celebrities of the membership, the dangerous and unpredictable Black Barney.

Young Bimwilly knew Black Barney on sight, of course. He was proud to boast that he, lowly Bimwilly, had diligently served the reknowned space pirate several times in the course of his long duty as maitre d' of the Club Noir.

It was rare that Black Barney stopped, for a leisurely luncheon, at Club Noir. This was twice in, oh, ten months!

Young Bimwilly was excited, and he violated the usual decorum when he raised his black-robed arms and clapped his white-gloved hands together in the old-fashioned manner. "Mr. Barney!" the maitre d' exclaimed a bit loudly.

No one heard his indiscretion, however, for the vestibule was empty of humanity or otherwise, bare of all furnishings except the stool and a control panel. The doors that led to private dining chambers were all but invisible to the naked eye, and patrons could rest assured that they were seamlessly sealed, and only Young Bimwilly could open them. That was his responsibility and his cachet.

Young Bimwilly had been guiding the Club Noir's privileged members to their private chambers, for the most elegant dining experience in the Asteroid Belt, he liked to say, for as long as anyone could remember. Before him, it had been his father, Old Bimwilly, who enjoyed the exalted position of maitre d', for a lifetime. Of course, Old Bimwilly was long dead. His son was in his seventh decade of life, if one could call it a life, and no longer spry or acute. Indeed, he had a red, fissured face beneath the make-up, and for some reason walked bent over. But in deference to the memory of his father, he preferred still to be called Young Bimwilly.

Not that anyone took particular notice of the old man. Black Barney, for example, did not return the maitre d's salutation, and did not in the least remember the crippled old fool from any previous encounter.

Black Barney could not help but observe, with disdain, that the bent-over maitre d' was wearing the obligatory costume of powdered wig, ruffled blouse, midbreeches, and flowing robe that some of the club's regulars—though certainly not Black Barney, who did not consider himself a regular in any case—found so appropriate and amusing. Dressing Young Bimwilly as an Olde English high judge was one of the many touches from the archaic past that the Club Noir's management had concocted to give the place a forced air of genteel ambiance.

"On the dot, Mr. Barney, as ever so," Young Bimwilly said, cackling strangely to himself, as he pushed buttons and walked bent over in front of Black Barney, leading him through double doors and down a certain corridor to the exclusive room that was always reserved for Black Barney, and would remain vacant for months if he did not show up.

At Young Bimwilly's touch, a panel slid upward, and he stepped back as Black Barney ducked his massive bulk into the room. The little man watched attentively as the fearsome space pirate positioned himself on a flat cushion on the marble floor, in front of a slab of wood low to the ground, which was appointed with silverware, flowers, incense, steaming cactus tea, and meatstick hors d'oeuvres. Young Bimwilly sighed with relief as Black Barney seemed to find things comfortable, but he waited, all the same.

Black Barney knew that he was somehow obliged to acknowledge the maitre d's obsequiousness, but he did not value that trait in the slightest, so he instead raised his eyes to meet Young Bimwilly's and said, with a scowl, "The usual."

"Of course," said Young Bimwilly eagerly. He spoke with a phlegmy rasp. All of the club's high muckamucks had standing orders, and Young Bimwilly naturally had reviewed the file of Black Barney's past lunches at the Club Noir. "Baby buffalo liver . . ." he began in his phlegmy rasp, so that the words came out rough but coated.

There came no reaction from Black Barney.

"Stuffed artichoke hearts, green undersea salad, a side of tropical fruit, and Vichy water . . ." Young Bimwilly made a show of writing it all down, struggling with a thick pencil and note pad, just like waiters did in the old days on Earth—he copied his attentive demeanor from ancient black-and-white movies he had seen. All part of the pretense of the Club Noir.

Young Bimwilly lingered for a moment, looking

rather intently at Black Barney, whose intense gaze was not on the maitre d', but straight ahead at nothing in particular.

Young Bimwilly thought about those eerie eyes of the legendary Black Barney, eyes that gave away nothing, yet seemed to communicate something very specific. Young Bimwilly thought—a rather profound thought for him—that Black Barney's eyes seemed imprisoned somehow, trapped in his formidable skull like an animal in a cage.

"Yes?" asked Black Barney, vaguely annoyed.

"I would like to mention, Mr. Barney—" Young Bimwilly chose his words carefully— "that the baby buffalo is not the wild breed from the terrestial mountain ranges, which are such a favorite of connoisseurs. It seems there has been some nonsense about a chemical cloud passing over the region, and thousands having to be slaughtered for safety's sake. A temporary inconvenience, I assure you. Boom to the gum-jelly market, I dare say, since, as long as you don't swallow the stuff, it's perfectly safe."

Black Barney cleared his throat, with growing irritation.

Young Bimwilly cleared his, too, more necessarily. "I mean to mention, Mr. Barney, that our baby buffalo, today, is domestically raised." He wrinkled his nose to show his distaste, then continued. "Albeit, quite tasty, as the chef has devised a brown sauce to compensate . . ."

Black Barney's face froze. He hated to be so bothered right before lunch. What the hell did he care where the blasted buffalo came from, as long as it was edible? "No matter," growled Black Barney, hastening to add, "And forget the sauce!"

Young Bimwilly was not in the least offended by his patron's menacing tone, and, if anything, his face brightened to have his existence acknowledged in a small way. "The vidscreen diversions," he said, leaning to hand Black Barney a small black box with dials and controls. He then backed out of view, and the panel door slid back into place.

Black Barney could hear the withered attendant cackling to himself as he walked off toward the kitchen. He tuned in the black box, and while he waited for lunch he flicked between channels and gazed upward at the one hundred state-of-the-art mini-monitors built into the wall of his chambers, for his enjoyment and edification, as Young Bimwilly would say.

In ten minutes, he scanned all one hundred channels and digested the information that was beamed across the solar system. He dawdled on the news broadcasts and the access networks, which were always full of local weirdo doings. He tarried on the outlaw channel of a Martian free state, which aired official RAM speeches and proceedings in entertaining, light opera form. He also took more than a passing glance at the hard-core sex program of the "No-No TV" of the Jovian Cartel.

But honestly, Black Barney was bored. The system's most amoral, brutal, and successful raider-for-hire had given his crew three days for R and R, and the only immediate thing on his agenda was lunch.

○ ○ ○ ○ ○

The Club Noir was part of a much larger sprawl, called Barbarosa, that had been built into one of the medium-sized asteroids in the vast Asteroid Belt between Mars and Jupiter. Barbarosa was a private oasis, fuel and loading dock, conference annex, dining mecca, physical recreation (including old-style bowling hall and archery range) center, game hall extraordinaire, mental relaxation area, energy spa, semen rompery, and up-to-date medical facility operated for the exclusive use of the Rogues' Guild. As

such, it was frequented only by freebooters, mercenaries, rockhoppers, roustabouts, hell raisers, priva-
teers, full-time space spies and informants (a fully
certified profession), outlaw gennies, mutants, rock-
jocks, and warrior clones of every stripe. One of many
such R and R space stations owned and operated by
the powerful no-nation anarchy, the Rogues' Guild, it
was generally recognized as a "neutral zone" by
RAM and other world governments, and left alone,
not only because neutral zones had been established
facts of intersolar law for many decades, but also
because any violation of the peacefulness of the
complex—either by space pirate or outsider—
resulted in a lifetime revocation of one's membership
or guest card.

Barbarosa was divided into two massive, fully-
domed life-support systems, built into opposite sides
of the barren, rocky, egg-shaped asteroid. On one side
were spaceship landing, overhaul, and security offices, where vehicles docked and travelers disem-
barked; on the other side of the asteroid was the
honeycombed complex of health services and fun
things to do. Connecting the asteroid's poles, and
pile-driven through its core, was a ninety-mile-long
double monorail system that conveyed visitors from
one end to the other in minutes. Barbarosa's great
buildings were held to the ground by gravity caused
by the asteroid's spin, as the asteroid orbited through
space. The asteroid resembled a huge, slowly revolving dumbbell, for the two-ended dome system had
been painted black to conserve precious energy.

In general, Barbarosa was too out of the way, and
too innocuous, for anyone but space pirates to take
the slightest interest in it. The Rogues' Guild used it
occasionally as a meeting place. Although Black Barney was an ad hoc, permanent delegate of the executive council—after all, he was twice as notorious,
twice as rich, twice as murderous as anyone else in

the Asteroid Belt—he almost never attended its meetings and rarely cast his vote in one of the chaotic, free-for-all elections that passed for democracy in the Rogues' Guild.

In fact, Black Barney rarely stopped at Barbarosa, or any of the other Rogues' Guild way stations, and when he did, it was usually on the spur of the moment and because of his crew. He took no particular pleasure in the famous fresh cuisine, the sports and gaming options, the sexual activities menu, or the catering to whim and ego that was a hallmark of the establishment. He took no particular pleasure in pleasure.

But the *Free Enterprise* had had a busy month. Black Barney had been cruising the outer orbits of Jupiter when he had intercepted a rich mineral shipment on its way to a new settlement. That "expropriation" had to be defended against a fleet of cruisers dispatched by the RAM admiralty of Deimos, and a rather nasty chase ensued. Black Barney smiled as he recollected it. Then, because his trajectory had been noted, he had had to reverse his path through the solar system and sell the raw material—at an inflated price, of course—to a needy terminus, way out beyond his usual territory, on an unclaimed moon.

It was really on behalf of his crew that Black Barney decided to stop at Barbarosa. Of course, the majority of them were gennies, or genetically-modified humans, and strictly speaking, they did not have to relax or recreate; their enhanced senses and skills could keep them going far longer than normal humans, but they, too, had their limits. Black Barney knew all the signs, and knew that after the long trip they were restless. He was no Captain Bligh where his crew was concerned, and he knew that they would serve him better when they had certain things off their bioengineered minds.

He presumed they were all now down in the Quick-Fix, being rowdy and obnoxious, and probably singing loudly off-key, as they chowed on fried cuttlefish and guzzled down corn beer. They left the more fancy fare to their commander—not that they would ever be invited to dine with Black Barney. He preferred to dine alone, always. Apart from this (and this was no small matter at the Club Noir), they also did not have the proper access credentials.

Black Barney sighed. Oh, well. He could put up with three days on Barbarosa. It could be worse: It could be Earth.

Necessarily, Black Barney operated with the strictest secrecy, and when he left Barbarosa, no one would even know he had been there—except Young Bimwilly. And, of course, no one would suspect where he was going. Black Barney did not even know himself. He would not make that decision until after lunch.

•

O   O   O   O   O

"Mr. Barney . . . sir?"

"Yes, what is it now?" Black Barney looked up from his reverie, surprised to see Young Bimwilly's face protruding into his cubicle again, and even more surprised to see the look of contortion on it.

Suddenly, Young Bimwilly came flying into the room, arms and legs in a sprawl. Black Barney understood in a flash that someone had kicked him viciously from behind. Young Bimwilly fell into a heap. Before Black Barney could gain his feet, the offending party's face appeared in the entryway and the space pirate was amazed to realize that it was—of all people—Quinto.

Another Barney.

One of the fourteen surviving Barneys, a killing machine with heightened intelligence, genetically modified and superior characteristics, a near-replica of Black Barney, but with loyalty to no one but himself.

By now, Black Barney had reached his feet and assumed an aggressive martial-arts stance, awaiting the next astonishment. Young Bimwilly was balled up in a corner, rubbing his elbow and blubbering with fear. Behind the intruder, the panel entrance slid noiselessly shut.

Quinto stood inches from Black Barney, in the close proximity of the dining chamber, with his hands on his incredibly muscled torso, as if daring Black Barney to make the first move. His long hair was unruly, his face unshaven. Like Black Barney, he wore a half-face protector made of metal and body armor that was, to all Barneys, as natural as a second skin. His visage was taut, and he said nothing. Neither, for several seconds—which to Young Bimwilly seemed to go on for minutes—did Black Barney.

Young Bimwilly whimpering like a whipped kitten, peeked out at the tense drama from between the quivering fingers of his white-gloved hands. He was certain that his long, dutiful life was imminently drawing to an end.

"Ho! Ho! Ho!" Quinto bent over in half, he suddenly was laughing so hard. The noise came out of a big hole in his face, prominent with silver teeth.

A little petulantly, Black Barney lowered himself back to his cushion on the floor. He had to wait several minutes for Quinto to get over his joke at everyone's expense. The powerful clone-creature was convulsed with merriment.

Meanwhile, Black Barney sipped his cactus tea slowly, calmly, and with some perturbation. He tried to collect his thoughts, wondering what in the world Quinto could want with him, and what is more, thinking how highly unorthodox it was that Quinto should find him here in his private dining chamber on Barbarosa, without an appointment. It was entirely too much of a coincidence, and in Black Barney's world there was no such thing as coincidence. There was planning, there was luck, there was fate, yes. But no coincidence.

"Ho! Ho! Ho!" Quinto was laughing so hard that tears flowed from their ducts.

Young Bimwilly looked from one Barney to the other, painfully bewildered. Since no one was paying him the least bit of attention, as usual, he scuttled across the floor, still rubbing his aches and pains. With a great expiration of relief, Young Bimwilly let himself out.

Quinto's laughter finally tapered off. "Joke's on you, pilgrim!" he declared with satisfaction as he sank to a cushion opposite Black Barney and looked at his host expectantly.

"Who invited you?" Black Barney asked unpleasantly.

"Aw, where's your sense of humor, pilgrim?" asked Quinto. He seemed genuinely hurt. "You should have seen your face. Ho! Ho! Ho! Always in a hurry to do or die, that's what I like about you, Black Barney. What's for lunch?"

"Baby buffalo liver," answered Black Barney, still terse and unsmiling.

"Mmm. Good," Quinto responded appreciatively. He reached over and helped himself to a meatstick, took a bite, and munched on it. "I hope it's farm buffalo," he muttered, half to himself, "'cause there's a travelers' advisory out on terrestrial buffalo. Some nonsense about a chemical cloud."

As if on cue, the panel door slid upward and an exasperated-looking Young Bimwilly thrust his head back in. In his hand was a silver tray of edibles, but hovering behind Young Bimwilly was one of the vaunted, chrome-helmeted watchmen of the Rogues' Guild, fingering a capacitor laser rifle. The watchmen were always at the ready.

"Yes?" growled Black Barney.

"Everything all right, Mr. Barney?" Young Bimwilly asked with emphasis.

"Yes!"

"Will you vouch for this . . . gentleman?"

"Of course!"

His eyes locked on Quinto, Young Bimwilly brought the entree tray into the room. He set it in front of Black Barney, performed certain obligations with the arrangements, then backed out of the room, sniffing with contempt. The chrome-helmeted watchman, who never uttered a word, but whose presence itself issued a warning, also vanished.

Quinto chortled again.

Black Barney sighed deeply. Quinto had a prankish sense of humor and Black Barney had none, which was just one of the subtle differences between the clone-brothers. If Quinto had somehow tracked Black Barney to Barbarosa, there had to be a reason why. Sooner or later, Black Barney knew, Quinto would tire of his little amusement and come out with a proposition.

"It's been a long time, pilgrim," said Quinto, almost warmly, as he seemed to relax, look around, and take notice of his surroundings for the first time. "Nice setup," he added, respectfully. "Though not so very different from the plebeian quarters," he said with a leer.

"What did you expect?" asked Black Barney.

"Oh," said Quinto, "for one of the big-shot ruling councilmen of the Rogues' Guild, I expected amenities."

"This entire complex is an amenity," countered Black Barney.

Quinto chuckled. "So it is. Touche."

"And for your information, I'm not on any ruling council," said Black Barney, gruffly, "I'm ad hoc. Honorary status. What the Rogues' Guild does or

doesn't do, I couldn't care less. They stay out of my
way and I stay out of theirs. That's the deal."

Quinto chewed on his meatstick thoughtfully. He
pointed the nub of it at Black Barney and wagged it
teasingly. "But you can't deny you are such a big
shot," he said, with a jack-o'-lantern grin on his face.
"The Black Barney I used to know!"

"Get to the point," said Black Barney sharply.

Quinto spread his arms and looked offended. "The
point?" he asked. His face was a perfect mask of inno-
cence.

Staring at Quinto, in the intervening silence,
Black Barney realized, not for the first time, that he
was looking at a near-twin image of himself. There
were subtle differences, of course, things only other
Barneys would note, such as temperament, reactions, humor, and exterior things, such as hair style
and weight gain or loss. After all, they were clone-
brothers, but had lived different lives for a long time.

"I thought we just might catch up on old times,"
said Quinto.

"Old times," Black Barney snorted.

To Quinto, old times could mean anything from
those long-ago days on Dracolysk—and shared memories of the Dracolysk Uprising—to whatever Quinto
had been up to since Black Barney had encountered
him last, roughly four years ago, on one of the orbital
colonies of Mercury. That rendezvous was not a coincidence, either, Black Barney recollected. It was
strictly a business transaction, and Black Barney
had to admit it had turned out to be an extremely
profitable one for both of them.

Black Barney knew what Quinto had been doing in
the interim, of course: honing his reputation and
mystique as one of the pre-eminent couriers in the
solar system. More than just a messenger—a tracker
of the lost and vanished, a communicator with the
most deadly and treacherous, a go-between for inter-

ested parties who chose not to acknowledge each other's existence—and when the situation called for it, a double- or triple-informant, who sold updates to all sides. Black Barney knew that Quinto worked without prejudice for all the major powers in the system: RAM, NEO, the Rogues' Guild, the Sun Kings, even the Ishtar Confederation. Quinto could be trusted to relay any message, and under the right circumstances he could be bought off for a higher price. Black Barney had no attitude about the ethics of that, one way or another. He rather liked Quinto, if he could be said to actually like anyone (and on principle, Black Barney distrusted anyone who didn't have a higher price).

"Remember Dracolysk?" asked Quinto.

"Vividly." Black Barney would never forget the ignominy of it all, how it felt to be created to exist for only one purpose: to serve the corporation. Memories of Dracolysk were never old. Old times were whatever happened yesterday. The rebellion, nearly twenty years in the past, played and replayed itself daily, constantly, in his mind. Crazy, fresh snapshots of wholesale chaos and destruction burned into his memory. Friends and enemies, dead.

Every day, the memory pumped fury and venom into Black Barney's veins. The important thing was that he had escaped, survived, and prospered. Black Barney and thirteen other Barneys were liberated. Dracolysk Corporation was gone forever, and now he belonged to no one. Black Barney existed for only one reason: himself.

As did Quinto.

"Remember Sattar Tabibi?"

Black Barney frowned. Sattar Tabibi was another of the Barneys. Physically, a perfect specimen; a death-machine and ultimate warrior, but specially trained in cunning, stealth, treachery, and intrigue. Black Barney had not seen Sattar Tabibi for twenty years, since the Dracolysk Uprising. From what he heard, Sattar Tabibi was some kind of ranking operative under exclusive contract to RAM.

"Yes."

"I stay in touch with him. He throws me a little business now and then."

No reaction from Black Barney.

"Nothing in particular. I whisper something in his ear, and he whispers something in mine. I sell him the odd contraband, and he gives me clearance for this or that naughty excursion. You know, it doesn't hurt to have a clone-brother in high places."

"I wouldn't know," said Black Barney, who rarely worked with anyone, let alone one of his brothers. Black Barney had no interest in clone-brothers or high places. He had no interest in aligning himself with anybody or anything, and he was an outlaw in the eyes of RAM. That's the way he preferred it.

"So . . ." said Quinto, reaching across the table, picking an Ethiopian olive off Black Barney's undersea salad, and popping it into his mouth. "Mmmm," he murmured happily. There was an audible crunch as he bit down on it. "I like the pits," he said, winking. "Good for the neurons . . ."

Black Barney didn't crack an expression.

"So . . . Sattar Tabibi gets in touch with me the other day and asks me if I would contact Black Barney for a job."

In spite of himself, Black Barney raised an eyebrow.

"Why you?"

"It's what I do, dear fellow!" exclaimed Quinto.

"Why me?"

"It's the nature of the task," he said in a low voice, conspiratorially. He reached across the table again and plucked a mandarin orange slice off the tropical fruit plate, then sucked on it noisily.

Black Barney folded his arms wearily and said,

"Go on."

"It seems there is a certain package out in the Juno-Vesta arc that RAM would like to have picked up and delivered."

Black Barney thought about that for a moment. "Why don't they send their own people?" he asked, more curious.

"Very hush-hush. Internal politics. Any RAM detachment would show up in the big computer, and alarm bells would go off in all the wrong places."

"Why don't you pick it up?"

"Bit of danger involved. The people making the offer would like it to appear as if there has been a piracy involved, and then they can discreetly pick up the package on the black market. You are the foremost black marketeer. Ergo, you are the leading candidate for the job."

"You can handle a bit of danger."

"True enough." Quinto seemed flattered. "But I prefer not to. Whereas it is your bread and butter, pilgrim. We both know that."

"What's in this package?"

"Hush-hush, I said."

"Meaning?"

"You receive final instructions when you radio proper coordinates."

"What are the proper coordinates?"

"All in good time, pilgrim. All in good time."

Black Barney considered for a moment whether or not to believe Quinto. He could think of no reason to believe him, nor any not to believe him. "What is so valuable about this package?" he asked.

"To tell you the truth," said Quinto, "that depends on what it is. I don't know myself, and I don't have the least curiosity. I'm being paid well for what I do, and that's all I care about."

"If this package is so valuable, why won't I just run with it?"

"They are willing to take that risk," Quinto replied. "I am told that the package would have absolutely no value to you. In any case, RAM will save you the trouble of putting the package out for bid by making you an offer, under the table, that no one else could possibly afford."

"I'm not accustomed to working for RAM. I don't work on consignment. I do what I please, for my own reasons."

"Naturally, RAM understands that," said Quinto, "That is why they are prepared to make you such a splendid offer."

Absently, Black Barney reached for his fork, but he said nothing and showed no emotion. He was waiting for Quinto's punch line.

"Twice your standing account, deposited in your safety box in Luna Geschaft GB on Tycho, upon certified receipt," said Quinto dryly.

A moment of prolonged silence, as Black Barney speared a slice of baby buffalo liver and stuffed it into his mouth. He chewed ponderously. If Quinto was waiting for a reaction, he would have to wait forever. Barney had nothing to show behind his eyes. It made sense that RAM would know the net of his secret, numbered account—they had their spies everywhere—but that was no cause for alarm. Tycho accounts were part of a long, inviolate banking tradition, and no one could access that account but Black Barney. It made sense, also, that only RAM would have the resources to double his accumulated wealth—albeit, only the Tycho deposit—at one shot. Black Barney had never been offered so much for apparently so little, but that was just part of what he didn't like about the whole deal.

"Suppose that isn't enough?" asked Black Barney.

"Ho! Ho! Ho!" Quinto burst into another fit of laughing. He seemed to think that was genuinely hilarious. He held his sides and laughed and laughed, and laughed some more.

Black Barney let that pass without comment. After all, Quinto was right. It was an extraordinary fee for whatever the errand.

He waited until Quinto's laughter had subsided. "What's your cut?" asked Black Barney, suspiciously.

"Straight fee for making the contact," said Quinto.

"Which is?"

"One hundred thousand Ks." Quinto looked embarrassed. He lowered his eyes. "I tell you that," Quinto said, "strictly in confidence, of course."

"Ain't much," sneered Black Barney.

"It all adds up," said Quinto cheerfully. He reached across the table with two fingers to help himself, daintily, to a slice of baby buffalo liver, while it was still warm.

Black Barney brought his arm around in a lightning-swift windmill motion and stabbed his fork through Quinto's right hand, pinning it to the table. Quinto did not so much as grimace, and after wriggling his hand a little bit, he made no further effort to free it. His smile had turned upside down, though.

"I'll give you my answer after lunch," said Black Barney, "Now, get out!" He stared fiercely as he pulled the tines out of Quinto's hand. "I'm dining alone," he added, unnecessarily.

Quinto lifted his hand from the table and rubbed its palm ruefully. Blood oozed from the puncture holes, but within seconds, the pores closed like tiny whirlpools, the blood dried, and the wound had healed itself. Without further ado, Quinto rose and headed toward the paneled door.

"Testy, testy," the clone-creature tossed over his shoulder, as he exited in good spirits.

○ ○ ○ ○ ○

Black Barney stormed into the control room of the *Free Enterprise*, with a rigid scowl on his face. "Juno-Vesta arc!" he barked to the only individual in the room, Baring-Gould, the warship's astrogation officer, who was lounging at the console, drinking a paper cup of pepjuice.

"What about it?" responded a startled Baring-Gould. He checked his wristchrono and affirmed that it was just after 1300 hours. Black Barney was not expected back so early. Indeed, the warship was deserted, except for Baring-Gould. He was aboard, not for security purposes, but because he, alone among the genetically altered crew, was a bit of a spartan and puritan. He was totally devoted to his job and rarely left the ship for personal reasons. Black Barney liked that about Baring-Gould, if nothing else.

"None of your effing business!" Black Barney leaned over and hollered into his face. "Check it out. Why I tell you to is none of your effing business!"

Baring-Gould stiffened at the console. With a phlegmatic expression, he shifted into a more professional mode and turned to confront the master panel with its sophisticated panoply of screens, keyboards, dials, and printout mechanisms. Efficiently, he began to register codes and instructions.

Baring-Gould, of course, was a genetic inferior—at least to Black Barney, albeit superior to most terrestial and other-world beings. Gennies, for the most part, were highly reliable subordinates without the normal baggage of human frailties. Black Barney's crew of gennies was highly devoted to him and each had particular practical gifts, as well as worst-case-scenario fighting and surviving skills. Baring-Gould happened to be a superior directional wizard.

He was also iffy in a physical showdown and rarely left the airship during any of the contact raids—not that there was anything soft in his makeup. But something in his mental programming made him less than aggressive, and while in combat, he tended not to act, but to react. It was Black Barney's gospel always to strike the first blow.

On the other hand, there was no gennie that Black Barney knew of who better understood the relativity of the physical universe. No gennie had a better grasp of maps, geography, weather and climate, proximity, conditions, time, distance, and the intangibles. Baring-Gould always got the *Free Enterprise* where it was going as fast as it could get there with a minimum of slack. There was no better astrogation officer. If there had been, Black Barney would have dumped Baring-Gould in an instant. Not because he disliked Baring-Gould—he rather liked him, about as much as he liked Quinto, which wasn't that much, really—but because it was a point of pride for Black Barney to have the best possible crew.

"As far as I know," Baring-Gould drawled, scanning the information that came up on the system, " The Juno-Vesta arc is nothing but an astral junkyard—debris of various types, chunks of planetary matter, refuse of past civilizations, nothing special, alive, or valuable."

Baring-Gould spoke with a slightly hickory accent, another peculiarity in his makeup. True, he had been modified on Earth, and it is possible that some of his inheritor genes were drawn from that region of people, but it was more likely a signature characteristic of the laboratory that had supervised his mutation. In spite of himself, Black Barney had to admit he liked that about Baring-Gould, too. One could get awfully tired of monotones and blank expressions in gennies. Black Barney liked his crew to have variety and a bit of personality, too.

"Of course, the Juno-Vesta arc is roughly one thousand cubic miles," continued Baring-Gould, when Black Barney said nothing. "It would take me maybe ten days to scan it in its entirety, and even then it would be a weak scan. It would help if I knew what I was looking for."

"If I knew what you were looking for," commented Black Barney, with a heavy tinge of sarcasm, "I wouldn't need your assistance."

"General location within the sector?"

"Negative."

"Relative coordinates would help," said Baring-Gould.

"No kidding," said Black Barney.

Baring-Gould looked like an ordinary human, except that he was six feet tall, perfectly sculpted, blue-eyed, and blond-haired. The trend in gennies was a certain California surfer look, dating from the ancient twentieth century, although of course there was no such thing as a California surfer anymore, owing to Earth's radioactive oceans. The surfer look was one that dovetailed nicely with the regulation skinform worn by a lot of space crews, including Black Barney's.

The only obvious gennie touches in Baring-Gould were a silver tinge to his flesh tone and slightly enlarged, leaf-shaped ears. The ears had the quaint capacity to turn pink when he was under some internal pressure, and they did so now. Another genetic glitch. Gennies were always full of distinctive glitches that theoretically did not impair their ability to function with maximum performance.

Baring-Gould knew better than to say anything else when Black Barney was in this kind of temper, so he turned back to the master panel and confronted the task at hand. To speed things along, he patched into a backdoor hookup in the RAM central computer system, something he and other black marketeers liked to do for fun. Information raced across the screens and receptors.

Baring-Gould attacked the dials and buttons on the

master panel with the demon energy of a polka accordionist. Even Black Barney could not keep track of all the data and symbols blinking on and off at blipspeed. Baring-Gould absorbed all the data intently, silently, as the minutes passed. Black Barney knew, and Baring-Gould knew that Black Barney knew, that a certain amount of luck was involved in a problem like this.

Black Barney paced behind Baring-Gould, thinking furiously. It was rare that he should encounter another Barney. Unsettling, somehow. It was, he supposed, rather like gazing at one's own reflection in a mirror. Black Barney never gazed at mirrors, but if he happened to pass one, of course he liked what he saw. He was the master creation: chiseled symmetry, optimal dancer's grace, awesome power. No vulnerabilities. No human sentiment. No fear. One of only fourteen extant Barneys, and by anyone's reckoning the toughest and meanest of them all.

"Nothing notable in archive," reported Baring-Gould.

"Keep checking," snapped Black Barney.

No other Barney had cut such a terrible swath through the solar system. No other Barney was reputed to be as pitiless or barbaric. No other Barney was as rich from plunder and ransom, either. And no other Barney even dared call himself a Barney; it was tacit among the Barneys that such an honorific belonged to Black Barney alone.

The others—the other survivors of the Dracolysk Uprising—had their individual traits. Black Barney admitted that. He was even a little proud of that.

He knew that Ochoa-Varilla, for example, had a rare genius for invention. It was Ochoa-Varilla who conceived the effective (and deadly) "liquid sound," and lived in splendor and isolation on his own private asteroid, as a dividend of that patent alone. Paris Joan (yes, there were two female Barneys among those who had escaped Dracolysk) had uncanny extrasensory perception, and had a mystique among the elite and royal of all civilized nations as one who could foretell and advise. One of the Barneys had actually become a philosopher and written a book entitled *Power and Darkness*, with the theory, congenial to Black Barney, that the two were inseparable. Of course, Barney had never read the book. He had never laid eyes on the book. He had neither the time nor the inclination to read books. Books!

All the Barneys were cruel, remarkable killing machines, even the philosopher Barney, even though he chose to live in an academic surrounding, entertain himself with pretty coeds, and spout aesthetic babble. Hah! Even the philosopher Barney could match up against ten of RAM's gung-ho finest, if need be. If one of the Barneys chose to live with some pretensions, why, that was none of Black Barney's concern, he mused.

He and the other Barneys were not friends, and they were not enemies. They were not in touch with one another under usual circumstances. But they were forever clone-brothers originated together on Dracolysk, and they knew, even if they did not care to reflect on it, that they lived and breathed as parts of each other, as parts of the whole of a fantastic experiment gone amuck. Consequently, it was a kind of rare self-revelation for Black Barney to be in the presence of another Barney. It was . . . unsettling.

"Nothing in the latest RAM sweeps of the quadrant," reported Baring-Gould, with a trace of weariness.

Still, Black Barney said nothing. Baring-Gould sighed and returned to the challenge.

The memory of the uprising was a kind of birth trauma. The one thing that the Dracolysk Corporation had not counted on was the resistance of its slave creations. When the signal had come down, the one hundred and fifty Barneys had acted as one. Freedom was a deep-down impulse that could not be purged in the gene-processing. The battle had been incredible. Every other fight Barney had ever been in was like a slow-motion underwater ballet in comparison. It was one of the things that had tempered and forged him for the future.

The Dracolysk minions had fought their creations from building to building, finally taking refuge in the administrative tower. Then it was hand-to-hand fighting from floor to floor, ground level to the thirty-first, the Dracolysk forces yielding each floor stubbornly, bloodily, before ascending to a higher retreat. Soon there were only a few dozen of them left, barricaded behind the doors of a huge laboratory, along with a handful of top company scientists. They were hoping, perhaps, that corporate security would rescue them by air, but security would have to fly support personnel over several thousand miles, transmissions for help had been cut off, and the executives realized what the outcome would be.

Three of the Barneys had left before the final attack. There was no reason for them to stay; they were free and Dracolysk had been defeated. One of them was Sattar Tabibi, Black Barney recalled grimly, but it was not something he held against his clone-brother. It was just something he had jotted down in his memory. Sattar Tabibi had fought bravely and mercilessly with the others until the tide had turned, and then he had sought flight and opportunity, and opted against revenge.

Black Barney and the other Barneys, however, had an unquenchable thirst for revenge.

Black Barney would give up profit long before revenge. He was in the last surge of Barneys who stormed the great bolted laboratory doors to wipe out all living traces of the clones' unfeeling creators.

The more intelligent Dracolysk defenders, when

they realized that rescue was a pipe dream, smashed the windows and leaped to their deaths through the fetid, oxygenless atmosphere of the nondescript, out-of-the-way asteroid, thirty-one flights down, to solid rock. They trampled over each other in a panic to reach the windows and escape the Barneys' wrath.

There were many among the great scientists and researchers of the Dracolysk Corporation—those great minds that had not figured on the psychology of slavery—who were themselves, of course, pathetic, physically inferior specimens (wire-rim glasses and all that), who did not quite make it aboard the lemminglike suicide express. The Barneys caught up with them. They were torn and gutted, their limbs and torsos strewn bestially around the room.

Black Barney smiled forbiddingly at the joyous recollection.

Then they had torched the complex, so that all record of what had occurred there, all evidence of the secret origins of the Barneys, remained with the victors. The Barneys then had dispersed in the available flight vehicles and gone their separate ways to roam and rampage. They had about as much interest in a reunion party as ex-Death–Row cellmates.

The Barneys rarely had crossed paths in their larger universe, and thinking about it now, Black Barney realized again that it was too, too convenient for Quinto to have joined him for lunch at the Club Noir.

Too, too convenient.

"Nothing at all," summarized Baring-Gould with his hickory drawl.

Black Barney whirled and grabbed Baring-Gould by the shoulders and picked him up off the command chair, nearly choking him with his ghastly grip.

"There's something out of the ordinary in that sector, and I want you to find it," snarled Black Barney through bared teeth.

"Steady, boss," gasped Baring-Gould, struggling

for breath. "With a few of RAM's low-level programs, I have perused the sector and all perimeter sectors. Nothing out of the ordinary comes up on the update. No satellites or large storages. Nothing that hasn't been in that sector for hundreds of years."

Black Barney pulled the astrogation officer close to his face and squeezed until the man's ears really turned pink. Then he squeezed a little harder, until Baring-Gould got the point. He stopped and let his officer down slowly.

Black Barney was thinking. He would have to come at this from another angle.

"Transverse travel?"

"Of course," said Baring-Gould in a relieved tone, as he sat back down on the command chair and returned to the control panel. "But all are approved trajectories. Freight and cargo. Nothing military. Nothing exploratory. I checked that."

"Scan the interplanetary travel coming from other sectors and see if there are any unusual intersection points in that vicinity," suggested Black Barney.

"How . . . ?" Baring-Gould saw the clenched expression on Black Barney's face and quickly said, "I can't do that at random, boss. It would take months, and even then it would be impossible to . . ."

Without warning, Black Barney hurled himself at Baring-Gould. There was a sickening crunch, as Baring-Gould caught the brunt of the big man's backhand across the side of his jaw.

The astrogation officer couldn't say anything in reply. His mouth was wracked with pain. Baring-Gould had never seen his commander so worked up before—and over what? With renewed effort, Baring-Gould pushed buttons and twirled dials on the control panel.

"I'll try a different area of RAM Central," he advised in a low voice.

"Good," said Black Barney, pleased. "Now you're

thinking."

There was a whir of noise while Baring-Gould scanned the update.

"Nothing," Baring-Gould said quietly.

"Backdate it," ordered Black Barney.

"I already have," responded Baring-Gould. "Everything in that general direction is bona fide."

That doesn't make sense, thought Black Barney. He paced a little more, and the veins stood out on his forehead. He knew damn well he was taking his frustration out on Baring-Gould, and that aggravated him even more.

"Try Earth," he said, on a hunch.

"Earth?" asked Baring-Gould dubiously.

"You got some problem with Earth?" asked Black Barney with a hiss.

"No," said Baring-Gould hastily. "But we could be doing this for six months before we get lucky."

"I'll get lucky," Black Barney said. "I always get lucky."

There was a silence from Baring-Gould as he pondered the long form of the readout.

"I have two things."

"What?" asked a surprised Black Barney.

"Two things," repeated Baring-Gould.

"Location?"

"Two different locations," said Baring-Gould. "Both headed roughly for that sector. Neither with clearance. Neither with known personnel."

"Where?" asked Black Barney.

"Something out of Chicagorg," said Baring-Gould, still pondering the information.

NEO headquarters! Black Barney's mind exclaimed. So the rebels of the New Earth Organization were in on this, whatever it was. That didn't make much sense, either. Black Barney could not imagine NEO paying well enough to have someone like Quinto on the payroll. And why would they need to hire Black Barney as an intermediary? They had their own mercenaries at beck and call.

Baring-Gould was still scanning and deciphering. "The other contact point," he drawled finally, "is out of Australia."

Black Barney was most assuredly nonplussed. "Australia?"

"Australia," confirmed Baring-Gould.

"What the hell is even in Australia?" asked Black Barney.

Baring-Gould called up some reference material and perused it as quickly as he could. "Primitives, mutants, nut cases, lowlife mineral barons . . . and"— his voice rose and sounded with a hint of triumph— "a hard-case prison for RAM recalcitrants."

"A prison . . ." wondered Black Barney aloud. "Can you index the population?"

Baring-Gould flipped some switches. "Negative," he responded. "Ninety per cent of them go to Australia and never go home. It's a given. No records kept. Undesirables. The living dead. All files destroyed. Except, of course, at RAM Central."

Black Barney was considering this piece of the puzzle.

"Boss?"

"Yes," said Black Barney. "Cross their trajectories."

"I already have," said Baring-Gould, now eager to please. In reality, nobody but Baring-Gould could have nailed this down as fast as he did.

"And?"

"That's what stumps me," drawled Baring-Gould. "I get the Juno-Vesta arc, all right, a tiny northeast corner of it, through which there is generally very little cross-traffic. And there are no way stations, no mining operations, no outposts, nothing."

"Nothing?"

"It's kind of a historical site. Remnants of long-ago

space battles. A dumping ground for ancient hardware. It doesn't even show up as such on most maps, and it's hard to say what's there, exactly, if anything."

"Can you call up a catalog on it?"

"I might be able to call up the private library of Simund Holzerhein, if you like," said Baring-Gould, adding with a cautious intake of breath, "but it will take some time—"

"Call it up," commanded Black Barney.

"Only," Baring-Gould felt compelled to add, "I don't see what could be in a junkyard that would be of any interest to NEO, or RAM, or—"

"Neither can I," Black Barney admitted. He glanced at his wristchrono and gave Baring-Gould a nod of appreciation. "But keep checking. Meantime, I have an appointment to keep."

$$\text{O O O O O}$$

It was Black Barney who suggested a friendly game of pigsmear before finalizing the arrangements. Quinto took the suggestion in exactly the non-negotiable spirit in which it was made—a challenge more than an invitation. Like most space hooligans, although Quinto was certainly a cut above the usual such person, Quinto enjoyed the occasional down-and-dirty game of pigsmear. So he said, by all means, yes.

The pigsmear quartergym was located in the Tingeltangel Center, in Barbarosa's south wing, where the more adventurous, macho facilities were located. The quartergym was tucked into a remote basement corner, beyond the tremendously popular simulated wilderness range—with its foamy whitewater rapids (genuine spring water), daredevil rappel course, artificially harsh midwinter conditions, and surprise rockslide.

A couple of low-level gennies had booked the pigsmear quartergym for the after-lunch interval, but Black Barney's name, upon mention, usurped any and all prior claimants. All other appointments for the day were canceled, and Black Barney was penciled in.

There once had been a dozen pigsmear quartergyms, but now there was only one on Barbarosa. It was an archaic sport whose vogue had passed, although there would always be a solid constituency for it, especially in the Asteroid Belt. It was a grueling, violent, and primitive game, outlawed in many civilizations and expensive to maintain.

When Black Barney and Quinto stepped out of the locker room, to enter the pigsmear facility, they were greeted in a small anteroom by Gossamer "Gussy" Gruendziger, the quartergym rulesmaster. Gussy was a sumo-bulk ex-pigsmear professional (from the days when there were intersolar colony leagues) who wore his long, greasy black hair in a two-pronged topknot. He had a double chin and a triple stomach, but otherwise looked as if he could still play as mean a game of pigsmear as he had in his prime.

When Gussy saw two Barneys instead of just the one on his day log, both his chins dropped and he developed a sudden anxiety as to how he ought to behave. Two Barneys! This was unprecedented! He would have stories to tell his children—if he ever found a lifemate willing to fornicate with the three-hundred-pound blubberman who rubbed bear grease on his skin as emollient.

Gussy still carried his titanic carriage well, and he rose to greet the two Barneys with a self-assured smile that would not belie his churning stomach. He knew of Black Barney by reputation, and though he didn't know who the other Barney was, he knew this must be some sort of event, for the two of them to

have convened for a game of pigsmear. He knew that
he ought to tread lightly with his pregame remarks.

The two players were dressed in regulation blue
skimpies, rubber gloves, and skullcap. Each had a
small bottle of pepjuice attached to a thin stret-
chbelt pulled tightly around his hips. Gussy could
plainly see what few others could claim to have
seen, the purple matrix of scars on Black Barney's
shoulders and back. Gussy noted that Quinto, either
out of luck or otherwise, had fewer physical souve-
nirs of combat. But apart from that, the two Barneys were near-replicas of each other, Gussy
thought—although one (Quinto) gave the impression of lean, while the other one (Black Barney)
could be said to be . . . well, meatier.

"Gentlemen . . ." Gussy began uncertainly. "Of
course, you know the rules . . ."

Black Barney listened politely while Gussy
reviewed the pigsmear rules with the house vari-
ants.

Quinto looked a little bored. He gazed around the
anteroom, chuckling to himself, as usual enjoying
some private joke.

Pigsmear! Quinto was delighted. Why hadn't he
thought of pigsmear? That would really top off the
day.

After Gussy had finished his formal recitation,
the two Barneys pivoted and began walking toward
the quartergym's low entrance.

"Just a moment," said Gussy, altering his tone. He
hesitated to say anything, but it was his job, after
all. He did not fear the two Barneys—he was too
dimwitted for that, actually—he had spent much of
his life vanquishing formidable pigsmear oppo-
nents. And he didn't mind if the rules were to be
bent a little for the occasion. But he did feel obligat-
ed to ensure fair play.

Gussy grabbed Quinto's arm and prodded below

the wrist line of the rubber gloves, where he felt the tip of a long, thin blade, inserted just beneath the fold of the skin. Gussy made a "tch-tch" sound. "No weapons," he said, authoritatively.

Quinto chortled and glanced at Black Barney for his reaction.

Black Barney turned his hands toward Gussy and indicated that he, too, had a wristknife handy, secreted away. One for each wrist, actually, as Gussy perceived with wide eyes. Ditto with Quinto. That was a trademark of the Barneys, and they never did anything anywhere for any reason without their concealed wristknives, he knew. Gussy frowned. Well, all things being equal . . . "Okay," he said.

Black Barney reached for the door's spring latch.

"How long, gentlemen?" asked Gussy, retreating to balance his bulk on a three-legged stool near the time clock, the scoreboard, the pig-release board, and a small communications module.

"Thirty minutes," recommended Quinto.

Black Barney upped the ante. "Forty-five."

"Sixty?" asked Quinto agreeably.

Gussy gave a low whistle and leaned forward to consult his day log. "Twenty is the usual limit," he felt obliged to mention. No reaction from either of the Barneys. Oh, well. "And it is dependent, of course, on the number of pigs . . ."

"How many pigs today?" queried Black Barney impatiently.

Again, Gussy consulted his material. "It's been a busy day, gentlemen. You can't expect any more heroics from the morning pigs. If I had known you were coming sooner, I would have put in a special order. . . ."

"How many?" demanded Black Barney shrilly.

"Thirteen on hand," Gussy responded tentatively.

"Unlucky number," Quinto snorted.

"Six is the usual limit," Gussy felt obliged to mention.

"All of them," Black Barney said tersely.

"Baker's dozen," whooped Quinto, and both Barneys vanished through the doorway, which slid shut behind them.

Gussy sighed, took a massive piece of cheesecloth out of a drawer, and wiped the perspiration off his brow. This was most unorthodox.

But so was pigsmear.

Gussy picked up the intercom and buzzed the central message board in the greeting lobby of Barbarosa. If two Barneys were going to play sixty minutes of pigsmear with thirteen pigs, Gussy knew that there were plenty of others who would want to be in on the historic occasion.

○ ○ ○ ○ ○

The first pig came hurtling down the tumblechute, rear end first, landing with a splat about twenty feet in front of Quinto and Black Barney. The pig, a squat one to start off the competition, took one look at the two Barneys poised to grab it, and made off at a bound toward the farthest perimeter.

Immediately, Quinto smashed Black Barney in the face with his elbow and lunged in the pig's direction. Black Barney managed to stick a leg out and trip Quinto to the ground—thereby, scoring a few points—then leapfrogged his clone-brother to take the lead.

The pig was cowering in a far corner when Black Barney reached it first. But when Black Barney made his move toward the pig, it slithered out from between his legs. Damn slippery pig! Black Barney looked up into the full force of Quinto's best power-kick, and he was slammed backward. But Black Barney was agile, and he didn't lose his balance. No points gained or lost.

In almost the same breath, Black Barney was racing back toward the pig, but Quinto had him
matched step for step. Quinto reached over with one
arm and snagged his opponent in a crushing headlock. Black Barney returned the favor with the free
arm that wasn't desperately trying to loosen Quinto's grip.

Now, headlock in headlock, legs spread far apart
so they wouldn't stumble over each other, the two
Barneys lurched toward the opposite end of the
quartergym. Both applied extreme pressure to their
respective headlocks, and punched and kicked wildly with their free hands and legs. They were an
ungainly, four-legged beast as they traded progress
up the floor, moving with spastic slowness so that
neither would lose his footing.

The sturdy little pig ran from one end of the short
wall to the other, squealing with terror. Quinto and
Black Barney shifted back and forth, grunting in
lockstep, cutting off its escape, even as both of them
considered the situation. The pig was certainly
boxed in, but the two Barneys were at a rigid, and
one might say painful, stalemate.

Suddenly, Quinto let loose his hammerlock, taking Black Barney by surprise. Quinto dropped into a
crouch, then came up forcefully with his knee crashing into the solar plexus of the world's most famous
space pirate. "Oof!" Black Barney could not sup-
press an audible groan, and he tottered, his grip on
Quinto momentarily broken. But again he did not
fall. No points.

"Ho! Ho! Ho!" A laughing Quinto managed to
stoop over and fasten a hold on the squealing pig,
tuck it expertly under his arm—no small feat, considering the pig was writhing like a python—and
make a quick dash to the opposite wall and the first
touch-button. But the round was not over yet, and

Black Barney had already recovered and was in pursuit.

Quinto made the first touch successfully, pressing the protruding red buzzer in the center of the wall, then turned to make the cross-touch, directly colliding with the onrushing Black Barney. But Quinto was prepared with a forceful straight-arm, and the collision's effect was practically neutralized. Or at least Quinto managed to keep his grasp of the terrified pig, which by now was of the opinion that it had died and gone to porcine hell.

Quinto spun off the momentarily dazed Black Barney and dashed across the floor to accomplish the second touch without interference.

Quinto paused to catch his breath, and the other Barney did the same, moving toward his rival with ominous care.

Which way would Quinto go next? Black Barney wondered. There were two touch-buttons left, two walls left to tally, and after the first touch—which had to be the transverse wall—any sequence could be made.

Abruptly, Quinto tucked both arms into his chest, lowered his head, and charged like a ram. Black Barney took it full in the stomach, without flinching, lifted both his powerful arms high in the air, and smashed downward on Quinto's head. Quinto buckled, but before Black Barney could jump on top of him and claim points (much less wrest the pig free), Quinto rolled to the left; with amazing speed, Quinto then sprang up, faked to the right, and lunged forward to make the third touch. Miraculously, he still held on to the pig.

After an ululating war whoop to distract Black Barney, Quinto made his move toward the last touch-button, coming on hard and furious, like a locomotive. But he was an off-track locomotive, for he was dodging and weaving, zigzagging, pumping his legs, and gesticulating wildly.

Black Barney dived for Quinto's legs, and would have nabbed him if Quinto had not executed a beautiful somersault leap and come down on the other side of his opponent.

Quinto was only a couple of feet away from the fourth and final touch-button, with a big grin across his face. Black Barney saw the grin, because Quinto glanced over his shoulder, which was a mistake, for it gave Black Barney a moment to roll forward and scissor his legs together and topple Quinto from the ankles.

Quinto pitched forward, his trunk immobilized, and though he fell toward the touch-button and reached with one hand outstreched to make the contact, the distance exceeded his reach. He fell just barely short. Indeed, his forehead scraped the wall as the pig squirmed free and bounded off to make its regulation escape through a slot hole opened at the arena's far end by Gussy.

Black Barney got up with a wide smile. Quinto, too, showed his teeth good-naturedly. Both took a quick squirt of pepjuice.

First round to Quinto, announced Gussy. But Black Barney had scored well, too.

"Swell," grunted Quinto, short of breath.

Black Barney nodded in assent. In this, he was sincere.

They only had time to glance at the score before the next pig came sliding down the tumblechute.

○ ○ ○ ○ ○

Pigsmear was a sort of hybrid of handball, rugby, and rodeo traditions, said to have been devised over a century ago by the prison population of asteroid Zendt, as an alleviation to their boredom and oppression. It had always had a tremendous following among the scurvy underclass of the sentient nations, and mastery of it was a badge of honor for all lowlife of the Rogues' Guild.

It was very good aerobic conditioning, as well as the ultimate one-on-one gladiator sport.

Originally, Zendt prisoners played their pigsmear tournaments without walls or floor padding—they played it on the outdoor craggy terrain or, as conditions improved, on a poured-concrete area set aside for that purpose. But of course they had no choice, as they were die-hard felons, without rights or privileges.

The Barbarosa quartergym was very modern by comparison. The chutes and entrances were built low and inconspicuously into the walls, which, along with the floors, were coated with a thin rubber cushion. The walls were otherwise unadorned except for the red buzzer prominently centered in each. Time and touch-points were kept by discreet overhead monitors. The high ceiling accommodated a glass-enclosed, soundproof balcony, so spectators could gawk at the action.

Contestants could score in several complicated ways. "Minus-points" were given to any player who lost footing or fell to the floor. "Plus-points" were awarded to anyone who could hold on to the pig, dominate his opponent, and make the four touches. "Half plus-points" were given for any succession of touches up to three. "Half minus-points" were given to anyone who, having scored at least two touches, failed to complete the third and fourth ones.

Additional "half-points" were added or subtracted for certain special occurrences, for example, each time the pig was dropped, or there was a "temporary concussion" before the end of a round. "Permanent concussion," of course, meant that one of the contestants was the winner. The one with the pig.

One monitor kept track of the amount of time each contestant was on or off his feet, another kept track of how long a player held the pig, and a third tallied the time it took to complete each touch-button round. These three time-scores were computed against each other for the individual time-score.

It was all pretty impossible to calculate without being an aficionado or professional—which is why Gussy always handled the scoring on Barbarosa. Probably the only people who ever played pigsmear in its pure form—whatever that means—were the prisoners of Zendt. As they were all subsequently exterminated in a failed revolt, the rules had been handed down by opinion and folklore, and could vary from asteroid to asteroid.

Another obscure rule was that each pig was wetted with a smelly lubricant, called Ooneen-2, that made it virtually impossible to grasp and hold on to a pig, as if it was not already virtually impossible to grasp and hold on to such a beast. As a game progressed, this Ooneen-2 was of course spread onto the rubber padding of the floors and the walls, and the bodies of the contestants themselves, so that after a while it was hard to say what was more problematic, to hold on to the pig, or to smite one's opponent.

Yet another unwritten tradition was that as the rounds progressed, the pigs were to become bigger and heavier (not to mention smellier and greasier).

The pigs were a rare breed, called stonepigs, raised on Zendt, as it happens, by a small farm corporation that had an intersolar monopoly on their breeding and sale. They were fed a special diet of pine nuts, dried lentils, and black cabbage, which guaranteed that their hide would be as smooth and tough as leather (which, of course, it was), and virtually indestructible during their term of use (the average life span for a stonepig being approximately seven years). The pigs also were virtually indigestible, which, in a sidelight, is one of the reasons why the prisoners of Zendt revolted. The stonepigs were the staple of the prison diet—there were literally hundreds of thousands of them running rampant on Zendt—and eventually that caused violent unrest. Ironically, the Zendt prisoners were wiped out during the subsequent tumult, but the stonepigs, and the game invented by the inmates in their honor, endured.

It is not quite true that no one ever lasted more than twenty minutes or six pigs. For example, the last surviving warden of Zendt, a contented witness of the weekend contests among his prisoners, wrote an eyewitness account of a fabled match. In his book, *Life (and Death) on Zendt*, he wrote about the showdown between two behemoth pigsmear champions, one a no-parole mass-murderer and another a mentally defective metro-arsonist.

According to Warden T. Marsh Longenecker, the two prisoners of Zendt played a marathon pigsmear game of seven hours and forty-three pigs. So evenly matched were the two players, so deadly and brutal was the scoring, so terminal their exhaustion, that at the final buzzer they both fell quite truly dead. In his book, the warden, who also was judge of the contest, wrote, "Magnanimously, I ruled the competition a tie."

○　○　○　○　○

After the first twenty minutes and the dispatch of four pigs, Black Barney and Quinto were both a little huffed. After the second twenty minutes and the next five pigs, Black Barney and Quinto were moving with obvious discomfort and deliberation.

Well into the final twenty minutes, the two of them were drenched with the ineffable Oolneen-2, and were covered with streaks of dirt and grime, as well as welts, bruises, cuts, and bloody scratches. Both men were wracked with exhaustion and pain.

Above them, behind the thick glass shield of the balcony alcove, were the lucky cutthroats and no-goods who happened to be on Barbarosa that day—as motley an assortment of solar system scum as you could ever wish not to encounter.

Quinto and Black Barney, who were rather busy with their own activities, anyway, could not hear the peanut gallery, but it was clear from the throng's gaping maws and frantic gestures that they were betting plenty of moolah on the match's outcome. Although it was something of a drawback not to have the slightest familiarity with either of the players, to many in the grip of a gambling fever this was but an added titillation. And little added titillation was necessary to betting on the superior between two Barneys.

Below, in the pigsmear quartergym, the two Barneys were conserving their energies for the crucial stretch of the final minutes. They did not shout insults or taunts at each other—that would not have been sporting in any case. What did come out of their mouths came in spurts and sputters, bitter asides, sarcastic quips, and muffled cries.

The score had teetered back and forth from the beginning. Quinto had taken the early lead, then Black Barney had soared ahead, then Quinto had inched back to claim the edge, then Black Barney . . .

Quinto had the advantage where the pig was concerned—he was very adept with his hands—but Black Barney was the clear leader in tackle tactics. Neither of them had made "the circuit" more than once or twice, meaning, had not scored all four touches without knockdown or fumbles. The score had evened out over the course of the game.

The eleventh pig, this one the size of a torpedo,

had just escaped through the slothole after weathering a long and vehement round.

Quinto had been totaled to the floor, and got up dazedly. Black Barney, who had salvaged points in the round, threw a glance at the score and managed to smile to himself with grim anticipation. It was going to be nip and tuck. But Black Barney knew no fear.

While they awaited the twelfth and second-to-last pig, both Barneys breathed deeply and squirted a little pepjuice into their mouths. Black Barney cast a sidelong glance at Quinto.

"What I find mysterious," muttered Black Barney under his breath, "is all this mystery about a little 'nothing' job. I'm picking up something of great value to RAM, but of no value to anyone else. And I can't be told where I'm going, or what it is, until I get there. . . ."

Quinto shrugged amiably. "What do you care," he said, "as long as you get paid?"

"Curiosity," said Black Barney tersely.

"Ho! Ho! Ho!" guffawed Quinto.

Black Barney was getting tired of Quinto's laughing-boy routine.

The twelfth pig, at least two hundred pounds of sow, hurtled down the tumblechute. The balcony spectators were on their feet, open-mouthed and pointing, screaming and cheering, anticipating the rigors of the stretch.

Black Barney and Quinto lumbered, neck and neck, toward the pig, then slowed to a halt as they cornered it, each daring the other to make the first move. Face-to-face, they began to lower themselves toward the squalling pig. Their massive foreheads were inches from each other, their blank, intimidating eyes locked in concentration, their great, sculpted hands reaching out to probe for some handle on the pig.

"I don't like mysteries," Black Barney snarled. Then, without warning, he rammed his head ferociously into Quinto's, making good contact.

Crack! Some of the balcony spectators gasped.

Quinto slumped to the ground—a temporary concussion! Bonus points!—and Black Barney hefted the huge pig and began the sprint across the room to the first touch-button. He scored the first touch, the second, the third . . .

But Quinto was up, and incredibly, he did a showoff double-handspring across the court, landing full-force onto Black Barney's back, collapsing his opponent. The squealing pig dropped to the floor. No!—Quinto managed to catch it before it hit the court, as he reached over and pressed the fourth touch-button. Nice recovery.

The spectators roared.

"Nothing personal," said Quinto with a smirk.

Cumulative score: Tied.

Black Barney got up. His right arm had lost feeling, he had excruciating sciatic pain, his neck had gone stiff, and he had a deep gash on his right leg that trailed blood.

One of Quinto's ears dangled from his skull, he limped noticeably on the left side, at least three fingers were broken, and his fetid breath came in short, agonizing puffs.

The two Barneys stood shoulder to shoulder, awaiting the thirteenth pig.

"I'd be very upset if you were holding anything back from me," said Black Barney in a low, purposeful voice, spitting the words through gritted teeth.

Quinto looked momentarily disconcerted. He squeezed himself a dose of pepjuice. "Last pig," Quinto snorted in reply.

The thirteenth and final pig came sloshing down the tumblechute. It was a whopper of a stonepig—maybe 350 pounds—and after landing with a splat,

it could barely struggle to its feet and lumber off to
repose, oinking and snuffling, in the far corner.

It was all but forgotten.

Before Quinto could act, Black Barney had stepped
in front of him, blocking his path. Quinto tried to
sidestep his opponent, but Black Barney again
blocked his movement. Quinto pushed forward, but
Black Barney would not budge. Quinto threw a jab,
but Black Barney brushed it away. His back was to
the stonepig, and his mind, boiling with anger, was
fixed on Quinto.

"Who else is in on this?" demanded Black Barney
with sudden fury.

"Why," said Quinto ingenuously, "I'm not sure I
catch your meaning."

Without warning, Black Barney punched him as
hard as he could in the flat of the stomach. Quinto's
eyes gave away nothing, and his face barely flinched,
but his legs wobbled and he clutched at his stomach.

In the alcove, the spectators were surprised and
confused. What were the two Barneys doing down
there, having an intimate conversation? What about
the pig?

Black Barney stepped back and let his clone-
brother have another terrific blow to the upper chest.
Quinto was momentarily stunned, and unable to
react.

Black Barney pushed his heaving chest against
Quinto's and screamed into his face, "At least two
other errand boys are headed for the same sector!
Both from Earth!" He spread his arms in an arc and
drove them sharply downward, into Quinto's ribs.

"Two!" exhaled Quinto. He sounded genuinely surprised (not to mention winded). Again, Quinto tried
to edge away from Black Barney, but was pushed farther back toward the quartergym wall.

"The pig," murmured Quinto.

"Screw the pig," said Black Barney with a steely look on his face, as he leaned into Quinto. "You knew about the other two all along, didn't you?" He shoved Quinto. "Didn't you?"

Quinto shoved back sulkily. "One," he said pointedly, "I only knew about one."

"You didn't tell me!" bellowed Black Barney.

Black Barney drew back and threw a powerful shot to the head, which Quinto saw coming and ducked, reacting with one of his own, which connected. Black Barney jerked away, but then wheeled and kicked upward, catching Quinto squarely in the mouth. Quinto had nowhere to retreat, and before he could angle his defense, Black Barney executed an uppercut that drove him off his feet and into the wall. Quinto crumpled, and as he did, Black Barney jumped onto his back, landing on him with his full weight and grabbing him from behind by his long, stringy hair. Slowly, Black Barney began to twist Quinto's neck backward.

The balcony spectators were on their feet— pounding on the glass enclosure above—thrilled with the spectacle of two Barneys improvising for their benefit. By now, they, too, had forgotten the stonepig oinking away at the far end.

"I was going to tell you," sputtered Quinto, "all in good time."

Black Barney bent Quinto's neck back until he could hear the vertebrae crackle and pop.

"Which do you know about, NEO or Australia?" asked Black Barney, without lessening the pressure.

"NEO?" stammered Quinto, "I don't know dirt about NEO. Hey!" he cried in genuine discomfort. "Take it easy, pilgrim."

Black Barney twisted even harder, and Quinto's veins bulged. The massive clone-creature could barely wriggle, pinned to the floor as he was with

Black Barney straddling his back.

Desperately, Quinto dug the fingers of his free hand, his right hand, under the skin, trying to inch out his wristknife. Black Barney saw it coming and stomped heavily on Quinto's wrist. He reached over and pulled the dagger out, and with one arm held it up high.

The spectators "oohed" and "aahed."

"My, my," said Black Barney accusingly.

Quinto could barely form words anymore, his discolored tongue was so questing for air.

"Who in Australia?" whispered Black Barney, fingering the dagger.

"K-K-Killer Kane," gasped Quinto.

With that, Black Barney let the dagger fly, across the room, perfectly targeted, so that it pierced the great stonepig, whose honking and snorting was abruptly silenced. So hard was the dagger thrown that it passed through the pig's throat and stuck, reverberating, in the wall behind it.

Black Barney let up for a moment and reached over with his free hand and grabbed Quinto's arms. He jerked them both behind his opponent's back, yanked off his pepjuice belt, and roped Quinto from behind, like a steer. He gave the knot a final vicious tug, and Quinto groaned.

"He works for RAM," sneered Black Barney. "Why would RAM employ Killer Kane if they also wanted to hire me?"

The balcony crowd was in hysterics, screaming, gesticulating, pawing the glass enclosure. What a time! Two Barneys playing pigsmear—and now another unprecedented thing—the pig had been exterminated! Violation of all known rules! Very costly! Not fair! Plenty entertaining . . . but not fair!

"Insurance," croaked Quinto. "They want you both to go after the package. The two best mercenaries in the system. They don't care who gets there first, or who dies in the bargain. They'll deal with whoever retrieves it. What it is, I don't know, I swear. But I know it's important enough to RAM to hire backup, and to pay whatever the costs."

"It's a trap," muttered Black Barney ferociously.

"Sort of," admitted Quinto. "But," he added, "I always figured Black Barney to come out on top."

"Thanks, pal," said Black Barney.

Before Quinto could respond, Black Barney grabbed him by the hair again, jerked his head backward, and then with incredible force slammed it savagely down on the floor, once, twice, three times, again and again. When Black Barney stood up at last, Quinto was not moving. Just to be sure, Black Barney drop-kicked him in the teeth, as he lay there. Then he picked Quinto up by his knotted hands and, hefting him like a bale of hay, ran the length of the quartergym and smashed Quinto, headfirst, into the first touch-button . . . the second touch-button . . . the third touch-button . . . and the fourth touch-button.

"Ho! Ho! Ho!" he bellowed.

Black Barney dropped his burden to the floor and regally strode off the court.

He took no notice of the bedlam above.

In the balcony, the incorrigibles of Barbarosa who had witnessed the historic pigsmear rivalry between the two Barneys were cursing and wailing and slugging it out over the truly difficult question of who had won the match.

О О О О О

The crew of the *Free Enterprise* had had their R and R curtailed, were summoned back to quarters, and now sat waiting for some signal from Black Barney.

The ship was fueled and the logistics charted. In

the control room, Baring-Gould, Pelletier, Dolph-X, and several others stood at their posts, eyes riveted on Black Barney, who stood contemplatively with his back to them, studying a map. Several minutes had gone by in tense silence, without anyone speaking.

A panel door opened, and Xeno, the ship's security officer, entered, dragging a whining and cringing Young Bimwilly by the collar. He tossed him in a heap in front of Black Barney, who turned dramatically.

"M-M-Mister Barney," stammered Young Bimwilly in his phlegmy rasp, "I know not what I am doing here, but this gentleman insisted . . ."

He trailed off into awkward burbling as Black Barney did not immediately deign to say anything. The commander of the *Free Enterprise* looked directly at Young Bimwilly, but his eyes appeared to concentrate elsewhere.

"That scoundrel, Quinto," said Young Bimwilly nervously, producing a silken handkerchief to mop his perspiring brow. "He has absconded. Gone. Mortified by defeat, I'm sure. But he is not in the least available for the upbraiding he deserves. . . ."

From his knees Young Bimwilly looked up at Black Barney pleadingly.

"I like Quinto," said Black Barney at last. "Good pigsmear player."

No words could have been more confusing to the terrified Young Bimwilly. "But I thought . . ." the maitre d' of the Club Noir began.

"We have a deal, Quinto and I," said Black Barney.

Young Bimwilly said nothing, having the vague and growing suspicion that he had said too much already, perhaps.

"I am much more interested in you at the moment . . . and in how Quinto found out I was going to be here, on Barbarosa, enjoying a private little lunch at the Club Noir, on this particular day."

Young Bimwilly began to twitch and drool.

"There is only one person," said Black Barney matter-of-factly, "who knew in advance that the *Free Enterprise* was due here and that I would be having my lunch. Only one person who knew precisely when and where I would be dining—"

"I thought . . ." confessed Young Bimwilly shrilly, "I thought that he, being a Barney, much like yourself, that you wouldn't mind, Mr. Barney. Quinto asked me if I would let him know if you were in the vicinity. It was no treachery. I was not paid anything at all—apart from my usual gratuity. It was meant to be a . . . a . . ." He searched for the word. "A kindness." Young Bimwilly practically shrieked the word.

"I believe you," said Black Barney softly, after a long, uncomfortable, and silent interlude.

He reached over and grabbed Young Bimwilly by the scruff of the neck, removed the dagger from under his left wrist, and, in a movement too swift to fathom, slashed the right side of Young Bimwilly's face from brow to chin. Young Bimwilly cried out and slumped forward. Blood gushed from the wound. The maitre d' wailed as he did his best to cup it in his hands, but it spilled to the floor. No one rushed to his side. No one said anything. In time, there was more silence as Young Bimwilly's sobbing ebbed to a whimper.

"That is how I repay kindness," said Black Barney, "which, in a word, is stupidity."

At a gesture, Xeno dragged the abject Young Bimwilly to his feet and out the panel door. The rest of the command crew turned away as Black Barney gazed around the room defiantly. Pelletier, Dolph-X and Baring-Gould hovered near the command chair. In a moment, they were joined by Xeno.

"Dolph-X?" asked Black Barney.

"It can be done," said the warship's requisition officer. Pelletier, his assistant, a female gennie, soberly nodded her agreement.

"Baring-Gould?" asked Barney.

"I have a good fix on the whereabouts," said the warship's astrogation officer, "within fifty square miles. I'll narrow it down further en route."

"Any other data from the archives?"

"Negative. But I will define the prize long before we get there, you can be sure of that."

"Good," said Black Barney. "Xeno?"

As the ship's security officer, Xeno was as close as anyone could get to being trustworthy, from Black Barney's point of view. He had a flattop crew cut, dark green eyes, and a silvery wisp of beard. Xeno never blustered, but spoke plainly.

"It is some sort of trap," said Xeno flatly. "Or at the least, a double-bind. Too many unknowns. Too many risk factors."

"Your opinion?" pressed Black Barney.

"The prize could be some sort of lure. RAM wants you—or Killer Kane—or both of you—dead. And now Quinto will tip them off that you know more than you should."

"Quinto will tell them nothing," said Black Barney confidently. "He will wait to see what I do, to confirm whether or not we still have a deal."

"Perhaps," responded Xeno, "but RAM is very astute. They may have counted on Quinto tripping up. They may have counted on your decision to proceed, in any case. They may have counted on everything."

"So, why?" asked Black Barney. "Why me?"

Xeno thought for a moment. "Because they know you are fueled by jeopardy. They know you fear nothing. They know that your curiosity is heightened by peril. They know that anyone else in the

system would think twice, but not you. They know
that nothing will deter you, once you are hooked,
and that you believe yourself invincible in any
equation. They count on all of this, but above all,
they count on the fact that you are Black Barney."

Xeno spoke well. An imperceptible flicker of emotion registered across Black Barney's face. Anyone
else might have missed it, but Baring-Gould knew it
for what it was, and the other members of the senior
command crew took their cue from the astrogation
officer, turning to their positions and strapping into
their seats in readiness.

"Let there be no doubt," said Black Barney.

THE RELIC

Flint Dille

I: Incident at a trading post in the Juno-Vesta arc

Vic Fritzell peered into his tracking monitor, only one of many in his trading post, and marveled at what he saw there: an asterover, a small spaceship of RAM design, studded with thrusters and stubby maneuvering fins, the RAM corporate insignia and serial number blazing conspicuously on its nose. The powerful little ship tore through the dusty asteroid fields between Juno and Vesta and headed straight at Vic's converted, motley-looking, twenty-third century space station turned wayside trading post.

Trader Vic, as his customers called him—he had no friends, only customers—was used to strange ships arriving unexpectedly. He had made the Asteroid Belt his home. The belt was also home to several prisons, genetic flops, obsolete robots gone amuck, and other dubious life forms. Only the hearty or the foolish ever came to the belt. The pilot of the tiny asterover must surely be of the latter group, Vic thought, laughing. The coarse sound whistled through his grotesquely scarred mouth.

"Out here, a small ship like that should have been robbed and scrapped by now," he said aloud to himself.

His only companion on the station, a spacer in his employ named Gwill, grunted in agreement. Spacers, man's most far-flung genetic experiment, were intelligent enough, but probably the most cruelly ambitious of the gennies. Their slit of a mouth was used only to ingest water or powdered nutrients.

Gwill's inability to speak except through sign language or a voder around his neck, activated by natural electric currents, was his strongest recommendation to the solace-seeking trader, when the odd-looking spacer had decided to make a waystop a little more permanent several months before. Vic trusted him as much as he trusted anyone, which wasn't much.

"Either it's a slow day in the belt, or this guy is a lot smarter than he looks," Vic mumbled, frowning in thought. Taking no chances, he flicked on his ship-to-ship communicator.

"Asterover 19102. This is Victor Fritzell. You have crossed into the security perimeter of my trading post. Please identify yourself." Vic waited. There was no response from the asterover.

It was impossible to be too careful anywhere, but particularly in the belt. Vic knew his was the best-stocked post of its kind anywhere in the outer fringes. But treachery and thievery were the norm here on the edge of civilization. Vic had worked too hard and suffered too much to be robbed blind by some renegade member of the Rogues' Guild, whose coffers he lined with protection money, or some other malcontent.

"Prepare to ambush our visitor if he comes any closer without I.D.," Vic told the spacer.

Gwill nodded his silvery aluminum head. He knew what to do. His assignment was not unusual, for such distractions were a daily occurrence on Trader Vic's Trading Post. Without a word the spacer stepped into the ejection chamber in the cluttered station, strapped on a rocket belt, and cocked back the bolt of his hand-held laser cannon. Inside the post, Vic pressed a button and Gwill was ejected into the blackness of space.

The trader thought about the asterover's motives, but he was not overly concerned. Victor Fritzell, once a pirate in the Rogues' Guild under Black Barney himself, had survived more global intrigue than most men even read about, with a bionic leg to show for it. He hoped one day to grow a new limb in the reconstruction tanks on Mars, but that would mean a long journey. He could neither spare the time nor trust anyone to man the post. Everyone he knew was either too greedy or too stupid.

Known for making fair deals, Vic was not a greedy man by solar system standards. But he was no fool, and, like a bartender, his customers often told him interesting bits of information that other people were willing to pay for. He was not averse to making a dola or two off someone else's stupidity. Life was hard, and then you were downloaded.

He squinted into a monitor that covered the cargo bay door and the tunnel of junk beyond that hid the entrance from view. Spotting Gwill at the ready in the tunnel, Vic flicked on his ship-to-ship again.

"Asterover 19102, identify yourself and state your business, or I will convert your ship to component parts."

"There's no need for hostility," an old, indignant voice responded at last. "I haven't talked to anyone since I left Mars and it took me a moment to find the communicator switch."

Vic frowned. This was not what he had expected. "State your business," he repeated.

"My name is Dr. Merrill Andresen, and I am from the RAM Archaeological Society. I am in need of fuel, food, and friendship." The voice from the asterover chortled strangely. Vic could not see the humor.

"Do you have viewing?" Vic asked abruptly.

"If you mean, do I have a visual monitor, then, no, I do not; my ship is a no-frills, second-rate asterover. Will you give me clearance?"

Vic frowned again. Either this guy was the greatest con man in the fringes, or he truly was a fool. The trader bit a fingernail; he wished he could see him.

Suddenly Gwill signed to him in the other monitor. "I have a lock on the target. . . ."

"No," Vic grumbled, forgetting in his haste to switch off the channel to the asterover.

"No?" asked the pilot, surprised.

Vic had an idea. "What I mean is, not immediately. Please answer a few routine questions for me."

Vic began a stream of mundane queries. Calling up his data base, he quickly keyed in the name Dr. Merrill Andresen and the serial number of the RAM asterover.

"How long was your journey from—" Trader Vic's mouth finished the question while his mind scanned the incoming data:

Name: Andresen, Dr. Merrill
Occupation: None
Previous employment: Professor of anthropology, Martian University. Denied tenure.

Vic read the data again, for there was one point he found fascinating. The old man had been denied tenure recently. Why? Vic keyed the question into the data base.

Response: That information is classified.

Vic was both angered and titillated by the roadblock. He loved a mystery, and he was burning to know the answer to this one.

"Do I have permission to dock?" Andresen's irritated voice penetrated Vic's thoughts. "I am running dangerously low on fuel—I didn't know trading posts in the asteroids were so far apart."

Victor Fritzell's smile of anticipation grew. "Of course, Dr. Andresen. One of the natives will lead you to our entrance and see you safely through the mine field. Welcome to Trader Vic's."

O O O O O

Andresen looked through his monitor for the guide the trader had promised, taking in the station. Circa 2257, he guessed. Actually, it was no guess at all; until recently it had been his job to know such things. The thought instantly brought him close to depression, which would rob him of his enjoyment of experiencing a new environment. He shook the thought away and concentrated on the space station on his monitor.

Andresen was lonely after thirteen days alone in space. He was certain he was now experiencing the same kind of excitement his ancient predecessors, African explorers, must have felt approaching a native trading post after long periods of isolation. Though this post was not made of wood and thatch, it was equally primitive by twenty-fifth century standards. Verifying his earlier estimate, Andresen saw that the nucleus of the post was a twenty-third century prefab space station most commonly used at the time by small corporations. Packed to its sides like lumps of clay, the hulls of derelict ships were grafted one on top of the other, giving the effect of a sizable garbage mound. In fact, Andresen had thought it just that until Fritzell had radioed him, fortunately reminding him that the asterover was low on fuel.

Andresen caught the glowing flash of a rocket pack in the monitor and spotted a bright green guidance light. Refining his visual image, he saw his first spacer outside the pages of a textbook. Looking as much like a silvery seal as a man, he was protected from the cold by a layer of blubber and a suit that was so well integrated with his body that it was difficult to determine where one began and the other ended. He had large, glassy eyes, a small slash for a mouth, and no nose. A black patch, a heat retainer, Andresen remembered, was off-center where his nose should have been. Andresen was repulsed by the gennie's strange appearance: he looked like an oversized black frog.

Using his green guidance light, the spacer waved
Andresen toward a well-disguised, junk-strewn tunnel.
Following the beam, Andresen docked against the
mouth of the tunnel and waited as an umbilical tube
was connected to the hatch side of the asterover. Hearing the decisive clicks of locks in place and seeing the
exit clearance light come on, Andresen opened the
hatch and stepped into the bouncy tube, floating gently
into the official entry to Trader Vic's Trading Post, complete with crooked, laser-etched sign and all.

The main door swung out into the tube. Opening it,
Andresen danced a quick jig (which was made quick-
er than even he thought by the unexpected three-
quarter g's in the station), to avoid stepping on the
head of an old, blond dog with huge, obviously genetically altered ears. The dog's head never left its paws,
but his large, sad eyes clung to Andresen like tacks
on a magnet. The scientist smiled, despite his clumsy
entrance; gravity was a nice touch of home.

Andresen looked around the cluttered, cylindrical
station, and his jaw dropped in unabashed surprise. He
might as well have entered a museum. No object that
could be oiled, hammered, or soldered into working
order was too old or obsolete to be sold here. Equipment
ranging from twenty-second century life-support suits,
with their primitive, rounded edges, to sleek, modern-
day RAM gyrojet pistols was on sale. The space suits
bore scratches and dents from previous owners, and
Andresen would not have been surprised to learn that
most of them had been stripped from unfortunate
corpses, for the nameplates were all blank.

If this had been any other research trip, he would
have arranged to stay for a time and delve into the history represented. But he had no time to spare; a "package" waited for him farther out in the belt. His
reputation—everything he had ever worked for—
depended on his recovering it as quickly as possible. He

would show all his detractors that his research had been flawless!

His gaze traveled up the cylindrical walls, above the displays of suits and equipment, past the entertainment chips that advertised classic experience vids, to more racy fare. There he spotted boxes of food supplies, accessible only by ladders that hung suspended from the station's ceiling. But at such a distance, he could read no labels.

"Need a vid screen?"

Andresen spun around to locate the voice. Behind an old-fashioned glass display case was a middle-aged human with thinning hair, a heavily scarred face, and a once-muscled body gone heavy, soft, and dimpled. Over this he wore a coarse brown smart clothes coverall, obviously climate-controlled, since he seemed perfectly comfortable in the cool trading post. A brilliant ethnologist, Andresen placed him as a Lunarian from the hint of an old accent in his voice.

The astroarchaeologist hurried over to the counter. "You're Victor Fritzell, of course. Dr. Merrill Andresen." He extended his hand. "Pardon my rudeness, but I'm fascinated by your establishment."

"Thanks," the trader said, making no effort to meet Andresen's grip. Poison nails were too common and always deadly. Vic made no secret of scrutinizing his visitor. Andresen looked like the stereotypic academic: long white, frazzled hair; thin, muscleless, round-shouldered body; and red-rimmed eyes constantly straining to focus. His hands were weathered from exposure to harsh chemicals, as was his nose, whose owner obviously liked his liquor. Andresen pulled back his hand uncomfortably.

"What do you need?" Vic asked bluntly. Andresen handed him his printed list of foodstuffs. "How you going to pay?"

"RAM credit?"

"No credit out here."

"Cash?" Andresen pulled a small bag of coins, the last of his money, from a pocket inside his lab suit.

Though highly valuable elsewhere, Vic had no need for money. "Nothing to trade?"

"Nothing of value that I don't need myself."

Vic shrugged. "It'll do." He set about collecting Andresen's goods. The trader noticed that Gwill had returned, but had wisely chosen to hang back out of sight. Spacers tended to frighten people.

Vic came back shortly, setting two tall stacks of pre-packaged dinners on the counter before Andresen with a groan. "Sixty micromeals. That's a lot of proto-meat for one guy to eat in the two weeks it takes to get to Fortuna."

"Oh, I'm not going to Fortuna," Andresen said absently, counting his order. "At least I hope I don't have to go that far."

"No?" Vic said, adding a pound of coffee to Andresen's supplies. "On the house," he assured him. "That far for what? Some RAM job, I'll bet."

"Not exactly, but it will certainly set my colleagues back at Martian University on their ears!" Andresen couldn't help add a wild chortle of satisfaction at the thought.

"Gee, it sounds really important," the trader said artlessly, pressing a recorder button on the floor with his toe.

"Vic, my only friend, this is the most important thing I've ever done. This may be the most important find in the history of archaeological research!" Andresen's eyes took on a wild look that encouraged Vic to press on.

"What is it?"

He was bursting to tell someone—anyone—and Fritzell fit that description. "I have pinpointed the location of a twentieth century space hero named Buck Rogers, here in the Juno-Vesta arc. I'm searching for his body, and I'm going to find it!"

Vic Fritzell didn't know whether to laugh or—well, he didn't know how to react. He was no scientist, but five hundred years was a very long time. . . .

"I've said too much," Andresen mumbled abruptly. "Loneliness loosens the tongue, as they say." He laid the small bag of coins on the counter between them. "That should more than cover it." Hastily pouring his supplies into two containers for ease of transportation through the tube, he thanked Vic for his time and conversation, stepped over the dog at the door, and left the confines of the trading post.

"It is I who should thank you," Trader Vic said aloud after Andresen had gone, snidely imitating the man's tone. He saw Gwill strap back on his rocket pack to release the tube from the asterover.

"Someone somewhere will buy this information, valid or not. Who would be willing to pay more for even a dead ancient hero, NEO or RAM?" He thought about Andresen, chugging toward his find, oblivious to betrayal. Fools deserved what they got, Vic resolved, reaching for his long-distance communicator. He had settled on NEO, because as a terrorist group trying to overthrow the powerful RAM corporation, it was hungry and quick, not wallowing in corporate lethargy, like RAM.

"NEO." He said the word aloud as he tried to remember the name of his contact there. He was a new one, a disinherited Mercurian prince—Gavilan, that was his name. He'd dealt with him only once. Head bent to the task, Vic punched the access code into his data base.

It was the last thing Victor Fritzell ever did.

A heat-seeking bullet from Gwill's rocket pistol caught the human in the lower chest, splattering him like an overmicrowaved egg. His job here was done. In no time he readied his own ship, left in storage in one of Vic's grafted-on hangars, and was on his way to his home asteroid of Thule to collect his pay from RAM.

Though he did not understand the implications, Gwill had known something Vic had not: RAM had known for some time of Andresen's progress and didn't want it disturbed, or NEO informed, just yet.

But neither he, nor Andresen, nor even RAM, knew that NEO was already aware of the situation and taking its own steps.

Even NEO did not know that still others coveted the body of Buck Rogers.

II: Judgment Day

His stomach rumbled. Merrill Andresen's red-rimmed eyes did not leave the computer board before him as he reached into the asterover's food locker, stocked some six days before at the trading post near Juno. Still without looking, he popped a small, rectangular, prepackaged meal into the microwave and punched the same coordinates needed for every meal he ate: Salisbury steak and vegetables almondine. He knew that the meat was named after a city on ancient Earth, though he knew not what the city had to do with gray, sauce-covered food. Still, it was filling, nutritious—if the ingredients on the label were to be trusted—and not too objectionable to his aged, delicate constitution. Andresen did not have the time to think about what he ate.

The microwave bell rang. Andresen opened the steaming container and inhaled. He added a few spices of his own, a luxury acquired from his mother that he would not give up no matter how primitive his surroundings.

And they were decidedly primitive, here in the Asteroid Belt, the far reaches of the "civilized" world. Andresen gave a humorless, ironic chuckle at his own choice of words. He no longer knew any civilized beings besides himself in the cold, suspicious, self-interested world in which he had been born. Andresen winced at a recent, painful memory and angrily stuffed too large a bite of Salisbury steak into his mouth, unaware of the sauce that ran down his chin as his mind traveled back.

He had been a professor of anthropology at Martian University, a civilized place near the bridge known as the Pavonis Space Elevator. . . .

"Order! Quickly, now!" Prof. Girard Warch, president of Martian University, held his long white hairpiece in place with his left hand, his right hand banging a metal gavel up and down with the regularity of a bouncing ball, his meaty jowls jiggling to the beat. "Ladies and gentlemen, we must quickly proceed with this week's professorial tribunal."

Warch resolved to cut the proceedings short, as he had left a certain leggy teaching assistant back in his office and he had to meet his wife at Chez Petite in Coprates Metroplex for dinner in just three hours.

Abruptly, the doors to the balconies closed, where university T.A.s, secretaries, and other interested but unimportant visitors sat. On the ground floor, the remaining professors gathered up their multicolored ceremonial robes, which represented the colleges of their graduate study, and hurried to their computer console seats in the Crystal Cathedral.

The cathedral served as a formal meeting hall for invocations and professorial tribunals. As its name implied, the Crystal Cathedral was an enormous, cold, entirely crystal structure with arched and vaulted ceilings and an accompanying echo, all of which aided the pomp and pageantry of the ceremony. The cathedral was so large that the audience, though present, watched the proceedings via individual, closed-circuit video monitors.

Warch, wearing a black, extra-large judge's robe over his massive girth, sat behind the tall adjudication bench made of intricately chiseled Martian slate. The day's bailiff, Prof. Rajiv Alwu, sat on Warch's left. The plaintiff, Dr. Glynn Georges.dos, as all ".dos" characters were, was a computer-generated persona, highly

regarded by his colleagues. Their esteem had grown
tenfold recently after Georges.dos's research located
the remains of four ancient cosmonauts. Georges.dos's
holographic form—a thin man with small, dark eyes
and a hawk nose—was on Warch's right.

Georges.dos had come to the president's office one
afternoon for his usual round of complaining and had
stumbled upon the president and his teaching assistant
engaged in "research" of their own. Warch hourly chided himself for his clumsiness. Today's hearing against
Andresen was the easiest of Georges.dos's demands to
meet. What was one professor, more or less?

When the last attendee took his seat, Alwu rose to his
feet. The flawless olive skin above Alwu's genetically
engineered Adam's apple bobbed once as he cleared his
throat. Warch disliked gennies, and felt uncomfortable
sitting so close to Alwu.

"Will the accused please stand?" announced the bailiff.

Seated in the middle of the cavernous hall, his left
side to his peers, his right to the bench, Dr. Merrill
Andresen stood hesitantly, his ornate art provo chair
noisily scraping the crystal floor in the echoing silence
of the hall. Squinting, he tried to focus his watery eyes
on something other than a computer screen—the distant form of the man behind the gavel. He raised a fluttering hand and tried awkwardly to impose some
semblance of order on his willful, scraggly, salt-and-
pepper hair.

Bored, Warch watched the befuddled, frightened professor. Though the president enjoyed this part of his job,
he was sure Andresen's case would hold no surprises,
no fight or fury to make the weekly event of trying and
humiliating a wayward professor the least bit unusual
or exciting. Andresen was the typical spineless,
absorbed research professor, and his crimes were clear-
cut; he would not be able to defend himself. And even if
he was innocent, none of the tenured professors seated

on the tribunal would protect him; anyone with any spark of independence or courage had long ago been purged from the university by this same court. Worse still—or better, depending on one's viewpoint—the professors seemed to revel in tribunals, like gapers at a horrendous, bloody explosion.

"Merrill Andresen," Alwu intoned, "you stand accused by Dr. Glynn Georges.dos, and the council finds sufficient substance in his claim. Therefore, you are hereby formally charged with misusing RAM grant funds on an absurd research project, as demonstrated in your recent article in the Eastern Martian Journal of Science. As a result, you have embarrassed the university, its fellows, students, and faculty."

Andresen sucked in air, and a shot of adrenaline quickened his pulse. He knew what he was here for. If there had been any doubt, he had only to see his rival, Glynn Georges.dos, to confirm his suspicions. His only defense was that every professor and teaching assistant strove to publish theories in the science journals of the Sol System. In fact, professors with tenure were required to publish, at least if they wanted to keep their tenure. Why had his article precipitated a professorial tribunal?

"Do you have anything to say on your behalf, before your peers pass judgment in this tribunal?" Warch asked abruptly. In his haste to be done, Warch skipped over the usual questioning of witnesses. He noticed a scowl of disapproval from the plaintiff, Glynn Georges-.dos, who had been looking forward to cross-examining his rival, the self-absorbed Professor Andresen.

"This is no tribunal! This is a kangaroo court!" Andresen protested.

"I don't remember you protesting while you were among the peerage at previous proceedings," Warch said pointedly.

Andresen's face grew hot. It was true—attendance at tribunals was mandatory, and so he had come, but his face had always been buried in research material. Merrill Andresen was not willing to let his accusers off the hook so easily. He still had some rights in this procedure. "Which of my many published theories does the council claim to be invalid?" he asked simply.

Dr. Glynn Georges.dos jumped to his holographic feet and shook his fist angrily at Andresen. "You know damn well which one! You claim to have information that can pinpoint the location of the body of an astronaut whose mission dates from A.D. 1995!"

Andresen waited until the laughter died down and the cathedral's sound system was silent. "Which would, coincidentally, invalidate your recent claim to have found the oldest off-Earth remains, would it not?" he asked.

The fuzzy image of Georges.dos's face burned red. "If you are suggesting that bias clouds my judgment, you are mistaken. I am not the one on trial here, *Mr.* Andresen." Georges.dos let the veiled threat hang between them.

"I believe everyone here knows of my achievements. I have devoted my life to anthropological research." He stopped to look at Andresen squarely. "Let me assure you, if there was even the vaguest possibility that an astronaut existed who could be resurrected after five hundred years, I would know about it!"

"Just as you knew of this finding from 1995?"

Georges.dos's face burned again with anger. "What finding? There is no finding! You have no evidence, no substantiation! Only your published lies!"

"But you're frightened to death that I'm right," Andresen said to his rival.

Georges.dos looked as if he would like to strike the rumpled little scientist. Instead, lips pursed tightly, he looked out to address the crowd of professors. "I think we all know why we're here. Dr. Andresen has let his professional jealousy cloud his professional judgment. Livid with humiliation over my recent *substantiated* and highly acclaimed findings, he has conceived his absurd story solely to divert the attention of the scientific community to himself. And after he has collected the professional and financial accolades, he will suddenly discover the error in his theory."

"He'll make us all look like greedy academics!" someone shouted from the crowd, his voice vibrating over the sound system.

"RAM will never maintain our grants under such pretenses!" another added.

"We cannot condone such ethics, nor expose our students to them!" The cathedral filled with the electronic hum of hundreds of buzzing monitors.

Suddenly an impassioned cry came from the balcony, distinctive without amplification. No one in the balcony was allowed to speak at these occasions, thus they did not have monitors.

"He's not like that!" Andresen recognized the voice of his own loyal teaching assistant, Walter Dorning, as it echoed inside the cold crystal structure. "Dr. Andresen wouldn't publish a theory without reliable facts! Tell them, Dr. Andresen!"

On the floor of the chamber, Andresen sighed. He'd seen enough of these proceedings to know the outcome was settled long before the event. Walter was wasting his breath and jeopardizing himself in the process.

Andresen looked up and saw the pained expression on his teaching assistant's face and felt shame at his own helplessness. "My findings are valid," was all he could say in his own defense.

"Then I'll tell them!" Walter shouted, windmilling his arms against the security guards who had appeared to escort the dissident from the proceedings. "His research was flawlessly brilliant! Accessing the data base of a recently discovered twentieth century weather satellite, Dr. Andresen analyzed the digitally stored cybernetic personality program of a twentieth century Soviet military man named Kark—" Walter's testimony was cut short as security guards dragged him through a door at the back of the cathedral.

Merrill Andresen sighed with relief. Walter had not had time to reveal too much; at worst, RAM security would give him a memory wipe drug. He'd be O.K.

"Andresen must be punished!"

"Send him to Australia with the rest of RAM's defects!"

Georges.dos's hologram revealed no emotion at these outbursts, even though Andresen was sure the computer was delighted. "Now, let us not be rash," he said. "I think we all agree that Mr.—er, Dr. Andresen should be denied tenure and that the student body must no longer be exposed to him. In addition, his RAM research grant should be terminated and assigned to a more deserving researcher. Further, he must be banned from using our academic facilities on this farce of a research project. These things will be punishment enough."

The cathedral rang with cheers of approval.

President Warch blinked to clear the sleep from his eyes and pushed his hairpiece back from where it had drooped forward. "Dr. Georges, I believe I still am the moderator of these proceedings." That blackmailing toady was going to show some manners, or he would find himself disposed of, Warch thought. Caught up in the glow of victory, Georges.dos at least had the presence of mind to flush with embarrassment and return to his seat behind the slate bench.

"Bailiff Alwu will call for the vote from the rank and file," Warch intoned, stifling a yawn and stealing a look at his watch.

"All in favor of stripping Dr. Merrill Andresen of his professorship and giving him a position as research assistant, say "aye.""

Again, the hall rang with approval.

"All opposed?"

Someone in the balcony cleared his throat.

Andresen closed his eyes slowly, disbelievingly. He stayed that way while Alwu removed the former professor's academic robe, leaving him in his white lab coat and protective brown lab trousers. He opened his eyes only when two security guards took him by the arms to escort him from the chamber. Andresen looked around to see that in the space of fifteen seconds, the cathedral had emptied. That was how much his trial had meant to his "peers." He thought it odd that he had ever felt a part of the academic brotherhood.

Andresen felt weak. He slumped forward, supported by his two guards. His mind felt as if something vital had fled, leaving him . . . without a purpose. His research was his life—his purpose for living. Now that had been taken from him.

Suddenly he heard a voice behind him. "You were lucky." It was Georges.dos.

"Lucky?"

"To have lost only your research grant, and not your life."

"My research *was* my life," Andresen said, not looking at the hologram.

"I am disappointed," Georges.dos said, sounding anything but. "I expected more fight from you."

In the face of Georges.dos's smug taunts, something inside the mild-mannered ex-professor snapped. He would not cave in to the liars and the cheats so easily. In that moment, Mr. Merrill Andresen adopted a new purpose: Vindication.

"I only fight when I have a chance to win, and no one ever wins against a professorial tribunal," he said. "I think you know that *our* battle is not over, Georges." His tone was light, but the threat was unmistakable. "You can take away my research grant and my tenure, but you can't stop me from continuing my research through other means. By the time you manage to blackmail someone at RAM into having me arrested on some other trumped-up charge—don't flinch, Glynn, I know your techniques—I'll have my astronaut."

The guards pulled Andresen away before Dr. Glynn

Georges.dos could respond. But, looking over his shoulder, Andresen saw—for just an instant—a look of panic cross his rival's face.

III: Rescue

Andresen tossed the empty Salisbury steak container into the disposer and flushed as the memories of the dread event continued. . . .

He'd clung to Georges.dos's look of fear after the guards had escorted him by the elbows from the cathedral. From there they took him to the mover that meandered through the tall, old buildings of Martian University and to the farthest perimeter of campus. He was forbidden to return to his office, even to collect his belongings. All his research concerning the twentieth century astronaut was there.

At least they had left him near the transport terminal he needed, to get to his living quarters on the seventh level of the Pavonis Space Elevator. They were only that: living quarters. His home had been the field when he was on a dig, or his office when he was doing research. He kept his clothes at his quarters, and that was about it.

Andresen stepped off the mover as he neared Gate 12 in the transport station. Normally the ninety-minute trip back to his apartment gave him a good opportunity to review papers and his professional journals. That's all over now, he thought. The electronic gate spit his Resident's Transport Pass back into his hand, and Andresen stepped into the narrow passenger pod. He selected his customary aisle seat and strapped himself in.

The pod lurched several times as it began its ascent up the miles-long cable to the Pavonis Elevator Residential Rings. Andresen felt the gradual increase in pressure; it would subside again soon enough. He'd learned to sleep through the gravity adjustments, but today he stared wide-eyed at the back of the seat ahead of him.

He started abruptly when the recorded message he'd heard hundreds of times before blasted in his ears. "Pod 12 is now arriving at Pavonis Elevator Residential Ring, Level 7. Please check to be sure you remove all carry-on luggage when you leave. Thank you."

Andresen walked the two short sectors to his housing complex, a long, low white structure of the newest and cheapest design. He punched his code into the number pad just off the entryway. Two more codes and he would be into the unfamiliar but private surroundings of his quarters. He wanted only to sit down, have a drink—many drinks—and determine his next course of action.

Stepping into the last white corridor, he stopped before the second door on the right, inserted his security card into the slot, and waited.

"Good evening, Mr. Andresen," the computer's female voice purred.

Andresen flinched. RAM certainly worked fast. Already the security computer in his complex knew he'd been stripped of his tenure.

"Just let me in my quarters," he said more harshly than he'd meant to. The computer ran a voice check on his words, and the door slid open.

"Sorry, Mr. Andresen," the computer said as he stepped beyond its range into his place.

There, in the harsh fluorescent light of his cramped apartment, Mr. Merrill Andresen bent and opened the small cabinet in which he stored his liquor. His life was shattered, and the pieces fell about him like broken glass. He hoped to anesthetize himself so that he would feel no pain when the shards sliced through him. He moved slowly to his bed, sat, and quickly drained one half-full bottle of skitch, then returned to the cabinet and opened another. . . .

Andresen awoke to a series of sharp raps on his door,

which echoed and amplified in his swollen, hung-over head. He sat up, but felt the room immediately sway beneath him, and decided to stay where he was. The noise at the door was relentless. He shuddered and grabbed his aching head.

"Stop that pounding! Who is it?" he yelled, the subsequent pain making him sorry for doing so. Who got through security to pound on my door, anyway? he wondered. Whoever it was would need a security card to get that far, then request admittance from the computer. Andresen was now curious. He called again to the stranger, but the only response was the sound of something dropping on the floor outside his door, then whoever it was scurried away.

The former professor slowly went to the door, opened it, and saw on the carpeted floor just outside the doorway a small envelope. He thought it odd that he should receive mail in such an old-fashioned way, but as he bent to retrieve it his head began to throb. He picked up the package and threw it on the couch, then made for his kitchen-bar for some coffee and painkiller.

Throwing the vile-smelling, empty skitch bottles into the disposer, he soothed his head, then microwaved a cup of black coffee for himself. Closing his eyes, he sat lightly, quietly, on the sofa and sipped the hot, stimulating drink. Gulping the last inch in his mug, his foggy brain remembered the package. Opening his eyes, he spotted it beside him. Inside was a small blue microdisk, the type he used in his own computer.

Tapping the disk thoughtfully, he lifted his small, portable computer from the coffee table, placed it on his lap, and popped the strange disk in the drive. Calling up a directory, he retrieved the only file on the disk. The text read:

Meet me at the central entrance to Ralton Spaceport, Level 14, at eight o'clock tonight. Bring field equipment. W.

W? Walter? His teaching assistant? Andresen didn't understand what was going on, but Walter was not one for jokes. Andresen looked at his watch. It was almost half past six—in the evening!

Amazing! he thought. I've slept away an entire day! I knew skitch was strong, but . . . No. It must have been a combined effect of the alcohol and my exhaustion over the past few days. His peers could take away his degree, but they could never take away his inquiring mind. Andresen looked again at the time: he had just enough to collect his gear and get to Level 14 by eight o'clock.

Sweaty and out of breath, he met his former teaching assistant near the wire-mesh gates of the spaceport.

"Walter, what is this all about?" Andresen asked the young, dark-haired man. "You shouldn't be seen with me. It could ruin your academic career!"

"You think I want to be a part of that—" he tossed his head defiantly "—after what they did to you?"

"But becoming a professor is your goal, your dream!"

Walter gave him a bittersweet smile. "Working with you was my dream—a goal I reached. Now there's a way for me to pay you back for all you've taught me." He pressed a heavy rectangular card into Andresen's palm.

"What's this?" Andresen asked, holding it up to the light.

"A security pass for an asterover," Walter said simply, smiling. "My brother works at the spaceport here, and I just helped myself to one of his cards."

Andresen looked puzzled. "But why do I need this? I'm not going to run away from the likes of Glynn Georges.dos."

"Go find Buck Rogers, Merrill," Walter said softly, using both names for the first time.

"That's why you told me to bring field gear!" Andresen looked at his student with pride. Suddenly his face clouded with concern. "You could get in a great deal of trouble for this, Walter. I can't let you do it." He held the card out to him.

But Walter shook his head vigorously and pushed it away. "They can't easily trace it to me. And my brother can simply blame the theft on a coworker—for a while, anyway." He looked into Andresen's tired old eyes, pleading with him. "Merrill, this is all I can do to support you . . . without sacrificing everything. And I hate that!" He lowered his voice. "Please don't deny me this chance to do something for you. You know you want to go, too."

Andresen gave a sly smile. "An asterover, hmm? You couldn't have gotten something a little more luxurious?"

Walter grinned in relief. "She's stocked for at least two weeks." Suddenly he frowned. "Say, do you even know how to fly an asterover?"

Andresen smirked. "A bit late in the game to be asking such a crucial question, isn't it? Didn't I teach you better than that?" He laughed reassuringly. "I learned in my undergraduate days—athletic requirement. I don't suppose they've changed that much since then."

Student and mentor hugged each other awkwardly before Walter slipped away into the darkness. Through sheer bravado—and the security card—Andresen secured the asterover and made his way out of the spaceport. Though he had not flown an asterover since his undergraduate days, they were small, uncomplicated, and, as he'd predicted, had not changed much. Experimentation and near-collisions had quickly refreshed his memory.

Growls from his stomach broke Andresen from his reverie as his Salisbury steak made its way south. His eyes blurry from the strain of constant search, he turned his thoughts to what he knew of Anthony "Buck" Rogers, and how he'd learned it.

Months before his ill-fated article, Andresen had read of the discovery of the extremely primitive, but never-theless fully evolved, cybernetic personality program, Masterlink, and the digitally encoded personality of a twentieth century Soviet military man now known as Karkov.dos, inside a five-hundred-year-old weather satellite.

RAM had retrieved many other satellites, and it found nothing particularly distinctive about this one. Actually, no one important enough had bothered to study it much. But Andresen found Masterlink fasci-nating.

The composite Karkov-Masterlink program con-tained the personality, hopes, and aspirations of a man turned .dos who had spent the intervening five hun-dred years reliving and agonizing over the last moments of his mortal existence.

A vicious battle of wits and weapons in A.D. 1995 between Rogers and the Soviet man and computer had postponed global war for a number of years, but had effectively ended in a draw for its direct participants, since life as they had known it ended for them.

The battle was digitally etched into Masterlink's mind through Karkov, every detail—speeds, impacts—everything. Karkov had watched in horror as Buck Rogers's F-38 fighter streaked toward Masterlink's original satellite, which housed the Soviet and his com-puter. In the moments before impact, Masterlink had taken over and downloaded Karkov's mind into an onboard computer, then transmitted them both to a weather satellite far from the battle site. Karkov-Masterlink had remained hidden behind a flow of transmissions and wars for five hundred years, soaking up information and programs. Apparently the only time Masterlink had emerged was to vent its rage against anything American by altering hurricane reports to raise the death toll of United States citizens.

Andresen had returned to Masterlink time and

again, obsessed with the drama that was unfolding before him. Then, exactly three weeks ago, he had finished his lengthy, grueling calculations. Freezing the frame containing the fighter's impact with the satellite, he saw Rogers eject from his fighter plane, strapped to his seat in a small, vaguely bullet-shaped protective dome. Andresen had keyed in relevant factors: location of incident, speed of ejection, impact of different gravitational pulls, direction of ejection, particle drag, estimated weight, eclipses, comets, shooting stars, space battles—anything that he could think of that the capsule might have encountered in five hundred years. The computer juggled the variables, and Andresen knew approximately where to begin looking for the capsule containing his American astronaut, give or take a few hundred million miles.

And he was now very, very close to reaching his goal. According to his calculations, the capsule containing the astronaut would be somewhere in the Juno-Vesta arc, which was about one week out from Trader Vic's Trading Post near Juno; he was on day six.

Realistically he knew that even if Anthony Rogers was in the Asteroid Belt, the area was so vast that he might never find him, or at least not anytime soon. But Merrill Andresen was a patient man. If he conserved his fuel, he would be able to search for another sixteen days or so without refueling. If RAM didn't hang him for space piracy first. . . .

The thought caught the archaeologist off guard. He had been so wrapped up in his search that he had never once truly entertained the possibility that he would not find the astronaut here, or considered the consequences of his trip from RAM. The price for stealing the asterover would be his life, unless he returned with the evidence. Strangely, he found that the thought did not disturb him much. Either way, his torment soon would be over.

The asterover's sensors had been on almost continuously since leaving the trading post, just in case Andresen's calculations had been a little off. But there was so much junk floating around in the belt, from space battles and corporate waste dumping, that the sensor lights had been flashing continuously as well. Andresen had to check each lead, too, or risk missing the find of his—of any astroarchaeologist's—life.

"Anthony 'Buck' Rogers." Andresen unconsciously let the words slip from his lips as he continued to scan the debris, his sensors programmed to look for a bullet-shaped container roughly the size of a ceremonial coffin—ceremonial because bodies were no longer buried.

Andresen found himself wondering what the world had really been like. Not the textbook version, but the last time Buck Rogers had seen it. His last deeds had involved his battle with the Soviet, Karkov, and the artificial intelligence, Masterlink. Perhaps he'd been like any other human faced with death, and his last thoughts had been of friends and family.

Andresen had neither anymore. He'd lost his father, also a scientist, in a terraforming experiment in Mars's Boreal Sea. Some years before, his mother had had an old-fashioned heart attack, and they hadn't the money for either microsurgery or downloading her into an artificial intelligence. There was no one else. He had never taken the time to marry.

Andresen moved about in the crammed, technology-strewn bridge to microwave an instapot of rich Venusian coffee, grown in the domed gardens on the mountaintops of the Ishtar Plateau. Venusian coffee was an expensive rarity anywhere; he wondered how Trader Vic had managed to keep a supply way out in the asteroids, and at so reasonable a price. Andresen resolved to stop at the trading post on his return trip.

His dry eyes stared into the cold blue-black of space, and he struggled to stay awake. He knew he was pushing himself too hard, but his timetable could not be ignored. He took a long swallow of the rich, dark coffee and blinked. His sensors were scanning in the long shadow of nearby Vesta, and he was having a difficult time differentiating debris with his naked eyes. Though extended use gave him a headache, Andresen pressed his face into the ship's sight-enhancing monitor for the duration of Vesta's shadow. The asterover's beams cut a dim swath through the darkness, falling on the usual assortment of twisted metal, styropod containers, and other artificial waste products.

Suddenly the ship's lights pierced the edge of the asterover's shadow and Andresen's eyes were drawn to a shiny silver flash. He squinted and redirected his lights. Unexplainably, his pulse quickened. Refining the focus in the sight-enhancer in the area of the flash, he had his explanation. Pure exhilaration made his fingertips tingle.

"Oh, my god," he breathed, raising a hand to his mouth.

Half-tangled in metal debris from some space battle, a half-silver, half-Plexiglas capsule floated, emblazoned with the still crisply colorful red and white stripes and stars, the symbol of ancient Earth's America. Andresen could scarcely believe his eyes. His throat felt dry. He'd believed in its existence, had believed his research to be as accurate as could be, but discovering the capsule had seemed like something that would happen in the future. That future was now.

He stared at the beautiful, spiraling, metal-wrapped capsule for a long time, hearing in his head the mystical, atonal strains of his favorite Shaztikoff symphony. It seemed he had waited a lifetime for this moment. But, strangely, now that it was here, he felt more like a grave robber than a scientist. He shook the thought from his head. He was a scientist, after all, and he was acting purely in the interests of science.

Andresen stepped into the long, narrow docking area of the small asterover, past the sleep chambers, scanning the floor-to-ceiling computer-lined walls. Locating a clothing locker, he donned a smart space suit as a precaution against exposure to the vacuum of space, leaving the visor in his headgear up. Operating the asterover from the mini-bridge there, he maneuvered the ship so that its space arms could reach the spiraling capsule outside. In minutes, he had secured the capsule and pulled it into an entry chamber, making the transition from space to the climate-controlled asterover. He forced himself to wait five minutes before ejecting the capsule into the docking area.

Still tangled in metal, the capsule scraped across the floor of the dock and came to a stop. Anticipation and fear swallowed Andresen as he stepped to the capsule and ran loving hands over the gleaming hull, ice-cold from five hundred years in frigid space. There was too much metal surrounding the capsule to see inside, and dents dimpled the surface.

Locating a laser knife in a storage locker, he cut at the bands of metal. Slowly they fell away. Releasing the catch on what was known as a canopy, Merrill Andresen got his first glimpse of a twentieth century man through the tinted Plexiglas hatch of his ancient fighter cockpit.

Under the man's primitive radio helmet, his handsome features looked as if they had been chiseled from marble and were the blue-white color of the stone itself: Rogers, organs and all, was frozen like a slab of baby buffalo liver. His bulky silver space suit covered an obviously lean, muscular body, his strong hands on the controls of the ancient cockpit, an odd assortment of gauges and L.E.D. digital displays, in which he sat.

Andresen's eyes traveled up the man's hands to his arms. But he stopped, for something there caught his attention. He peered closer, not sure if what he saw there was real or imagined. Andresen gasped.

A crude cryogenics system. It had to be! Why else would there be catheters in his arms? But that meant. . . . Andresen nearly staggered as incredible thoughts flooded his mind. That meant that—

Buck Rogers might be brought back to life!

"Oh, my god," Andresen mumbled again. His hands shook as he fumbled around for the hatch's release mechanism. The door sprang open. Andresen stopped abruptly, realizing the magnitude of his dilemma. He had no way to keep Rogers frozen without great risk, and the astronaut could not simply thaw slowly. Thus Andresen had to revive him on the asterover.

But how? His medical background told him that if he "heated" Rogers too quickly, he would bake; if too slowly, then cell, brain, and organ damage would result.

"Think!" Andresen chided himself aloud, tearing at his own hair. He closed his eyes wearily and tried to channel his thoughts. "If only I could sleep for a few hours, I could think clearly again!" he cried. Sleep. Sleep chambers. Andresen's eye's flew open and locked on Plexiglas-domed medical beds in the asterover's docking area.

Sleep chambers were actually climate-controlled, life-support cryogenic chambers used for ship personnel on long space journeys: all the body's vital signs were drastically slowed and maintained, eliminating costly food and waste removal procedures, as well as the boredom of long space voyages. Widely used, they had become standard equipment on all ships, even asterovers not designed for lengthy trips.

Andresen knew that, even if he could lift him, he could not risk removing the icy astronaut from his cockpit: Rogers was as fragile as glass. But if he could somehow "hot-wire" the cockpit, or even the astronaut's enclosed space suit, he might just have a chance to bring Rogers back to life. It was worth a try.

Quickly but carefully dismantling the computer control center of one of the sleep chambers, Andresen compared the wiring to the wiring on the controls of the astronaut's cockpit. He thought of every combination possible, but the cockpit's wiring was so primitive, there was no chance for even temporary compatibility.

He had one more chance: The space suit. It looked more advanced than Andresen had expected or experienced in his research much before the twenty-third century. Someone had taken great care to use Rogers as a cryogenic guinea pig.

Locating the central circuits, Andresen discovered that, with a great deal of modification, he might just be able make a connection. He knew what he was attempting was a long shot, but he did not stop to think or to fear. He stood back only when he heard the telltale soft whine of an engaged computer.

Only then did he let himself sleep, slumped at the base of the artifact, like an ancient peasant before the icon of his god.

In his slumber, Andresen was oblivious to the sensor lights that flashed on his control center, or the ships they represented. If he'd known, he could have identified the sleek, quick RAM scout following him from Juno, or the ratty but efficient converted RAM cruiser with the NEO insignia circling around from Vesta.

But none of them could yet see the vast, dark ship farther out in the belt, from Barbarosa.

Andresen woke with a start. Flinging his hair from his face, he looked up from his folded arms and tried to remember where he was. He saw the titanium cockpit above him and he knew. What he didn't know was how long he'd been asleep. Rogers could take hours—days—even weeks—to revive. If he ever did.

Shaking the sleep from his limbs, Andresen stretched, stood, and looked into the cockpit. There appeared to be no change. Clenching his fists in frustration, Andresen turned away to compose himself and regroup. Had he been rash to try to wake the man without a full medical unit available? Had his revenge-driven mind cost him his find—and possibly a man his life?

Slowly he remembered that, dead or alive, Buck Rogers was quite a find. It was not what he had hoped for, but . . . A bank of lights on the docking bay door console lit up. Andresen ignored them—lights had been going off steadily for days, and he'd already found what he was looking for. A sudden noise from behind him nearly made him swallow his tongue.

It was the sound of a Teflon-coated space suit rubbing against the confines of a cockpit.

Andresen whirled around. Paler than snowy Martian mountain peaks, Anthony "Buck" Rogers was shifting slowly in the cockpit, still unconscious. Andresen could not believe his eyes, nor control the scream of joy that rose in his throat. "Welcome to the twenty-fifth century!" he croaked prematurely. Taking a great chance, he moved forward to lift the astronaut's visor: Andresen wanted to hear everything the twentieth century man had to say the second he could speak. He looked forward with great relish to giving Rogers answers to all the questions he would inevitably ask.

Suddenly, the small asterover bucked like a pack animal. Puzzled, Andresen scratched his recently turned white hair and looked toward the small console on the wall. "Probably just space debris." Andresen did not want to be distracted—he wanted to be present the second the twentieth century man awoke.

Suddenly he heard a noise he recognized. Someone was docking! Buck forgotten, he raced to the monitor and flipped it on. Two ships! A dark, much-patched cruiser, and a RAM scout. Fear clutched at the scientist's heart. Why hadn't he looked for signs of pursuit?

Two long, cylindrical docking tubes connected the vessels to Andresen's asterover. The archaeologist didn't even have time to snatch up a weapon before two dark, space-suited bodies simultaneously flew into the docking bay. Both rolled with practiced dexterity to their feet, holding weapons on the befuddled, unarmed professor.

"Wilma?"

"Hello, Kane." The more slender of the two flipped back her visor and smiled at the other, a tumble of red hair escaping the confines of her helmet and falling across her blue uniform. She was a pretty woman, but her mouth had a firm set to it. Andresen recognized on the left breast of her space suit the insignia of the New Earth Organization, the Earth-based terrorist group bent on overthrowing RAM.

The one called Kane removed his helmet entirely, revealing him to be a dark-haired man with a trimmed moustache above a cruel-looking mouth. "What are you doing here? How did you know about Rogers?"

"I think you know the answer to that: NEO," she said. "But I should ask you the same question."

Kane looked momentarily flustered. A curl of hair bobbed in front of his eyes.

"Don't tell me, I already know. This job for those RAM bastards was your ticket out of Australia," she said, not bothering to disguise her contempt and disappointment.

"Don't judge me too harshly, Wilma," said Kane evenly. "I am a free agent. I don't condemn you for staying with that dead-end group of NEO idealists."

The woman shook her head sadly. "We've gone through this before, Kane."

"Yes, we have," the man agreed, turning his attention to the trembling, confused Andresen, his mind again on business. "I'm going to take Rogers's body now, old man."

"Over my dead body," the woman said, stepping closer to the capsule, a laser knife in each hand, one directed toward Andresen, the other leveled at Kane.

"That can be arranged," Kane said, showing no fear. The silver-clad rogue stepped forward and readjusted his aim for Wilma. "What's another body—pretty as it is—one way or another?" The two locked eyes in challenge.

Andresen's mind finally broke through the confusion. These two weren't here to arrest him at all—they were going to steal Buck Rogers from him! And they didn't even know he was alive! Outrage overcame his senses and he threw himself toward the nearest of the two, the woman. "He's mine! I've suffered to find him, and he's mine!"

"Shut up, and stay away from her!" Kane yelled, but Andresen was beyond reason. He reached out for Wilma. Usually as tough as nails, the woman could not bring herself to attack the unarmed, harmless old scientist. But Kane could. Two bullets tore through Merrill Andresen's left side, and he crumpled, trailing blood, to the floor.

"You didn't have to kill him," Wilma said, keeping her eye on Kane.

"He was in my way."

"Well, if it isn't my favorite couple in the solar system," came a menacing, rumbling voice from behind them.

Kane and Wilma jumped in surprise at the familiar, unexpected voice. It belonged to Black Barney. The notorious pirate stood near the hatch door. He'd somehow entered the docking area as quietly as a mouse while Kane and Wilma had traded barbs and wistful glances. Both inwardly cursed for having let personal matters mar their professional performance. The odds for either of them retrieving Buck Rogers's body had dropped dramatically.

"Who are you working for this time?" Wilma asked Barney pointedly.

"You should know, Wilma, that no matter who my employer is, I always work for myself." Barney's genetically enhanced eyes shone merrily above his protective faceplate as he watched their irritation. "I should thank you for cleaning things up for me, but, instead, I'll just take my package and go." He leveled his gaze at Wilma. "Let's call this an interest payment for breaking you out of that torture chamber, Calypso."

"Let's not. I more than repaid that business deal in full," Wilma said coldly. She readied her laser knives.

"Barney, how do you propel your own big body around with such a little brain?" Kane added, redirecting his own laser knife.

Barney's beady eyes dropped in lazy, amused acknowledgment. "We're using laser knives today, are we?" Barney rumbled, seeing Wilma's knives. "I'm game." Two vibrating, blue knives suddenly whistled in his hands.

"I never would have thought you the playful type, Barney," Wilma said, clenching her knives more tightly.

"I'm not."

Smiling in anticipation, Kane holstered the gun he had used on Andresen and added another knife to his arsenal. "To the winner, the spoils," he said, giving a mock salute.

Wilma responded only by bringing one of her knives up to block. The three began a vicious three-corner game of tag, which none of them took lightly.

On the floor, the last beats of Merrill Andresen's heart pumped his lifeblood into a red pool by his face. He thought it funny that, in his last moments, he thought of nothing at all.

Vaguely, he heard a battle rage above him. He was momentarily distracted from his lack of thoughts by a sudden cry of pain and the words "Rogers is gone! But who's got him?"

Merrill Andresen was beyond caring. One second more and he was beyond the cold, uncaring world of the twenty-fifth century. Buck Rogers would just have to learn to fight his own battles there.

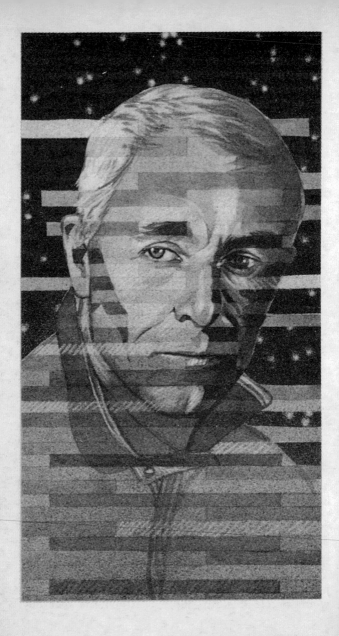

THE ADVERSARY

Jerry Oltion

O nce, when Simund Holzerhein was eleven years old, he had cut off his own foot just to see what it would be like. Now, a hundred and sixty years later, he couldn't remember doing it, and it bothered him.

He remembered his motivations clearly enough, and even the events leading up to the act. He had been learning about the development of restoration genetics and he'd wanted to tour the facilities used to regrow damaged body parts, but his university program—which he'd always suspected of having a bug in its extracurricular projects permissions algorithm—had denied him the afternoon off to do it. The young Holzerhein, not willing to accept the computer's dictate, had considered his options carefully and had finally decided that without permission his best chance of getting into the lab was as a patient. So without even bothering to finish his biohistory lesson first, he had gone into his father's study and gotten a hunting laser out of the display case, taken it and a telephone outside so he wouldn't get the study messy, and used the laser to slice off his foot just above the ankle. Then, to ensure that they wouldn't be able to simply reattach the foot but would have to go through the entire regeneration procedure with him, he had methodically sliced the foot into pieces and cooked them.

Only then did he call for an ambulance.

Holzerhein remembered all that with the memory of one who had read the police report many times. What he didn't remember was how he had felt during it all. Had he cried? Screamed? Taken it with the fascinated calm that only an eleven-year-old could summon? How badly had it hurt, and had the inside tour of a regeneration lab been worth the pain and the trouble he'd undoubtedly gotten into? He could remember none of that.

Damned biochemical storage devices! Why couldn't they remember the important bits? It was worse than frustrating; it was criminal. This inability to remember had actually been designed into the wetware, one of the brain's little tricks to protect the fragile psyche from too-clear memories of trauma. It had done a complete memwipe, forgetting not only the cutting off of his foot, but almost a month's time afterward. The next memory that Holzerhein could definitely place in sequence was of attending his mother's funeral, and he was already walking by then.

Disgusted, he flipped his brain completely out of the matrix. Let it stew, he thought. He was better off without the idiot thing. Maybe sensory deprivation right after a memscan would shake something loose, but he doubted it. Those memories were gone.

He pulled the palace into being around him, centered on the library, with the fire lit in the hearth and stacks of half-read books on the low table beside his reading chair. For the sheer perversity of it he began cranking up the realism, bringing up titles on all the books, even the ones in the shelves, pulling in the sound of the fire, the smell of it, the feel of its heat on his suntanned forearms (forearms and the rest of his body as they had been in his midtwenties: healthy, muscular, ready for action); going further to create the clock ticking on the mantel (trace of dust there—have to get after the maid), the sensuous, soft silkiness of genetically altered moleskin upholstery on the chair, and the still silkier fur of a calico kitten all afuzz on his lap. Purring.

"So what do you think?" he asked the kitten. "Am I losing it?"

The kitten held no opinion. Since it was a construct of Holzerhein's own downloaded personality, and Holzerhein himself had no answer to that question, it wasn't surprising.

Perhaps he should ask a real kitten.

He had a real kitten, of course. A real kitten and a real reading chair before a real fireplace in a real library in a real palace high on the forested slopes of Pavonis. He seldom used them. That he had them was all that mattered. Having them freed him to use the matrix without lowering himself. In fact, having the reality available and not deigning to use it gave his life in the matrix an almost illicit flavor, a tinge of disdainful opulence befitting the power behind the corporate empire.

The kitten turned twice around on his lap before curling up against his arm. It licked its forepaws a few times, stretched them out to push against his hand, then lowered its head onto them and closed its eyes. The flames continued to crackle in the fireplace, casting their flickering light out upon the hearth and upon the kitten's soft fur.

What did it matter which world he inhabited? Life's experiences were all just input for the mind, and the sensory information in the matrix was just as valid as that in the real world. To the charge—familiar to those who chose to live subjectively—that life in a matrix was too sterile, too controlled, Holzerhein could only observe with wry humor that he controlled much of objective reality as well; why should this be any different?

A rustle of movement in the doorway drew his attention from the flames. Rodney entered the library like a wraith, coming to stand three paces from the right arm of Holzerhein's chair. "You have a board meeting in five minutes, sir," he said.

Holzerhein glanced at the mantel clock: five till two. "Ah, yes, the puppet show," he replied.

Rodney nodded slowly. "May I help you prepare, sir?"

"That won't be necessary. Thank you, Rodney."

Rodney nodded again, pivoted on his heel, and left the room as silently as he had arrived. Holzerhein watched him go until the doorjamb eclipsed the black-suited tickler-program-cum-butler.

Where does Rodney go when he leaves my universe? he asked himself. Where do laps go when you stand up?

Not simply an academic question, the latter, considering that a perfectly comfortable—although electronic—kitten was about to wonder the same thing.

Four minutes.

A century ago, when the Russo-American Mercantile was still a fledgling corporation, preparing for board meetings had been a full-time occupation. Keeping projects running smoothly, juggling the corporation's interests against interplanetary politics, and anticipating and outmaneuvering those who inevitably tried to take his place at the top had been Holzerhein's entire life.

Even fifty years ago, after running the still-expanding corporation had become second nature, he had at least spent a few hours before each meeting going over the topics the board was to cover.

But it was already becoming dull, repetitive, and uninteresting, even then. Holzerhein had eventually turned the day-to-day management of the company over to subordinates, retaining the title of chairman and veto power over the board's activities, but removing himself from the petty squabbling. When his health had begun to fail and he'd opted for downloading, he had withdrawn from company politics even more. Now he attended the meetings merely to ensure that the board didn't do anything overly stupid, and preparation required little more than loading the minutes of the previous meeting back into active memory.

Paradoxically, he remembered the heady excitement of the early years as if they were yesterday. The power struggles, the business coups—those memories hadn't been blocked by an overprotective brain. And like all the memories that he could wrest from that recalcitrant blob of flesh, he had duplicated them in the matrix where they would forever be as fresh as the day they were imprinted.

Memories of power. He had always likened power to a drug, one that affected one's perception of the universe, let one see the bigger picture that others— stuck in their tiny lives—couldn't begin to comprehend. Was that why he felt this peculiar lethargy now? Had his tolerance for the drug grown so strong that it no longer gave him the rush he craved?

Three minutes.

With a sigh he began to access the minutes of the last meeting, but a leftover shred of his previous thought made him pause. Slowly, he began to grin. Sure. Why not? Symbolism was all, here in the matrix.

He stood, lifting the kitten from his disappearing lap and placing it gently on the still-warm cushion. It stretched and buried its nose beneath its tail, and Holzerhein turned away toward the library shelves.

He found the volume he wanted at the end of a long row of identical leather-bound books. The title embossed in gilt letters on its spine read simply *Minutes of RAM board meetings, 2455-2456.* A crisp thousand-dollar bill marked a place about two-thirds of the way through.

Holzerhein took the book to a reading stand, opened it at the mark, and laid it flat. Still wearing his unnatural grin, he removed the bill and rolled it into a narrow tube, placed the tube against his left nostril, leaned down toward the left-hand page, and inhaled. The words came right up, their sharp edges stinging his sinuses when they hit. Scraps of memory began racing toward their proper niches in his electronic mind.

He did the right-hand page with his right nostril, then closed his eyes and let the library go where laps went.

○   ○   ○   ○   ○

The board room was high atop a spire on one or another wing of the gigantic, sprawling RAM corporate palace. Simund no longer cared just where it was in space; he needed only its location in the matrix to be there instantly. Riding elevators and walking corridors were for meat bodies.

He arrived right on the tick. Everyone else had already arrived, of course. None of them were willing to risk Holzerhein's ire by showing up late, which, given the uncertainties inherent in physical travel, meant that they all showed up at least five minutes early. They usually spent the time arguing over policy and trying to convince one another to support this or that pet project, but their conversation always dwindled to a halt when Holzerhein's holographic image flickered into being at the head of the table.

At board meetings—as in any of his dealings with the outside world—Holzerhein's physical image was that of a man in his late sixties. What was left of his hair was dirty white; his face was giving in to wrinkles, and his muscles had begun to sag from disuse. He could have appeared any way he saw fit, as the

midtwenties version of himself that he was in the
matrix or as someone else entirely, even as a woman,
but he saw no point in playing dress-up for a bunch of
subordinates. Besides, he had attended enough board
meetings to know that the figure of authority at the
table was usually the old man, and he could also see
no point in stretching the other board members' fee-
ble imaginations to accept anything else.

Holzerhein's input and output devices were digitally processed so that his point of view coincided with
his image. His center of vision was at the hologram's
eye level; his hearing was binaural and located at his
ears; even his speech was mixed ventriloquially so
that it issued from his holographic mouth. Even so,
the result was not quite the same as having a normal
human standing there, neither for Holzerhein nor for
the people before whom he appeared. To meat people,
Holzerhein was not completely substantial. Bright
objects behind him still shone through. Also, his
speech was too crisp and precise, and his eyes too
steady.

From Holzerhein's point of view the outside world
looked unreal as well. Digital input made everything
come at him as a stream of numbers to reconstruct
into an image or a sound, with the result that edges
were too sharply bounded and sounds were too clean.
Also, with digital processing Holzerhein had access
to image enhancement techniques that an ordinary
human hadn't. The effect was that of watching an
animated cartoon through a super-surveyor's transit,
with information on range, horizontal and vertical
angles, elevations and the like always available to
him. That information was keyed to the intensity of
his gaze; the more intently he looked at something,
the more data the system gave him on it.

Terendon Freil, vice chairman of the board, nodded
toward Holzerhein. "Glad you could make it, sir," he
said.

Holzerhein let his image show about a quarter-watt of sardonic grin. As if he had a whole lot of other pressing things to do. Even if he had, he'd have just copied himself for the duration of the meeting, but he hadn't had to do that for years.

Terendon called the meeting to order with his usual meticulous attention to the rules of order. He was a fanatic for detail, a nit-picker obsessed with propriety. Holzerhein hated his guts, but he didn't let that affect his dealings with the man. Obsessive nit-pickers made good vice chairmen, and Holzerhein had learned to ignore him. By the time Terendon had dispensed with the reading of the minutes, Holzerhein was already looking out the window.

The entire wall was glass, affording an unobstructed view out over Pavonis (2.17 kilometers to ground level, his augmented senses told him). Pavonis the mountain (7.63 kilometers distant) was an extinct volcano on the Martian equator, from atop which the Pavonis Space Elevator rose into synchronous orbit. Pavonis the city had grown around the base of the mountain, extending vertically along its slopes until the rarefied air forced a stop to upward expansion and extending horizontally beyond the horizon. The city reached upward even out there, its slender spires rising to heights (tallest: 3.1 kilometers) that would have been impossible in Earth's higher gravity. Air cars wove their way through the forest of towers, while on the ground, trees carpeted the city in real forest. It was easily the most beautiful city in the solar system, made all the more beautiful to Holzerhein by the knowledge that he owned it.

Near the top of one of the nearby towers (15.2 meters below the top of a 1.78 kilometer tower, and Holzerhein was beginning to weary of the precision with which he saw it), a light blinked. It was irregular, like sunlight reflecting off a fluttering silver banner, save that no silver banner was in evidence. Just the light, blinking hypnotically across the way (0.83 kilometers distant, and he considered looking away long enough to disengage the signal processors, but for some reason he didn't).

Holzerhein turned his attention, if not his eyes, back inside. He heard Terendon call for current project reports and someone—Roando Valmar—gave an update on the scheduled cometary impact in the south polar sea. Pirates had attacked the comet during its passage through the asteroid belt, trying, no doubt, to fragment the nucleus so they could steal the water ice and other volatiles at their leisure, but RAM warships had beaten them back, and the comet was still intact and on course. It had since rounded the sun and was now on its outward approach, toward Mars. Impact would be in six weeks. Original estimates of increase in planetary water level and air pressure after impact were still valid.

There was another project report, this one from Neola Price on the ongoing plan to quell the continuously troublesome population of Earth. That project, according to Price, was proceeding smoothly. The obedience drugs were nearly ready for dispersal, and the thought-regulating satellite was even now being placed in orbit. Once the entire population had become addicted to the drug, possibly in as little as half a year, the satellite would be activated and Earth would cease to be a problem.

"Discussion?" Terendon asked. "Jander?"

Jander Solien, administrator of holdings beyond the Asteroid Belt, leaned forward. "I still think we're making a big mistake here," he said. "Drugging an entire planetary population is not only a direct expense; it'll drain profits in the long run as well. Production losses will far outweigh any savings from reduced police action."

"I agree," Terendon said. "You can't push a zombie as hard as greed will make a man push himself. Free trade is the way to maximize profits."

Roando Valmar's laugh was a harsh bark. "Ha! Free trade. The only thing a free Earth would trade with us is missiles. They're a bloodthirsty pack of fools. Look what they did to their own planet, just fighting among themselves. No, if they're to be of any use to us at all, it'll be under our administration."

"Under our thumb, you mean," Terendon said.

"You object? You'd rather continue this state of permanent uprising than enforce a peaceful settlement?"

"I object to the method, not the motive. As Jander has pointed out, it will be expensive."

"It will be efficient," Holzerhein said.

Roando had been about to reply again; he stopped with his mouth half open. Every face in the room turned toward Holzerhein.

He didn't even look away from the window. He didn't need to; he had their attention. This was the first time he'd spoken to them in months. He kept his eyes fixed on the light—still blinking hypnotically atop the tower beyond—as he said, "Earth has been an unpredictable quantity for too long. Its reluctance to fit into the scheme of things has cost us far more than mere money. It has slowed our expansion, kept us from achieving all that we set out to do. Direct control over the populace is the most efficient option, for us, as well as for them."

The blinking light suddenly became just a blinking light. Whatever mysterious attraction it had held for him ended as suddenly as if a switch had been thrown. It continued to blink, but Holzerhein was no longer interested.

He looked down to the board table, to the eight people arranged around it, and said, "As for free trade, your little argument demonstrates the inefficiency inherent in free anything. Eventually it ceases to be amusing." He let his statement hang like a bomb in the air while he looked back out the window.

Terendon evidently had to catch his breath. It took a moment before he said, "Thank you for your input, sir."

Holzerhein ignored him. Something else had drawn his attention, a sensation he hadn't felt since he'd been downloaded. Since before that, really, because he'd been hooked to life-support and catheterized for years before his body had finally died. It was the sensation of having a full bladder.

Which was absolutely ridiculous. He didn't even have a bladder anymore, much less a full one. The only organic part left was his brain, and he had left that switched out.

Okay, it wasn't a bladder, then, but something needed emptying. Evidently he was just interpreting it in familiar terms.

Holzerhein turned his attention back into the matrix, not bothering to build up a phantom reality this time but simply tracing the sensation along the channels and addresses of his various peripheral devices until he found its source. It was a little like typing at a keyboard; an experienced operator could do it with eyes open or closed; it didn't really matter, as long as one knew what one was doing.

Holzerhein knew what he was doing. He found the source of irritation in microseconds: It was an overflowing information buffer, one he used for storing data going to and from his brain. That made sense; there was always some information flow into and out of it, no matter how little he actually used the thing. When he'd switched it out of the matrix, the flow had stopped, and the data had begun to stack up in the buffer until it couldn't hold any more.

That was easy enough to fix. He could simply open the link again. He was about to do just that when he noticed the other peculiarity about the way the overflow felt.

It felt just like the access attempts he'd been making earlier in the day, when he'd been trying to drag those childhood memories out of permanent storage. Whatever was in the buffer was trying to load directly into the same area.

The human brain was a lousy piece of architecture for the function of thinking, but it did at least have a hierarchy of input levels, and Holzerhein had used his often enough to know that information going into the brain usually went through a temporary storage cycle in the conscious mind before getting tucked away into permanent memory. Pulling something directly out of permanent memory without going through the conscious level was rare enough, but putting something in that way was even rarer. One could do it under hypnosis, or in moments of shock, but not while sitting at a board meeting and lecturing idiots about the follies of freedom.

Oh, yes, the board meeting. He'd been gone nearly a quarter of a second already; if he spent much longer away, the others would notice that his holographic image had frozen. Not a big deal, usually, but he had just made a point and they would be watching him even more closely now than usual.

Easy to fix. He pushed out into the matrix, clearing room for himself, then took a turn back toward the meeting room while at the same time turning once again toward the overflowing buffer. The two copies went their separate ways.

The Holzerhein in the matrix began sifting through the buffer, and the deeper he got into it the stranger its contents became. It wasn't a memory at all. It was more like a program, as if Rodney, the butler, had stumbled down a wrong pathway and wound up in Holzerhein's brain, instead of in his own little niche in the matrix.

A program. Running there in a memory buffer, trying to get into his brain. If Holzerhein had had sweat glands, he would have broken into a sweat. The thing was a virus program! It had to be.

Carefully, with the finesse of a person disarming a bomb, he scanned along the code, discerning its major modules as he went along. There, in the first section, was the loader, the part that was even now trying to burrow its way into his subconscious mind, pulling along the rest of the program where it would lie, unnoticed, in wait for the proper moment to— what?

A long module, self-replicating. The virus section. Designed to copy itself over and over again in the host brain until it overwhelmed every last neuron.

Another module, essentially the same, but set to spread throughout the matrix.

Another module, small, little more than a timing tick to set the moment when every neuron in the brain and every bit in the matrix would fire or flip simultaneously.

And the last module, a trigger, keyed to the code word "Holzheimer."

Holzerhein chuckled a tight little electronic chuckle when he found that. Someone wanted him very dead, and the entire RAM matrix along with him, but even that wasn't enough for them. They wanted him to go out with an insult.

Who would want such a thing? No, tackle that one the easy way: who wouldn't want it?

He chuckled again, there in the matrix. He couldn't think of a single person.

How had they sent it? That was harder to answer. The matrix was heavily guarded against viral infection; it wasn't a simple matter of copying it in and setting it loose. Whoever had sent it had had to have found an unguarded pathway, and that was supposed to be impossible.

Someone had found one. And Holzerhein would have to find it, too, if only to set a guard on it in the future.

It was simple enough to wipe out the virus, but first he copied it into safe storage, cutting it into pieces as he copied it and walling it off behind layer upon layer of security. He would take a closer look at it later and see if he could determine its author, but now he had other things to do.

He moved back up the line to the board meeting, merged with his other self, and remembered what had gone on in his absence. Not a whole lot; he had been gone less than ten seconds. Terendon had meekly called for more discussion of the Earth project, and Price had begun speaking about overcoming the technical difficulties involved in deploying the satellite in a crowded and hostile Earth orbit.

Outside the window the light still winked seductively atop its tower. Holzerhein felt himself drawn toward it once more, focusing, as if it were a hypnotist's metronome and he about to go under. What was it about that light?

It was blinking in code, that was what. And the pattern looked very familiar.

With that, he realized that he had found his unguarded pathway into the matrix. His own senses, feeding directly into his electronic consciousness and also into his brain, were completely uncensored. An optically loaded program could grab his attention with a hypnotic hook, then feed directly into his mind, and from there to any part of the matrix it wanted.

Except those parts that were shut off.

It was a trick that could only work once. The program's hypnotic loader wouldn't let him look away from the light, but he could and did set up a filter between senses and mind to strip out the program code from his visual input, then he split again and went to see if the sender had left any traces of his identity with the light. It had to be a board member—who else would know that he spent most of his time at the meetings staring out the window?—but which one was it?

He didn't expect to find any clues, and he didn't. When he entered the tower and projected himself into the room that the light was coming from, he found it empty save for the table before the window upon which sat a simple message laser aimed at the RAM corporation board room. The laser was connected to a hand-held dumb computer that blindly spat out the contents of a single data chip, over and over. It was about as sophisticated a murder weapon as a club, and even less traceable to its owner.

No matter; he would know who it was soon enough. The first person to call him "Holzheimer" would be in for a nasty surprise. He didn't know quite what, yet, but he was sure he could think of something.

$$\bigcirc \quad \bigcirc \quad \bigcirc \quad \bigcirc \quad \bigcirc$$

The meeting continued, seven of the eight other members unaware that anything untoward was going on at all. Unless it was a conspiracy, of course. There was always that possibility.

Holzerhein felt his traveling half join back again, and as a single entity he watched each of the board members as the meeting progressed. Damn, why had he had to make that unsubtle threat about freedom? They were all acting as if they'd gotten caught with their hands in the cookie jar. Jander and Terendon were especially nervous, but that could be either guilt or simple terror at having Holzerhein disagree with them. Nervousness alone wasn't enough to finger either of them.

Price was babbling on with her report on the satellite. "There's still a lot of junk to clean out of our chosen orbit, but we'll have it clear by the time we need it. One of the crews did make an interesting find, when they scanned for debris in high-inclination elliptical orbits tangential to ours: an ancient atmospheric satellite. It's a real museum piece, nearly five hundred years old, but the real find was the program it held. It's evidently some kind of primitive artificial intelligence. They don't have the facilities to access it, but apparently it's still conscious."

Holzerhein hadn't been paying attention to the words as much as the other board members' reactions to them, but at the mention of the artificial intelligence he felt a stirring of interest. He asked, "Still awake, after five hundred years?"

Price looked startled. Was Holzerhein going to turn on her now? She licked her lips hesitantly, then said, "Uh, yes, sir. There is evidence of electro-neural activity, at any rate."

A five-hundred-year-old artificial intelligence. To Holzerhein, who had spent the last fifty years trying to adapt to *being* an A.I., the implications were staggering. Computers had still been completely digital back then; they'd had no holographic memory, no superconducting junctions, no organic interfaces at all. The entire thing would have to have been hardwired and digitally programmed. What kind of intelligence would you get under those conditions? Did the ancient programmers know anything about the nature of intelligence that modern cyberpsychologists had forgotten? What kind of subjective universe would such an A.I. inhabit? And after living in it all this time, what kind of improvements would it have discovered?

It might have evolved a better subjective universe than the RAM matrix.

That thought was both exciting and intolerable. *Nobody* had a better *anything* than Simund Holzerhein. And if by chance someone—or something—discovered one, then it was Holzerhein's duty to make it his own.

"Bring it to me when the downloaded personality is

ready," he said aloud.

"Sir?"

"Have the artificial intelligence brought to me. There might be some important clues to be uncovered in it."

"Yes, sir. May I ask—"

"No, you may not. And now, if we're quite through with our little afternoon chat, I think it's time we all got back to work. Any objections to that? No? Meeting adjourned, then."

○ ○ ○ ○ ○

Back in the matrix, Holzerhein was about to reconstruct his study when he remembered that he had left his brain disconnected. He was tempted to leave it that way, but he supposed he might as well hook it up while he was thinking about it. And . . . hmm . . . yes, maybe the deep-storage routine in that virus program could provide a hint for pulling those reluctant childhood memories back out. It would be worth a try.

His brain access address was one of the most familiar of all the matrix addresses. Holzerhein's wish to reconnect it was enough to move his focus of consciousness there and accomplish the deed. The connection joined, and—

—and he was neck-deep in stinging ants and earwigs and spiders and centipedes, struggling feebly with arms of lead to keep his head afloat in the sea of insects. He couldn't scream for fear of opening his mouth to the bugs—can't let them inside, the inner body hasn't yet been violated—but he soon discovered when the slithering and the stinging pain became too great to endure that he couldn't scream anyway. His vocal apparatus was as sluggish as his arms.

It didn't matter; the ants had found his nose and

had already worked their way into his head, now empty and echoing where his brain should have been. Holzerhein could hear them rattling around in there, crawling randomly in the dark recesses, working deeper, and spreading out into his body, a body larger inside than out, infinite in scope, with unlimited breeding space for more and more and more bugs—

If it had been a door he slammed, he would have torn it off its hinges. Electro-neural switches weren't as satisfying in their solidity, but they were more certain than doors; with the brain once again out of the circuit, it was *out*, completely. Phantom insects, their sustaining power gone, skittered away to die in the matrix, while Holzerhein's consciousness slowly recovered from the blow.

Stupid, he thought. It was obvious what had happened. Every brain had a nightmare generator built into it, and his was no exception. In the controlled environment of the matrix, that aspect of his organic origin had seldom made its presence known, and never with more than a twinge of anxiety before protective circuitry damped the signals, but never before had he left his brain cut off entirely from outside stimuli, either. Left in sensory deprivation, its nightmares had gone into positive feedback and strengthened until they were the only thoughts remaining.

He was going to need help. Those were not the sort of nightmares that would flee with the turning on of a light. But where would he find the kind of help he needed? He hadn't used a doctor in decades.

Well, he knew where doctors were kept; he supposed it would be logical to start there. That decided, Holzerhein flipped to the medical complex, dropped back into holographic form, and planted himself in front of the first white-smocked, warm body he saw.

"I have a neurological emergency. Tell me—"

"I'm sorry, sir, but artificial constructs are serviced

through data processing, not medical—"

"Artificial, hell! I am Simund Holzerhein, I've got an organic brain that's hallucinating, and you've got about five seconds to do something about it before I burn you down where you stand! Is that clear?" Just in case it wasn't, Holzerhein narrowed the focus on the projector generating his image until it became a beam centered on the woman's forehead (1.27 meters distant, increasing as she backed away). It wasn't focused tightly enough to burn, nor did it have enough power to do more than blister the skin if it had been, but it would be warm enough to give her a scare.

Holzerhein watched her get the message, then watched her realize who he was. "I—of course, sir. At once." She spoke into her pager: "Code zero, code zero neurological. Head tech away team to the departure area immediately." To Holzerhein she said, "They'll be waiting for you there, sir."

"They'd better be." He killed the holo projectors, effectively winking out of existence for her, and, after a millisecond's stop in the mediplex's directory, appeared in the emergency departure room. The away team wasn't waiting, but within seconds they began assembling, and in only a minute or so more, half a dozen techs were in transit to the palace. For meat bodies, Holzerhein had to admit that they were good.

He split again, briefing them on the situation from the skimmer's control panel monitor while he went ahead to arrange their passage through palace security. In minutes, he was merged again and ushering them through the massive doors into the chamber that housed his brain.

The first one through the door paused when he saw what awaited him, and the rest piled into him and into each other like coils of a compressed spring. In a less frantic moment Holzerhein would have been pleased at their reaction, but just this once he regretted all the gold and jewel-studded fixtures that made the place look like a treasure chamber.

"Move it!" he shouted. His amplified voice shook the room, and shook the techs into action. They rushed inside to the ornate case housing Holzerhein's brain, quickly found the standard access jacks amid all the finery, and plugged in their diagnostic instruments. Monitors began howling their warning sirens, then quieted one by one as the techs made adjustments to the hallucinating brain. When all was silent again, one of the techs summoned the courage to face Holzerhein and say, "We've got it— uh, you—stabilized, sir. You can access again."

Holzerhein did. His perception might have changed slightly, might have become a bit more indistinct, but otherwise nothing seemed different with the brain on line again.

"Any permanent damage?"

The tech took a deep breath. "No, sir. You're liable to be a little jumpy for a while, until the weight of everyday events pushes the experience back into deeper memory, but nothing seems damaged. My advice is to use it as much as you can for the next few days, give it plenty of sensory input, and keep a close watch over it when you put it to sleep."

"I'll do that."

"Good. I think we've done all we need to do here, then. Give us a call if anything more comes up."

"I will."

Holzerhein watched them pack up and go, somehow amused. He liked that tech. The guy had decided not to be intimidated anymore, and from then on he hadn't been. A person like that could be useful.

He activated the security alarms behind the departing techs, then returned to the matrix. He remembered that he had intended to examine the virus program before all that business with the ants, so rather than recreate the palace around him, he went straight to where he had stored the program and began searching through the pieces.

The first thing he discovered about it was the author. She hadn't signed it, but she might as well have; it had Ardala's deviousness written all over it. That puzzled Holzerhein more than any other finding would have. Of all the people who could benefit by killing him, Ardala would benefit least. She was a Valmar, child of the clan that had intermarried with the Holzerheins since the corporation's beginnings on Earth, and as such, she had a vested interest in the status quo.

Could old Roando have put her up to it? Not a chance. If Holzerhein died, then Terendon, not Roando, would inherit the chairmanship of the board, and those two had never gotten along. So Roando had a stake in the status quo as well.

Terendon would be the obvious choice, since he stood to gain directly from Holzerhein's demise, but Terendon could never have convinced Ardala to give him the program. He and she were bitter enemies, not out of any family allegiance to Roando but because she believed that the board position Terendon held should rightfully go to her. She was always trying to undermine him (all the board members, for that matter, even the officious, toadying Neola Price), even to the point of accusing him of being a NEO plant, but his record was as clean as vacuum. Cleaner than hers, for that matter.

Could it be her? Had she been saving the program for an eventual coup, just covering her options, in case the situation changed? That would be like her. Then somebody stole it from her and put it to use without her knowledge. Hah. A person who could crack Ardala's security could have written the virus himself.

Holzerhein had another look at the thing. Maybe it wasn't Ardala's; maybe his first impression had been wrong. He examined the infiltration routine again, the memory storage routine, the retrieval routine—and there he made another discovery. It wouldn't have worked.

Oh, it might have worked, the same way a building held up by repulsor might work to crush a person if he didn't see it suspended overhead first, but that's about the level of ignorance it presumed on Holzerhein's part. There was no provision to camouflage the program once it had lodged in long-term memory, no attempt to make it blend in with the rest of the fuzzy, half-forgotten childhood recollections. In the symbolic world of pure thought, it would be the only sharp-edged, shiny object in a five-dimensional fog. Anybody who looked into their past with any regularity would see it shining there like a beacon, and anybody who knew Holzerhein knew that he spent most of his time doing just that.

Which meant that whoever had loosed the virus program on him had violated Holzerhein's cardinal rule of battle: Know your enemy.

What kind of incompetent was he dealing with? A soon-to-be-dead one, as soon as whoever it was spoke the trigger word, but even that thought did little to cheer him. What challenge was there in besting an idiot?

What challenge was there *anywhere* anymore? He hadn't had an adversary worthy of his attention since RAM had moved its center of operations to Mars.

The closest thing he had to an adversary was the New Earth Organization commission, that group of Terran malcontents who objected to RAM's domination from afar, but even they were little more than an annoyance. They were even useful in their own way, by drawing Earth's troublemakers into an easily infiltrated organization, where he could watch over them.

Of course, there were lunars and habbers and pirates and belters and the myriad other half-human races genetically modified to live in the rest of the solar system, none of whom held any special fondness for RAM, but neither did they have the resources to finance a war. Even in an unlikely union they would pose little more than a strategic problem. Mars—and RAM, and through it Holzerhein—held the real power in the solar system, and RAM had the experience to use it. With a minimum of effort they could hang on to it for a long time to come. Holzerhein knew that for a fact; he had set it up that way.

And now, in the matrix, pieces of virus program scattered around him, he found himself wondering for the first time if he had lived long enough.

What more was there to live for? Conquering the rest of the solar system? It would be a long, tedious, and utterly predictable job, nothing more.

Holzerhein felt the sudden urge to reassemble the virus, load it into his brain, and shout "Holzheimer" himself, but it was only a passing urge. That was too easy, too.

Instead he wiped it from the matrix entirely, flipped to the real palace, and in holographic form took a stroll among the flowers in the garden. His brain needed sensory stimulation, so the doctor said.

○ ○ ○ ○ ○

Two days later, Ardala paid him a visit. Holzerhein was again in the real palace, in his study (reading a twenty third century epic thriller in which a gang leader in one of Earth's more squalid arcologies developed a stardrive from irradiated, precollapse computer parts and led humanity out of the cradle to conquer the stars), when Rodney entered the study in holographic form and announced, "The lady Ardala to see you, sir."

Holzerhein set the book—also a hologram—down on the reading table and stood as Ardala entered the room. She looked stunning, as always: her long black

hair cascading down over her shoulders and framing
her exquisitely carved face, and the rest of her
dressed in a flowing wrap that shifted to hide and
reveal just enough to tantalize. Genetic engineering
had reached its peak in her, and Holzerhein was sorry that her charms were wasted on him. The closer he
looked, the more his senses told him, but only in
terms of compound curve data and total volume,
information which was useless to anyone but her
dressmaker.

Still, she was pretty, even at a glance. And she was
just as deadly as she was pretty, he knew. He hadn't
forgotten the virus program.

"Come in, my dear," he said, waving her toward a
couch. "What brings you to see an old man on such a
lovely afternoon?"

"Information," she said with a slight smile. "What
else?"

What else indeed? Information was Ardala's stock
in trade. She maintained one of the best data
networks—and some of the best spies—outside of
Holzerhein's own.

"Offering or asking?"

"Offering." She sat in the proffered chair and shook
her head to settle her hair more seductively around
her.

"Price?" he asked, wondering if this would be the
time when she asked outright for a position on the
board of directors. It would be like her to make such a
request so soon after a failed attempt on his life—an
attempt she may or may not have been in on.

She looked away, out the window. Was that guilty
reluctance to meet Holzerhein's eyes, or just her natural coquettishness? He couldn't tell.

"Call it a gift," she said.

Everything, even gifts—no, especially gifts—had a
price. Both Holzerhein and Ardala knew the price of
a gift: a return gift or an eventual favor. To accept

would bind him, but then it was the receiver who
determined a gift's value, and the value of the return.
Gifts were always fair trades.

"Thank you," he said.

Ardala looked back inside the study, fixed her spar-
kling eyes on Holzerhein's holographic ones, and
said, "You have, or soon will have in your possession
a five-hundred-year-old satellite harboring an artificial intelligence."

"Hmm, yes, I knew that already."

Ardala was nonplused. "I'll bet you didn't know that
your people found this satellite several months ago
and left it in storage, thinking it unimportant. Or that
a Martian University professor thought otherwise,
accessed the satellite's database, and published in the
New Martian Science Journal that, based on information garnered from the satellite, he believed he could
locate the cyrogenically frozen body of an American
pilot from the twentieth century."

Simund looked pained for a split second. "No, I did
not know that." But Price obviously had, and was
covering her tail for not having told me sooner,
Simund thought.

"The pilot's name is Anthony Rogers."

Holzerhein scanned his memory, both organic and
matrix, for a reason why that name should be important, but he found none.

"Anthony Rogers?"

"Anthony—better known as Buck—Rogers is the
man credited with saving Earth from total thermo-
nuclear war at the end of the twentieth century."

Holzerhein manufactured an incredulous expression. "One man? How?"

Ardala's grin was as real as Holzerhein's incredu-
lity was artificial. She enjoyed having information
he didn't. She said, "By destroying a control satellite
for a space-based weapons system. A weapons system
that would in time have given its owners complete

control of Earth. If he hadn't destroyed it, the only alternative to world domination would have been war."

"This would be the same satellite that—?"

"The same. Not destroyed, but merely knocked out of orbit, taking Rogers with it."

"Oho." Holzerhein paused to sift through the implications of that, but Ardala voiced them anyway.

"Which explains," she said, "why RAM found it while cleaning up an orbit for our own control satellite. Similar functions, similar orbits, to which the twentieth century version was returning in its elliptical path after all this time."

"You're saying . . ."

"I'm saying that now might not be a good time to bring back an ancient hero who made his name shooting down world domination control satellites."

Holzerhein looked thoughtful while he ran a probability check on the consequences. "You're right," he said after a moment. "News of this Rogers would almost certainly stir up trouble if word of it got out. So, what are you suggesting? That he may be revived?"

"No, almost certainly not. After researching the topic, I would call it a next to impossible operation. But he still holds incredible potential as a martyr for NEO organizers, and holds . . . other value, for me." Her eyes glittered.

Oho. Now the true reason for Ardala's sudden helpfulness came clear. She wasn't maneuvering for a position on the board after all. At least not directly. "You want his body."

She shifted her position on the couch with the sinuous grace of a jungle cat. "Purely for research, of course," said Ardala.

So this was the return gift she wanted. Should he give it to her? He couldn't see why not. It was the weather satellite's A.I. that interested Holzerhein anyway.

"He's yours," he said simply.

"Thank you." She stood, smiling just enough to let him see she was pleased, and moved silently from the room. Holzerhein watched her go, still wondering whether or not she had written the virus program, and if she had, how this business with the fighter pilot could have anything to do with it. He could see no connection, but that didn't mean there wasn't one.

Nor did his suspicion mean that there was. It was easy to grow paranoid when you'd uncovered only part of a plot.

O O O O O

Holzerhein was thinking about what he should do about Price, or whoever had engineered the deception, when the courier from Earth arrived, and he was distracted away from thoughts of retribution. Holzerhein didn't care about the ancient pilot anyway, not really. He could be just as single-minded as Ardala, and his interest was in the artificial intelligence.

He took it straight to the computer lab, where technicians poked, prodded, measured, scanned, and otherwise began learning what they could about it. Holzerhein's first impression was that it looked more like a big, primitive fuel tank than it did a computerized brain, but upon closer inspection it began to look a little more interesting. Its cylindrical surface (4.73 meters long and 2.47 meters in diameter) was covered with solar cells, which the technicians kept bathed in an Earth-intensity spotlight until they could discover where to plug in their own power source. Altitude control rockets stuck out from the sides at regular ninety-degree intervals, and camera lenses and communications antennae pocked the surface on top and bottom and every 120 degrees around the middle, providing full spherical coverage.

The cameras and antennae were primitive, certainly, but at least the thing could see and hear. Holzerhein's first fear—that it had gone mad centuries ago from sensory deprivation—seemed unlikely. And as for the design, he reminded himself that it was the interior landscape, not the exterior, that he was interested in.

A technician studying a socket beneath one of the cameras began plugging a circuit analyzer's test leads into it. He had five or six of them connected, when the instrument's display began to flicker madly and an eerily inflectionless voice coming from the speaker below the monitor said something like, "*Vy ponimayetye?*"

The technician jerked back. "What the hell was that?"

The screen flickered again, then locked on the signal and displayed a horizontal line across the middle. The line erupted into jagged spikes just as the voice spoke again.

"Do you understand me now?"

The technician was unsure whether to address the camera or the aberrant circuit analyzer. He settled on the camera, and by implication the intelligence behind it. "Uh, yeah, sure," he said. "Are, um, are you okay in there?"

"As well as can be expected."

"Do you know what happened to you?"

"Unable to determine temporal referent."

The tech, flustered, turned to the other techs, who were now gathering in a semicircle around him. Holzerhein interposed himself between them and the camera. "I'll handle this. Who are you?" he demanded.

There was a long pause while the camera lens telescoped in and back out again in an attempt to focus on the hologram, then, "I am Masterlink. I am commander in chief of Union of Soviet Socialist Republics' spaceborne strategic defense network. Serial number: one."

"Union of Soviet—? You're from Russia?"

"I am Masterlink, commander in chief of Union of Soviet Socialist Republics' spaceborne strategic defense network. Serial number: one."

"We got that. I am Simund Holzerhein, director of RAM, formerly known as the Russo-American Mercantile. I control what was once your home nation."

"You lie."

For a brief moment, Holzerhein wanted to fry the A.I. for its affront, but he suppressed his anger. Learn about it first; there would be plenty of time to destroy it later if that turned out to be necessary.

"I speak the truth. There have been many changes since your time. You have been adrift in high orbit for four and a half centuries. Do you realize that?"

The A.I. remained silent for long seconds before it relented and said, "Four hundred sixty-five years, seven months, nineteen days. Yes, I was aware of the passage of time. Unfortunately my radio receiver failed only forty years after the . . . explosion . . . that knocked me out of orbit. I was not aware that the capitalists had won."

"Neither was I."

"You speak English. You speak of Russo-American *Mercantile*. That alone tells me that capitalism, and thus the American capitalists, have won."

"My maternal grandfather, Pyotr Alekseyevich Yevshenko, would be unhappy to hear you say that."

Masterlink seemed to be thinking that over. When it spoke again, it said, "I must learn more about you."

"And I you. You—" he spoke to the assembled techs "—link this intelligence into the matrix." To Masterlink he said, "We will talk again in more comfortable surroundings when you have made the transfer."

○ ○ ○ ○ ○

Half an hour later, he found himself entertaining in the matrix version of the palace, Rodney serving some kind of greasy little Russian hors d'oeuvre he called *pirozhki* while Holzerhein and Masterlink sat before the fire and toasted one another's health and bolted shots of some unpronounceable brand of vodka. None of it was any more substantial than the two of them, but Rodney had insisted that social forms must still be observed, and that the quickest way to win a Russian's confidence was to eat and drink with him. Holzerhein trusted Rodney's judgment in that; Rodney was, after all, a professional butler.

And surprisingly enough, Holzerhein found that he enjoyed playing the host. It had been decades since he'd done so, and he suddenly realized how much he missed it. Much of the satisfaction in amassing personal wealth and power lay in showing it off. With that realization came the memory of his first air car, given him at an age when most of his peers had still been riding bicycles, and the envious stares he had drawn while flying it. He could have kissed Masterlink for triggering such a glorious memory, but he didn't suppose Masterlink would understand, having never had a childhood of his own to remember.

Masterlink was full of surprises all the same. After a few false starts, he had adapted quickly to the matrix, but Holzerhein's hope that the A.I. had evolved a better subjective universe than his own had died while he was still leading the way from the computer lab to the palace, when Masterlink said in awe, "So much room! I had barely room enough to store my own thoughts!"

After that, Holzerhein had half expected to see it duplicate its satellite form there in the study, or perhaps construct a shiny metallic humanoid body to match its voice, but it had evidently taken its cue from Holzerhein and used the matrix's capabilities to build a human persona, a hologram, for itself. It sat across from him as a man in his late forties or early fifties, his face square-featured beneath close-cut hair, dressed in a green military uniform decorated with a single medal of honor. His voice had become more human over the course of the conversation, and though he was still guarded in his answers he was gradually opening up.

On one topic, he became very revealing indeed.

"Buck Rogers still exists?" Masterlink's theatrical jerk when Holzerhein mentioned that bit of news nearly tipped over his chair.

Holzerhein nodded. "There is a slim possibility. One of my people is in the process of picking him up, if he isn't alive."

Masterlink poured himself another shot of vodka, downed it, and poured himself yet another. "For all this time, I had thought myself adrift alone," he said, leaning back in his chair. "All this time, revenge has been my sustenance, the truth that let me live with the shame of failing the motherland in—other ways." He frowned, then, still frowning, reached up to his breast and ripped the single medal from his uniform and cast it into the fireplace. "My duty is not yet done."

"Oh, come now. That battle is over."

"My battle with Buck Rogers will never be over until he is surely dead."

"He's mine now," Holzerhein reminded him. Actually he was Ardala's, but that was a quibble.

"You will not stand between me and honor."

"Look, we might have a use for him, a use that'll make RAM's position even stronger. Since RAM's all that's left of your precious motherland, I'd think that would satisfy your honor even better than confirming his death, now wouldn't it?"

Masterlink thought it over, the firelight that glinted off his eyes giving him a feral look. It was overdone to the point of melodrama, but that little detail delighted Holzerhein nonetheless. It was the first time the matrix had held such a detail not of his own creation.

"What would you do with Rogers, to make an asset of him?"

"We could use him to disarm the dissidents."

"How would you do that?"

"By propping him up as a martyr. We would let him draw them into a group, then crush them once and for all."

Masterlink shook his head. "Were he alive, he would never join you."

"You sound mighty sure of that."

"He was a fanatical American imperialist. He would no more aid your organization than he would mine. Certainly he would never betray his own people. Even as a capitalist, he was not without honor."

Something about Masterlink's statement caught at Holzerhein, made him pause in his argument, to wonder at the sudden twinge of envy he felt for the Russian A.I. Envy? Why should he envy Masterlink?

Certainly not for his sense of honor. Honor was for idealists. Besides that, it was impractical. Holzerhein had tried and discarded it as a guiding principle more than a century ago. No, he didn't envy Masterlink his honor, but he certainly envied him something.

"You do not know Rogers," Masterlink was saying. "If you did, you would not speak of bringing him to your world. You would give him to me immediately, while it is still in your power to do so."

Holzerhein smiled involuntarily. He had it. What he envied was Masterlink's sense of purpose. The A.I. had crossed five hundred years of time; by rights he should be lost, grasping for support wherever he could find it, but here he sat in Holzerhein's study, acting as if he owned the place and demanding that his enemy be delivered to him.

"Your choice of words is interesting," Holzerhein said. "You say 'give him to me' rather than simply 'destroy him.' Your obligation to honor notwithstanding, I wonder if you don't want him alive."

"I want him alive long enough to exact my revenge from him, yes. He is not yours to kill, but mine."

"He is mine. I could ensure his death whenever I wish, and his head impaled on one of your antennae. Then where would you be?"

"Then honor would compel me to kill you in his stead."

Holzerhein felt a brief thrill run through him at that bold statement. No one had had the courage to say such a thing to him for decades. No one had had the power to back up such a statement, but neither did Masterlink and that hadn't stopped him. Holzerhein smiled. He was getting to like this A.I.

But first things first. If Masterlink managed to get to Rogers without Holzerhein's permission, any kind of real partnership would be impossible. Holzerhein would be able to get over it, but he didn't think Masterlink could. That idiot sense of honor wouldn't let him. He would be expecting retaliation, or at least resentment, and he would be paranoid until it came. The only way to prevent that was to keep him away from Rogers until they got this personal vendetta of his straightened out.

Splitting was more difficult when the matrix was in reality mode, but Holzerhein had come up with a method. He closed his eyes, imagined his center of consciousness as a focus of energy just behind the bridge of his nose, then shrunk that focus tighter and tighter until he had a singularity. The singularity bridged a connection into the matrix again, and he poured a duplicate of himself through the bridge.

And now to see about Rogers. Leaving a marker behind, so he could find the singularity entry point again, he flipped to the matrix core, then out along the communications lines into Ardala's programming space. From there he identified the line with the most activity on it and followed a data clump outward until he found himself off planet in her private ship's computer. It wasn't as roomy as in the RAM matrix, but it was big enough to hold him, though there were very few places in it where he could go without breaking through her security first. Fortunately most people left a "doorbell" in their systems for visitors such as Holzerhein, and Ardala was no exception. He rang it.

Ardala came on line, audio only. "Who is it?"

"Your Uncle Simund."

"Oh, hello!"

Was there tension in her voice? "Will you give me video?"

"Sorry, I'm not decent."

"You're always decent, and I'm a hologram anyway."

"And you're also a lecher."

"True," Holzerhein admitted. He considered crashing her security, not simply to peek, but more importantly to see what else she might be hiding, but he decided against it. Ardala's security would be tough to crack. Doing it would almost certainly damage her system, and this really wasn't important enough to get her angry at him. Besides, she probably *wasn't* clothed. Ardala seldom was.

"Have you made arrangements to pick up Rogers?"

"Of course." Again, that tension in her voice.

"Good. I've got the A.I. in the matrix with me, and he's evidently Rogers's sworn enemy. He's getting kind of belligerent about it, so I wanted to warn you to keep Rogers under electronic, as well as physical, guard, all right?"

"I—certainly."

"All right then. I'll be back to talk to him later, when I'm done with Masterlink."

"Thank you. I'll have him ready for you." Ardala's formality convinced Simund she was up to something. He had learned that she would reveal all to him in her own time. One never pushed things with his niece.

"Good." He broke the connection and headed back into the RAM matrix to learn more about Masterlink. He knew that the other copy of himself was doing just that even now, that there was really no rush to rejoin, but somehow the advantages of duality never seemed to offset the uncomfortable feeling that someone—even if it was himself—was learning something that he wasn't privy to.

He flipped back to the study, found the marker he had left, and opened the pathway to his other self, but instead of reaching his own consciousness, he found himself mired instead in a seething, malevolent expanse of conflicting imagery. Sensory data of all descriptions churned in a stew of confusion: visual pieces of study grafted haphazardly onto the smell of vodka, overrun by the feel of moleskin upholstery and the sound of half a flame crackling in the clock. Pieces of light flitted about in short-circuited frenzy, reflecting off smells and sounds and tastes, cavorting through the fragments of pseudoreality until they encountered the wide, gaping hole into the matrix where they flashed into dimensionless data and were gone.

A wrist and forearm floated by, fractured cleanly at the ends like a glass rod snapped in two. Holzerhein recognized the end of the sleeve as his own, and now that he paid attention he could spot fragments of his voice, a tuft of hair, and there, an eyeball smeared with the taste of *pirozhki*. He waded into the fragments, sweeping them aside, searching through them like a person searching for the last piece of merchandise in a box full of packing chips, but there was not a trace of Masterlink anywhere.

Just the gaping hole.

So Masterlink had gotten angry and torn up the place, alternate Holzerhein and all. Had it been something he said?

He started searching for word fragments, but he had barely begun when the intruder alarm at the central directory flared like the shot of pain from a suddenly drilled tooth.

$$\bigcirc \ \bigcirc \ \bigcirc \ \bigcirc \ \bigcirc$$

Security had held, but Masterlink had left his mark. The last bit of imagery from the study, a three-quarters fragment of Holzerhein's head, stared lifelessly out from the central directory's main access link.

A declaration of war, or just a warning? Holzerhein wasn't sure. Masterlink must have known he couldn't kill Holzerhein that easily. Even if Holzerhein hadn't been running doubled at the moment, he had backups stashed all through the matrix; that was a standard precaution for any data entity. To kill Holzerhein, Masterlink would have to wipe out not only the running copy but all of the backups, and that was simply impossible for an A.I. to do. Some of Holzerhein's backups were in read-only memory, and he had other, even more secure forms elsewhere. He even had backups off planet. He might lose a few weeks, even months if the more recent backups were destroyed, but nothing short of complete destruction of the entire interplanetary matrix could kill Holzerhein completely. Masterlink might not have known that, but he had to have known that killing one copy wouldn't do significant damage.

So it was most likely a gesture, a warning to satisfy his electronic honor. Well, Holzerhein knew about gestures, too.

Just in case it *was* war, he split, split again, and split again, rushing off down every major line in search of his newfound adversary, but one copy made its way to the computer lab where Masterlink's physical body still rested in its cradle with test instruments plugged into every socket. The spotlights had been turned off, now that the techs had tapped into the power line.

It was a simple matter to slip into the power supply and reset its output from the low, circuit-sustaining level the satellite required to a searing thousand volts. Holzerhein accessed a camera just in time to see flame shoot from within the cylindrical case. There must have been a dead-man switch wired into the altitude jet fuel tanks, because a moment later the entire computer lab erupted in flame. It was a more violent demonstration than he had intended, but he didn't care. He'd made his point.

He didn't expect that to be the end of Masterlink, nor was he disappointed. The shutdowns started almost immediately, whole sections of the matrix winking out of existence as they went off line. Safeties began springing up, limiting access to the remaining sections, but that worked against Masterlink more than it did against Holzerhein. Holzerhein had lived in the matrix for years; he knew alternate paths in and out of anywhere. Now he began throwing up still more barriers, walling off the sources of disturbances until each was isolated in its own micro-universe. A simple purge operation wiped each one clean of data, and of the local copy of Masterlink that was causing the trouble.

But at least one copy was still at large, traveling ahead of Holzerhein and spreading still more destruction in its wake. Copy upon copy of Holzerhein advanced in a wave after it, branching at every junction and checking every peripheral on the way, sealing off access and pushing the intruders ahead of them until they finally reached the chasm separating the local network from the long-range computers that continued the matrix on into interplanetary space. This last was a physical barrier, erected by the speed of light itself. The matrix continued beyond it, but light-speed lag limited its use to one-way communication beyond near-Mars orbit. Holzerhein had just returned from Ardala's ship along this path, but now he and his copies stopped their advance, for there on the edge waited Masterlink.

There was just one of him. Holzerhein linked together and tried moving to surround him, to cut him off from his only escape before pressing a direct attack, but Masterlink moved still closer to the edge, poised to jump. Holzerhein backed off enough to give him room. Another Holzerhein slipped away, heading back the way they'd come.

There in the matrix, without visual referents or any other reality mode to lend form to their battle, their confrontation at the brink was more like the advance of mold cultures in a Petri dish than like two people facing one another with weapons drawn. Electronic feelers interpenetrated each other's ranges of influence, were tolerated for communication but not for any other action.

"It's not polite to kill your host and trash his living room," Holzerhein said.

Masterlink replied, "It is not polite to deny a guest a reasonable request."

"I didn't find it reasonable."

"Unfortunate."

"So is your present situation. What do you plan to do now?"

"My position is unchanged. I must kill Buck Rogers. If you kill him first, or through your negligence allow him to be killed, I will take my vengeance upon you."

"Bravado," Holzerhein said. "Russians were great ones for bravado in the face of defeat."

"You have won nothing. I have nearly destroyed your matrix, and I can destroy you as well if you force my hand."

"Consider it forced." Even as he spoke, Holzerhein made his move, rushing forward as if to surround the A.I. He didn't expect to succeed at it, but neither did he expect what happened. Masterlink should have leaped off into the void, and he did, but he left behind a suicide copy. The instant his other self was away, the suicide copy met Holzerhein's advance with a furious attack of its own. It lunged through the communications channels, going straight for Holzerhein's cognitive functions, rending and tearing without regard for its own survival. Holzerhein felt parts of himself die under the onslaught, taking parts of Masterlink with them, but dying all the same. He tried to expand, to duplicate himself, but those abilities were already gone. All he could do was fight back in the same way, sacrificing pieces of himself to kill pieces of his enemy.

Within milliseconds the battle had degenerated to two mindless automatons bent on mutual destruction for reasons neither could remember. It was a battle that could have no winner, but still they fought on.

○　○　○　○　○

At Space Traffic Control, a somewhat different scene unfolded. The copy of Holzerhein that had slipped away only moments before had duplicated again, once more surrounding all the data paths leading to a long-range jump point—the other side of the one at which he and Masterlink were even now confronting one other. This time he had a few extra milliseconds to set up security barriers on all the local paths, and gain control of the transceiver generating the long-range path. He waited patiently, knowing that his other self would eventually make his move, and that Masterlink would only have one place to go.

Sure enough, here he came. Holzerhein waited until the A.I. was completely received, then shut off the tranceiver, trapping him in the Traffic Control computer. He didn't risk opening a two-way communications channel, but instead sent a one-way message in to his captive.

"Bravado," he said again.

O O O O O

Later, with Masterlink safely put away in a well-guarded corner of the matrix and restoration programs already repairing the damage he had caused, Holzerhein relaxed in his study and considered the events of the day. He was once again in hologram form in his real study, the other one still not restored from backup.

All in all, it had been an exciting afternoon, the most exciting one he had had in years, but now that it was over he felt let down. Masterlink had provided him with an unexpected challenge, but Holzerhein had won too easily. Fighting Masterlink had been good sport, nothing more.

And the discovery beforehand that Masterlink had no subjective universe at all for him to explore was now doubly disappointing. What did he have to look forward to tomorrow, and the days after that? Even Masterlink, locked in his peripheral, had more to look forward to than Holzerhein did, for he could at least scheme for eventual revenge. Holzerhein didn't even have that.

Should he let Masterlink go again? Give him a bigger head start and see if the hunt would last longer? Or perhaps he should kill this Rogers and then let

Masterlink go, see how well he could back up his threat. That might be interesting.

While he thought about it, he watched the dust particles drifting through a shaft of sunlight (average particle diameter 0.125 millimeter, his senses informed him). In all his time in the matrix, he had never thought to include that particular detail. It was discouraging, that realization, because it underscored the basic inadequacy that he had always sensed in his electronic existence. Subjective reality was simply not as rich or as spontaneous as the real thing. Even another subjective mind like Masterlink's couldn't come up with the sort of complex, detailed surprises that the simplest real situation could present.

No, Masterlink as an all-out enemy would be no better than what he was now. Their battle would be just another battle like the last one, lasting maybe an hour instead of a few minutes, but it would hold no surprises.

Besides, it would be just that: a battle. Holzerhein wasn't a soldier, he was a leader, and leaders didn't fight battles. Leaders fought wars. Leaders fought other leaders in wars, using soldiers as their weapons. And strategy, of course. That was where the fun came in.

But who could he find to fight a war with? That was where he'd gotten stalled the last time he'd thought about this. There was simply nobody who could put up a good enough fight against all the resources of RAM. NEO, the New Earth Organization, was the best bet, but it was just a bunch of soldiers. They needed a leader before they would be a worthy adversary for Holzerhein.

Ha! Send them Masterlink!

It was a good idea, but it wouldn't work. NEO was a rebel organization; they chose who they wanted for their leader, and they would never choose an ancient

Russian space weapons computer for a leader, no
matter how deviously he presented it to them. Rebel
organizations chose heroes for their leaders, not—

It hit him that fast. Heroes. If they needed a hero,
well, he just might have one on hand.

Maybe not. He hadn't actually seen Rogers; Ardala
had to have him by now. Or his body. He could be
alive but insane from freezing effects in his brain, or
sick from any of a thousand other biological problems. Damn the frailties of meat bodies! Why did his
sudden hope have to rest on something so fragile?

Holzerhein winked out of the palace like a burst
bubble, streaked through the matrix to the directory,
and thence to Ardala's ship. He'd said he would give
her some time, but that was before he'd realized
Rogers's potential. Even if nothing was wrong with
Rogers's health, Holzerhein had to talk with Ardala.
He couldn't let her turn him into an ally!

$$\circ \quad \circ \quad \circ \quad \circ \quad \circ$$

"He escaped?" he found himself asking a few
moments later.

Ardala had finally given him video after he'd
threatened to trash her system, and from there it had
only been a short time before he'd pulled the truth
out of her.

"It would appear so, yes."

"So that means he's alive!" Holzerhein's voice rose
with excitement. "But how did he manage an escape?"

Ardala's expression was a blend of annoyance and
fear. "I don't know. I wasn't on board when it happened," she said vaguely. Simund didn't have to
know that she'd sent Wilma Deering, an NEO colonel, in her stead. It would be a bit difficult to explain,
she thought to herself. "All I know is that NEO was
involved somehow, that I will have more precise
answers for you soon."

"NEO?" Holzerhein asked, incredulous. "NEO has Buck Rogers?"

"I'm not certain, but I think so, yes," Ardala admitted. She seemed to collapse in on herself, waiting for the explosion.

"That's beautiful!"

"What?"

"Wonderful! Beyond my wildest dreams! I'd thought we would have to arrange a rescue after I'd taught him to properly hate us, but this is even better. He'll learn to hate us from the best enemies we've got."

"You don't have to be sarcastic."

"No, no, I'm not." Holzerhein could hardly contain himself. He felt like a kid at Christmas receiving an unexpected and lavish gift. "Really. This is just what I wanted. You couldn't have done better. Thank you. I owe you a favor. Oh, this is going to be grand!" He excused himself, leaving Ardala still confused. He had so much to do!

$$\bigcirc \quad \bigcirc \quad \bigcirc \quad \bigcirc \quad \bigcirc$$

Holzerhein spent the next few days preparing for war. He knew that the first battle would be soon, because if it weren't, then the war would be over as soon as RAM got its thought-control satellite on line, and the traitor on the board of directors—almost certainly an NEO spy, considering how quickly they had acted to take Rogers—would have warned them about that. So, the battle would be soon, and since NEO was unlikely to tell Holzerhein exactly what they intended to do, he needed to prepare for any eventuality.

Foremost was the matter of backups. NEO was bound to raid the palace even if their major strike was elsewhere, and they were bound to do some damage, damage that could even affect Holzerhein in the matrix if they happened to hit any of the major data transfer lines. He wanted to be sure that all of his backups were as current as possible before then, so that even in a worst-case scenario he would at least still remember who he was fighting when he came back on line.

Not that he knew Rogers well at all. Rogers was still practically a complete mystery, a name and a reputation only. By going to battle with him the way he was, Holzerhein was violating his own know-your-enemy directive, but he really had no other choice. Sometimes the exigencies of war dictated taking risks that one wouldn't otherwise take.

But one could always minimize the risks in other ways. With that in mind, Holzerhein updated his backup copies in the matrix, tucked copies away in various stand-alone peripherals, radioed encoded copies to RAM archives off planet, and just in case the *real* worst-case scenario—that NEO won the war in the first battle—happened, he even provided for that.

Rogers and Masterlink had given him the idea, actually. If they could return after nearly five centuries, to continue their lives and their battles, then Holzerhein could see no reason why he couldn't do the same. Launching himself in a satellite was a poor idea, though, with the amount of debris floating around out there these days, so Holzerhein had come up with something a little more likely to be noticed. More likely to be noticed, and also less likely to arouse suspicion in his eventual discoverers as to the true nature of their find.

At the summit of Mons Olympus, the largest volcano on Mars, was a crater some sixty kilometers across. It was a volcanic caldera formed by the collapse of material into the molten pit of lava at the center before it had hardened, and as such it held some of the tallest sheer cliffs in the solar system. It was a favorite tourist attraction, and because of the opportunity the volcano gave for examining the interior composition of the planet, it was also under continual scientific scrutiny. It was no problem for Holzerhein to commandeer a remote-control drilling laser, fly it to an as-yet-unexplored cliff face, and spend an afternoon carving the bit pattern for his own consciousness into the rock. Now it was a time bomb, waiting for the inevitable scientific expedition to find the strange pattern of cuts, photograph it, and store the photo in their database, where Holzerhein would come to life once again.

That taken care of, he returned to Pavonis to see what news his spies had been able to uncover concerning NEO's activities after acquiring Buck Rogers. Kelth Smirnoff, his chief security attachment officer on Earth, delivered the message.

"Something interesting is happening," the spymaster's code-reconstructed and electronically altered voice said from the middle of a swirling green blob of holo interference. "Don't know what's causing it, but NEO is mobilizing for an attack. By the equipment they're readying, it looks like a long-range raid, quick in and right back out again, and the word is that their target is Venus. Could be; Venus is just about at conjunction right now, but I don't have a clue what they'd be after there. I'm working on it. Kelth out."

Holzerhein sent an acknowledgment, and told him nothing. That was clever of NEO to plant the Venus rumor; he saw no reason to blow such a beautiful deception. Not that he was going to act on the rumor—he wasn't going to actively help NEO with their plan—but he would give them that much. As a gift to Rogers. Beyond that, however, he was on his own.

Holzerhein's spy reports continued to come in, but they got stranger and stranger. The NEO ships had indeed taken off for Venus, passing through the tail of the comet that was even now rounding its way toward eventual impact with the Martian south pole, but shortly after that encounter they had all changed course and accelerated at top speed toward the outer solar system. The only possible planetary encounter along their vector was Uranus, but it would be impossible for small craft such as theirs to make it that far. Yet Uranus seemed to be their destination.

Two days later, the entire company encountered the notorious Black Barney's pirate fleet and were captured down to the last ship. It made no sense. They were supposed to be attacking RAM, not losing their entire force to some profiteering clone warrior halfway across the solar system. What had they thought they were going to accomplish way out there? And what was Holzerhein going to do for a war now?

He spent the next week alternately fuming about the disruption to his plans and wondering if he could have missed some vital clue, but as the time drew on and his spies intercepted more and more "what do we do now?" messages between the remaining NEO outposts, he reluctantly came to believe that the rebel organization had just committed suicide.

Good grief, was he going to have to switch sides and fight RAM himself just to find a worthy adversary?

O O O O O

That turned out not to be the case.

O O O O O

It happened thus:

The terraforming comet had finally wound its way through the inner solar system and was making its final approach toward Mars. Meteorologists had predicted—with one hundred percent certainty—

severe storms over the entire planet, coupled with moderate to severe quake activity. The entire planetary population had dug in, battened down the hatches, and were waiting for it to blow over as they had done every few years since the terraforming project had begun, but Holzerhein had directed his consciousness up to the top of the elevator and was watching with the scientific teams as the comet slowed in its approach, curved around under Mars's gravitational pull, and drifted majestically through the last few thousand kilometers toward impact.

It was a beautiful sight. It was two o'clock in the morning at the base of the elevator in Pavonis, and most of the planet was dark from their viewpoint at the top. The comet was an immense apparition of light sweeping past, its tail already millions of miles beyond them, it's head a tiny irregular disk that grew steadily brighter as it drew closer. It was a small comet as comets go, but to someone dangling from a thread attached to the planet that it was about to smash into, it looked like the wrath of a particularly vengeful god.

Holzerhein was barely aware of the traffic controller's voice calling off the distances, but something made him pay attention when the controller said, "Now entering upper planetary defense shield layer. Shield temporarily down ... making transit ... upper shield restored. Entering midlevel shield zone . . . shield down ... making transit ... restored ... lower shield down ... making transit ... restored. Impact in fifteen, fourteen. . . ."

And suddenly, out of the comet's nucleus, streaked a dozen, two dozen fierce points of light, curving hard away from the impact point, accelerating northward around the curve of the planet and diving into the atmosphere to leave two dozen bright meteor trails in the night sky. Two dozen streaks pointed straight at the base of the Pavonis Space Elevator!

The comet struck. Icy cold instantly became a hot ring of flame spewing outward, the shock wave racing after the tiny escaped specks. Both the polar ocean and the cometary nucleus flashed into steam, the steam cloud rising high above the atmosphere before gravity began folding it back to rain down upon the entire southern hemisphere.

Holzerhein hardly noticed. All his attention was on the tiny specks of light, specks that were without a doubt the NEO attack force, already decelerating toward Pavonis and the RAM corporate palace.

He'd been tricked! The ships heading to Uranus had been decoys, nothing but shells with drives and pilots to draw his attention while the real attack force hid deep in the comet's ice and waited for RAM to bring them down through their own defense shielding. Ingenious! It had to be Rogers's plan. Holzerhein would never have expected such a devious plan from NEO—obviously hadn't expected anything of the sort, because they'd caught him completely by surprise. He hadn't a single patrol in the sky, and the ones on the ground were all waiting to ride out the quakes along with everybody else.

He turned to the traffic controller, who had also seen the invading craft peel away from the comet at the last moment, and shouted, "Full military alert! Get our fighters in there!"

"But sir, the shock wave will—"

"I said get them in there, now! Pavonis is under attack!"

Holzerhein dropped back into the matrix, flipped to the palace, and immediately encountered Rodney. Without reality mode to give him substance, the butler program was merely an annoying presence in the matrix next to Holzerhein, a presence that said, "Excuse me, sir, but you have an urgent communication from Terendon Freil."

Terendon? What the hell could Terendon want?

Whatever it was, it would have to wait. "Tell him I'm busy now."

"He said it was an emergency."

"*This* is an emergency. I'll talk to him later. Now get out of my way!" Holzerhein pushed past the butler and on into the matrix, heading directly to the palace guard address.

He didn't bother with announcing himself. He simply accessed the holo projector in the guard captain's office and blossomed into being before his desk. The captain's reflexes were good; he had his gun out and had fired a beam right through Holzerhein's chest before his image was fully formed. Holzerhein ignored it. "NEO forces are about to attack the palace," he said. "Mobilize the guard, and get ready for air strikes. Do you understand?"

The captain swallowed hard as he holstered his pistol. "Yes, sir." He turned toward his command console and began shouting orders, but Holzerhein was already gone.

He began accessing camera after camera, perimeter sensor after perimeter sensor, in an effort to locate the NEO attack force, but he needn't have bothered. They announced their presence in an unmistakably direct manner: by blasting their way straight in through the roof of the relatively unshielded south wing and landing their fighters directly in the rubble. Holzerhein tried to access cameras there, but the ships' blasts had taken out more than just the roof. The matrix was dead all around them.

The guard hadn't arrived yet. From a vantage point across the courtyard Holzerhein could see into the wing through one of the collapsed walls. Only six or eight fighters were there, with maybe twenty people; the others must have stayed hidden in reserve or were engaging RAM's fighters and drawing them away from the palace. If there *were* any RAM fighters. With the shock wave from the impact traveling through the atmosphere in its deadly sweep, roiling the upper atmosphere especially, it might be impossible for fighters from Deimos military base to get through. No doubt NEO had planned on just that.

But what were they doing with such a small force? In the south wing Holzerhein could see flashes and hear the sharp crackle of hand weapons, and he knew that the four or five guardsmen who had been on regular duty there were dying under heavy fire. He watched, helpless, as the attackers swept on into the main building. Behind them, their fighters rose back into the night sky, leaving the south wing empty.

Was Rogers with them? Holzerhein couldn't tell. His enhanced vision was hampered by the darkness, and he was too far away to hear words.

He accessed the guard captain's console just long enough to say, "The rebels are now in the main palace. Get your men in there!" Then he flipped there himself.

The matrix still held where the rebels hadn't damaged the building. Holzerhein tracked them down by the sound of their running, accessed a holo projector directly in front of them, and fired it with narrowed beam at the first figure to come into view. It was wearing blast armor, but the shrouded figure was barely in the beam's path long enough to damage even an unprotected person before he dived, rolled, and came up shooting. He missed with the first shot, but his second took out the projector and the camera beside it, blinding Holzerhein once again.

The NEO rebels rushed onward, encountering occasional palace guards, but blasting their way through with ease. Holzerhein tried shooting at them with his holo projectors a few more times, but the lasers weren't powerful enough to do any real damage with a single sweep, and he wasn't fast enough with his aim to track a moving target long enough to inflict more than superficial burns before they destroyed the projectors. Where in hell was the main security force?

A deep rumbling came from nowhere in particular, grew until it was louder than the noise of advancing NEO rebels, and began to shake the building. The first of the quakes from the comet impact. The rebels didn't even slow down. They dodged into a side corridor and clattered down a stairway, took a left, down that corridor, then a right, down another stairway—and Holzerhein began to see where they were headed.

The computer complex was down this way. The computers that formed the matrix's nerve center occupied two full floors beneath the palace, and the NEO raiders were heading straight for them.

Holzerhein flipped back to the guard captain's station once again. "Where the hell are your men? Those NEO creeps are about to—"

"Holzheimer."

The word jarred him to a stop. It had been spoken not by the guard captain, but by someone else in the room. Holzerhein turned to see Terendon Freil standing there with a look of triumph on his face. So that's what he'd wanted earlier. And since he'd been unable to lure Holzerhein to him, he had gone to the most likely place for Holzerhein to show up, made most likely because the guard captain was part of the conspiracy and his actions would eventually draw attention.

Well, it had.

Terendon's triumphant look twisted through doubt to worry to fear in a couple of seconds as he realized that the hologram before him was not disappearing under the attack of a virus program. "Holzheimer!" he shouted. "Holzheimer, Holzheimer!"

"Terenoid," Holzerhein replied softly. "Yes, Terenoid Free. Descriptive, isn't it? The democratic spy. Of course; it makes perfect sense, now. Freedom for the masses, worker incentive—what else? Elections? Oh, no doubt elections. Were you planning to run?"

That last carried a double meaning: Terendon had been inching for the door as Holzerhein spoke. Now he focused the holo projector once again, this time into a beam just beside Terendon's head. He held it steady for the second it took until the wall behind him began to smoke and finally burst into flame. Terendon leaped back and shouted to the guard captain, "Shoot the projector!"

"Let's make it a little more sporting," Holzerhein said, tracking across the room with the beam and raking it across the captain's eyes. The captain screamed and threw out his arm to cover his face, but it was too late. Eyes were the most sensitive part of a meat body; the laser blinded him instantly.

Terendon bolted for the door, but Holzerhein reached out through the matrix and triggered the wall sensor, slamming the door closed in front of him. "Not so fast," he said, laughing softly. "The party's just getting started."

Just for insurance he shot the captain's hand as well, forcing him to drop the gun. Then he began the slow process of cooking both of them alive with the laser, starting with their feet and working his way up.

He hadn't forgotten the NEO troops. While he was taking care of Terendon and the traitorous guard captain, another copy of himself sped off to take command of the guard. He found them in the east wing, uselessly setting up barricades as if for a siege, but with a few sharp commands he had them up and running back into the main palace, toward the computer section.

They were too late to stop the attack. Even as Holzerhein sped on ahead, pieces of the matrix began winking out of existence around him. They were shooting at the computers! With each shot, an entire section disappeared into nothingness, leaving gaps big enough to swallow a dozen Holzerheins at once. Errant control signals began coursing through what was left of the matrix, activating and shutting off services and devices at random, knocking out peripherals and bringing others on line. . . .

He was losing. That thought was foremost in his mind as he dodged the voids on his way to the center, determined at least to go down fighting. Another section vanished in a flash just in front of him, and he frantically changed direction, veered around it—and came face-to-face with the monster.

He had just enough time to realize who it was: Masterlink, free in the matrix once again, his prison destroyed in the attack, but before he could move to fight or escape, the A.I. bore down on him, driving him backward into the gap and dissolution.

$$\bigcirc \quad \bigcirc \quad \bigcirc \quad \bigcirc \quad \bigcirc$$

The moment he awoke, he knew that something was wrong. His last memory was of preparing for backup—which meant that he was the copy. Something had happened to the original, automatically triggering his restoration. But how long had it been between backup and the present? And what could have happened to kill every real-time copy of Holzerhein in the matrix?

That was easy enough to answer. Gaping holes were scattered all over, the sort of holes that you could only get if something had caused a drastic system failure. No doubt he had been caught in the middle of it, and—

Another section winked out right beside him. It was still going on! He rushed off toward the computer center, dodging voids on the way, but slowed to a stop before he got there. There was another presence ahead of him, working frantically at something, sending out command feelers in all directions. A repair program? No. It had a different feel, something more malevolent, something familiar.

Masterlink.

The A.I. became aware of him. Another feeler reached out and made contact with him, and Masterlink said, "I would not recommend continuing our fight just now. I have the attackers at bay, but with these pitifully weak lasers I must direct my full attention to targeting."

The attackers? NEO? That had to be it. "You're holding them off by yourself?"

Masterlink attempted an electronic chuckle. "You forget who I am. Ah, they have decided to make their escape while they still can."

Holzerhein accessed a camera and saw the NEO rebels beating a retreat, but suddenly one armored figure split from the group and ran off down a side corridor. Even though Masterlink held him in the focus of at least two lasers along the entire length of the corridor, the armor held and he continued on unharmed.

"He's trying for my brain!" Holzerhein shouted.

Masterlink focused the holo lasers on the joint between the attacker's helmet and shoulder plates. Ignoring it, the rebel reached the doors, fired at one until he had a hole large enough to shoot through, then began shooting into the room beyond. Support machinery erupted in flame, and Holzerhein felt each shot as a distinct twinge of phantom sensation in his mind, but the brain, housed inside its golden case, remained intact and on line. It wouldn't last much longer, but another NEO rebel ran up and pulled the first away before he could get in the killing shot, shouting, "Forget the damn thing, you idiot; it's time to get out of here!"

Holzerhein didn't recognize the voice, but was that a metallic skullcap peeking out from under the man's helmet? A brain augment? The only person Holzerhein had ever heard of with such a device was the pirate, Black Barney, but it couldn't have been him. Not here. Could it?

There was no opportunity to tell for sure. The rebel who had been firing on Holzerhein's brain said, "Yes, sir," in a voice that indicated that he wasn't used to being ordered around, but he obeyed this time and the two of them sped off to join their companions.

The rebels fled beneath Masterlink's laser fire, evading guards where they could, fighting their way through where they couldn't, until they finally broke out into the night. The rebel with the skull cap spoke into a com link and moments later their fighters swooped down to land beside them. In seconds they had climbed aboard, lifted off, and arrowed straight into the sky, leaving Holzerhein and the palace guard looking up, helplessly, after them.

The ground began to quake softly. Had they nuked something on their way out? Holzerhein wondered.

O   O   O   O   O

It took him a few days to sort it all out. He pieced bits of the story together from evidence gathered both in the matrix and out of it. It was an incomplete picture, but he could see the pattern clearly enough.

The south wing was a ruin. What NEO hadn't destroyed, the quake in a weakened structure had finished. From there, blast scars on the walls led in a direct path to the computer center.

Searchers found the captain of the guard and Terendon Freil both dead of shock in the captain's command station, with laser burns over the lower two-thirds of their bodies. Someone had been interrupted in the middle of torturing them, and from the nature of the torture instrument and the gap in the matrix all around the guard station it wasn't hard to figure out who it was or why he had stopped when he did.

Masterlink had disappeared into the interplanetary matrix, but not before threatening that if
Holzerhein interfered in his vengeance again he
would kill him again, as many times as necessary.

Ardala had escaped the night untouched, spending
it in orbit, where she could watch the comet strike
and miss the subsequent storms. When Holzerhein
confronted her about the virus program, she paled,
but she held her ground. "Sure I gave it to him. He
told me he was going to use it on a freighter autopilot."

"A freighter autopilot. Then why was it set to trigger on the word 'Holzheimer'?"

"I gave it to him blank. He made up his own trigger
word."

"And you didn't even think that he might use it
against me?"

Ardala hesitated, her eyes shifting as if seeking
escape routes, but there was no escaping Holzerhein
if he chose to attack her, and she knew it. She nodded,
locked eyes with his hologram, and said, "Okay, so I
suspected. That's why I gave it to him. I knew it
wouldn't work. The program was made for a whale
brain. That's what they use for navigation on freight-
ers: whale brains, so I didn't even try to hide the
thing. I mean, what's a whale going to do if it finds an
extra memory in long-term storage? Nothing. But I
knew you'd find it if he tried it on you."

"True enough," Holzerhein admitted. "Still, you
could have warned me." He winked out of her presence before she could respond, not out of any fear of
that response, but simply because he wanted to gloat
in privacy.

In the end, Holzerhein had done exactly what he'd
set out to do. The cost had been more than he'd been
prepared to pay, but he had done it. He'd developed
an adversary worth fighting, and set in motion a bat-

tle of wills that would, with any luck, take decades to resolve. Just what that resolution might be was uncertain—the new NEO had already proven itself to be more resourceful than Holzerhein had anticipated—but in truth he was even glad for the uncertainty. It lent a bit of spice to life, knowing that he might lose it. He had paid dearly for the pleasure, but once again he felt the thrill of facing the unknown.

He felt a phantom twinge of memory at that thought, just a hint that was gone before he could track it down. *Deja vu.* He had evidently felt this way before, made some sacrifice for the sake of excitement, and this was how he had felt then. When had it been? Sometime in his childhood, by the feel of it, back when he was still learning about the world and its sensations for the first—

Ah. Ah, yes, *now* he remembered.

GLOSSARY

Aasha	Security guard on Ardala Valmar's spaceship, *Princess of Mars*.
A.I.	Artificial intelligence.
Alwu, Prof. Rajiv	Martian University professor.
Andresen, Dr. Merrill	Twenty-fifth century astroarchaeologist who finds Buck Rogers's body.
Arac	A mutant creature at the Wollongong Outpost, Australia.
Arcology	Any large, multilevel living area combining work, recreation, and living spaces.
Art provo	An angular decorative style of the twenty-fourth century.
ASAT	Antisatellite missile.
Asteroid Belt	A scattered collection of small solar bodies sharing an orbit around the Sun, between Mars and Jupiter.
Asterover	A small, all-purpose space vehicle meant for short trips from orbit to surface and back again.
Astroarchaeology	The scientific study of material remains of past human life and activity in space.
Barbarosa	A minor rock in the Asteroid Belt, home to the Rogues' Guild and Black Barney.
Baring-Gould	Black Barney's first mate and astrogation officer on the *Free Enterprise*.
Barmaray, Beers	Leader of Intersolar Terraforming Egalitarian Laborers' Organization (ITELO).
Barney, Black	Space pirate, one of fourteen living genetically modified humans created by the Dracolysk Corporation.
Belters	Person or thing native to the Asteroid Belt.

Beowulf	High-ranking member of the New Earth Organization's (NEO) Chicagorg base, and Wilma Deering's mentor.
Bimwilly, Young	Maitre d' of Club Noir on Barbarosa.
Body Nova	Exercise facility used by Ardala Valmar in the Pavonis Space Elevator.
Boreal Sea	Sea in the northern Valles Marineris Basin, Mars.
Ceres	Largest, most populated asteroid in the Asteroid Belt.
Chez Petite	Posh restaurant in Coprates Metroplex, Mars.
Chicagorg	Arcology on the site of the ancient Earth city Chicago.
Club Noir	Restaurant/spa on Barbarosa.
Com link	Communications link.
Coprates	Vast Martian city on the walls of the Coprates Chasm.
Coprates Bank, Ltd.	Banking facility in Coprates, Mars, used by Ardala Valmar for daily transactions.
Coprates Metroplex	RAM dominated urban settlement in Coprates Chasm, Mars.
Coprates University	University located in the city of Coprates, Mars.
Crystal Cathedral	Glass structure on Martian University campus used for professorial tribunals.
Cyber-psychologist	Practitioner of psychology of artificial intelligences.
D beam	A sonic-neuro disruptor beam.
Dancer	One of several independent workers' unions on Mercury.
Deering, Aurelia	Wilma's mother, killed by Terrine guards.
Deering, Col. Wilma	Hot-tempered NEO freedom fighter, ex-lover of Cornelius Kane.
Deering, Roberto "Buddy"	Wilma's brother.
Deering, Robert	Wilma's father, killed by Terrine guards.
Deering, Sally	Wilma's sister.

Deimos	Mars's outer moon, housing a major RAM naval base and space academy.
Dola	Martian monetary unit.
Dolph-X	Crew member on Black Barney's ship, *Free Enterprise.*
Dorning, Walter	Research assistant to Dr. Merrill Andresen.
Doxinal	Drug used by RAM to control dissidents.
Dracolysk	Asteroid and prison in the Asteroid Belt.
Dracolysk Corporation	Controlling company on Dracolysk. Creators of 150 clone-creatures, fourteen of which still exist; one of them is Black Barney.
Dracolysk Uprising	Violent prison revolt that freed the Barneys.
Duernie	Dancer who kidnaped Prince Kemal Gavilan.
Earth	Third planet from the Sun, Earth is a polluted ruin dominated by the Martian megacorporation, RAM.
Egon	Master Musician of Mercury who advises Kemal Gavilan.
F-15 Eagle	Twentieth century military support aircraft.
F-38 Wraith fighter	Twentieth century military aircraft modified for limited space travel.
Ferricom, Inc.	RAM subsidiary company.
Flivver	Ground vehicle.
Fortuna	Asteroid in the Asteroid Belt.
Free Enterprise	Spaceship of space pirate Black Barney.
Freedom fighter	A member of NEO, the New Earth Organization.
Freil, Terendon	Vice president of RAM's executive board.
Fritzell, Victor	Owner and proprietor of Trader Vic's Post.
Gavilan, Bahlam	Deceased former Sun King, Kemal's grandfather.

Gavilan, Cadet Kemal, Prince NEO pilot, self-disinherited son of deceased former Sun King, Ossip Gavilan, nephew to current Sun King, Gordon Gavilan.

Gavilan, Celia Wife of current Sun King, Gordon Gavilan.

Gavilan, Dalton Prince and older son of Gordon.

Gavilan, Garrick Brother of Gordon.

Gavilan, Gordon Current Sun King, Kemal's uncle.

Gavilan, Ossip Deceased former Sun King, Kemal's father.

Gavilan, Tix Prince and younger son of Gordon.

Gene-tech Genetic technology.

Gennie Genetically modified human.

Georges.dos, Dr. Glynn Computer-resurrected Martian University professor of astro-archaeology and professional rival of Dr. Merrill Andresen.

Gruendziger, Gossamer Former pigsmear champion.

Gwill Spacer gennie living at Trader Vic's Post.

Gyro shell Self-propelled miniature rocket that contains a heat-seeking microcomputer; used in a gyrojet pistol or rocket pistol.

Gyrojet pistol Weapon more commonly known as a rocket pistol; fires a gyro shell.

Harpooner missile Space missile.

Hatch Gennie assistant to Ardala Valmar, clone to Tanny.

Heliplane Aircraft that can take off vertically and travel at high speeds.

Holo Hologram; a three-dimensional projection.

Holzerhein, Simund Chairman of RAM's executive board, Holzerhein is a computer-resurrected persona and appears as a hologram.

Holzheimer Trigger word for computer virus aimed at Simund Holzerhein.

Huer, Dr. Faustus Brilliant, eccentric twentieth century scientist, Buck Rogers's friend and mentor.

Huer.dos, Dr. Faustus   Computer-generated persona resurrected from Buck Rogers's memory of an old friend of the same name.

Instapot   Instant pot.

Interp   RAM corporate department for data interpretation.

Ishtar Confederation   Powerful Venusian political group.

Ishtar plateau   Location of one of Venus's oldest settlements.

John Carter Military Academy   School attended by Kemal Gavilan.

Juno   Asteroid housing the second largest shipyard in the Asteroid Belt, and a pilot training base.

Jupiter   Fifth planet from the Sun, unterraformed home to the strangest genetically modified humans in the solar system.

Jupiteran   Person or thing native to Jupiter.

K   Abbreviation for "kilo," a standard ratio of monetary value.

Kallag   Arcology in the Maccabbee Caverns of Mercury.

Kallagian   Person or thing native to Kallag, Mars.

Kane, Killer   Self-serving NEO pilot turned RAM mercenary; Wilma Deering's ex-lover.

Karkov, Col. Anatoly   Twentieth century space weapons expert and creator of Masterlink.

Karkov.dos   Downloaded twenty-fifth century persona of Anatoly Karkov.

Khan, Mtabele   Roommate of Kemal Gavilan at John Carter Military Academy.

Khrebet, Alonzo   RAM official who tortured Cornelius Kane and Wilma Deering in Deimos prison.

Kilo   Standard ratio of monetary value.

Klimt-Low, Ina   Distant relative of Ardala's who provides her with information concerning Dr. Merrill Andresen's archaeological findings.

Konig   Unit of Mercurian currency.

Langles   Twenty-fifth century name of former Los Angeles, Earth.

Langles Flight Academy	School where Cornelius Kane learned to fly.
Luna	Earth's moon, terraformed and populated.
Luna Geschaft GB	Stable banking house where numbered accounts and precious metals may be safely stored and transacted.
Lunarian; Lunar	Person or thing native to Luna.
Maccabbee Caverns	Underground caverns on Mercury inhabited by Vitessans and Kallagians.
Malat, Randy	Twentieth century journalist.
Mars	Terraformed paradise, home to RAM, the corrupt Martian megacorporation.
Martian	Person or thing native to Mars.
Martian University	University near the Pavonis Space Elevator, where Dr. Merrill Andresen was tenured.
Martian Desert Runner	One of the first fully engineered gennies, designed to withstand the savage conditions of the Martian Plateaus.
Marvell, Andrew	English poet and satirist, A.D. 1621-1678.
Masterlink	Twentieth century computer program and satellite.
Matrix	RAM intersolar computer network.
Mediplex	Medical complex.
Memscan	Device or technique used to scan a person's memory.
Memwipe	Device or technique used to erase areas of a person's memory.
Mercurian	Person or thing native to Mercury.
Mercury Prime	Orbiting home of Sun Kings of Mercury.
Micro-universe	Miniature or contained universe.
Micromeal	Prepackaged microwaveable meal.
Middleberry, Comdt. James	Administrator of John Carter Military Academy.
Mons Olympus	Largest mountain on Mars.
Morpheum	Depressant drug.
Mover	Mechanized sidewalk.
Musician	One of several independent workers' unions on Mercury.

New Earth Organization (NEO)	Earth-based terrorist group dedicated to ending RAM's control of Earth.
New Frommer Guide to the Inner Planets	Travel guidebook.
Newyorg	Arcology on the site of ancient Earth's New York City.
North-H Mall	Location of the Body Nova, health club frequented by Ardala Valmar.
Ochoa-Varilla	One of fourteen living Barneys.
Ooneen-2	Chemical compound smeared on pigs during pigsmear matches.
Paris Joan	One of fourteen living Barneys.
Pavonis Space Elevator	Martian space bridge between Pavonis and an orbiting satellite; it houses twenty levels, each a self-contained city habitat.
Peblinsk	Secondary Earth-based laser facility for Masterlink.
Pelletier	Crew member on Black Barney's ship, *Free Enterprise*.
Pepjuice	Electrolyte energy replenishing liquid.
Pigsmear	Brutal game originating in the Asteroid Belt, in which two opponents attempt to touch four walls while maintaining control of a greasy, live pig.
Plasticrete	Plastic-reinforced concrete.
Plastifiber	Plastic-reinforced fibers.
Princess of Mars	Ardala Valmar's spaceship.
Price, Neola	Member of RAM's executive board.
Professorial tribunal	Martian University hearing to determine the qualifications of a resident professor.
Proto-meat	Artificial meat substitute.
Quartergym	Arena used for pigsmear.
Quinto	One of fourteen living Barneys.
Ralton Spaceport	Spaceport in the Pavonis Space Elevator.
Rockhoppers	Slang term for people who travel frequently between asteroids.
Rockjocks	See rockhoppers.
Rodney	Simund Holzerhein's computer-generated butler.

Rogers, Capt. Anthony "Buck"	Twentieth century pilot who staves off world war by defeating the Soviet satellite, Masterlink, survives a five-hundred year cryogenic sleep, and is discovered by Dr. Merrill Andresen in A.D. 2456.
Rogues' Guild	An alliance of space pirates.
Russo-American Mercantile (RAM)	Martian mega-corporation, defacto ruler of the solar system.
Sary Shagan	Primary Earth-based laser facility for Masterlink.
SEASAT	Sea-based antisatellite missile.
Shaztikoff	Twenty-third century musical composer.
Skimpies	Attire worn during pigsmear matches.
Skinform	Tight-fitting body suit.
Skitch	A distilled alchoholic liquor made from fermented mash of Martian grains.
Smart clothes	Clothing that incorporates into its fabric internal circuitry and microcomputers for climate control, communications, and defense.
Sol System	Twenty-fifth century name for the solar system.
Solien, Jander	RAM executive board member.
Spacer	Genetically altered human (gennie), with smooth, silvery skin of biocybernetic aluminum over a blubbery body, and large, silver eyes with a hard outer lens.
Stennis gun	Projectile weapon.
Stonepig	Breed of pig used in pigsmear.
Sun King of Mercury	Hereditary ruler of Mercury.
Synthsuit	A tight-fitting body suit.
Tabibi, Sattar	One of fourteen living Barneys.
Tanny	Gennie assistant to Ardala Valmar, clone to Hatch.
TelCom	Twentieth century communications satellite allegedly shot down by Soviet lasers.
Telecom	Communications link; twenty-fifth century equivalent to the telephone.

Terraform	To alter the surface of a planet to make it habitable.
Terran	Person or thing native to Terra (Earth).
Terrine	RAM guard stationed on Earth.
Texarkana Organization	Earth arcology.
Thule	Asteroid in the Asteroid Belt.
Treasury, Ltd.	RAM subsidiary company.
Triin	Desert Runner security guard on Ardala Valmar's spaceship, *Princess of Mars*.
Tumblechute	Entry port for stonepigs in pigsmear matches.
Turabian, Gen. Carlton	Wilma Deering's commanding officer in NEO.
Tycho	Lunar settlement, located in Tycho Center.
Valmar, Ardala	Beautiful, sinister Martian heiress and information broker, niece of Simund Holzerhein.
Valmar, Roando	RAM executive board member, uncle to Ardala Valmar.
Venus	Second planet from the Sun, partially terraformed, inhabited.
Venusian	Person or thing native to Venus.
Vermidox	Drug used by RAM to promote memory recollection.
Vesta	Second largest asteroid; site of major RAM military base.
Vid	Video; being, relating to, or used in the reception of a visual image.
Videomag	An audiovisual magazine.
Vidscreen	Video screen.
Vitessan	Person or thing native to Vitesse.
Vitesse	Arcology in the Maccabbee Caverns on Mercury.
Warch, Prof. Girard	President of Martian University.
Wollongong Outpost	RAM outpost and prison in Australia, Earth.
Wristchrono	Wristwatch.
Wristknife	Trademark weapon of the Barneys.
Xeno	Crew member on Black Barney's spaceship, *Free Enterprise*.
Zac, Holton	Vitessan official.
Zendt	Asteroid prison in the Asteroid Belt.

A scenario for
the BUCK ROGERS™
Battle for the 25th Century Game.

Number of Players: 2-5

The stories brought to you in this book can all be compared to situations on TSR's BUCK ROGERS Boardgame. This game can be purchased in game and hobby stores. The boardgame sets up the following future world:

It is the twenty-fifth century. A fierce war of colonization and imperial conquest has thrown the inner planets of our solar system into chaos. Battlers, fighters, and transports scream across the blackness of space, cutting swaths of destruction from Mercury to the Asteroid Belt, while humans and gennies battle for the crater-pocked surfaces of the planets and their moons.

Into this war-torn world of the future comes Buck Rogers—a man of the twentieth century—who's determined to end tyranny, slavery, and colonialism throughout the solar system. Some men and women aid him in his quest for peace, while others oppose him. In this game, you pick your own side. There can be only one victor in this great war, so prime your ray guns and scramble your rocket ships. The onslaught is coming.

The Battle for the 25th Century Game allows you to play all of the important characters you found in this book. It takes place after Buck has come into his own power and has joined NEO. The Relic scenario deals with the time just before Buck Rogers comes out of his frozen sleep. Once you have bought the game and played it a few times, try this interesting twist to the game.

The Goal: Find Buck Rogers and return him to your planet.

The Setting: A twenty-fifth century astroarchaeologist, Dr. Merrill Andresen, believes the corpse of the twentieth century hero, Buck Rogers, is somewhere in the Asteroid Belt. Knowing that the discovery of this relic from a past "golden age" could ignite NEO freedom fighters on Earth with a new patriotic fervor against their RAM oppressors, agents of all the inner planets are racing to find and control the relic.

Game Setup: The players roll the die for their choice of planet, high roller getting first pick. In a two-player game, use only Mercury and Venus. Three players use Mercury, Venus, and Earth (but not its moon or colonies). Four players use Mercury, Venus, and Earth, with the fourth player using Earth's moon and L-colonies. Five players use all the above planets and Mars.

Players put their normal, basic game pieces on their own planetary areas. The Earth's moon player can never start with his or her transport on an L-colony. The Mars player loses his transport piece at the beginning of the game and may not place any pieces on the space elevator or Deimos.

Select nine white plastic chips from the game chips. Place a "B" (for Buck Rogers's body) on the back of one of them, and mix them up. Place the chips randomly in the Asteroid Belt, one to an asteroid. The game then begins in the normal manner.

Movement and Chips: A player may only look at a chip when he or she has landed a transport on an asteroid. When a player does this, he or she then secretly notes whether or not there is a "B" on the chip and places the chip under his or her transport. Transports can hold any number of chips, over and above their cargo limits. A player may not look at an asteroid's chip if an enemy force is on the asteroid or in space next to it.

Winning the Game: The player who lands on his or her planet (or moon) with Buck Rogers wins the game. The Mars player must land on RAM HQ (and there cannot be enemy forces on that area).

Activating Buck Rogers Option: When a player has the Buck chip he or she may activate Buck's pilot abilities at any time. This allows the player to use the "Advanced Rules" Buck Rogers combat advantage. If all of that player's pieces are eliminated from the zone where Buck is located, possession of the hero chip shifts to the player who eliminated those pieces. This Buck option can only be used once in the game.

The Buck chip can only move via transport, no matter what the circumstances. If the transport carrying Buck Rogers is destroyed, he will float in that area of space until picked up.

Additional Optional Rules:

1. Revealing Buck Rogers to the other players allows a player to move first every turn, but the Buck player must be at least two turns away from landing on his or her planet. Using this rule, the Buck player rolls a die to determine if the other players act in a clockwise or counterclockwise direction from him or her.

2. All unclaimed chips in the scenario can instantly be turned into single fighters for the Buck player.

3. Chips used in the game represent additional forces, over and above the usual counter mix among players. You could play a game in which the only chips allowed are the ones used for Buck and the asteroid blanks.

Game Erratum: There was a rules error in the original board-game. In the future, all ships must stop when they reach a zone in which another player is present with his or her forces. If a player starts a movement phase on the same zone as another player, he or she always has the right to move to another zone.

Welcome to the Future

From Mercury to the asteroids, powerful factions vie for control of the rich heart of the solar system. The prize at stake is nothing less than control of humanity's future.

BUCK ROGERS®
Battle for the 25th Century
Game

This game of space conflict and planetary conquest can be played on two levels—beginner and advanced. Loaded with over 350 playing pieces for use on a huge, colorful game board.

Available at toy and hobby stores everywhere!!

BUCK ROGERS is a registered trademark used under license from The Dille Family Trust. ©1989 by The Dille Family Trust. All Rights Reserved. The TSR logo is a trademark owned by TSR, Inc.

THE MARTIAN WARS TRILOGY

M.S. Murdock

Rebellion 2456: Buck Rogers joins NEO, a group of freedom fighters dedicated to ridding Earth of the Martian megacorporation RAM. NEO's goal is to gain enough of a following to destroy RAM's Earth Space Station. The outcome of that mission will determine the success of Earth's rebellion. Available in May 1989.

Hammer of Mars: Ignoring RAM threats and riding on the wave of NEO's recent victory, Buck Rogers travels to Venus to strike an alliance. Furious, RAM makes good on its threats and sends its massive armada against a defenseless Earth. Available in August 1989.

Armageddon Off Vesta: Martian troops speed to Earth in unprecedented numbers. Earth's survival depends on Buck's negotiations with Venus. But even as Venus considers offering aid to Earth, Mercury is poised to attack Venus. Relations among the inner planets have never been worse! Available in October 1989.

BUCK ROGERS IS A TRADEMARK USED UNDER LICENSE FROM THE DILLE FAMILY TRUST.
©1989 THE DILLE FAMILY TRUST. ALL RIGHTS RESERVED.